Praise for the novels of
New York Times bestselling author
Heather Graham

"Graham is a master at world building and her latest is a thrilling, dark, and deadly tale of romantic suspense."
—*Booklist*, starred review, on *Haunted Destiny*

"Intricate, fast-paced, and intense, this riveting thriller blends romance and suspense in perfect combination and keeps readers guessing and the tension taut until the very end."
—*Library Journal* on *Flawless*

"Graham is the queen of romantic suspense, and her latest is proof that she deserves the title. What makes this story more fun than most is the relationship between Kieran Finnegan, who wants nothing more than family harmony and a functioning restaurant, and FBI agent Craig Fraiser, who wants justice. Sparks fly, and it's electric."
—*RT Book Reviews* on *Flawless*

"The Krewe is back! Graham excels at weaving history, finding the proper balance between past and present and keeping a story fresh and authentic, with *Haunted Destiny* being no exception. The chaos and camaraderie of the characters are captured with vivid detail, and the identity of the killer will keep you guessing until the very end."
—*RT Book Reviews* on *Haunted Destiny*

"Riveting mystery...interesting history, sweet romance with a second chance at love."
—*Fresh Fiction* on *Darkest Journey*

"Graham stands at the top of the romantic suspense category."
—*Publishers Weekly*

"An incredible storyteller."

P9-CDX-715

Also by HEATHER GRAHAM

DARK RITES
DYING BREATH
A PERFECT OBSESSION
DARKEST JOURNEY
DEADLY FATE
HAUNTED DESTINY
FLAWLESS
THE HIDDEN
THE FORGOTTEN
THE SILENCED
THE DEAD PLAY ON
THE BETRAYED
THE HEXED
THE CURSED
WAKING THE DEAD
THE NIGHT IS FOREVER
THE NIGHT IS ALIVE
THE NIGHT IS WATCHING
LET THE DEAD SLEEP
THE UNINVITED
THE UNSPOKEN
THE UNHOLY
THE UNSEEN
AN ANGEL FOR CHRISTMAS
THE EVIL INSIDE
SACRED EVIL
HEART OF EVIL
PHANTOM EVIL
NIGHT OF THE VAMPIRES
THE KEEPERS
GHOST MOON
GHOST NIGHT
GHOST SHADOW

THE KILLING EDGE
NIGHT OF THE WOLVES
HOME IN TIME
   FOR CHRISTMAS
UNHALLOWED GROUND
DUST TO DUST
NIGHTWALKER
DEADLY GIFT
DEADLY HARVEST
DEADLY NIGHT
THE DEATH DEALER
THE LAST NOEL
THE SÉANCE
BLOOD RED
THE DEAD ROOM
KISS OF DARKNESS
THE VISION
THE ISLAND
GHOST WALK
KILLING KELLY
THE PRESENCE
DEAD ON THE DANCE FLOOR
PICTURE ME DEAD
HAUNTED
HURRICANE BAY
A SEASON OF MIRACLES
NIGHT OF THE BLACKBIRD
NEVER SLEEP
   WITH STRANGERS
EYES OF FIRE
SLOW BURN
NIGHT HEAT

* * * * *

Look for Heather Graham's next novel
A DANGEROUS GAME
available soon from MIRA Books.

HEATHER GRAHAM

WICKED
DEEDS

mira

mira

ISBN-13: 978-0-7783-3036-3

Recycling programs
for this product may
not exist in your area.

Wicked Deeds

For questions and comments about the quality of this book, please contact us at
CustomerService@Harlequin.com.

www.Harlequin.com

Printed in U.S.A.

For my oldest son, Jason Pozzessere,
and for Kari Stewart, a true delight to have in our lives.
Also for her folks, Kelly and Gail Stewart—
simply wonderful people.

CAST OF CHARACTERS

Griffin Pryce—special agent with the FBI's Krewe of Hunters

Victoria (Vickie) Preston—historian and author

The Krewe of Hunters

Adam Harrison—head of the Krewe of Hunters

Jackson Crow—field director, Krewe of Hunters

Angela Hawkins—special agent, married to Jackson Crow

In Baltimore

Franklin Verne—popular bestselling author

Monica Verne—his widow

Myron Hatfield—Baltimore medical examiner

Carl Morris—detective, Baltimore Police

At the Black Bird restaurant

Gary Frampton—restaurant owner

Alice Frampton—his daughter, hostess at the restaurant

Lacey Shaw—gift shop manager

Liza Harcourt—president of the Blackbird society,
a Poe appreciation group

Brent Whaley—writer, member of the Blackbird society

Alistair Malcolm—Poe expert, member of the
Blackbird society

Jon Skye—waiter

At Frampton Manor

Hattie Long and Sven Moller—housekeeper and caretaker

Prologue

In Dreams

It was dark, and it was night, and she was following along a strange wooded path.

Vickie Preston fought against it; good things never started this way.

But she wasn't in deep woods. She was not far from some kind of a city—she could see light through the trees.

The light seemed strange. It wasn't the contemporary, bright luminescence of electricity that shined with such fervor that it was easily seen from space. This was different. Soft light. As if it came from candles or…gas. Gas lamps.

She had, she thought, stumbled into a different time, a different place. She made a turn, and the darkness was gone, things changing suddenly in that way of dreams; she was in a city, and it was day, late afternoon perhaps, with evening on its way.

People were rushing about, here, there and everywhere.

"Vote! Fourth Ward polls!" someone called out.

A woman with a big hoop skirt pushed by Vickie, dragging a man about by an ear. "Harold Finder! Voting is no excuse for my husband to show himself in public, drunk!" she said angrily.

Harold was twice his wife's size, but Mrs. Finder seemed to have an exceptional hold on his ear!

They had just come from what appeared to be a tavern. Vickie looked about, wondering why no one noticed her. They were all dressed so differently; men in frock coats and waistcoats and cravats and women with their tightly corseted tops and great, billowing skirts. Granted, she was sleeping in a long white cotton gown, "puritanical," or so Griffin had teased her.

No, no, oh, yuck! You know how I feel about our dear historical Puritans! she'd told him.

Vickie, like Griffin, had grown up in Boston. She'd become a historian and wrote nonfiction books. Despite trying to understand the very different times they had lived in, she just didn't care much for the people who had first settled her area—they were completely intolerant.

Griffin could usually just shrug off the past; he'd been a cop when she'd first met him and he was an FBI agent now. The past mattered to him, but mostly when it helped solve crime in the present.

He'd been sleeping next to her, of course. They were on their way to Virginia from Boston, ready to start a

new life. But they'd stopped in Baltimore, at a hotel...
They'd laughed as they got ready for bed, he'd teased
her about the nightgown...

She did not look like a Puritan!

Griffin had assured her that she wouldn't wear the
"puritanical" gown long, and she hadn't, but then,
freezing in the air-conditioning of their hotel, she'd
put it back on...

She was glad, of course. Otherwise, she'd be walking stark naked around this unknown and bizarre
place.

Where was she?

She turned to the doorway of the "polling place"
where Harold and his wife had just departed. She could
hear all manner of laughing and talking. It was definitely a tavern. Gunnar's Place.

And there was nothing indicating Puritan Massachusetts here—she wasn't in Massachusetts and these
people certainly weren't Puritans.

She walked in, wondering if women were welcome.
It didn't matter. No one seemed to notice her.

The place was smoky and dusty. Barmaids were
hurrying about, handing out drinks. Men were being
solicited for their votes.

There was a lone man seated on a wooden bench at
a table, head hanging low. But when Vickie entered,
he looked up, and he beckoned to her.

"I've been waiting for you," he said impatiently. He
stood, wavering.

He was a small man, just a little shorter than Vickie,

maybe five-eight to her five-nine. His hair was dark and a curl hung over his forehead. His eyes seemed red-rimmed and sunken in his face, which was quite ashen, with a yellow pallor.

She knew him.

She'd seen his picture throughout her life; she'd loved his work. She'd loved that he'd been born in Boston—even if he had come to hate that city. There was a wonderful statue of him now, a life-size bronze figure of the writer, hurrying along with a briefcase and a raven.

She knew his face from so many pictures and images, a man haunted by demons in life, most of those demons brought about by his alcohol addiction. She'd always wondered if more knowledge during his age might have helped him; a really good therapist, a good program...

"I'm hallucinating you, you know. Delirium tremors," he told her gravely. "But I have been waiting for you, Victoria."

"I love your work!" Vickie said. She flushed. It was a dream, or a nightmare, and she was having a fangirl moment. She needed control and decorum.

"Yes, well, then, you are brighter than my insidious detractors," he told her. "But here's the thing. You must stop it. I am being used—my work, my memory. It was good—it was all good, until I came here, until I reached Baltimore. Then, they...were upon me."

"They who?" she asked. "No one knows—it's still a mystery."

"They were upon me," he repeated.

Vickie reached across the table and set her hand gently upon his. He was trembling, she realized, violently. "You're not looking very well," she said.

And he turned to give her a rueful smile. "No. I will not be here long, you see. But I'm glad that you made it, so glad that you're here. It's happening again. And you must do something. You must stop it. No one will see, because it's much the same. Do you understand?"

"Not a word," she assured him.

He looked across the room and seemed concerned; he stood suddenly and hurried toward the door. Vickie raced after him.

She didn't see him at first. He was on the ground, slumped against the building. She tried to reach him, but there was already a man at his side, attempting to help him. She noted an address then, Lombard Street.

As she stood there while the one man tried to help, people continued to hurry along the street. Hawkers shouted out their wares—and their candidates. Drinks were promised for votes; there was laughter, there was a rush of music, someone playing a fiddle…

She tried to reach the fallen man, thankful that at least someone was helping him.

Across the bit of distance between them, he opened his eyes and looked at her.

"I have to go now," he said.

"No…!"

"But I must. And you…"

"Yes?"

"You must pay attention." He laughed softly. "Don't let it happen again."

"What's that?" she asked.

A loud cawing sound seemed to rip through the air.

He looked at her sadly and said, "Quoth the raven—
nevermore!"

1

"There's been an incident, a very bizarre incident," Jackson Crow said.

His voice over the phone as he spoke to Griffin Pryce was steady—as always. Jackson had pretty much seen it all. As field director of a special unit of the FBI—unofficially known as the Krewe of Hunters—Jackson *had* just about seen it all, although he'd be the first to say they'd probably never "see it all."

The "bizarre" was usually the reason the Krewe got called in.

"What's the incident?"

"You've heard of Franklin Verne?" Jackson asked.

"The writer? Yes, of course. Kind of impossible not to have heard of him—he likes to do his own commercials. He's known for action books with shades of horror, right?"

"Yes, that's right."

"What about him?"

"He's dead."

Griffin frowned, thinking about the night before.

He'd actually heard mention of Franklin Verne's name—he and Vickie had stopped for a damned good dinner and some excellent wine at a spectacular new Baltimore restaurant. Their waiter had mentioned that Franklin Verne was in the city and they were hoping to see him in the restaurant for a meal—and, of course, an endorsement!

"Griffin?"

"Yeah. I'm thinking that you're about to tell me how he died, and since you're on the phone with me, and you know we're in Baltimore, I'm assuming he died in Baltimore?"

"Yes, last night. He was found in the wine cellar of the Black Bird, a new restaurant—"

"What?" Griffin said. He knew the restaurant—pretty well! It was, in fact, the posh place where he'd taken Vickie last night.

"The Black Bird," Jackson repeated.

"We ate there last night."

"Oh. Well, that's convenient. You know right where it is."

"I do. Fell's Point, not far from where we're staying. You know Vickie—we found a really great old historic hotel. Blackhawk Harbor House. In fact, I'm standing outside. It's so wonderfully old and historic, though I can't seem to make a cell phone call from inside." He glanced up at the building. It had been built as a hotel in the 1850s—built with concrete and care. It would probably withstand any storm. The hotel was handsome and elegant, and Griffin enjoyed it—but he still found it annoying when he couldn't get a decent signal on his phone from his room.

"They sure weren't expecting Franklin Verne at the restaurant," he told Jackson. "They talked about the fact that they hoped that he would come in. His patronage would be great for business."

"I imagine. Well, he was there—is there. Sadly, he's dead. At the moment, they're calling it an accidental death."

"Okay. So. How did he die? *Was* it an accident, possibly...?"

"A combination of over-the-counter drugs and alcohol," Jackson said. "That's a preliminary—the ME, of course, will deny he suggested any true cause as of yet. You know how that works—they won't know for certain what caused it until all the tests are back. I take it you haven't seen any news yet?"

"Jackson, it is 7:30 a.m. This was our last weekend before settling in—me back from a long stint in Boston, and Vickie moving to a new state and an entirely new life. Hey, it was *supposed to be* free time. We were out late last night. Vickie is still sleeping."

"Okay, you haven't seen the news. Anyway, Franklin Verne used to be quite the wild man, drinking, getting rowdy with friends, playing the type of hard-core character that appears in most of his books. His wife, Monica, put a stop to it a few years back—when the doctors told her he wouldn't make it to old age. But his body was found in a wine cellar. According to Monica, Franklin had been clean for two full years."

"You know all this because...?" Griffin asked him.

"Because Franklin Verne gave generously to a lot of the same causes our own Adam Harrison holds so dear," Jackson said.

Adam Harrison was their senior advisor—he was, in fact, the creator of the Krewe, and a man with a phenomenal ability to put the right people together with the right situation.

"Naturally," Jackson continued, "he's quite good friends with Monica, so… Well, there you have it. He'll wrangle us an invitation into the investigation eventually—you know him and his abilities with local police." Jackson hesitated a minute. "Even if we wind up having to tell Monica she lost her husband because he slipped back into addiction, she'll have the truth of the situation. For the moment, I need you to go make nice with Detective Carl Morris."

"Carl Morris, sure," Griffin said.

So much for the incredible plans he'd had with Vickie for the day!

"Addiction, a friend, temptation… It could have been an accident," Griffin said.

"Yes. Except that none of the waitstaff saw him in the restaurant, much less down in the wine cellar. And, as I said, Monica—who claims she really knew her husband—is calling it murder."

"Ah. Okay, are you coming up?" Griffin asked Jackson. Krewe headquarters was only about an hour and a half—two hours at most—from Baltimore, even counting Beltway traffic.

"Maybe, but Adam wants to move delicately with this. We're not invited in yet—Franklin Verne's death isn't even considered to be a murder at the moment. But of course, the way the man died, there has to be an autopsy and an investigation. Get started for me, and then give me a call. Let me know what you think."

"All right. When did this happen?"

"He was found about an hour ago. Adam got the call from Monica immediately after she was visited by the police and informed that her husband was dead. If you head in quickly, you'll see the body in situ. Oh, and one more thing."

"What's that?"

"Well, it is Baltimore, and Poe is buried there, and, hell, the name of the restaurant isn't Raven, but it is Black Bird…"

"What?"

"He was found gripping a little bird. Yes, a raven, of course. It's the kind you can find just about anywhere they have Poe souvenirs. Cheap, plastic, black—on a little pedestal with its wings out, beak open…and the word *nevermore* written on the base."

"Like you said, you can buy those souvenirs anywhere."

"Yep. And, sorry. Just one more thing again."

"What's that?"

"He was surrounded by three dead blackbirds. Naturally, of course, no one can figure out how Franklin Verne—or the birds—got into the wine cellar."

Vickie opened her eyes.

For a moment, she was disoriented.

She wasn't at all sure where she was!

And then she realized that Griffin was there, looking down at her with concern. A half grin curled his lips, though that grin was far more rueful than amused.

Grim, even.

"A nightmare?" he asked her gently, a trace of worry crossing his bronzed face. There wasn't a reason for her to be having nightmares—at the moment. The Krewe cases with which she'd been involved had come to their conclusions.

She was in the wonderful hotel in Baltimore's Fell's Point where she had enthusiastically suggested they stay on their trip from Boston to Arlington, Virginia—even though they hadn't really needed to make it an overnight trip, much less a weekend one.

But she and Griffin had wanted time together. Fun time, sightseeing, before Griffin reported back to headquarters; Vickie was preparing to enter the FBI's training academy at Quantico.

Eventually, they'd both be working out of the main special offices of the Krewe of Hunters unit. But for now, Griffin would be getting back to work, they'd both be settling in to living together—and Vickie would be starting up with the next class for twenty weeks of training that would lead to her graduation and an official position with the Krewe.

Vickie could have told Griffin about the dream. The Krewe were more than simply dedicated and well-trained agents. They had been gathered together carefully because they all had unique abilities, the center of those abilities being that they could communicate with the dead.

When the dead chose, of course.

She and Griffin had both known for years just what the other was capable of. While they had only rekindled their relationship recently, they had first met almost a decade ago—when a serial killer had nearly taken Vickie's life. It had been a ghost, the older brother of the child she was babysitting, who had saved her by sending her running out of the house to safety, straight toward a young Officer Pryce. He'd been a cop before becoming an agent, though he had now been with the Krewe of Hunters for quite some time. He'd always known that he wanted to be in law enforcement.

It wasn't that way for Vickie.

She loved history. She'd been a guide, leading youth-group tours as a historian, and she was an author of history books. She was proud to say that she was good at it—the most important reviews to her were the ones that said she had a way of making history fun for the reader.

It was only the cases with which she had recently become involved that had made her want to veer in a new direction. Not a change—an addition. There had been a case in which an incarcerated serial killer had managed to reach out to strike again, and then another where modern-day Satanists had tried to bring the devil back to Massachusetts.

She was now determined to do her best to become an agent herself, and it was a decision with which she was really pleased. It was odd to realize that she had once been embarrassed by her secret talent—the ability to speak with the dead. She hadn't wanted to admit that it could be real. But she'd learned recently that her

so-called curse allowed her to actually make a difference. She might have the ability to help in more bizarre
cases—to save lives. And that mattered. To that end,
she'd applied for and been accepted to the academy at
Quantico. The Krewe might be a special unit, but even
so, the agents were required to go through the academy.
Vickie had passed the necessary tests on paper and
made it through the grueling physical regimen necessary to become an agent.

Griffin already had an apartment in a wonderful old
row house in Alexandria. For him, it wasn't a move—
just a return to his home of the past several years. He
had only been back in Boston—where he and Vickie
both were born and raised—on assignment.

Vickie had gone to college at NYU and then lived
in New York for several years, but never farther south.

It was, she'd assured him, exciting to move.

But she was aware that Griffin believed it had to be
a tug on her heartstrings as well—she was leaving a
lot behind.

And she was. But she was also happy to be moving forward.

"A nightmare?" he repeated, and the note of worry
seemed higher.

She smiled, staring into his dark eyes. Griffin was
fine with her decision to become an agent; the Krewe
was composed of both men and women, and he knew
women were every bit as efficient and excellent as
agents as men.

It was just her—but of course, he loved her. It wasn't
going to be easy for him to accept her walking into the

same danger he did daily. He would, however, get used to it—and she loved him all the more for that fact.

"No, not a nightmare!" she told him. He far too quickly became concerned for her. All it had been was a bizarre dream. It might well have been due to the way they'd overindulged in some delicious blue crabs at dinner last night.

She would stay mum. For the moment. After all, she was in Baltimore. Edgar Allan Poe was buried here; he'd died here. Having dreams about him didn't seem the least bit strange, actually.

But for the moment...

"It was a dream, and rather a cool one. I was walking around Baltimore..."

"We're in Baltimore, so that seems...normal, maybe?"

She grinned, rolling onto an elbow to better face him—he'd already gotten up and showered and dressed for the day. He was an early riser—alert and ready to face the world as soon as he opened his eyes.

Vickie...not so much! But she was getting used to early mornings.

"Perfectly normal," she told him. "It wasn't a nightmare. It was just a dream. About beautiful old Baltimore— hey, it's an important city, right? And we are going to go and do some cool things today, aren't we?"

"Absolutely," he promised. "Fort McHenry, the Inner Harbor, Federal Hill—"

"Don't forget the aquarium!" she said.

"I wouldn't dream of it. But I thought we might want a full day for that. We can do whatever you choose, my love. Anything you would like."

"You've done it all too many times before?" she asked him.

He laughed. "No. I mean, I have done it all before, but not with you, so it's as if it's the first time, right?"

"That is an incredibly good suck-up line if I have ever heard one!" she assured him.

She thought that the line might take them somewhere, but he smiled and stepped away from the bed.

"I just have a couple of hours of work first," he said.

"What?"

"Work. But there's not much involved at the moment, and not much I can do." He added quietly, "Franklin Verne—you know who he is?"

"Yep. I'm living and breathing and have ears and eyes. You can't miss him. What about him?"

"He died last night."

"Oh, that's too bad—terribly sad! I've seen him speak. I mean, I write nonfiction and he writes fiction, but I've been at a number of conferences where he's been a speaker on a panel. He was charming and very funny…helpful, giving. He's actually written some historical fiction, and while Verne tended toward horror—some action, some sci-fi and some mystery—he was a wonderful researcher as well."

"Always the writer!" he teased.

"That's not going to be a problem, is it?" She'd spoken with other agents and she believed that—assuming she did make it through the academy—she'd still be welcome to write on her own time. It seemed that Krewe agents were, in fact, encouraged to keep up with any previous pursuits.

"It's fine!" he assured her quickly.

"So what happened to Franklin Verne? I know that he was ill a few years ago—in fact, he joked about it sometimes when he spoke, saying that his wife taught him how to have fun and not be totally boring without a dip in a whiskey vat."

"Yes, I had heard that he was supposedly as clean as a newborn babe."

"Supposedly?"

"He was found dead in a wine cellar."

"In a wine cellar—he didn't have a wine cellar. I don't think he even drank wine. When he did drink."

"Not his wine cellar. But how do you know he didn't have a wine cellar?"

"He was very open about his health problems, about his wild days—and his love for his wife," Vickie said. "So, if not his own wine cellar—where then?"

"The Black Bird."

"What?"

"Amazing. That was my exact reaction when Jackson told me. Want to come with me? I'm on my way there now. Heading off to kowtow to a local cop named Carl Morris."

Vickie rolled out of bed. "Ten minutes," she told him.

He nodded; he knew she was telling the truth.

Vickie and Griffin had both thoroughly enjoyed the Black Bird the night before; the service had been wonderful and the food had been delicious.

Vickie had especially like the decor; the building was 1820s Federal style, and the restaurant had the first two floors and the basement of the building while the remaining three floors above were given over to office space. Upon entering a long hall of a foyer with exposed brick walls and plush red carpeting, you came to the hostess stand. From there it went through to the bar area.

The bar was lined with portraits of Poe and his family; there were framed posters of quotations and more, all having to do with Edgar Allan Poe.

Stairs led from behind the bar to several sections of seats and a few party rooms of various sizes. The main dining room was the first floor, and tables and booths were surrounded by bookshelves.

Of course, not even the master could have written enough to fill the restaurant's shelves; it was an eclectic mix of secondhand novels. The venue had charmingly been planned on the concept that every diner was welcome to take a book, and, naturally, you were welcome to leave a book or books as well.

New editions of Poe books were sold in the gift shop, which was conveniently on the way out, at the back of the restaurant. Of course, one could leave through the front door, but the bookshop was like a minimuseum, and Vickie sincerely doubted that many people ignored it. Their waiter—he'd introduced himself as Jon—told them that though the restaurant was comparatively new, they attracted a lot of local, repeat clientele, for which they were very grateful. But locals didn't tend to shop for souvenirs, unless they were entertaining out-of-town friends. Since they were happily playing tourist, Vickie and Griffin made sure to visit the shop. Lacey Shaw, the woman working the little boutique, was a bit of a Poe aficionado, and she assured them that even the locals loved to come in and chat.

And their waiter was also quite the enthusiast. "Seriously, poor Poe was much maligned in life, but most of the time, the people who wrote about him were seriously jealous competitors, so of course they tried to make him out to be nothing but a drunk with delusions of grandeur. In truth? He was brilliant. You do know that we credit him with the creation of the modern detective novel? 'The Murders in the Rue Morgue'! What an imagination the man had!" Jon had told them, eyes bright with his admiration. He might be a waiter there, but he truly loved the works of the man and had studied his life.

"I promise you, we'll not argue Poe's brilliance," Griffin had assured him.

Jon had gone on, "But people love the restaurant because of the library. It's not a new idea but what a great one—bring a book, take a book! Or just take a book. Well, okay—buy a shiny new one in the gift shop, too. I love working here! Gary Frampton—the owner—is a wonderful man. I'm crazy about him. Alice—the lovely girl with the long blond hair who greeted you as a hostess tonight—is his daughter."

It wasn't "lovely Alice" who met them then, though, by light of the next day.

It was an officer in uniform.

Griffin produced his credentials, and the officer gruffly told him to go on downstairs to the wine cellar.

The stairs were brick, as old as the building, but well

maintained. As they descended, the air got cooler. The cellar was climate controlled but obviously didn't need much help. It was stone, deep in the ground near the harbor, and naturally protected from the heat of a mid-Atlantic summer.

A tall, slim man who somewhat reminded Vickie of Lurch from *The Addams Family* was standing quietly in the center of the main room. Crime-scene techs—easily identifiable by their jackets—were moving about, collecting what evidence could be found.

The body of Franklin Verne remained, giving Vickie a moment's pause.

She had known him in life. She had seen him when he had smiled, gestured, moved and laughed.

And now, of course, the man she had known—if only casually—was gone. What remained, she felt, was a shell.

She glanced at Griffin. They both felt it.

Yes, Franklin Verne was definitely gone. Nothing of his soul lingered.

At least, not here.

The dead man was seated in a chair near a desk; it was a period piece, Victorian era, she thought. Fitting for the place, but it had a modern computer with a nice monitor, along with a printer/scanner, and baskets most probably from Office Depot that held papers and mail and more.

The desk, however, was next to an old potbellied stove. In winter, it might have warmed up the place a bit, for those condemned to keep the wine company on a cold night.

Franklin Verne had died slumped back in the chair. His eyes were eerily open. A man in scrubs and a mask worked over him—the ME, Vickie assumed.

"Detective Morris?" Griffin asked, stepping forward to introduce himself. Vickie knew that Griffin would follow every courtesy, thanking the detective first and then speaking with the ME.

The Lurch-like man turned toward him, nodding, studying him and then offering him a hand.

"Special Agent Pryce?" Morris asked.

"Yes, sir. Thank you for the courtesy. Our supervising director is friends with Mrs. Verne, as I suppose you've heard."

"Yes," Morris said, looking at Vickie.

"Ms. Victoria Preston," Griffin said, introducing her. "Vickie is heading down to start at the academy in a few weeks."

"Excellent," Morris said, nodding. He lifted his hands. "Sad thing. I've been standing here, looking around, hoping that something brilliant might come to me. I can't say I knew Mr. Verne—he was local, but he and Mrs. Verne were only in residence part of the year these days. He's a popular personage around here. There are wild tales of him back in the day, but he never stopped giving to the city police, and he was involved in a number of charitable enterprises."

"I've heard he was a very good man," Griffin said. "Vickie knew him."

"I didn't exactly know him," she corrected. "We met several times at conferences. I write nonfiction books," she explained.

It was certainly not something that was at all impressive to Detective Morris. "Perhaps this is uncomfortable for you," he said, "being in here. Since you know the victim. And you are a civilian."

"Accepted into the academy," Griffin said.

"I'm fine," she assured Morris, glad that Griffin had so quickly—and indignantly—come to her defense.

Morris turned to the man working with the corpse. "Dr. Myron Hatfield, Special Agent Pryce, Ms. Preston. Dr. Hatfield is, in my opinion, one of the finest medical examiners to ever grace the Eastern coast," he said.

Hatfield straightened. He was tall, too, probably about fifty, with steel-gray hair and a good-sized frame; he was built like a linebacker or a fighter. But he had a quick—if slightly grim—smile. "Nice to meet you. Sorry about the circumstances. I'd met Mr. Verne, too, at a fund-raiser for a local children's hospital. He seemed a good man. And…well, the night I met him, he looked great." He looked as if he was about to say more. He shrugged. "I really won't know much of anything until I get him into the morgue."

"Doctor," Griffin said. "My field supervisor suggested that he died of a mix of alcohol and drugs."

Hatfield hesitated. "His mouth… Well, a layman could smell the alcohol. The condition of the body suggests a catastrophic shutdown of organs. But we need tests. I need to complete an autopsy. I hope that my words haven't gone any further."

"No, sir," Griffin assured him. He turned back to Morris. "No one saw him come down here—they've spoken to all the employees?" he asked.

"It was a late night. The manager didn't close up until almost three in the morning," Morris said. "The place was, according to him, completely empty. We're still trying to contact all the night staff, but the last thing the manager does is check the basement—the wine cellar here—and see that the shelves are locked for the night." He pointed. "Master switch there. You can see that most of the shelves have cages. Some of these wines are worth thousands of dollars."

"And there's no other way in than by the stairs? What about cameras?" Griffin asked.

"None down here, but there are cameras at the front door and the back door, which is really more of a side door, by the gift shop."

"We were here last night," Vickie said.

"Oh?" Morris asked, a brow politely raised a half notch.

"Yes, but we were early birds, comparatively. We were gone by eleven," Griffin said. "Ironic—our waiter was wishing that Franklin Verne would pay a visit and endorse the restaurant."

"He's endorsed it now, all right," Hatfield said.

"So tragically!" Vickie said.

Morris grunted. "Yes, but people are ghouls. The place will be booked for years to come now—it's where Franklin Verne mysteriously died!"

None of them could argue that. "Detective, may I walk around?" Griffin asked.

Detective Morris nodded. "I've been here almost two hours. Can't figure it myself, but I don't believe he vaporized or said, 'Beam me up, Scotty!' There's something here. I'm mulling. You knock yourself out."

"We're about to take the body," Hatfield said quietly.

"Thank you," Griffin said. Vickie kept her distance. She was startled when she heard Griffin ask Hatfield, "I heard he was holding a raven?"

"The kind they sell in the gift shop, right upstairs," Hatfield said.

"Bagged it as evidence," Morris said. He pointed to the desk, where the raven lay in a clear plastic evidence bag.

"Thanks," Griffin said. He lifted the bag. He and Vickie both studied it.

Vickie had noted other ravens just like it at the gift shop the night before; they were cheap plastic, cost no more than a cup of coffee—perfect little souvenirs that brought back a memory and made you smile.

"There were three dead blackbirds by the body?" Griffin asked.

Morris lowered his head in acknowledgment. "They're in the evidence bags at the end of the desk. Take a look—knock yourself out. I guess what's going to matter is how they died, and that falls in Dr. Hatfield's territory."

"Actually, it's a necropsy—but we have a fellow on staff who deals with all animals that aren't of the human variety," Hatfield said. "And we'll keep you apprised every step of the way."

"Thanks," Griffin said. "They are blackbirds, right? Not young crows or ravens?"

"Blackbirds," Hatfield agreed. "The size alone gives us that."

Vickie held where she was, watching Griffin's broad back as he headed down the rows of carefully shelved wine.

After all, he was an agent; she wasn't sure what procedure would be. It was best in this situation to let Griffin move forward without her.

And…

For a moment, she felt dizzy, remembering her dream.

Poe—Edgar Allan! She had met him at a tavern that wouldn't have been far from here…the tavern he'd been found near, delirious and wearing clothing that wasn't his.

He'd been missing three days. Some said he'd been kidnapped for his vote—and thus the different clothing that he wore. Some said that it had been the drink, that he'd met up with friends and the alcohol had quickly cost him his life.

Some said it had been a murder plot, perpetuated by relatives of the widow he'd planned to marry when his business was accomplished…

But the author and poet had not died in a wine cellar. Rather, one of his immortal characters had done so!

"Miss?"

"Oh! I'm sorry!"

Men from the medical examiner's office were there to take the body. She quickly moved out of the way.

Griffin came back from walking up and down the racks of wine.

"I'll know soon enough what I suspect, even if it

takes a bit longer to be official," said Dr. Hatfield. "Special Agent Pryce, you're welcome to come by this afternoon with Carl. I'm afraid that this gentleman will be bringing me in to work all day on a Saturday."

Griffin shook hands all around and gave Detective Morris a card; Morris returned the courtesy. Then Griffin set an arm on Vickie's shoulder and they started back up the steps to the restaurant.

They walked outside.

Vickie stopped dead.

There were birds everywhere.

"Ravens!" she gasped.

"Blackbirds," he said. "I had an uncle who loved birds. Crows, ravens, rooks and blackbirds—all confused for each other, but all different birds. Ravens belong to the crow—or corvids—family, but not all crows are ravens. Blackbirds belong to the thrush family. A raven, however, is about the size of a hawk and a crow is about the size of a pigeon. Those guys..."

He was looking up; he suddenly stopped speaking.

"How bizarre!" he said.

"What?" she asked.

He pointed high where a bird glided over the street, far above the little blackbirds that gathered on buildings and wires.

"That one—that one *is* a raven," he said.

Vickie wasn't at all sure why—the sun was brilliantly shining—but she shivered. She stared at the bird.

It flew over the area, again and again, before lighting on the roof of a nearby building.

Griffin looked at her. "Come on. Let's go see Mrs.

Verne. I'll report to Jackson. Maybe we can still get in a trip out to Fort McHenry."

"Actually…"

"What?"

"I think we should visit Poe's grave," Vickie said.

"Haven't you been before?"

"I have."

"It's just… It's a grave," he reminded her.

"Yes, but fitting today, don't you think?" She shrugged. "It is one of those things you do in Baltimore, you know."

The hardest part of the job wasn't dealing with the dead.

The dead didn't weep like the living.

Griffin hadn't met Monica Verne before, but thanks to his conversation with Jackson, he knew that Adam Harrison was friends with her.

Adam was careful about the friends he chose.

Griffin and Vickie reached Monica Verne's palatial home on the outskirts of the city right before noon.

An attractive young woman wearing a black dress, functional pumps and a bleak expression opened the door.

"Police?" she demanded. She had an accent. She was most probably from somewhere in Eastern Europe.

"No, ma'am," Griffin began.

"You are despicable! You are horrible. Poor Mrs. Verne. She's just learned about this unspeakable tragedy—*from you people*! And you are hounding her!"

"Ma'am!" Griffin said. "We're not the police. We're

FBI—and Mrs. Verne requested that we be here. Please, we're here on behalf of Adam Harrison."

"Oh, oh, oh! Do come in! This way!"

She led them to the widow. Monica Verne was seated in the enclosed back porch of the home, which sat on a little hillock. Picture windows looked out on beautiful gardens, a pond and a small forest.

Monica was slender, almost ethereal. She was no trophy wife; while very lovely, she'd done nothing to correct the changes of time. She was obviously in her late sixties, and still beautiful. Great bone structure, huge powder blue eyes and a quick smile for them— even through her tears.

"I'm so grateful that you're here and that you've come so quickly! I knew that Adam would help… I knew. The police are going to get this all wrong. It's such bull! Franklin was, of course, a player when he was young—some drugs, a hell of a lot of drinking, partying. That's how we met—back when I was modeling he was just becoming known as an author. Struggling! Wasn't making much of anything at the time. I was actually the far more prestigious person! We met at a party where I was a guest—and he was working for the catering company!" She wasn't boasting when she spoke; she was laughing. She choked slightly, more tears spilling from her eyes.

Vickie reached out and set her hand over Monica's. "I'm so sorry."

Monica looked at Vickie and nodded. Griffin thought that Vickie's ability to empathize with others and offer them real comfort was going to be one of her greatest assets in joining the Krewe. It was also going to be one of the most difficult parts of the job for her to learn to manage. He lowered his head for a moment; it was an odd time to smile. And, an odd time to think just how lucky he was. Vickie was beautiful to look at— five foot nine, with long raven-black waves of hair and blue-green eyes that could change and shimmer like emeralds.

She was also so caring—honest and filled with integrity.

He truly loved her. Watching her empathy and gentle touch with Monica, he knew all the more reason why.

"My husband didn't kill himself!" Monica whispered fervently.

"I don't think it's been suggested that he killed himself. I believe they're considering it an accidental death," Griffin began.

"Accidental death, my ass! If there's any last thing I can do for Franklin, it's going to be to make someone prove that this was no accidental death!" Monica lashed out, furious and indignant. She wasn't angry with Vickie—who was still holding her hand. Her passion was against the very suggestion that her husband's death had been through a simple slip—some misfortune.

She wagged a finger at Griffin. "You listen to me, and listen well. We were the best, Frankie and me. I swear it. When all else fell to hell and ruin, we still had one another. I had nothing against his friends, all the conferences, all the fun—some I went to, some I didn't. I trusted him. I was glad of his buddies—his writing friends, men and women. I'm a reader, but I can barely string a decent sentence together. Frankie needed other people who could write and talk about it. But when it all threatened his body, I put my foot down. No drugs whatsoever—not even a toke off someone's joint. No alcohol. None. And he listened to me. Because he wanted to live, and he loved and respected me. He loved us—he loved living. Adam sent you to me because he knows, damn it! Accidental death! No way. And you will find a way to prove it."

"Mrs. Verne, what happened yesterday? Was he home—did you not notice that he wasn't with you until the police came to tell you that…that he'd been found? What went on here yesterday?"

"What do you mean?" Monica asked indignantly. "There is no lie to this. You may ask anyone anywhere who knows the two of us, from friends to associates, to—"

"I'm not suggesting anything was wrong between you," Griffin said, interrupting her softly. "What we're trying to do is figure out where he was during the day, how he came to be where he was last night. Where was he when you went to bed?"

"Next to me, lying right next to me!" Monica said.

"What time was that?"

"Early. We'd been at my cousin's house the day before. Her grandchildren were in town. We were literally exhausted—in bed by eight o'clock!"

"And when you woke up this morning—he wasn't with you?" Griffin asked.

Monica shook her head. "But there was nothing unusual to that! Franklin loved to head out for walks first thing in the morning. He always told me that the longest and hardest part of writing was all in his head. When he went for his morning walks, he was really working. Of course, he'd say that with a wink, so what was and wasn't really true…"

"Did he mention anything about going anywhere? Meeting up with someone? Any arrangements he might have made to meet up with a friend later—and he didn't tell you?"

"He had no reason to lie to me!" Monica said. "No reason. Ever—and he knew it."

"But he did keep up regular correspondences with friends, right?"

"Of course. The police took the computer from his home office. And—"

She broke off, sighing.

"What is it?" Vickie asked gently.

"They asked for his phone. But I don't have it. They didn't find his phone anywhere. And I can't find his laptop, either."

Griffin glanced at Vickie. Missing personal devices were suspicious.

Because there might be evidence on them.

"Franklin did not meet up with a friend! He did not break in to that cellar to drink wine! I'm telling you, I knew my husband, he…"

She broke off, gritting her teeth. She was trying not to cry. The woman was truly in anguish; she was also furious.

"I don't know when he went out. I don't why he went

out—or how he wound up at the restaurant. I do know one thing."

"What is that, Mrs. Verne?" Vickie asked.

Monica Verne startled them both, slamming a fist on the coffee table. "My husband was murdered!"

The motion seemed to be a cue.

In the yard, a dozen birds took flight, shrieking and cawing…

Griffin could see them as they let out their cries, sweeping into the sky.

A murder of crows…

And an *unkindness of ravens*…

As poetically cruel as the death of Franklin Verne.

2

"I feel just terrible for Mrs. Verne," Vickie said. "I mean, it was obviously quite a love match. I don't think that she's going to be quiet about this—she's going to let everyone out there know that she thinks that this was a murder."

Griffin glanced at Vickie as he drove, taking them back into downtown Baltimore. She was incredibly—and very sweetly—a *people* person. She felt bad for Monica Verne, and seemed to understand both the woman's pain and her determination.

"Yes, she will let everyone know exactly what she thinks, including everyone in the media. The problem is that she's going to demand answers before people may have them. The ME is no one's fool, and certainly in no way a yes-man. He will not give his report until he has every single test in. So..."

"I guess any ME has to be careful. I mean, a writer isn't exactly a Michael Jackson, Heath Ledger or Prince, but..."

"Bite your tongue!"

"I'm serious—who recognizes writers? Stephen King, maybe. And okay, James Patterson—he does a lot of his own commercials, too. But—"

"People knew Franklin Verne. He was very popular—he gave to so many charities. He and his wife had no children, just one another—and all their good deeds," Griffin said.

"But you're saying it's going to be a while before the ME will even say if it was a murder or an accidental death?"

"He will test for every poison out there, for every possibility," Griffin said.

"So, what do you think?" Vickie asked.

"What do I think?" he repeated.

"That was, yes, indeed, the question," she said.

He glanced over at her again as they drove. Vickie was serious and thoughtful. He gritted his teeth, reminding himself that she'd already been through two heinous cases. She'd never panicked; she behaved rationally.

She was about to go through the academy. It was a smart thing for her to do, the right choice; since they were staying together, she was going to get involved in his cases. He was glad she'd been accepted into the program.

And still…the worrying—the wishing he could keep her from all danger—did not go away.

"I think," Griffin said, "that we're way too early in this investigation to have any idea as to what is really going on. For one thing, I'm disturbed by the fact that no one can explain how Franklin Verne got into the restaurant—much less down to the wine cellar."

"And the way he died... Well, I think they'll find out that it was drugs or alcohol poisoning. So similar to Poe—though there are many theories on exactly what happened with Edgar Allan Poe, too," Vickie said. "Some people believe he was just taken by pollsters—it was an election time, and in the 1800s, voter fraud certainly existed. One theory is that Poe was kidnapped by ruffians so that he could vote and then vote again—and that could be why he was dressed in clothing he hadn't owned."

"That sounds like a possibility," Griffin said.

"Ah! But some people believe it was a murder plot by the brothers of the woman—Sarah Elmira Royster Shelton—whom he was about to marry. History is still undecided about whether they were or weren't officially engaged when he died. She denied it sometimes, and sometimes said that it was true. I guess it was an understanding. She had been his first love, and his last, certainly. But she would lose the inheritance from her first husband if she married again."

"Motive!" Griffin said.

"Yes. A thickened plot," Vickie agreed. "Then again, some think he just got into a bar brawl, changed clothing for some more whiskey money—and died in his delirium because he was an alcoholic and, therefore, finally drank himself to death."

"And that sounds possible, too."

Vickie looked unhappy again. "Poor Monica. People *will* assume that Franklin Verne fell off the wagon, got started on a binge and managed to sneak down to the restaurant's wine cellar."

"Maybe we'll get a lucky break. There are cameras at the front door."

"They won't see Franklin Verne on those cameras. I'm assuming the cops are checking them now, right?"

"Yep."

"They won't find him."

"You're so sure."

"I am absolutely certain," Vickie said. She hesitated, drawing in a breath and holding it. "I believe that he was murdered."

There was something about her voice that made Griffin look over at her quickly. She was definitely deeply disturbed by something that went beyond their current speculation.

"What is it?" he asked her softly.

She glanced back over at him, thoughtful, yet appeared hesitant.

They'd originally met under horrible circumstances; Vickie had been just seventeen, he in his early twenties, and she'd been attacked by a serial killer.

They'd met again when a new serial killer was terrorizing Boston, and since then, they'd worked together to rescue a friend and save the lives of many people, including—in the end—Vickie's own life.

They knew each other deeply; knew they saw and felt what most others did not.

And, still, sometimes Vickie seemed timid, as though afraid that when she spoke aloud what she had to say would sound ridiculous.

"Vickie!" he persisted. "It's me!"

"Okay!" she said, and smiled. She took a breath. "Remember this morning? You asked me if I was having a nightmare."

"Yes." Griffin didn't press.

"I was. Kind of. I was dreaming about Edgar Allan Poe. I was here—in Baltimore. But it was way back in time—on the day that he was found in delirium before he was taken to the hospital for the few days before he died. Poe was talking to me. He warned me not to assume that it was like what had happened to him."

"This was before I heard from Jackson?" he asked her.

She nodded gravely. "Yes, Griffin. Before. I mean, I thought I was dreaming about Poe because we were in Baltimore, because we had enjoyed that great dinner and the Black Bird and our waiter had kind of inundated us with Poe. But..."

Griffin sat quietly.

The "gift" or "curse" that united Krewe members—that had sent Adam Harrison on his quest for his special teams—manifested in different ways. For most of them, it was simply seeing and speaking with the dead.

But because of what Griffin had seen and encountered over the years, there was little that he denied as possible.

Oh, he doubted most people! He was a horrible skeptic. He'd learned to be, since the world was far more filled with fake seers, psychics, mystics and mediums than most people would ever imagine.

But there were also those who truly had a sixth

sense—and it did, sometimes, manifest itself in the world of dreams and nightmares. This wasn't the first time Vickie had communicated with the dead in visions while sleeping.

"So, under these circumstances, your nightmare meant something. We'll assume that you had the dream for a reason—and that it wasn't an Edgar Allan Poe overdose at the restaurant. Did you see in this nightmare that the cameras at the front would get nothing?"

Vickie shook her head. "No, I just saw Poe himself in the nightmare. Maybe Poe was witnessing it, or... I don't know. But I believe that Franklin Verne was murdered, and that his murderer is too smart to be caught on film. There's also a delivery entrance. There's a driveway that goes down to the basement at the back, remember? Receiving for the kitchen is next to the wine cellar, right through one of the little doors."

"Yes," Griffin told her. "I walked the whole thing. So, tell me—how did he get in through the receiving door?"

"With a friend. Or a so-called friend."

"A friend? So you're thinking accidental—or depraved indifference?"

"No," Vickie said again, emphatic. "I think that Franklin trusted this person—and shouldn't have. I don't think that he set out to drink. I believe he loved his wife as passionately as she loved him. She had no problem with him being a wild Hemingwayesque writer—she didn't care until his excesses started to kill him. Only then did she put her foot down. And I believe he knew that everything she did was because she loved him."

"Wow. You did *just* meet her, right?" he asked, smiling—but with a sardonic tone.

"Oh, ye of little faith!" she said. "I am good at reading people."

He laughed. "I have faith. I buy what you're saying, too. I never heard anything other than that those two—Franklin and Monica—had a beautiful marriage."

Griffin shifted his attention for a moment to navigating the one-way streets throughout downtown around the University of Maryland campus.

"And, we can't forget the Poe mania around here—and Poe's stories!" Vickie said. "There's 'The Cask of Amontillado'!"

"Ah-ha!" he said. "The cask of Amontillado. Wine? A cask of wine. Saw lots of bottles down in the cellar, but no casks. Something I didn't notice?"

Vickie nodded gravely. "I'm not talking about wine—it was a short story by Poe, circa 1846. The narrator of the story is a man named Montresor. He's very angry with and jealous of an acquaintance, Fortunato. Fortunato has insulted him gravely, you see. The story is haunting and gothic and creepy—Montresor is dressed for the carnival season in black, and Fortunato is in all the colors of the jester. Anyway, to make a long story short—"

"Too late," Griffin assured her, which earned him a glower.

"Montresor tricks Fortunato with wine, promising him a most unique sherry—and saying that if he's too busy, he can get one of Fortunato's competitors to come try it. Fortunato is too vain to allow someone else to try the wine. Montresor never explains what the insult was that he's so angry about—he's just on a vendetta and he explains how he's become judge and jury. In the end, he walls poor Fortunato up in a crypt—and we learn he remains there, undisturbed, for fifty years. Pretty harsh."

"He gets away with it?" Griffin asked.

"You never read the story?"

"Um—no."

"What? How did you manage to neglect Poe growing up? You're from Boston. Okay, so Poe hated Boston, but he was actually born there."

"Hey! I know some of Poe's work," Griffin protested. "Everyone knows 'The Raven.' I absolutely loved Vincent Price. And Peter Lorre and—"

"You're talking movies, not the written word!"

Griffin laughed. "Yeah, well? Without Poe, we wouldn't have had the movies. A few years back—I don't know how many—there was a movie with John Cusack playing Poe. In that version he died to keep his love from being murdered."

"That's not how he died! That was a movie."

"Ah-ha! But you see, no one knows how he did die—that's the point, isn't it?"

"Yes, but the movie had him engaged to a pretty *young* thing. In reality, he was about to be married—as I was telling you—to Sarah Elmira Royster Shelton, she with the brothers who might have been murderers, and with whom he'd been in love when he went to college. Her father hadn't approved and he'd destroyed all of Poe's letters to her, and so young love had been thwarted. Anyway, years later, her husband was dead and Poe's wife, Virginia Clemm, was dead, and Poe and the woman he'd loved in his youth met up again. Poor man, he was just forty when he died. But Sarah Elmira was no sweet young innocent—she was about his age, a mother, all grown up."

"Killjoy," Griffin told her, and Vickie laughed softly.

"I don't mean to be. I love a John Cusack movie, too. I think I would have found a different way to explore what had really happened. I mean, he was found delirious in clothing that wasn't his! How did that happen? He'd joined the temperance society before he left Richmond, but of course, no matter how you look at it, the man was an alcoholic—though it seemed that he was a binge drinker rather than a habitual drunk. I can't help but think sometimes that he might have had a much better life if he'd lived in our day and age. So much information disappeared right along with him regarding the days he was missing! His death was as much a mystery then as it is today."

"'Once upon a midnight dreary, while I pondered, weak and weary...'"

Very determined, Griffin went ahead to repeat a good section of the famous poem. What he couldn't remember, he thought he faked with a tremendous amount of panache. Vickie was grinning as he gave her his dramatic interpretation, so he was pretty sure that she knew when he was doing his ad-libbing.

"Well, you know the title, you know it's a poem and

you know it's by Edgar Allan Poe," she said, amused. "I'm totally impressed."

"Wait and see how I wow people!" he told her.

He pulled into public parking near Westminster Hall and Burying Ground. "Poe's grave, at your command, my love."

She looked at him and smiled. "So you're going to wow the dead people with your Poe-etic license?" she asked him.

"Sometimes," he reminded her, "dead people are far more important than the living."

"Sometimes," she repeated.

The old Presbyterian church itself—long since deconsecrated and now known as Westminster Hall—offered tours on certain days of the week with reservations, and special tours when prearranged. The catacombs and the inside of the structure were only available through those special times and reservations. But the burial ground surrounding the old church was open to the public, and historical markers identified many of the notable dead.

"Poe was buried in the back at first," Vickie said, walking quickly ahead of Griffin.

She wasn't heading toward the back, though, but rather toward the place where Poe had been moved when admirers of his work had finally gotten together to manage the creation of a fine monument to him.

"In an unmarked grave!" she said. "He had a cousin—Neilson Poe—in the city of Baltimore. Neilson was finally contacted after Poe was found and brought to the hospital. But the thing is, Poe never came back to his senses. He was delirious from the time he was found to the time he died."

There were other visitors to the burial ground, some wandering around to view other notable graves, some hovering by the monument to Edgar Allan Poe.

"Miss, excuse me—is he really here? Or is this just the monument? You seem to know a great deal."

An attractive woman of about forty or forty-five had stopped in front of Vickie; she'd apparently heard her speaking.

Vickie flushed. "I don't know that much. I just always loved his work. I do know that he was exhumed and moved here—with other members of his family, Virginia Clemm, his wife, and Maria Clemm, her mother. You can see their names if you walk around the monument."

The woman thanked her.

Others were gathering. Some came with curiosity— and some with absolute reverence, bowing their heads, speaking softly and then just standing there, as if by gathering at his grave they could breathe in some of his brilliance.

Griffin noticed that a boy standing near the monument suddenly jerked—as if he'd been startled or touched by someone unseen.

He looked around the monument, but saw nothing but other visitors who had come to pay their respects to Baltimore's famous poet.

Griffin walked around the monument himself, then stopped short.

A man stood there, with dark hair and a sad face. He seemed to be dressed oddly for the day and the time.

The man saw Griffin. He lifted his hand in a salute, staring at Griffin gravely.

Griffin had never been the Poe reader that Vickie was. Of course, he'd never been any kind of a historian, either—able to rattle off names and dates with such amazing conversational ease.

But even he recognized the figure.

For a moment, he thought that the man was an actor, out to entertain Baltimore visitors at the burial ground.

Then the man disappeared, as if he'd faded into the stone itself.

And Griffin could only presume that he had just seen the real Edgar Allan Poe.

The news was out; it was everywhere.

Baltimore had lost another great writer, and how oddly, how eerily! He had died in a wine cellar—at a restaurant called the Black Bird, a restaurant that entirely honored the great writer Edgar Allan Poe.

Boston claimed Poe for its own—and had just added a life-size statue of him with a raven on Boylston Street. But in life, Poe hadn't much loved the city of his birth. To be fair, he had lived and worked more in Virginia and Maryland. It seemed, however, that just as "Washington slept here" was a common refrain, Poe was also coveted. And it was only right. New York City had quite a claim on the man, too—in the Village, and up in the Bronx, where he had last lived, and where his mother-in-law, Maria Clemm, had been waiting for him to come retrieve her.

Right now, Baltimore had renewed their claim on the man—and was musing over what facts were known about his death—and how they compared with the death of Franklin Verne.

Griffin and Vickie had come to the police station to meet up with Carl Morris, having given up the illusion that they were on any kind of a vacation or even off for the weekend.

Maybe they had been on the job from the moment the dream had first plagued her that morning, Vickie thought. And, if not then, they had become completely involved once Jackson had called, or even as soon as Monica Verne had reached out to Adam.

Monica's resolve and passion couldn't be ignored. Vickie just wished that she hadn't brought that passion to the media so quickly.

Monica Verne was offering a hundred-thousand-dollar reward to anyone who could lead her to the true cause of her husband's death.

"Great, just great!" Griffin muttered. "Now we'll get calls from every demented soul in the city."

"Well, maybe someone will come forward with good information," Vickie told him.

They were standing with Morris and a group of officers in the center of the work floor of the station; one of the officers had brought up the live footage on the large screen that hung from the room's ceiling, available anytime there was some type of video footage that should be witnessed by all.

Monica must have called the local news station just minutes after Griffin and Vickie had left her home; any self-respecting journalist would have hurried to her with all possible speed.

Phones were always ringing, lighting up, at the police station. It almost appeared as if an alien ship sat above them, there was such a display of sound and light as the show aired.

Morris looked at Vickie, shaking his head sadly. "We can hope, but…for the most part? This kind of thing takes up hours of work, and yields little. But yes, we can hope."

"Well, Monica is convinced her husband was murdered," Vickie said.

"And she's probably right," Griffin murmured.

"Sorry!" Carl Morris called, his voice deep, rich, loud—and extending to the different officers and detectives in the room. "Answer all calls—do your best to sort the wheat from the chaff."

"You're going to love this one, Detective!" an officer called out, holding up one of the police station's yellow crime-tip forms. "The Martians are here. They learned how to beam people places by watching *Star Trek* reruns for hours and hours. They killed him because they had to suck out his brain."

Morris waved a hand in the air. There wasn't much laughter. There were far more sighs.

Morris motioned to Vickie and Griffin. They followed him into his office.

There was a monitor screen at the side of his desk. Morris picked up a remote control and hit it. "Maybe you can see something I missed. I've gone over the digital video or whatever the hell it is from the front-door cameras a zillion times."

Nothing happened on the screen. Morris swore softly. "Hang on," he told them. "I have to go find a kid."

The kid—Officer Benedict, who appeared to be about twenty-five—hurried in after Morris stood at the door and yelled out.

"Here, sir!" Benedict said to Morris, glancing at Griffin and Vickie with a grimace. "This, sir, turns it on. Then just hit this arrow, and it will play. The arrow is Play. But the device must be powered on."

"I got it this time, I got it!" Morris said. "Hey, these things are new. We just got them in a week or so ago. Thanks, Benedict."

"Yes, sir," Benedict said.

"Stay, will you? These special agents might want the footage slowed down."

There was only one real agent there at the moment—Griffin. But he didn't say anything and Vickie kept quiet as well.

"We have footage from the opening at eleven o'clock all the way through the night," Benedict explained. "So, it would take hours to watch it all."

"Go ahead, start at the beginning," Griffin told him. "I'll have you speed it up—but please, Detective Morris, Officer Benedict, please let us know if you see someone coming or going that we should know about."

"Of course," Morris told them.

They began to watch the footage. They saw Gary Frampton, the owner, opening the door and looking out on the day, then closing it again. His daughter, Alice, arrived. A small cluster of men and women who'd been identified as kitchen staff showed up. Then later, Lacey Shaw, the Poe lover/gift shop manager, and then their waiter from the night before, whose full name was Jon Skye. More staff ambled on in. Then came the customers.

"There! Stop it. Back up a bit!" Morris told Benedict.

The young officer did as he was told. Morris leaned in to the screen, pointing at people as he said, "There. Naturally there is a major Poe literary society here, a national Poe society and others. Among them is one actually called the Blackbird Society, and they're dedicated to all things Poe. Franklin Verne belonged *nominally* to a number of societies, and among them was the Blackbird Society. That woman there, Liza Harcourt, is the president. The man at her side is Alistair Malcolm, vice president of the society, and with them is…" He paused, staring at the screen.

"That's Brent Whaley," Office Benedict said. "Another writer. He's probably best known in science fiction circles, but he loves horror and Poe. Oh, and he belongs to several societies, the Poe one here, and also an H. P. Lovecraft one up somewhere in the northeast, probably Rhode Island, where Lovecraft was from and where he's buried."

They all looked curiously at Officer Benedict.

"You have great information," Griffin told him.

Benedict flushed and shrugged. "My parents are kind of armchair members. They pay their dues and they love to read all the different stories and articles that go out. They're just kind of homebodies."

"They all went in together," Morris noted. "I've met Liza and Malcolm, just not Brent Whaley."

"Well, they must be friends. They're society friends, at least," Benedict said.

Other diners came and went. Benedict sped up the recording, and people on the screen began to look like little ants.

Liza left the restaurant at about three thirty in the afternoon.

Malcolm left a few minutes later.

Brent Whaley didn't seem to leave.

"Take it all the way to the next morning," Griffin asked.

They watched as the evening diners—including Vickie and Griffin themselves—came and went. They watched as the staff left, including their waiter, Jon Skye, gift-store maven Lacey Shaw and finally Alice Frampton with her father, Gary. Then nothing. Just a few late-night stragglers walking past, but the front door didn't open again, and the time stamp on the video rolled into the next day.

"Did you see Brent Whaley leave?" Griffin asked, looking at the others.

"Let me run the footage back," Benedict said.

Morris pointed at the screen when a large group was leaving together. "Is that Whaley there? I think it's the same man—the top of his head appears to be the same. But maybe not."

"You have to be right," Benedict said. "Yeah, that

has to be him. He's just surrounded by that big crowd—looks like it was a rehearsal dinner for a wedding. Guess Brent got into the middle of it."

"Maybe—or maybe not," Griffin murmured.

"We'll find out. Because if he was still in the restaurant… I guess we'll pick up Brent Whaley. If he tells us he walked out in a crowd…we'll know for sure. But even with the cameras, there are things that can be missed. And there is the delivery door… Oh, we'll be really nice. We'll ask for help from him," Morris said wearily. He shook his head. "Would one writer kill another? Out of jealousy, anger or a perceived insult?"

Griffin looked at Vickie. "I don't think it involved writers, but… 'The Cask of Amontillado,'" he said.

"Oh, yeah, man! I read that one," Office Benedict said, enthused. "So cold! So precise… But our victim wasn't walled in."

"Poe liked to wall people in, huh?" Morris asked, shaking his head. "'The Black Cat.' He liked burying people alive, too. 'The Premature Burial'—and others, I'm sure."

"Everyone is a Poe expert," Griffin murmured, looking at Vickie a little bit baffled. She had to smile. "Detective, Mrs. Verne said that you took her husband's desktop computer. Have you been able to find anything on it, any references to him planning to meet up with anyone—anything at all?"

"Our tech people are on it—and they're good," Morris assured him.

"I'm sure they are," Griffin said. "We'll be in touch

then," he said. "Will you let me know if you're able to find Brent Whaley?"

When they left a few minutes later, Vickie whispered to Griffin, "That really was a great rendition of 'The Raven' you gave earlier."

He laughed, squeezing her hand and smiling at her. "Yeah? Well…"

He looked away. Something was bothering him, she thought. "My turn," she said. "What? What's going on?"

"I saw him."

"Him—who?"

"Him—Poe. Edgar Allan. He was at the burial ground."

"The ghost of?" Vickie asked, frowning.

"Looked just like Poe—and disappeared in the wink of an eye. In my experience that means, A, I've worked at this job too long, B, there's a really amazing magician at work in Baltimore, or, C, the ghost of the master of horror and mystery himself, Edgar Allan Poe, is walking among us!"

3

Vickie stood on North Amity Street, looking at the building that Edgar Allan Poe had once called home.

She was on her own; Griffin had headed to the morgue with Carl Morris. The medical examiner—Dr. Myron Hatfield—was going to start right in on Franklin Verne.

With the uproar in the city over the very unusual passing of such a man, it was imperative that he give a cause of death as quickly as possible. He had already been approached by various media outlets, of course.

He'd said he could not give out cause until he had received results on every test that must be considered when such a death had occurred.

Bravo, Myron! Vickie had thought. She was sure that certain things might quickly be obvious. She was glad that the man intended to be thorough—and that he wouldn't be pressured into speaking before he was ready.

Morris had, she realized, kept a number of pieces of information from the press. There was no mention of the dead blackbirds found by him, nor the little souvenir-style raven Verne had been holding so tightly in his hand.

Vickie looked up at the house. She had downloaded and printed some information about the residence while at the police station.

While the home wasn't furnished, it was on the National Registry of Historic Places, and, according to her reading, very much the same as it had been during the years Poe had lived there between 1833 and 1835. A Poe society had struggled long and hard to preserve the building and had managed to do so. Through time—and due to the expense of keeping up the old property—city organizations took over. Now Poe Baltimore, an organization dedicated to keeping alive the brilliance of the man who had lived and written some of his most amazing work in the city, took care of the house.

The house was a small brick row house in a line of other similar houses.

A friendly docent welcomed her and explained some of the rooms and the exhibits. The museum was proud to have Poe's writing desk and a number of other important artifacts, some china, glasses and more that had belonged to the family. Vickie admired the objects—those that had belonged to Poe's father, and those that were simply from the correct period.

Walking the rooms, halls and stairways of the house and studying the exhibits, Vickie wondered about the fact that Griffin had been the one to see Poe—while she had dreamed about him. She wondered if she was a little bit worried that the ghost had shown himself to

Griffin rather than to her—or if she was just disturbed because her dream had been so real. She had nearly felt the dirt of the road; she had heard the noise of the tavern as if it had been real. She'd much rather simply see the man—or the specter of him—than face dreams that made her feel she was right there with the clip-clop of horses' hooves and the dust that stirred in the air.

The staircases in the house were wicked—with twists and turns and very narrow. Vickie smiled and stepped out of the way for a mother with a young son to make their way up.

Vickie followed; the house was mostly empty, but there were displays here and there.

She studied Poe's family tree and felt she got a sense for why he loved the Virginia and Maryland areas so much more than Boston. Both of Poe's parents had been actors. He'd been born in Boston, but his father's grandfather had been a Revolutionary hero and the Poe family had settled in Baltimore even before the fighting had begun. And while his foster father had been in Richmond, Poe had found love in the arms of his cousin, Virginia Clemm. His mother-in-law/aunt had loved him, too. He'd formed a family here. According to one exhibit, Poe had considered himself to be a "Virginia gentleman."

And yet, in the end, Baltimore had claimed him.

She was reading another placard when she felt an uneasy sensation. The mother and little boy were near her, along with an older couple and a small group of young women who appeared to be high school age. She looked around.

And then she saw him. He was standing behind the young women. He was watching her with what seemed to be tremendous enjoyment. As she stared at him, he smiled deeply, and then gave his attention to the pocket watch he drew from his waistcoat. He pointed a finger at her, as if he was mocking her. And then he disappeared.

She blinked.

She had seen him. She had definitely seen him.

And she was suddenly angry; he was playing with the two of them. Somehow, he had haunted her when she'd been sleeping! And now he was playing the mystery out with his appearances and disappearances.

If he had something to say, he needed to say it!

She turned and strode across the room, eager to get down the steps—very eager to leave the house. On the very narrow stairway, she felt something—as if a hand pushed her. She gritted her teeth, really angry—until she realized that she hadn't been pushed, she'd been grasped.

Vickie managed to swing around just in time to catch the little boy, who had hurried ahead of his mother and tripped on a step.

She steadied him, mentally mocking herself.

Poe's ghost had not been trying to push her down the stairs. She was glad to have rescued the overanxious boy and was quick to assure the boy's mother that it was nothing—she might have tripped on the stairs herself!

Outside the small museum, she muttered beneath her breath as she headed for her car.

Glancing up, Vickie couldn't help but note that while it was afternoon, the sun was still up in the late-summer sky. It had been a long day, and it seemed almost ridiculous that so much could have happened and it still be the same day. But it all had moved quickly. They had gone from the wine cellar at the Black Bird to see Monica Verne. From her house, they'd gone to Poe's tombstone, then to the station, and from there, Griffin had gone on to the morgue and she had come out to the museum.

The afternoon was waning, but…

There was still sun.

And shadows, she thought, going into the parking garage. For a moment, she paused, turning quickly. She had felt certain that she was being followed.

She saw no one. But since she couldn't see anyone, she spoke aloud.

"You wretched little bastard! If you're following me, just show yourself. And if you can't have the manners to do so, well, shove the hell off!"

No one replied. She tensed, hearing a footstep. It was just a man in a hoodie, hands deep in his pockets. He looked up at her as if she was crazy, shaking his head. He didn't speak to her, but muttered beneath his breath.

"I'm not following you, lady. Take a pill."

Wincing, Vickie let out a breath and hurried to the elevator at the parking garage, and then across the asphalt to her own car. She got in and set her key in the ignition.

It was then that he spoke.

"Good afternoon, miss."

She nearly broke the key in the ignition, switching it off, turning to stare at the ghost.

It wasn't that she was in the least afraid of the dead. Dylan Ballantine—the teenaged ghost who had saved her in high school—had taken it upon himself to be her near constant companion and torment her through a great deal of her college years. Now, he had a lovely girlfriend, Darlene—a young woman sadly lost to killers, but who had reached out to Vickie to help solve her case. She was used to having spirits around.

It had nothing to do with fear. It had everything to do with Poe's ghost following her around and popping up in her car.

He was now seated next to her in his suit, waistcoat and an ascot. A curl of his dark hair fell over his forehead.

"Ass!" Vickie muttered, so startled that she was shaking. She was glad—at least—that he had spoken before she'd driven out into traffic.

Then she realized that she had just called a man who had created work she had admired all her life an *ass*.

But he did not seem to be offended.

Rather, he grinned at her with sheer pleasure.

"Wonderful! You do see me, and quite clearly!" he said. "I mean, one must face it. There were times, indeed, when I might have been compared to the lowliest of the beasts of burden! But I beg of you, believe this! I can be charming and sincere and offer the utmost assistance as well. And, my dear Miss Preston— oh! First, forgive me being so forward, but I observed some of the most recent events and heard your name. I am, of course, Edgar Allan Poe—and I do believe that *you* need assistance!"

"Sir, I will tell you this," Vickie said, irritated and

amazed that a ghost could make her feel so aggravated, "I see you clearly."

His pleasure increased; his dark eyes twinkled. "I'm quite overcome—so deeply pleased. Why, it hasn't been since…perhaps 1921 or so, when Mr. Abraham Grisham was in the city that I was able to speak so simply and easily with the living. He was a charming man—quite well lettered. He spoke to me at the burial ground. Oh, you mustn't think that I spend my days sitting melancholy in the cemetery—despite the words I wrote. I… Well, I'm not at all sure what I'm doing here, but, my dear young woman, I dearly hope that you realize I wrote fiction, and that I was no ghoul!"

"No, of course not. I had a dream about you, about the day you died," Vickie said.

"You seem like an intelligent young woman. I'd not have whispered in your ear as you lay sleeping had it not appeared so. I listened at the restaurant… You were knowledgeable. I was so pleased. So many people see me in such a sad light. As if I did nothing but haunt old, decrepit, decaying houses crumbling apart! Graveyards by night… They seemed to think I was a drunken, broken man, even in death, wasting away on a tombstone. That was that wretched Griswold—Rufus Griswold." He stared at Vickie, as if waiting for her to say something.

She did. "Rufus Griswold. You attacked him with some rather pointed criticism of his work. When you died, he found his revenge. But you see, in the end, of course, you won. People became enamored of your work more and more with each year. I can assure you, very few people today would know the name Griswold—but there is probably no one who has ever attended a school in America who has not heard of Mr. Edgar Allan Poe."

"Bravo, Miss Preston, and words most kind. Far sweeter to my ear than those I heard before! Imagine— those that came harsh upon the ear before as you traversed the garage! Such rude words to fall from such rose-like lips!" the ghost said, shaking his head. "Dear me! Not that I have not known my share of opinionated members of the gentler sex, but...you can be quite hasty and devilish in your speech!"

She narrowed her eyes. "Trust me, I've said worse. Usually, when your kind makes acquaintance with me, it's because they need help. If you wish for some kind of assistance, Mr. Poe, it's not good manners to pop up here and there, and then disappear, testing the sanity of the living."

He still looked at her, amused.

"Should I care? I'm afraid I'm quite beyond help, though, to be honest, I don't at all understand this existence." For a moment, he looked stricken—he had an expression that suited every description of him as a haunted and miserable man who had led a life of substance abuse, scraping for an income, continually plagued by death and misfortune in those around him. "My Elmira has gone," he said. "All those I would call beloved, or friend—or even enemy. So...you, Miss Preston, surely need help. Not me. Therefore, I am at my leisure. You may do the groveling, if you so choose."

"You may get out of my car, if you wish to be so rude," she said.

He smiled at that. "My apologies! It is not my intention to be rude. You have no grasp of what it is like to be among the dead. Here on earth. Quite uncomfortable— I mean, those unused to being critiqued and disparaged would barely make it! People walking through you, not seeing you, not noting a pleasant, 'Good morning!' And those of my kind. Oh, the wailing and lamenting! Quite enough to give one a dreadful headache—I mean, had one actually had a real head that might ache!"

She had actually been really angry—as much as she admired Poe. She'd simply seen the dead most of her adult life, and there was one thing she knew for a certainty. They were very much like their living selves. Some were giving, some needed help, some were kind—and some were self-absorbed and self-righteous and not so nice.

"Do you know what happened to Franklin Verne?" she asked him.

"Most sadly, I do not," he told her. "But of this, I'm quite certain. He did not kill himself. He did not fall back into the ways of sin or the flesh or into a vat of wine, as they might well say! I knew Franklin Verne. Well, I did not *know* him as those who called him friend might know him—I know the man because I observed him. He was a good man. A good writer. He loved his wife very much. I felt that we were kindred spirits."

Vickie studied him, waiting. It had been, she knew, way too much to hope that the ghost of Poe, having appeared in her dream and now in her car, had all the pat answers she might need.

"He loved his wife, and she loved him," Vickie said.

He nodded, grave now, not taunting or teasing. "You see, he reminded me of where I was when… Well, I don't know what happened at the end myself, but I am referring to the point when I left this earth. When I died. I was on a train…and then I was dead. I have been listening to theories ever since. But that is no matter now. It is far too late to be solved. But so—here is one truth. Sarah Elmira Shelton was my first love. We were so young…and in love as only youth can be in love. Her father betrayed us. I went on. And believe me, I did love my Virginia. Dear, sweet, innocent Virginia! So very lovely! And yet, she was gone. And then I was back in Richmond, and there was my Sarah Elmira, a widow herself. She was no flushing young rose; time lay between us. Time had taken a toll upon us both as well. For her, I joined the temperance society. I gave up drink. And I did not die in a drunken stupor—to that I swear!" He was passionate, but he stopped suddenly, smiling at her. "I knew love, and that is what I mean. And I have seldom seen such a deep, rich, selfless love as that which Franklin Verne bore his wife, and which she bore him in return. He told her he would not drink. I told Sarah Elmira that I would not drink. I meant it— so did Franklin Verne. I came to you because the truth must be proved for him—he did not run down to a wine cellar and drown himself in a vat of wine!"

"No," Vickie said.

"You must understand—"

"I do."

"What?" He frowned. "You really believe that?"

"I believe he was murdered. I met Franklin Verne a few times. I also write. History."

"Ah, nonfiction." He studied her. "Not poetic at all, but…"

"Excuse me! It's not easy, laying down facts and figures, making it interesting and keeping the reader going. Well, okay, sometimes history is so bizarre that it is all quite intriguing, but…"

"Back to me! And Franklin, of course. How are you going to prove the truth?"

"Griffin will find the truth. Griffin and the FBI and the police," Vickie said. "I'm not an agent yet. I have no real power."

"You don't need power," he told her.

"No?"

He lifted a hand into the air dismissively. "I am credited with creating the first mystery novel, you know. Detective novel. 'The Murders in the Rue Morgue.'"

"Yes, I know the story. But Franklin Verne wasn't killed by an ape."

"Neither was I, my dear, neither was I. The point is this—one needs to merely follow the clues to discover the truth."

"And you know how to follow the clues?"

"Indeed, I do. My dear Miss Preston, I did not write the first such novel without having some knowledge of the quest for such forensic knowledge."

Vickie smiled. "Well, then." She turned the key in the ignition once again.

"Where are we going?" he asked her.

"To the morgue."

"I will not go in."

"I'm not going in," she told him. "Griffin is there. And I believe that Dr. Hatfield is very good at what he does. If there is something that we need to know, we'll know it."

"Yes." The ghost of Poe looked thoughtful and concerned. "If Verne drank, someone forced that drink into him!"

"Possibly." Vickie hesitated. "He did smell like wine."

Poe lifted his hands. "I don't— I can't smell anymore, so..." He smiled at her. "I would think, Miss Preston, that you wear the sweetest perfume."

"Well, thank you. I think," she murmured. "We'll go and get Griffin. He's seen you, of course, you know."

"How rare. How delightfully rare. Two of you! And it's almost as if..."

"As if?"

"As if I were living again. If only..." He paused again, then seemed to straighten. "But we will not be waylaid in our quest. We will find the truth. Franklin Verne was a fine man. I believe that too often in life, he received slings and arrows for reviews. I think others were jealous of him."

"Everyone gets bad reviews now and then," Vickie said, and chuckled softly. "Anyone can review a book now and so many people do. I can't think of an author who doesn't get a bad review somewhere along the line—even if out of jealousy or sour grapes. Perhaps deserved—perhaps not. Books being digital and reviews online mean that… Well, like I said. Everyone gets a bad review now and then."

"Rufus Griswold," Poe said. "Rufus Griswold, too, is long from the world we both once knew. But what people see as the legend of *me* is largely through that man's words. Yes, I could overdo. I was temperamental. I had an ego. I was prone to dive into alcohol. But I wasn't a perpetual drunk! And I did join the temperance league, and I wouldn't have gone against Sarah Elmira…"

"You think that Rufus Griswold murdered you?" Vickie demanded.

"Only on the page, my dear. Only on the page. I was somehow murdered. And while my thoughts on that pompous bastard with a total lack of imagination regarding coherent verbiage are dark, I don't believe he murdered me. Did someone cause my death—other than myself, as sometimes assumed? Yes. But…even in death, I can't find the truth. That's why I feel that I must hound you and your lawman until the two of you find out what happened to Franklin Verne. If I can't find justice for myself, I will strive to see that the words and opinions that cast ill on memories of me do not fall upon him as well. He mustn't be maligned. For him, the truth of this matter will be known!"

There would never be anything *nice* about an autopsy.

The morgue was, however, as clean as one could imagine. The scent of decay was well washed in that of disinfectant. Stainless steel seemed to glint against tile, and while the dead lay silently upon their gurneys, the living moved among them with purpose and determination.

Franklin Verne was not the only corpse awaiting the tender mercies of the medical examiner.

At the moment, he was, however, the one who apparently commanded the most attention.

Photographers were still at work when Carl Morris and Griffin arrived; the body of the man had been stripped and cleaned and the first incisions had begun. Dr. Myron Hatfield spoke as he worked; he didn't take notes by hand but rather had a microphone hanging above the body, recording. He acknowledged the arrival of Morris and Griffin, noting the time as well. He urged them forward, lifting a lock of Franklin Verne's hair. "At this point, I am directing the detective and agent to notice the hematoma rising on the left side of the forehead. Such bruising does not appear to have formed as the result of any fall, but rather it appears to be the result of a strike by a hard, blunt object. Bruising is also beginning to appear around the mouth, specific points of such bruising appearing as if perhaps fingers and a thumb pressed the mouth open. Previous to the body being stripped and washed, the smell of wine was abundant upon the corpse and clothing, indicative of a great deal of wine being poured on the face and spilling over."

Hatfield went on with his observations; then the typical Y incision had to be made. He continued to comment on the state of his subject.

Franklin Verne may have cleaned up his life, but he had done damage, and such damage Hatfield noted.

The heart was enlarged.

The liver bore witness to overindulgence.

But what cruel injury Franklin Verne had done himself in life had been on the mend. There was nothing visible that would have immediately taken his life. Samples were taken from the stomach, of the hair, and so on; they would be sent for analysis. An as-yet-unknown poison might have been the actual cause of death, but if so, that substance would be revealed with time.

The man's heart had given out, perhaps due to the damage of an imbibed or otherwise ingested substance, perhaps due to the brutal strike on the head, or a combination thereof.

Finally, Hatfield fell silent. He looked down at the man he studied, his expression sad. He asked his assistant to please care for the body.

Then he turned off the microphone and stepped away with Griffin and Morris.

"So...no definitive cause of death?" Morris asked him.

"Well, there will be. As of right now...no. We'll wait for the test results."

"But what do you think?" Griffin asked him.

"What do I think?" Dr. Hatfield turned and looked at Griffin, studying him up and down for a moment. "Damn it, I don't want to say anything official yet. If I were to suggest something, it could become rumor, and too many people take rumor as truth. Then you learn something different from forensic tests—and you have to explain what is proved far too many times. But between us? I think that some person or persons unknown set up Mr. Verne. I think that he was struck on the head with some blunt object. He was somehow spirited down to the cellar of that club, and wine and other substances were forced into him. Will I say this yet for the record? No. Yes, the man might have fallen, gotten up, stumbled in—and drank a ton of wine or whatever. His wife might have pinched his face. He might have pinched his own face shaving. I will not go on record yet. But neither would I have you waste your time assuming this to be the man's own downfall or an accident. I suggest you begin your hunt for a killer now, gentlemen. And I believe, as in all such cases, the sooner one suspects the worse and seeks the truth, the better. Mrs. Monica Verne is no fool—her husband was murdered."

Vickie waited outside the morgue for Griffin. She could have gone in; she chose not to do so. For one, Poe didn't want to go in. She explained to him that there was a reception area that was corpse-free at most times, but he wasn't interested.

For a ghost, he was pretty squeamish.

"Thankfully," he told her, "there is something about the body and the tragedy of the decay that befalls us all. Rot is not, nor never has been appealing, as well I should know, since I have a talent for description of all that is foul and ghoulish in the extreme. That one can find the words to create the tremendous discomfort and fear to be found in such sadness does not mean that one enjoys…rot!"

And so they stood outside on the sidewalk.

At length, Griffin appeared, exiting the building with

Detective Carl Morris. Morris noted her first, pointing her out to Griffin.

Griffin surely saw Poe at her side, but he barely batted an eye.

Griffin was skilled at seeing the dead—and not appearing as though anything strange was going on.

"Why, Vickie!" Morris said, smiling as he approached her. "There is a cool and comfortable vestibule, though I had thought—since you are about to enter the academy—you might have chosen to join us within."

Vickie didn't reply to his words but rather smiled and asked, "Did you learn anything?"

"Well, we learned that our illustrious ME believes that the man was murdered. He's waiting on test results to discover just what caused the death," Griffin offered. He kept from looking at Poe. "He was apparently struck on the head with a hard, blunt object."

"And forced to drink," Morris added. "Only tests will explain exactly what caused the damage to his organs," he added, "and they'll let us know what they discover."

"He was somehow brought downstairs to the wine cellar of the restaurant—as we, of course, suspected. There—or perhaps to get him there—he was struck on the head. A good, hard blow. It might have rendered him temporarily unconscious. Wine—and possibly other substances—were forced into him. We saw the bruises on the cheeks that suggest his mouth was forced open. As far as poison or some other deadly substance being forced into him, yes, the tests will tell," Griffin said.

"Dear God—too much like my own wretched demise!" Poe said. He looked at Griffin, a strange expression on his face. His words had been dark, but there was almost a smile on his face. He was testing and teasing Griffin—and her!

Griffin didn't react.

The ghost was completely aware that Griffin saw him.

And aware, too, that Morris did not.

Beyond a doubt, something of the mischief maker had certainly remained with the soul of the man.

"Well, Franklin Verne was dearly beloved by many— and therefore had hidden enemies somewhere," Morris said. "I'm going to the office. We'll be speaking with Monica Verne and looking into Franklin Verne's known associates. And you?" he asked Griffin.

"I think we'll return to the restaurant," Griffin said.

"It's closed until tomorrow," Morris said. "I'm studying the architect's old layout for the building, trying to decide if there was any other way in. I may be sending crime-scene techs back in."

"Of course. I'd like to look around now, if you don't mind," Griffin said.

"Not at all. I don't give a damn who solves this—I just want it solved," Morris assured him.

"My sentiments exactly, sir," Griffin said.

Morris made a saluting movement with his hat. "We'll keep in close contact," he said, and then he left.

Griffin turned immediately to their ghost once Morris was out of earshot. "Mr. Poe. A pleasure," he said. "I am a tremendous fan of your work."

"Intelligent lad," Poe informed Vickie. "FBI!" he continued. "Such an institution did not exist in my day.

People were not fond of the federal government being in their business, you know."

"Nor are they today," Griffin assured him, "but then, there are times when the abilities of a far-reaching body to coordinate with offices everywhere is often beneficial. The world is easily traveled these days—the worst criminals can quickly hop from state to state."

"Yes, yes, of course, I have been observing. Enough about the rest of the world. Let's move back to dear Mr. Franklin Verne. You must prove that he didn't go to that cellar and drink himself silly. You do have a plan, of course?"

"I do, yes," Griffin told him.

"I shall help in any way I can."

"Help would be most greatly appreciated. So to begin, what is your concern here? Do you know anything of what happened?"

"Do I know the killer?" Poe asked Griffin.

"Yes."

"Don't be daft, man!" Poe said, irritated. "If I knew, do you not think I'd have shared such information by now?"

Vickie hid her smile. Griffin looked downward for a minute.

The ghost had gotten him.

He looked up. "We are heading back to the restaurant."

"Fine. I shall, when appropriate, tell you what I know of the people there."

"You do know them, then?" Vickie asked him.

"Know them? Ah, to know one infers that there has

been an actual volley of information, affection and ideas. Know? I know what one can from observation of people," Poe said. He seemed to puff up a bit. "After all, they are part of a *Poe* society. Naturally, I find the members intriguing, and, of course—with all humility—I cannot help but admire their taste in the subject matter they choose to honor!"

"With all humility!" Griffin said to Vickie, but he was smiling, and she knew that he was fascinated—delighted that they had actually been able to meet the ghost of the poet and author.

"Touché!" Poe said softly. "Well, then, if you'll excuse me, I have a bit of detective work I'd like to be doing on my own. I trust that you two will be avidly pursuing leads, and when we meet again, an exchange of information will help build the bridge to the truth!"

Poe turned and walked away. They seemed to see him…

And then they did not.

He had moved on.

"Where to now?" Vickie asked Griffin.

"Back to the scene of the crime," he told her. "Where's the car?"

Vickie led the way. Griffin was thoughtful. He glanced at her as they reached the car, and he smiled again.

"You're driving? I'm driving?"

"Whichever. Here, you drive. You know Baltimore better than I do—and the way to the Black Bird." Vickie tossed him the keys; he caught them deftly. They got in. For a moment, he paused.

"Poe!" he said.

She smiled. It wasn't that often that she saw Griffin impressed.

"Poe," she agreed. She hesitated. "It's great—and it's sad, too, really."

"What's sad?" Griffin asked, pulling out onto the street.

"Well, he had a hard life. His parents died. His foster mother loved him, but died. He argued with his foster father, who didn't support him through college. He fell in love and the girl's father hid his letters. He fell in love again, and his bride died. And then, as far as his own death went…no one really knows. And now…he's still running around, haunting Baltimore," Vickie said.

"Many times, life can be sad. And sometimes, it's as they say—life is what we make it. Poe was incredibly talented. He did have an ego the size of Texas. He argued with people. He was a drunk."

"Not as bad as his biographers might have made him out to be, Griffin!"

"Hey, I agree he was talented, and I think it's great he's helping on this," Griffin told her. "But there was something dark about him—he did provoke a lot of his enemies. And there you go—there's your next project. A book on Poe—in his defense."

Vickie thought about that. "I'm not so sure I can do the research the way it should be done while I'm in the academy. But…yeah! You're right." She laughed. "And now I have insight." She fell silent, hoping that they were able to find the truth—and that in doing so, they might, in a way, help the long-dead author as well.

Griffin pulled into the parking lot for the Black Bird.

"Showtime!" he said softly.

"Showtime?"

"Well, I would bet that we're going to discover that Franklin Verne was killed by someone who knew him well." His expression was grim as he looked toward the restaurant. "I believe he was killed by a friend, the worst kind of betrayal. And perhaps..."

"Perhaps it was the same with Edgar Allan Poe as well."

4

The officer nodded to Vickie and Griffin and opened the door for them to enter. The restaurant was closed that day out of respect for Franklin Verne, and because it was an active crime scene.

While the restaurant was shut, Gary and Alice Frampton and Lacey Shaw from the gift shop had still come in.

Gary, a man of about fifty with salt-and-pepper hair, a medium build and an easygoing manner, was sitting at a table near the bar, frowning as he read the paper.

Alice was drying glasses behind the bar, inspecting them for spots.

Lacey was opening boxes. They were filled with little bobblehead statues of Poe and little ravens.

The same as the little raven Franklin Verne had been holding when he'd died.

But of course, no one knew that but the crime-scene technicians, the ME, Detective Carl Morris—and whomever he had shared with at the BPD—and Griffin and Vickie. Lacey Shaw certainly had no way of knowing that Franklin Verne had been holding one of the little bird models.

Unless, of course, she had killed him.

Lacey, along with Alice and Gary, looked up and ceased their activities when Griffin and Vickie arrived.

"Hey!" Alice said, seeming relieved that they were there.

"Hey, how are you all doing?" Griffin asked.

"Handling the situation the best we can," Gary said, his mouth a grim, glum line as he finished speaking.

"Sad, sad, so sad!" Lacey said. Then she pointed to the TV screens above the bar and groaned. "Have you seen this yet?" A reporter was interviewing Monica Verne.

Alice hit a button on a remote control; the volume increased. Monica was an excellent subject for the TV news. She was bereft, and she was passionate, promising that she'd pay for any information leading to the truth behind her husband's death, and vowing that she would get to the bottom of the situation. Her husband's murder would not go without justice.

The reporter suggested that there had been no murder, that Franklin Verne might have fallen back into his old ways.

That brought another flurry of passionate denial from Monica. So much so that the reporter turned red and took a step back.

The bar phone rang shrilly, making everyone there jump.

"Don't answer it!" Gary Frampton groaned. "It's another kook." He looked at Griffin and Vickie and sighed as if with great exhaustion. "We reopen tomorrow. Staying closed today as the police asked, but we're already booked solid for tomorrow, from the first seating until midnight. I don't get it. I wanted Franklin Verne's patronage—I sure as hell never wanted him to die here! Now the phone rings off the hook already! And half the calls are from mediums, certain that they can contact Franklin Verne and that when they do, they'll solve the mystery of his murder."

"Mediums. Nice," Vickie murmured, gazing at the phone. "Shall I?" she asked them.

"Please!" Alice said.

She answered the bar's landline. "The Black Bird, may I help you?"

"No," came the answer. "But I can help you!"

"I don't think I need any help at the moment," Vickie said. "The restaurant is booked for tomorrow. Perhaps you'd like to make a reservation for a future date?"

"I'm Liza Harcourt!" the voice said indignantly.

"And Liza Harcourt, you are...?"

Lacey, Alice and Gary moaned before the woman could answer Vickie.

"I'm the head of the Blackbird Society!" the woman said indignantly. "And I can come over right now and we can set up a séance. I will channel my spirit guide, and will take us all to the night and point us all in the right direction of the murderer!"

"Ms. Harcourt," Vickie said, looking out at the others, "I'm so sorry. The police have closed the restaurant for the day and while the crime-scene tape stays up, the restaurant is closed to everyone except for law enforcement and the owner."

The woman went off with such virulence that Vickie held the receiver away from her ear.

"You can hang up on her if you want," Lacey suggested.

Alice looked at Vickie wide-eyed and shuddered.

Vickie let the tirade go on. When it seemed that the woman was forced to pause for breath, she quickly cut in. "The restaurant will reopen tomorrow. At that time, you're welcome to speak with the owner about a séance."

Gary Frampton let out a grunt of disgust.

"Well, excuse me! And who, exactly, are you— answering the Black Bird's phone?" Liza Harcourt demanded.

Vickie hesitated. She was tempted to tell the woman that if she had psychic power, she should figure it out herself.

"I'm with law enforcement," she said simply. That, of course, could be taken many ways, but it wasn't a lie. "Good afternoon, Ms. Harcourt," she said. And then she hung up the receiver.

"Hmm," Griffin murmured, watching her. He looked at Gary Frampton. "And just who is this woman, Liza Harcourt?"

"As she said, she's the head of a society—the one based here, in and through the Black Bird," he added with a sigh. "I love books—and I love Poe, as you can see by the restaurant, I imagine. So, of course, I'm a member myself. I encouraged the creation of the society—at the very beginning, it was all that guaranteed me I'd have a customer now and then."

"And she's really harmless," Lacey said. "A snob—but harmless."

"She's very wealthy," Alice explained. "She really is a snob—elite, you know. Above all the rest of us. She doesn't like me at all."

"Why?" Vickie asked her.

"Probably because I'm not an aged and dried-up old bat!" Alice said.

"No," Gary said softly, looking at his daughter with pride. "You're beautiful, my dear—the spitting image of your mother, just as lovely!" His smile was poignant; Alice's mother was apparently deceased. Gary cleared his throat.

"Liza! She's filthy rich and…well, it was her husband's money. But she's managed to convince herself that she was the one born into privilege," Lacey said.

"She considers herself an expert on Poe and his work. Oh, and, of course, she thinks she's a wonderful poet herself. She did a reading one night—dreadful! But," Gary added ruefully, "she filled the place. She is loud, cantankerous and full of herself. Still, she can be a great deal of fun and very supportive of the society, Poe—and my restaurant."

"And that's why we're all nice to her!" Alice said, glancing over at Lacey and shaking her head.

"And she's a medium?" Vickie asked.

Lacey laughed at that. "She's a medium now? I mean, she's come in here with a crystal ball and a Ouija board, but to the best of my knowledge, she's never awakened anything but a few dust motes! Still, she believes that she has special communications with Poe."

"I guess she thinks that she can contact Franklin Verne, too," Alice said. She sighed softly. "She's… okay. Really. You just need a lot of energy when she's around."

"And she knew Franklin Verne?"

"Quite well, yes," Gary said, glancing over at his daughter and Lacey. "They both…had a lot of money. They gave to a lot of the same local charities. She always told me that she could get Franklin Verne in here."

"Do you think that she did?" Griffin asked seriously.

"Do I think that she got him in here?" Gary asked. He seemed perplexed, and then his eyes widened. "Oh! I see. Do I think that she lured him here, that she plied him with wine…? Well, she's a little bit of a thing. If she did lure him, she'd have had to have *lured* him, you know what I mean?"

"She didn't carry him down any stairs," Lacey said flatly. "She's ninety pounds, tops."

"Were they friends or acquaintances?" Griffin asked.

Gary stood and stretched. He sighed deeply, putting his hands on his hips, then he looked steadily at Griffin. "We were all *acquaintances*. Over time, through festivals and readings and what have you—book signings— we all knew Franklin Verne. Liza had been talking to him about coming to a meeting here, and she could be a very good friend—I'm sure that she intended for him to endorse the restaurant."

"We didn't know him nearly so well," Alice said. "In passing, he might recognize us, and he might smile or wave. He wasn't going to insist we come for Sunday coffee, or anything like that."

Lacey had a distant look in her eyes. She was holding one of the ravens she had unpacked and looking thoughtfully toward one of the walls. "He was all right," she said softly. "I talked to him now and then. Of course, I carried his new books in the gift shop. But I would actually talk to him now and then. Sometimes he'd call me—just to make sure that I wasn't having any trouble getting his work from the distributor or the publisher. Of course, no one had trouble getting his work. He was very popular."

"Like Poe," Alice murmured.

"Poe did gain a great deal more popularity in death," Gary said.

"As will Franklin Verne!" Alice said softly. "Sad, huh?"

"Who do you think would have hurt him?" Griffin asked. "I mean, I realize that Liza was the one who knew him, but you were all in or involved with the society. Any ideas at all?"

No one had a chance to answer him; they heard a hard pounding on the outside door, past the hostess station.

"What the hell? I have a huge sign out there!" Gary said.

"I'll go," Vickie volunteered. "It's a bolt?"

"Yes, several, actually, no alarm on. Just twist the bolts. We are not open!" Gary said.

Vickie hurried to the door, leaving Griffin with the others.

There were three bolts on the door—not easily opened. But she didn't believe that Franklin Verne and his murderer had entered by the front, anyway.

She unlocked and opened the door. And she stared into the face of Jon Skye, their young waiter from the night before.

"Hey!" he said, obviously very surprised to see her there. "Um…what are you doing here? I got a call this morning… I saw the news. But I figured that Gary and Alice were here, and I felt that I had to help and…why the hell are *you* here?" he asked.

"Griffin is with the FBI," Vickie explained quickly.

"Oh. Oh, the FBI! But…I'm so confused. So, he didn't just die. He didn't sneak in to do a suicide thing, huh? He was murdered. Like his wife says? Still, I don't get it. Oh, but yeah, Franklin Verne was so well-known. It's national news—worldwide news, really. Is that it?"

"Actually, we don't know anything yet," Vickie said. "Any such death has to be investigated, and Monica Verne is very good friends with Griffin's director," she explained. She was still blocking the door. She hesitated, and then stepped aside. He'd come to lend support to Gary and Alice, much, she assumed, as Lacey had done.

Or because he was curious. But Vickie decided she'd let the others sort that out.

"Thanks," Jon told her, entering. He nodded and strode ahead of her into the bar area.

The group there all greeted him. Alice seemed to perk up, glad to see Jon.

Griffin nodded at Vickie. Apparently, it had been the right thing to do, letting him in.

"I came by to see if I could help in some way," Jon said.

"Sure, thanks. We're all just sitting here a little shell-shocked. Appreciate you coming," Gary said.

"It's terrible about Franklin Verne," Jon said. He looked over at Griffin. He shook his head. "I do understand that any unexplained death has to be explained. But…FBI? Does this all mean that Franklin Verne was murdered? That he didn't just sneak in to give it all up, go on a binge—and die?"

Griffin didn't answer the question but rather voiced one in return. "Do you know of anyone jealous of him? Someone who would want to hurt him—for any reason?" he asked.

Gary, Lacey, Jon and Alice all looked at one another. Then they all looked at Griffin and shook their heads in unison—almost as if it had been rehearsed.

"Whoever it was—if there was a *whoever*," Alice said, "they hid what they were feeling. I mean, at least as far as we know."

"But you will want to talk to Liza," Lacey said.

"Yes, he'll need to talk to Liza, of course," Gary said.

"Dad, what, you think she'll rouse the truth with a séance?" Alice asked sarcastically.

"She knew him," Gary said, ignoring his daughter. "She can do her ridiculous séance. Who knows—maybe she'll come up with something."

"Oh, it will be great," Alice murmured darkly.

"Liza is going to do a séance?" Jon asked. "I mean,

they may want to talk with Alistair Malcolm and Brent Whaley, too. I'd say the three of them are the core of the Blackbird Society," he said. "Others come…but not with the same passion and continuity. And Alistair and Brent were also friends with Franklin Verne," he said, looking earnestly at Griffin.

"Thank you," Griffin said.

"Yes! Special Agent Pryce will need to speak with Brent Whaley and Alistair Malcolm as well," Lacey said, sudden energy in her voice. "Whaley is a writer! Part of the Poe society, but a writer, too. I mean, he actually writes for a living. He does a mystery series about a Baltimore detective. And, like Liza, he knew Franklin Verne! I'm sure Brent considers himself to be a friend of Franklin Verne—or, at least, he did," she added awkwardly. "In fact, he and Liza have been known to get a bit snippy when discussing him. And Alistair is about the only one who can put little Ms. Liza Harcourt in her place. He owns an amazing collection of Poe memorabilia. Liza is quite jealous of it. There's no way out of it—Alistair is very knowledgeable and he writes as well. He's had some articles published and is always working on a book."

"Thank you. I look forward to meeting these people," Griffin told them. He looked at Gary then. "How do you think that Franklin Verne came to be down in your wine cellar?"

The man sighed deeply, shaking his head. "I don't know. I know that we have an alarm system. You'd have to have the code for the front door or the delivery entry."

"How many people have the alarm code?" Griffin asked.

"You know, we've been through all of this with the police already," Lacey said, sounding somewhat aggravated.

"We're chatting here," Griffin said softly. "When you haven't found the answers, you keep going. And sometimes you find them because you just keep talking, and someone suddenly says something that helps that they didn't even know that they knew," he told her, his voice deceptively gentle.

Lacey sniffed. "I have the code, of course."

"And we have the code, too—of course," Alice said, coming to stand by her father.

"And who else?" Griffin persisted.

"No one else should," Lacey said, looking at her employer.

"Hey, I *don't* have it!" Jon said.

Gary winced.

Griffin and Vickie both looked at him, waiting.

He sighed.

"All right—Liza Harcourt has it."

"And?" Lacey prompted.

"And Alistair Malcolm and Brent Whaley," Gary finished, grimacing. "Liza left something here one night— her cell phone, I think it was. Anyway, she was with Brent and Alistair at the time. So, I'm assuming they all have the code. I thought about changing it, but…they are the people who first made this place *the* place to go. They're good, smart people—even if they are eccentric and dramatic. I don't believe that any of them lured Franklin Verne to his death in my cellar!"

"Oh! You don't believe evil of anyone. Not to mention that you left the code written on a Post-it on your desk," Alice said sweetly. "Love you, Dad, but you do know that you're far too trusting!"

"If you'll excuse us," Griffin said, "Vickie and I are going to take a look down at the wine cellar again. Mr. Frampton, not to worry. We'll be very careful."

"I'm not at all worried," Gary Frampton said. "We haven't been down there. The police have tape across the doorway. They said they might return. I understood clearly that any of us cutting, moving or ignoring that tape in any way would be considered hampering the investigation. We have not been near it."

"Thank you. I'm working in accord with Carl Morris," Griffin told him. "We appreciate your consideration."

"The police and the crime-scene people were down there for ages and ages," Lacey said. "I can't imagine what you think you'll find."

Griffin smiled. "Neither can I. But then, that's the challenge, isn't it?" he asked politely. He continued to gaze at them all for a moment with a very pleasant expression. "We will, however, find out exactly what happened," he said softly. "We do sincerely thank you for your cooperation."

He turned to leave them all, heading for the stairs down to the wine cellar.

Vickie quickly went after him.

At the bottom of the stairs, Griffin stopped, pulling her to his side so they didn't collide.

He waited; she held silent. She smiled suddenly, aware that he was waiting to see if they were followed.

And, indeed, they were. One by one, four heads appeared, looking around the wall. When they saw they'd been spotted, Gary, Alice, Lacey and Jon all came to stand on the landing, looking awkwardly down.

"Just making sure you're okay," Gary Frampton said.

"Thank you!" Griffin told them.

"If you need anything, just holler, okay?" Alice said.

"Anything!" Lacey added.

"Will do!" Griffin said.

The door to the cellar at the bottom of the stairs was closed.

It was sealed with crime-scene tape. Griffin slipped out his Swiss Army knife and slit the tape; he opened the door.

There were "night" lights on in the cellar: small lamps with low-wattage bulbs that had been crafted to look like old gas lamps.

They burned softly now.

The dead man was gone. All that remained was what the crime-scene people had left behind; traces of powder here and there for lifting fingerprints and footprints, sticky remnants of spray—even a sense of violation.

There was nothing about a death investigation that suggested kindness or gentility toward possessions, property or space.

"What else do you think you're going to find down here?" Vickie asked. "This place has been gone over and over. The crime-scene techs were here for a good five hours."

"Yes," he said softly.

"You just wanted to see if they thought you could find a clue?" Vickie asked.

"Something like that."

"They did all follow us," Vickie said.

"Yes, they did."

"Conspiracy?" she asked him.

"I don't know, Vickie. Right now I can't believe any of that crew is guilty."

"Because they seem so gullible?"

"Gary Frampton does appear to be a trusting man. He created a business that he really loves. The man is obviously a literature fanatic."

"A very nice thing," Vickie said.

"Question is—and something we'll look into, of course—just how well is the restaurant doing? This kind of place is someone's dream."

"You think that Gary Frampton might have killed Franklin Verne—*just to make his restaurant famous*?"

"You did hear them. They're completely booked for tomorrow."

"True. But…"

"We both know that sometimes the murderer proves to be someone we just can't believe—or don't want to believe!" he reminded her.

"Lacey," Vickie suggested. "She's…opinionated."

"And there's the very lovely and sweet Alice!"

"You just said you don't believe that any of them are guilty," Vickie reminded him.

"At the moment, I don't. I just like to keep watching—and not eliminate suspects too quickly. That said…"

"What?"

He laughed. "I can't wait to meet Liza the medium!"

Vickie went back to the doorway and looked up the stairs. The little troop was gone.

"Our resident ghost chose not to join us here," she said.

"He seemed to have a plan of his own that did not include us," Griffin said. "I imagine that Mr. Poe might well be visiting either Liza Harcourt, Brent Whaley or Alistair Malcolm. He's lurking around to see if any of them is acting suspicious—perhaps gleefully watching television, especially when a newscaster is of the opinion that Franklin Verne fell off the wagon."

"When do you think we'll see him again?"

"When he wishes to be seen!" Griffin reminded her softly.

Griffin started to pace the room, going around and around the rows of fine wine.

Vickie found herself looking at the foundations—close to two hundred years old, she reckoned. But the cellar had an air about it that suggested that it had always been part of the present, always part of life. It was a special place now—housing exceptional wines. Years ago, it might have held wine, barrels of beer, salted meat, canned vegetables—and even farm implements or farm animals.

There were doors—built-in niches—in the brick here and there. They had all been opened.

One housed bottle openers, and one coasters and

various other accessories necessary to the restaurant trade. Some were long—as if they had once held rakes or brooms, perhaps, or something of the like. Some were even deep.

Griffin called to her, "There's an entrance just over there—the double doors at the service entry."

"There is? I don't see it!" Vickie said.

"Come!" he encouraged her.

She followed him around a few of the racks. She thought she was staring at more brick; Griffin pushed at it and the brick, she realized, was a false door. It wasn't even anything like the other brick in the foundations; it was lightweight, only a shell. And when pushed, it opened to a narrow hallway. Down the hall were the double metal doors that led to the delivery drive.

"I believe they came in this way," Griffin said. "There is no video camera here. I don't know if maybe, just maybe, we can see some kind of vehicle if we look at the security footage from the front again. I don't think that a ninety-pound woman did this—at least, not alone. I'm pretty sure that Franklin Verne was incapacitated before they came here, that wine was forced down his throat and that his killer gloated while he died."

"Horrible," Vickie murmured.

"The thing of it is," Griffin said, "at the very least, I think I've figured out the *how.* I'm going to call Carl Morris, have him come back here. I don't know if Gary Frampton even knew he had a false wall down here. These old buildings have all kinds of secrets, and new buyers—and real estate agents—don't always know what those secrets are. Someone knew about the wall, of course. The delivery doors lead straight into the prep kitchen, so the back-basement passage isn't as well traveled as it might have been. But…I do believe we definitely have the *how*. I really wish we knew *why*."

"The *who* would be extremely useful as well, too," Vickie reminded him.

He gave her an exasperated look and then inclined his head and smiled. "Yes, of course. Well, we'll find out soon, won't we?"

"We will?"

"Of course," he told her cheerfully. "We're going to pay a visit to the medium!"

They were greeted at the door to a palatial estate by a traditionally clad dark-haired young maid who spoke English with only a slight foreign accent. Griffin couldn't quite place it, but she hailed from somewhere in Eastern Europe, most probably a country that had once been part of the Soviet Union.

They asked to see Ms. Harcourt, and the young maid left them in the foyer as she hurried away to find her employer, Griffin's card in her hand.

"Spiffy, huh?" Griffin said. The foyer was an octagonal shape. The hardwood floor was inset—maple and pine, he thought—and handsomely designed. Crown moldings adorned the ceilings, and vases—collectible or historic pieces, most probably—filled niches around the room.

"Spiffy?" Vickie asked. "Been watching too many classic movies?"

He grinned and spoke quickly, aware of heels clicking toward them on the hardwood floor.

"Nick and Nora. I love classic movies!"

Liza Harcourt arrived in the foyer on her own. She was petite and elegantly slim. As they had learned at the Black Bird, she was tiny. She was also close to seventy, Griffin knew—he'd called in to Krewe headquarters and had the woman researched. She was apparently a fanatic about physical fitness—and he had the feeling that she would maintain her attractiveness at any age. If she'd had any kind of plastic surgery, it had been done very well.

"Excellent work—subtle, not pinched!" Vickie whispered to him, winking as the woman approached them regally.

"Hello?" Liza said, looking from one of them to the other as they stood there, waiting for her.

"Ms. Harcourt, my name is Griffin Pryce," Griffin said, offering his hand. "Special Agent Pryce. I'm with the FBI."

"Yes," Liza said. "I saw that on your card."

"And this is my associate, Vickie Preston," he continued.

"We spoke this morning," Vickie said.

"Oh. Oh!" Liza said, and her eyes were disapproving as her gaze focused upon Vickie. "Hmm. So, what do you want? What are you doing here?"

"Well, of course, we were incredibly impressed!" Griffin said.

"By…?" Liza asked carefully.

"Your abilities. And, of course, we're here because

you were such good friends with Franklin Verne. We're hoping you can help us shed some light on what happened—either through things you remember, or through a séance," Griffin said.

Liza seemed to brighten at first, but then her eyes narrowed suspiciously. "You're mocking me, sir."

"Oh, no, not at all!" Griffin assured her.

Liza stared at Vickie. "You, young lady, are rude."

"I'm sorry, Ms. Harcourt," Vickie said. She glanced at Griffin, evidently realizing that complete pandering and flattery were the best tools they could use with the woman. "I didn't mean to be. Please understand, they've been upset at the restaurant by the amount of fake psychics who have been calling in. I answered the phone specifically because of that situation—and then, of course, afterward they explained to me who you were."

Liza Harcourt sniffed. "Well, all right then. You may come in."

She turned and walked through the large double-arched doorway that took up two sides of the octagon shape of the foyer. They followed her to an immense parlor with a large fireplace and carved wooden mantel as the focal point—with the famed painting of Washington crossing the Delaware above it. The sofas surrounding the fireplace were modern and comfortable, as were the glass-and-chrome tables between them. An elegant winding stairway sat to the back-left side of the room, while to the right Griffin could see a formal dining room. He saw that the fireplace was double-sided, and that it serviced the great room that stretched behind the parlor as well.

She led them on through.

The back room offered a circular table with a beautiful large crystal ball set upon it.

Liza Harcourt took her "powers" very seriously.

She stretched out a hand, indicating that they might take seats at the table.

They did.

"We thought that we might begin with asking you what you might know about Franklin Verne—or his acquaintances and friends—that we might not know yet," Griffin said.

"You've spoken to Monica, of course," Liza said.

"Yes, but sometimes a wife can see no ill in her husband. Monica has publicly declared that her husband was murdered. What do you think? I mean, you, as a friend, might have known if he...well, if he was falling back into old ways," Vickie said.

"Friends do know—often—what wives do not," Liza said, shaking her head sadly.

"What is your opinion?" Griffin asked.

"Overrated!" Liza said. "Sorry, I'm talking about his work, and the body of his work is the man, really. I mean, I do beg your forgiveness, and I know that I am judging harshly perhaps because of the dismal standards of our day, but Franklin—while a good and generous person, if saddled with personal demons—was overrated. Now, I do realize that men such as Shakespeare, Dickens and even our dear Poe were, in a way, the popular fiction of their day. I just don't believe that Franklin's drivel will come to be known as classic literature. The man had blood and guts and lots of technical skill, but to my mind, at least, no heart—no soul. Ah, but still his death is so tragically sad."

"Sad. Hmm. So you don't see his death as a murder, either?" Griffin asked.

Liza waved an elegant hand with heavily ringed fingers in the air. "Monica is distraught. She doesn't want to believe that her dear beloved husband, was, in truth, a dreadful addict. He was found in a wine cellar, for God's sake. And that's it with people like that, you know—one drink. Maybe it was a lark for him, slipping down to the wine cellar. He was probably jealous that the restaurant was dedicated to Poe—and not him. Ah, yes, sip a bit of secret Amontillado! And a bit... well, it's poison to such a man. He went on to kill himself. That Monica. She will have the police running in circles. She will not be able to accept the truth."

"How do you think that he got down to the cellar?" Vickie asked.

"What do you mean?" Liza countered.

"He hadn't even been to the restaurant before. How would he know the alarm code?" Griffin asked.

"Well, that's no great mystery," Liza said.

"No?" Vickie asked.

"Gary Frampton," she replied, shaking her head. "The poor man has no sense. He is a reader—a sweet fellow, and semidecent as a restaurant entrepreneur. But what an addle brain when it comes to trusting the people in his life. That daughter of his! Why, it's quite amazing she isn't in jail. I'm sure—just sure—the girl shoplifts. Not to mention the smoke going in and out of her lungs—from all kinds of sources, if you know what I mean. And Lacey... Oh, she's so convinced she's an expert. But almost anyone else can tell you more about Poe."

"I see. But what does that have to do with the alarm?" Griffin asked.

Again, Liza sent a hand flying into the air, bedazzling them with the sparkle of her jewels. "Well! That Lacey is an addle brain, too. And God knows! Alice is a criminal. She might have sold that number to anyone out there!"

"The alarm code to her father's restaurant?" Griffin asked. "It's her livelihood as well, and, I'm assuming, she is her father's heir."

"Her mother left when she was just about three or four," Liza said. "She had no guidance."

"She left—and she never saw her daughter again?" Vickie asked.

"The woman died—and I do believe she willed herself to die!" Liza said dramatically. "I mean, that was her way of leaving. At the time, Gary Frampton was trying to make it as a writer. But he just couldn't sell. It was a very sad state of affairs. And so, with no guidance, Alice grew up more than a bit of a mess. She was a wild child in high school. Gary did manage to sell a few short stories—not a lot of money there. Then he sold a couple of nonfiction books—and he bought the restaurant."

"What kind of nonfiction?" Vickie asked her.

Naturally, Griffin thought, Vickie was keenly interested. She loved working on her own books, he knew—she'd recently completed a piece on Cotton Mather for a university press—but she also loved hearing about other biographies and just about any kind of history. She might have determined that she was going to join the agency and become part of the Krewe of Hunters, but history—and the people who created it—would always have a tremendous role in her life. And it all fit in nicely with being part of the Krewe of Hunters.

Liza laughed softly. "Cookbooks! Regional cookbooks. But hey…nice pictures. They do sell. I'm surprised you didn't see them or hear about them in the gift shop."

"Friday night—it was quite busy," Vickie told her.

"Even without Franklin's patronage!" Liza said. "Imagine!" she added dramatically. "It was just hours before poor Franklin would find his way there—down to the cellar, down to his death!"

"Yes, just hours before," Vickie murmured.

"So! Shall we?" Liza asked.

"Shall we what?" Vickie asked, frowning.

Griffin forced himself not to laugh. Vickie had forgotten all about the fact that Liza was more than willing—anxious, even—to have them engage in a séance.

"See if we can speak with Franklin himself!" Liza said.

Griffin had to admit that she took even him by surprise when she suddenly clapped loudly twice—and most of the lights in the room went out. Only small, rose-shaped night-lights remained on with a very soft glow.

"Let's join hands here, shall we. Just fingertips touching!" she advised.

Vickie glanced at Griffin, frowning. He shrugged.

They were on either side of Liza Harcourt, pinkies and thumb tips just touching.

Liza asked for no more.

She began her speech.

"I speak to the powers of the darkness and the night! I speak to those who hover in the veil, that place of mist between life and death. I speak to friends who may need my help or my guidance. I speak to friends who just might need their story told. I am your light. I am your way. I will be your voice and I will speak for the dead!"

"What rubbish! What complete and utter rubbish!"

This time, Griffin managed not to jump. At his side, Vickie started violently.

It was Poe. Leaning with one elbow on the mantel this side of the double fireplace, he stared at the three of them at the table, his eyes registering absolute disbelief.

"Yes!" Liza cried excitedly, feeling Vickie's movement. "I can feel you—we feel you. Franklin, is that you, dear? Can you tell me, in any way—give me a sign? I feel you, and I know that Vickie feels you. You are here among us!"

They waited. Poe let out a sound of disgust.

"Can you give us a sign, Franklin?" Liza asked.

Still nothing, but Liza said, "I know, Franklin. I will do my best. Poor Monica! Addiction is a true curse, Franklin, and we all loathe it and loved you… I will see that she knows."

Vickie stared at Griffin. Then she glanced over at Poe. He'd moved; he'd walked over to the table and placed himself between Vickie and Liza Harcourt. He waved his hand in front of her face; he touched her cheek.

"Franklin, you are here!" Liza said. "I see you. I feel you."

Poe let out another grunt—this time, sounding aggravated. He looked at Vickie and winked.

"Indeed, alas, the seers of the world must take care! This woman is a medium!"

He walked away then, leaning upon the mantel once again. "I must say, I do wonder what will come next in her dog and pony show!"

Liza closed her eyes tightly; she seemed to fall back in her chair—almost as if she had passed out. But she quickly opened her eyes and stared at the two of them,

"Did you see him, did you hear him?" she asked them, sitting straight.

"Franklin Verne?" Griffin asked.

"Yes, of course, Franklin! He was here, poor man! Desperate for me to somehow convey to Monica how he loved her—and to beg her pardon that he so woefully failed!"

"He woefully failed?" Vickie asked.

"He couldn't help himself, you see," Liza explained. "He'd been asked so many times to come to the restaurant—and he meant to, of course. I mean, I had asked him and he would have been happy to have done me a favor. But you know, as John Lennon said, 'Life is what happens when we're busy making other plans!' So, Franklin thought that he'd slip in and maybe grab a selfie or the like to show that he'd been to the Black Bird and loved it! But then…he went down to the wine cellar. And there was his undoing! Like Fortunato, he couldn't resist the call of a good Amontillado. And thus, so sadly, he perished! But you see, I can tell his story. I can say that he meant just to be there and show the world what a lovely place it was."

"May heaven help us and save us from fools! And they say that I suffered from delusions!" Poe suddenly expounded. "How dare this would-be poet! Oh, that's something that she had not told you. Fool woman is forever spouting poetry, yet—by the saints who strive to preserve us—very little has been published. There she is—vilifying Franklin Verne." He pushed away from the mantel and strode toward the table, staring from Vickie to Griffin. "You will put a stop to this! You will find the proof. The man was murdered!"

"Yes," Griffin heard himself promise.

Poe swung around and disappeared into the woodwork.

"So! You did see him, you did hear him—and you know the truth, as I do!" Liza exclaimed.

"What?" Griffin asked, frowning.

"You just said yes," Vickie reminded him sweetly.

"Did I? I'm so sorry—power of the moment. No, Ms. Harcourt, I'm afraid I saw nothing, heard nothing and certainly felt nothing of Franklin Verne." He stood quickly, and Vickie followed his cue, doing the same. "I'm very sorry, and we thank you sincerely for your time."

She stood as well, looking baffled.

"But—but you jumped!" she told Vickie.

"I did. Just a muscle spasm, I'm afraid," Vickie told her.

Liza sighed. "It's so incredibly hard to find anyone with the least tinge of the gift, of the sixth sense," she said. "Hardly your fault. Perhaps tomorrow, at the restaurant."

"Perhaps."

Soon they were out the front door. And when they were, Griffin slipped an arm around Vickie, pulling her tight. "Oh, dear God! Can you believe it! She thinks she's turned her family room into a portal through the veil by using the *Clapper*! And Poe was there, right there…"

"One damned good ghost," Vickie said.

"What else would he be?" Griffin asked. "I mean, he's—Poe!"

"And not at all what I expected."

"Well, he was egotistical and more than a bit arrogant."

"But still—his biographers were not always kind. Anyway, I'm going to look up everything I can about him again. Friends of his did something of an investigation." She paused. "Griffin, he has reason to be so upset about people—like Liza—being so certain that Franklin fell back into his old ways. Maybe Poe is hanging around because he's desperate to prove that he didn't fall back himself. There are a number of theories. I want to work on them."

"We do have to solve the current murder, you know. The death of Franklin Verne," Griffin reminded her.

"I think that they will go hand in hand," she said. "Anyway, where to now?"

"The hotel. It has been one hell of a long day. Dinner—and bed."

"Dinner, lovely. Bed, lovelier!" Vickie said.

She smiled. And his heart, and his libido, seemed to catch fire.

5

Vickie thought they were lucky to catch the last few minutes of the dinner hour at the Italian restaurant just down the street from their historic hotel; she was ravenous, since they hadn't given much thought to food throughout the day.

While she wasn't Italian herself, it had been almost impossible to grow up in Boston and *not* fall in love with an Italian restaurant or two. This one was excellent; their pasta was homemade and the piece of parmesan-crusted cod she had was out of this world.

Griffin had chosen a giant appetizer tray of oysters.

Vickie watched him enjoy the oysters.

"You don't know what you're missing," he told her.

"I'm sorry. They look just like—"

"I know what they look like."

She smiled.

"It's what they taste like that matters," he assured her.

"So I've heard," she said.

"And you never know if it's true or not, you know," he said softly.

"What's that?"

"Prowess, so they say," he told her seriously.

Vickie couldn't help but burst out laughing. Griffin shook his head sadly. "Great!"

"No!" She laughed. "Hey, it's just… Hmm, well, you know, you're far too much a manly man already—no oysters needed!"

"Good save," he said, looking around for their waitress to ask for the check.

Ten minutes later, well fed and thus feeling the length of the day even more, they teased one another as they headed down the hall from the old elevator to their room.

Griffin threw open the door, making a leading remark about oysters and leaning in to kiss her when she jumped back, gripping his arm.

"Hey!"

They weren't alone.

The ghosts of Dylan Ballantine and Darlene were stretched out on the bed. They had apparently been watching television.

Dylan was a massive fan of *The Walking Dead.* He would watch whole seasons over and over again if there were no new episodes or discussion groups going. He was a talented ghost, having worked hard to manage certain *spectral feats*, as he called them. Turning on the television was one of them.

"What are you doing here?" Vickie asked.

"You're not happy to see us?"

Dylan was truly puzzled.

"We're just surprised to see you. In our hotel room. In our bed," Griffin said.

"We left you back at the Ballantine house," Vickie reminded him.

"Oh, Dylan, I told you that we shouldn't come!" Darlene said, gently touching his chest. "I mean...they're on their way to a new life, they aren't really involved here, they stumbled into this... They don't need us, Dylan."

"The man was killed—kind of like Poe!" Dylan protested. He grimaced, and Griffin and Vickie frowned, looking at one another. "Hey, I watch the news, too, sometimes. We saw everything about the murder. Well, if it is a murder. But I say it is. And I say that we can help!"

"I'm sure you can," Griffin said politely. "But...this is a hotel room. A little awkward, you know?"

"Oh, yeah, yeah...we've got our own room. We just needed to let you know that we're here," Dylan said.

"You have your own room?" Vickie asked.

"Well, of course, Vickie, you know we're not rude... that we would never just pop in on you unannounced... awkward, awkward, really, I mean, we're not voyeurs... or..."

"You're lovely ghosts, always polite," Griffin assured her. "But I think what Vickie is asking you is—how do you get your own room?"

"Oh, well, we look, of course! We check registration, and find out what rooms aren't taken. Believe it or not, it's easy to figure out what rooms won't be taken, which are given out last at any hotel. Such as this one!" Dylan said.

"They've redone most of them," Darlene explained. "Except for this floor at the other end of the hall. We'll be down there. In fact, we're going now."

"Hey, is Edgar Allan Poe hanging around here by any chance?" Dylan asked.

"Here? No," Griffin said quickly.

"I don't mean in this room," Dylan said. "I mean..." He let his voice trail as he looked from Griffin to Vickie. "He is! Oh, my God. He's here! Well, maybe not a surprise—he died here. Not that hanging around where you died is a cool thing, but...maybe he's looking for something. Of course, he's looking for a way to clear his name. Wow. Oh, wow. Poe. A real writer!"

Vickie couldn't help but clear her throat.

Darlene gave him a ghostly jab in the ribs; apparently, he could feel it. "Ouch! Oh, I'm sorry, Vickie. But he created incredibly wonderful and creepy tales. He's legendary. He's a mystery. Amazing. He's...Poe!"

"And I'm sure he'll be glad that you're so enthused," Vickie said. "Tomorrow."

"So far, he doesn't hang around our *bedroom* at night!" Griffin said.

"Oh, we're going, we're going right now," Darlene said. "We didn't think you'd be this late. We hopped a train down and just wanted to let you know. That we're here, I mean. We're going now."

"See you," Dylan said.

Darlene had his hand. She was dragging him out of the room. Though they could pass through any substance, Vickie and Griffin moved, allowing them to exit.

"They're gone," Vickie whispered, smiling.

"Ah, but they're here. In Baltimore," Griffin said.

"Out of our room."

"Yes."

"Time to let the oysters kick in," she told him, leaning close, then turning away and shedding her clothing as she headed for the shower.

He joined her shortly.

There was hot water.

Steam.

Deliciously slick and bubbly soap.

Teasing words about all that oysters could do for a man...

And then they were laughing and slipping and sliding a little too much, and Griffin managed an impressive lift to bring them both out of the shower. They dried each other and wrapped up in the massive fluffy towels, and then laughter faded and they were touching and kissing and the towels were discarded.

And then they were together in the bed. It had been a very, very long day.

And yet the nighttime activity seemed to wash it away.

They made love, and whispered, and curled together.

They made love again.

And then they drifted, drowsy, replete. Vickie thought that she would surely sleep, and sleep deeply. That she wouldn't dream. She didn't need to *dream* about the ghost of Poe; she had already seen him. Certainly she would see him again on the streets of Baltimore, once the sun rose and the dawn became another day.

But...she did dream. She dreamed again that she

was walking in darkness. And then she heard distinct sounds—the shouts of political advocates, declaring for their candidate. The clip-clop of horses' hooves on the streets.

There were smells that came to her...

Nasty ones, for the most part. Sweat and dirt and manure of horses and other animals in the streets.

Someone shouted, "Guard-a-loo!"—an American bastardization of the French for "watch out for the water" as they tossed a chamber pot.

"They're in the street. Do you feel them, do you sense them?"

Vickie looked to her left. Edgar Allan Poe was walking by her side, looking at her soulfully with his large eyes. "Since I came here, to Baltimore...I have felt them. You understand? I felt eyes on me, felt that wretched discomfort one feels when they know that they are being watched, and watched with malicious intent!"

And then, of course, she did sense it. She turned quickly—and it was as if whoever followed them had slipped straight into the shadows.

She felt her heart pound.

Yes, they were being followed...!

They turned a corner. This street was very dark; no one was shouting. She could hear no horses' hooves.

"Hurry... What a fool I am. We're on the wrong street... Hurry!" Poe urged.

She quickened her pace. Somehow, she and Poe had become one. She felt what he had felt, once, long ago; her heart beat, as his must once have beat.

A *tell-tale heart*!

And then...

She heard the flurry of footsteps behind her. She tried to turn; tried to fight them off. But there was something suddenly thrown over her head. It was rough and coarse—a burlap bag, she thought. It smelled of coffee. It was stifling and she could barely breathe. Then she realized that there was some other scent in it...something sweet. Some kind of opiate...

It made the world spin.

She couldn't fight.

She was falling, and rugged arms were catching her.

No!

But she had no power, and she could only scream silently in her mind.

"Vickie... Vickie! Vickie!"

She was tossing and turning—and fighting an invisible enemy. She was, in fact, so determined that she would win her war that she managed a not-too-shabby right hook to the jaw on Griffin as he tried to hold her still and awaken her.

He'd woken early. Showered and dressed for the day, he'd been sitting at the desk, messaging with Angela Hawkins—one of the first Krewe agents and Jackson Crow's wife—when he'd heard Vickie start gasping and moaning and fighting the pillows and the sheets.

"Vickie!" he said firmly, trying to grasp her and draw her to him, stop her from the violence of the war she was waging with the bedding.

Her eyes flew open and she looked up at him, letting out a gasp. She seemed to stare at him and not see him for a long moment before she blinked—and then moaned and cried out his name softly. "Griffin!"

"Dreaming?"

"He was kidnapped, Griffin."

For a moment, he was confused. "Franklin Verne?" he asked tensely. "You saw something that had to do with Franklin Verne?"

"What? No, no. I'm sorry. Poe. He was on the streets downtown. There was a dark and heavily shadowed alley…gaslights, but the lights didn't help, they just made shadows."

"Poe?" he said.

She nodded at him, very seriously.

"Okay," he said softly. "You're okay. You're awake now."

She threw her arms around him and he realized she was trembling; that wasn't like Vickie. She was really shaken.

He held her tightly. Touched her cheek gently and let his hands smooth down her hair.

"I'm here," he said, his tone still quiet. "I'm here."

Her dreams, he'd learned, could tell them things. They went above and beyond the usual, Griffin thought, but then, it was hard to say what was normal. The agents with the Krewe of Hunters were extraordinary—even before whatever their mystic talents might be. And for some, the talents were stronger, and for some, those talents included seeing the dead—and therefore, events around them—through their dreams.

Her trembling slowed.

She pulled back, looking at him, stressed and confused. "I'm sorry! I don't know why I'm not getting anything on Franklin Verne…just Poe. But I think that he may be around because everything written about him was wrong…it was a lie. He did keep his promise—he meant to keep sober. That's why Poe wants to help us. If I can follow his path, figure out what happened to him…"

"Of course, I hope that…I hope that you can."

"You're disappointed."

"No, I'm not!" he said firmly. He was only lying a little. Hell, it would be just too nice if she actually *saw* what had happened to Franklin Verne, even in a dream. Then all they would have to do is prove what happened. As it stood…

So, okay, he was disappointed. He was truly sorry, but Poe was long dead. His killer was long past a time when justice might have been served.

Franklin Verne…

Wasn't even in the ground yet.

"Hey. We've just begun our investigation," he told her. "And that's what we do—investigate and get to the truth." He offered her a smile. "Krewe members aren't just, as they like to say, ghost busters, Vickie, you know that. You're about to go through the academy. It is hard training. Lots of people don't make it."

"Are you suggesting—"

"No! I'm saying that we do know how to work as the rest of the investigators around the free world work. We talk to people, we look for clues…we *investigate*. And we both know that whatever is going on here with Poe *haunting you*—night and day—might help in the end. I just don't like to see you so shaken. It's good when the dead can help. They don't always. We're still damned good at what we do."

"I know."

"You're okay?"

"I'm okay. It took a minute. It was just strange, Griffin. It wasn't as if I was with him when it happened—it was as if I *was* him."

"As if you were—Poe."

"I felt it happening to me."

"Well, if he doesn't know, you can tell him that you know he was innocent."

"If we see him again."

"I'm sure we will."

He kissed her forehead and pulled her close again. They stayed together for a moment. Then, he moved away from her. "Shower quickly, please. I want to get over and see Alistair Malcolm and then I'd also like to meet with Brent Whaley."

"I'm up, I'm up," she promised.

She was. Her hair was tousled; her body seemed to be glistening.

Griffin turned and headed toward the door. "I'll go downstairs and get a couple of cups of coffee."

"Great! Thank you. How sweet."

"Not so sweet—avoiding temptation!" he told her, grinning.

She grinned, too. She was all right. She dashed for the shower while he let himself out, made sure the door locked behind him and headed down for the coffee.

* * *

Alistair Malcolm was evidently quite wealthy, too.

He lived in a mansion on a hill, but he opened his own door. He had the benefit of expecting them; Griffin had called ahead. But it was evident that everything about the man was different from Liza Harcourt.

Alistair Malcolm was a big man, not fat, but sturdy, with a strong jaw, a bald head and bright blue eyes that looked steadily on. Griffin noted that the handshake he gave Vickie was just as strong as the handshake he received himself.

"Family money," he said, ushering them in. "I'm kind of a simple guy myself. As you see, sadly, I haven't a whit of design sense about me—this stuff is the old Victorian trappings my mother kept about. I think her grandmother kept it about, too. Anyway, I'm glad to meet you. I hear that the cause of Franklin Verne's death is being held back pending an autopsy. But surely, if you're here, being FBI, there must be grave suspicion— no pun intended—that Franklin was murdered?"

"It's a possibility, I'm afraid."

Alistair Malcolm seemed to be open, forthright and solid as a rock. He would obviously form his own opinion. He led them into the parlor with the old, almost shabby, Victorian furniture and indicated that they should sit and be comfortable.

He did have his own opinion and he was ready to voice it.

"You ask me, it's impossible. Impossible that the man walked down to a wine cellar and drank himself silly. Franklin loved Monica, I mean, he really loved Monica. The two of them had something special. You know, some kids don't do things because they don't want to get punished—some don't do things because they don't want to disappoint their parents. Well, Monica wouldn't have left Franklin or anything if she'd caught him drinking. He just wouldn't have done it because he wouldn't have hurt her or disappoint her in any way. Not only that, but if he was going to go crazy and start drinking again, it sure as hell wouldn't be wine. The man would buy himself some kind of really fine single-malt scotch." He paused to sigh. "I'm sure Liza is convinced of the opposite, of course. Maybe it's not her fault. She was married to a total ass. Rich man, complete jerk. He's dead—sorry about that, but he wasn't a good man. Liar, cheater, rude…ass. Anyway, she can't accept the good in any man, so… But hey. I'm talking and I don't know if I'm answering anything at all."

He appeared eager to help them and perplexed—and sorry. It was nice to see someone—besides Monica—who seemed so sorry that a man was dead.

"You're actually doing fine," Griffin told him. "But here's the real question—who would have killed him? I keep hearing that he didn't have any enemies."

"That's what is so strange. Hey, sorry, I don't like people hovering around me so there's no butler or housekeeper—would you like coffee or some iced tea or something? It's a bit early, but some people are different. I have a full bar in the basement, too," Malcolm said.

"We're fine, thanks!" Vickie assured him. "Can you tell us more—anything that comes to your mind, really?"

"I wish there was more! I mean, Franklin Verne knew literally thousands upon thousands of people. He loved conventions—writers' conventions. He would autograph at stores around the country. He was generous and giving and people loved him. Thing is, of course, you just never know. There could have been someone out there who was jealous—no matter how they behaved toward him. I mean, he was fun—even on his commercials. He knew he wasn't beautiful, or the funniest guy. He played upon his own weaknesses. He never said he was brilliant—and I don't believe that he thought he was. He thought he was lucky, getting by."

"What about here—in Baltimore?" Griffin asked.

"What do you mean?" Malcolm asked.

"Do you know of anyone here who was jealous of him?" Griffin pressed.

Alistair Malcolm lifted his hands, pursed his lips, and shook his head, at a loss. "He was always friendly when he was in town. He would have eventually come by the Black Bird for dinner, and I'm sure he would have endorsed the restaurant."

"But he wasn't friends with anyone from the restaurant?" Vickie asked.

Alistair Malcolm took a moment and then thoughtfully shook his head. "Franklin Verne was hot stuff around here. He might have traveled a lot and he might have owned property elsewhere. But he was still a native son. Over the years, he'd been at dozens of events. He'd been out in public, at bookstores, at other venues. He's a friendly guy—was a friendly guy. I'm sure he might have met everyone associated with the restaurant. But to the best of my knowledge, he was actually friends with me, Liza and Brent."

"You're a writer, too, I understand," Vickie said.

He shrugged. "I try my feeble best. I've had non-fiction articles published. And, yes, I'm working on a book."

"Nice," Griffin murmured. "We're going to talk to Brent Whaley, too," Griffin said. "But we haven't been able to reach him."

"Brent travels a lot, too. But I'm sure, wherever he is, he'll let us know. I mean, we're all supposed to be at the séance today," Malcolm said.

"Liza Harcourt's séance?" Vickie asked.

Malcolm rolled his eyes. "Yeah. The woman is eccentric, to say the least. She really thinks she has some kind of special power—she's convinced that she'll raise Franklin's spirit and he'll just tell us what happened to him, and solve it all!"

"So—she sent out invitations to her séance?" Vickie asked.

"She did. To the Blackbird Society," Malcolm told them. "Are you going to be there?"

Griffin glanced over at Vickie. She turned and smiled at him.

They hadn't been invited.

They were definitely going to be there.

Vickie smiled at Griffin and turned to Alistair Malcolm. "Of course," she said sweetly. "We wouldn't miss it."

"You're going to a...séance?" Carl Morris asked. He had a good poker face—he stared straight at Griffin, betraying little of what he was surely feeling. "A séance?" he repeated. "And you think that the dead are going to talk to you?"

"It's not what I'm hoping to find out from the dead," Griffin said, silently adding, *Though if they did choose to speak, it would be damned nice!* "I want to see what we can learn from the living."

"Of course," Morris said. They'd met up outside the Black Bird. They'd met there so that Griffin could show him the false wall and explain his theory—the only workable theory in his mind—as to how Franklin Verne had come to be in the wine cellar.

Morris agreed. He and his men had been scouring the streets for witnesses. None had come forward and none had been found.

"You know, he could have just been killed by any jackass out there who knew about him and had a Poe hang-up," Morris said. "Or an obsessed fan. Random. Then…well, hell, you know how hard it is to find a random killer."

Griffin asked, "You haven't picked up Brent Whaley yet, have you?"

"No, he's not home. Whaley belonged to a ton of groups, too," Morris explained. "He could be at any number of conferences…or just on a research trip. We haven't been able to find him. He lives alone, so there's been no one to ask."

"Okay, so, we've got nothing! A séance couldn't hurt."

Morris made an odd sound of revulsion. "You won't mind if I leave?"

"Not in the least. I'll keep you posted—if there's anything," Griffin told him.

They were in the cellar—near the chair where Franklin Verne had been found. Morris looked up the stairs and visibly shuddered.

"You do that—you keep me posted," he said. He gave Griffin a grim smile. "Back to the streets. Someone out there had to have seen or heard something. Of course, the tip lines are ringing off the hook."

"Yes—they're getting a lot of folks calling here, too. Including Liza Harcourt—who is about to conduct our séance," Griffin said.

Morris rolled his eyes and shook his head.

He turned to head up the stairs and Griffin followed him.

At the landing, Morris didn't stay; he lifted a hand to acknowledge Gary Frampton, who was behind the bar, and he hurried out the front door.

The restaurant wouldn't open for another hour and a half. That didn't matter. Liza was gathering her select few while the others—just *ordinary* employees who understood nothing of just how special Poe had been—were busy setting up for business. Liza, Griffin knew, was in one of the private dining rooms. It had a round table with a bust of Poe for decoration in the middle. The table could seat twelve, but there wouldn't be that many of them. Liza wanted only those who mattered—herself, of course, and then Alistair Malcolm, Brent Whaley—if anyone had managed to find him—Alice, Lacey and Gary. And, since they seemed to be intruding here and wouldn't go away, Griffin and Vickie were reluctantly welcomed. That made for a table of eight, which, in her mind, was an excellent number.

"We might as well get on with it," Gary told Griffin.

"Sure. Lead the way."

Gary did so.

Liza had candles set all around the dining room. That it was daytime hadn't bothered her in the least—ghosts didn't tell time, she'd assured them.

It might as well have been night. The private room was enclosed by the restaurant itself and when the lights were out, it was pitch-dark. It was a special-occasion room, used most often for family celebrations, Gary had told them, and sometimes for meetings. A replica of an 1850s Persian carpet sat over hardwood flooring; the walls were covered with an intriguing mid-nineteenth-century paper as well—replica, but extremely well crafted and really beautiful; it was white with delicate little gold hourglasses creating a pattern of lines. A number of serving mantels in rich wood lined the walls. One of them held a long metal lighter, used for table candles on regular days, Griffin imagined, and useful in here for Liza's séance as well.

"This won't do. I really thought the number was perfect!" Liza said, as he entered the room.

Vickie was by her side. She had been listening to Liza go on and on already, Griffin was certain, but she was standing her ground without screaming or running.

There was little one could do with Liza—other than listen.

Alice and Lacey had been seated at the table; Lacey looked annoyed and bored.

Alice had her head on her arms on the table—napping, possibly.

Alistair Malcolm had arrived, and he nodded to Gary and Griffin from his position at the table across from the two women.

"No one has talked with Brent Whaley yet," Liza said. "I don't begin to understand how the man isn't aware of just how important this is! He's ignoring the death of a great author!"

Vickie looked at Griffin pointedly. He nodded to her. The powers that be were aware Brent Whaley was unaccounted for.

"Just bring in Jon. He's out there setting up," Alice said. "Jon Skye."

"But he's no real part of the restaurant or the shop—he doesn't belong to the Blackbird Society!" Liza protested.

"He loves Poe!" Lacey argued. "We talk all the time. And I'm certain he has at least read a Franklin Verne book, which I'm sure that not everyone else here has!"

"I've read many of Franklin's books!" Liza said indignantly.

"I didn't say you. Agent Pryce, have you read a Franklin Verne book?"

"I'm sorry to say I haven't," Griffin said. "I do believe that Vickie has enjoyed a number of his novels."

Vickie waved a hand in the air. "Yep. I have!"

"And we're trying to find out what happened to Franklin—not Poe!" Gary said, his tone aggravated.

"All right, all right. Bring Jon in. Then we'll have eight. Lacey, Alice, Gary, Alistair and me, and then

Agent Pryce and his assistant, Vickie, and Jon. Fine. Not perfect, but as good as I'm going to get. Okay, we have eight chairs at the table. Let's make sure the candles are lit and the lights are off and the door is closed. Then place your hands on the table. We don't have to join hands—just see that your fingertips are touching."

"I'll get Jon," Alice said.

She disappeared out the door. As soon as she returned with Jon—who looked baffled but not unpleased—they all took their seats; Liza spent a moment assuring herself that the candles in the room were burning. Then she turned off the lights and closed the door to the room.

"We won't be disturbed, right?" Liza asked.

"We won't be disturbed," Gary assured her impatiently.

Vickie was to Griffin's left side; Liza was to his right. Alistair Malcolm was across the table from him. He grinned at Griffin and rolled his eyes.

The room was eerie in the candlelight. The Poe bust in the center of the table cast some uncanny shadows about the room. Not bad for atmosphere, Griffin thought.

"We have gathered here today in the name of humanity, in the name of love, in the name of the great universal care that we give to one another as human souls. We have gathered here to speak with our dear friend, a special friend, a friend now lost to us in our earthly coils!" Liza said dramatically.

Lacey coughed; Griffin was pretty sure the sound had become a cough, that it had been Lacey's way of controlling her laughter.

"I call upon the great power of the universe, that power that we call God! I call upon the saints and angels who guard the gates of heaven and hell!" Liza continued.

"Franklin Verne, dear friend! We have gathered near the very place where you drew your last breath, where you went into the eternal land of the dead. Please, let us hear you. Let us know you again. Let us help you tell the truth of your story."

The sound that came to Griffin then was light. It sounded like a tapping, or a knocking. No one else seemed to notice, so he assumed that it had something to do with preparations for the busy restaurant day that were going on beyond the private room.

"Dear friend, we have not come to judge! Whether pain became intense, whether you were lured, tricked… murdered! We are not here to judge. We are here to love you in death if leaving this earth was your choice. We are here to find who did this, if you were taken from us!"

The tapping sound had grown louder. Griffin looked around the room. No one else seemed to be paying it the least heed. But by his side, he felt Vickie twitch. Her fingers—just touching his—moved, falling over his.

He looked at her. She was frowning.

Yes, Vickie heard the sound. She returned his look and slightly hiked her shoulders, telling him that she had absolutely no idea what it was.

"I feel you!" Liza Harcourt suddenly called out. "Yes, I feel you, Franklin. Remember, in life, I was your friend. You may still come to me. I will always do what I can for you."

Thump-thump, thump-thump-thump-thump...

What the hell?

"A slight chill has wrapped around me, Franklin. I know that you are here. I know that you may as yet not be able to tap or make the lights flicker...if you cannot, you mustn't worry, Franklin. We know that you are with us—we will be steadfast!"

"I think it actually is colder!" Lacey murmured incredulously.

Griffin didn't feel cold. He didn't feel anything unusual at all.

But the sound was nearly driving him crazy. How was it that none of the others seemed to hear it?

"Yes!" Liza exclaimed. "We feel you, Franklin. My dear man, you may try, do your best...let a candle go out...let us hear a soft tap, telling us that you're near."

"Tell us that he's near!" Gary exploded. "No! We need him to tell us what the hell happened! Did he just come in here by himself? Was he lured here? Was he forced to drink wine? Liza, if he's here, we need some answers! If he's here! What the hell am I saying?"

"Dad!" Alice admonished.

"Well, it's true."

"I do feel...cold, too!" Jon Skye said.

Thump-thump, thump-thump, thump-thump...

Griffin stared around the room.

Why was no one else mentioning the sound? How the hell didn't they hear it?

"Franklin, dear, Gary Frampton is a terrible doubter.

I know that you are with us. Perhaps you could find a way to flicker the candles—oh! You could even turn the lights on and off if you wanted. You could tap on the table, shuffle something on the floor, or perhaps make a rapping sound—"

"Make a rapping sound!" Vickie suddenly said, her voice explosive. "What is the matter with you all? It sounds as if legions of the dead are trying to break out of the floor! What the heck is wrong with your hearing?" she demanded.

All around the table, their fellow séance participants just stared at Vickie. Then they stared at one another.

And then back at Vickie.

Then, to Griffin, the sound was suddenly so loud that it was painful.

Thump-thump, thump-thump, thump-thump, thump-thump, thump-thump...

"All right, that's it," Griffin said, keeping his voice level and calm. He stood. "That's the end of this. I—"

"She's crazy, right?" Alice asked in a small voice.

"What?" Griffin said.

"There's no sound! There is no sound!" Jon Skye told him.

But there was. Griffin looked at Vickie.

Yes, there was a sound. Maybe they were the only ones who could hear it, but...

"Everyone up, please," he said.

"What?" Lacey murmured, still surprised apparently that she believed she felt the cold.

"Huh?" Alice said.

"I don't know—" Gary began.

"Please. Up," Griffin said firmly.

They all rose and stepped back. Griffin had adrenaline going for him; he gripped the edges of the round table and pulled it to the side. It sat on the handsome reproduction period rug he had noted earlier.

"Now, hey! This is my restaurant!" Gary said indignantly.

Griffin ignored him, ripping up the rug.

Several of those in the room gasped softly.

And then, for a moment, they all stood as if frozen, and stared.

It was evident that the floorboards beneath had been crudely ripped out.

And even more crudely replaced.

Griffin hunkered down.

"What in God's name…" Gary said. "Who did this? Who would have done this? This is my restaurant. Why…? I'm so confused!"

Griffin wasn't particularly worried about Gary's feelings at the moment. He looked around the room for something to use as a crowbar.

It wasn't much, but Vickie had seen the long metal taper that had been used to light the candles, still lying on one of the serving mantels by the wall. She passed it to him, coming down on her knees, ready to get her fingers beneath the wood as soon as she was able to do so.

"You've got to be careful! You're going to totally wreck the place on me!" Gary said. But his protest was weak.

As if he was afraid of what they would find.

But then, they were all afraid of what they were going to find.

The floorboards had been carelessly nailed. As poor a tool as the lighter might have been, it fit between the boards. Griffin wrenched, and one of the boards began to give.

Vickie got her hands beneath it; Jon Skye fell by her side and helped her pull.

Griffin twisted on another as the first gave to Vickie and Jon.

They reached for the other.

And then there was another gasp.

And everyone froze again.

Finally Lacey said, "Oh, my God!"

Griffin sat back on his haunches and looked around the room. They all appeared horrified.

"I believe," Griffin said quietly, "that Brent Whaley isn't missing anymore, and that he has attended your séance after all, Liza."

6

"Franklin Verne might have snuck in somehow and indulged in the wine cellar," Carl Morris said drily, "but it's most unlikely that Brent Whaley snuck in and buried himself beneath the floorboards."

He looked around at the group gathered just outside the private room.

His gaze, at the end, rested on Vickie. He looked tired, she noted. Tired—and yet resigned, as if he'd known that the strange case of Franklin Verne's murder had been going to get much worse before it got better—if, indeed, it got better at all.

He had been quick to arrive—it almost seemed he'd been expecting a call from them, as if he'd anticipated the drop of the other shoe. He'd arrived within minutes. Followed closely by the medical examiner and a slew of crime-scene technicians.

They were outside the room where the séance had taken place because Griffin had seen to it that they all stepped out immediately after the discovery of Brent Whaley's body in the floor. At that point, no one had any clue as to how long the body had been there and just how much had gone on in the room since the body had gone in beneath the boards.

Griffin had been trying to preserve whatever they could of the crime scene. And while none of them knew just how long the man had been deceased—or how he had arrived at his end, Griffin had whispered to Vickie that it couldn't have been too long.

If so, the smell of decay would have alerted everyone to the presence of the dead.

And not in the spirit.

Gary was stunned and disheartened, slumped at a table outside the room. The restaurant had already been closed down again. Police were lining the streets around it.

"Rather an Oscar Wilde moment, wouldn't you say?" Alistair Malcolm asked. "I mean, finding one corpse might be considered tragic bad luck, but finding two… What did Wilde call losing two parents? Sheer carelessness."

"You're not in the least amusing!" Lacey chided him. She wiped her eyes and blew her nose loudly. "That's Brent! Our friend Brent. And he's dead. Stuffed in the floor!"

Alistair Malcolm appeared to be angered by her words. Vickie saw his hands ball into fists at his sides and his words were fraught with emotion. "They were my friends, Lacey. My real friends, both of them. Not acquaintances from some autographing or another. I cared about them both."

"Oh! As if I didn't!" Lacey said.

"Far more my friend," Liza said. "Yes, of course, he was a member of the Blackbird Society. But he was an author. He did well. He was a very good friend. And he's dead…here."

"Boarded up in a floor rather than a wall, but still—à la Poe!" Alice noted.

"Quit with the Poe!" Gary said, his voice torn between hurt and anger. "I wish to hell that I'd never heard a single poem by that wretched man. I mean, what is this? What's going on? Why is this happening here?"

He sounded truly broken, Vickie thought. But his daughter was still quick to send a stinging remark his way.

"Dad! Get over it—yes, you'll close today. Maybe even tomorrow. A man is dead. Someone is doing something terrible here. In the end, rather sadly and ironically, you will win out. This place will be more popular than a theme destination!"

"Actually, it kind of is a theme destination," Jon Skye pointed out. "We do have Poe here, there and everywhere."

Alice shook her head, turning. It looked as if she might walk away.

But she was not going to be allowed to do so.

Carl Morris said, "No, no, no. No one is going anywhere. You'll take a seat here in the dining room somewhere until my men have had a chance to take a statement from each and every one of you!"

There was grumbling, of course. And denial.

Liza, first. "This is outrageous, Detective," she told Morris. "We had nothing to do with poor Brent being found in the floor. Well, other than that my séance did something that made Agent Pryce suddenly decide to go crazy and rip up the place."

"He wasn't alone," Lacey said, pointing at Vickie. "*She* was in on it."

"What? Sorry—in on what? You're suggesting Agent Pryce and Miss Preston had something to do with… stuffing a man in the floor?" Morris asked incredulously.

"They've been questioning us!" Liza said. She stared at Vickie rather than Griffin. Maybe she thought that she could intimidate Vickie with great ease.

Vickie stared right back at her, shaking her head.

"Wow," Alistair Malcolm murmured, looking at everyone, amused. "Wow."

"Hey!" Alice said. "They were here—the first time any of us ever saw either of them, they were here for dinner. Then we found Franklin's body, and then we found Brent's body." She pointed across the room at Vickie. *"There were no bodies here until the two of them came around!"*

"Alice, hey," Jon Skye said. "It's a dangerous thing to start suggesting that a federal government employee might have been involved in such a thing."

"Conspiracy!" Lacey said.

"So right!" Alice said. "Where were you when you left the restaurant on Friday night? How do we know that the two of you didn't come back here with Franklin Verne *and* Brent Whaley and kill them in this horrific manner?" she demanded.

Vickie started to answer—something angry and defensive and incredulous, she was pretty certain.

But Griffin answered—calm, and not in the least defensive or angry.

"When we left, we went through the front door," he said calmly. "I have a service record that's hard to match, Miss Frampton. Nor are we any part of this community. I'd take care throwing accusations at a federal agent."

"You take care. We left by the front door, too!" Lacey said.

"Okay," Griffin said politely. "Let's see, we returned straight to our hotel—where security camera records will prove we entered the establishment before midnight and did not go back out until the morning. Key cards at the hotel are also programmed to show every time a door opens and closes. We were back in our room well before midnight."

Lacey just stared at him. "Oh," she said coldly, turning aside.

"I wonder if you'll have as much proof of your whereabouts," Griffin said.

"I believe that everyone is upset," Vickie said, stepping in. "And we should be upset. A man is dead. A second man is dead, a friend to many here. Let's try to remain…" Remain what? She wondered herself. Remain decent, calm and nice? What was the right word—when one of them might be a killer? "Controlled," she finished. "We'll find the truth. Honestly, we will."

"Killers get away all the time," Liza noted.

"Not this time," Vickie said.

"Sit, please. Get yourselves coffee or drinks if you want. No one leaves here until we get a statement from them about this morning."

"This is so dumb!" Liza protested. "We were having a séance. Those two started freaking out. Agent Pryce went crazy ripping up the floor, helped by Miss Preston here. And then…then we saw Brent. That's it. In a nutshell. And how the hell did they know to look under the floor unless they were somehow responsible for him being there?" she demanded.

Everyone looked at Vickie and Griffin.

"How did you know?" Carl Morris asked.

Griffin was silent just a beat too long—and Vickie realized that she didn't have a believable answer at all.

Liza gasped with pleasure and clapped her hands. "It was me! It was my séance. I brought Brent Whaley's spirit into the room, and Brent told them that he was under the wood. That's right, isn't it?" she asked gleefully.

"I had a hunch about this room," Griffin said, looking at Carl.

"A hunch?" Morris asked.

"There was a strange wrinkle in the rug," Griffin said. "It wasn't right. It just wasn't right. I figured we had to move the table and see the floor."

"I see," Carl said. He didn't see at all, but he wasn't going to argue with Griffin in front of the others.

"Liar!" Liza accused Griffin. "You felt his presence— more than we did. Admit it! You heard him, you saw him!"

"Liza," Alistair Malcolm said. "Please! Everyone will think that we're all…"

"All what?" Liza demanded.

"Kooks!" he exclaimed.

"Ass," she told him lowly. Then she turned and stared at Griffin and then at Vickie with total disgust. And she walked away, her back to them as she took a chair across the room, folding her arms over her chest.

"Bitch," Alistair muttered beneath his breath.

No one argued.

"May I go to the store, clean up a bit?" Lacey asked quietly.

"As long as you don't leave the premises," Morris told her. "I'll be sending officers in to speak with each of you, take statements from you."

"What? We were just there when they found him," Liza protested. "His death obviously had nothing to do with us."

"We're here, and he was found here," Jon explained gently. "They have to question us, or, at the least, take our statements."

"Okay, so here's my statement!" Liza announced. "Some vicious freak killed poor Brent by stuffing him in the floor. I am a medium. I brought his spirit forth, and Agent—whoops, sorry—*Special* Agent Pryce found him in the floor."

"I thought Brent was our friend," Alistair Malcolm said very softly. "I am happy to answer questions that you may have."

"An officer in uniform will come to each of you,"

Carl Morris said. "He will only take a few minutes of your time."

"Of course," Alice said. "Because we've all been questioned about Franklin Verne already. I guess we're all going to have about the same answers."

"Except…" Alistair said.

"Except what?" Gary asked dully.

"We don't know yet when Brent died, so…we're not at all sure what date we'll need for our alibis!"

Two officers in uniform with notepads had come to stand behind Carl Morris.

"People, if you will, please? This can be quick and painless. You can do what you like—the officers will come find you."

"Then I'll help Lacey?" Alice asked, looking at Morris.

Morris nodded.

"Me, too," Jon Skye said. "I need something to do."

Lacey shrugged and said, "Whatever. Can't usually get any help—might as well use it now while I've got it."

"You got copies of Poe's 'The Tell-Tale Heart' in there?" Alistair asked.

"It's a story in an anthology in the shop, of course, yes," Lacey said impatiently. Then she paused. "So that was it, huh? A tell-tale heart. Agent Pryce heard that heartbeat, huh?"

"Hard to hear the heartbeat of a dead man," Jon Skye noted.

"Yeah, truly curious, huh?" Lacey said, staring hard at Griffin and then Vickie again.

"I want to refresh myself on the story," Alistair said.

"Maybe *help* law enforcement," he said. "Bring me a copy? Put it on my bill? You know I pay."

"Sure," Lacey said. She couldn't just leave it. She had to stare at Griffin and Vickie yet again before she headed for the gift shop, Alice and Jon in her wake.

One of the two officers followed them as well.

Gary hadn't seemed to have heard much of anything. He'd fallen into a chair and seemed to simply be in shock now. He wasn't speaking or moving—he was just staring ahead.

The second officer asked him, "Sir, come along with me?"

And Gary nodded and went with him to another table nearby.

The medical examiner appeared at the door to the private room; he nodded to Carl Morris and Griffin, indicating they were to come back in.

The two men did so, Griffin looking at Vickie in a way that she took to mean she should keep her eyes on the entire assembly around them—even though they had gone off in different directions.

Alistair Malcolm pulled out a chair for her. "I guess I'm next!" he said. "I wasn't here when Franklin was killed. I mean, I didn't have dinner here or anything like that. There were no meetings. But…"

"But?"

"I have no alibi!" he said.

"Are you innocent?" she asked.

He grinned sadly. "They were both my friends. This is devastating. But so odd. Two friends of mine—good friends—have been killed. And it isn't sinking in because I could be a murder suspect. I was home alone. I was working. Hey, maybe that's an alibi!" he said, brightening. "The computer will show that I was working."

"I think it will, Mr. Malcolm," Vickie said. "But for them to accuse you of murder, they'd need more than the fact that you just don't have an alibi."

He nodded glumly.

The officer finished with Gary, and they returned to the table. Malcolm rose. "My turn," he said, nodding to the officer. "I can only tell you what I know, but I am happy to do that."

"Thank you, sir," the officer said politely.

The officer left with Alistair Malcolm. Gary took a seat. He looked at Vickie and shook his head and buried his face in his hands.

"Two men, one a friend, one…one famous! Dead. Here. À la Poe. And I thought that I was honoring talent, giving people a bit of a history lesson. I never meant this!"

"Gary, the restaurant didn't kill anyone," Vickie said.

No, the restaurant hadn't killed. But it did belong to Gary Frampton. Was he very good at pretending to be so stunned and heartbroken? He did know the place backward and forward. He owned it. He was naturally a suspect.

As if he could read her thoughts, he said, "I swear! I had nothing to do with any of this!"

"The police and the Bureau will find the truth," Vickie said simply.

She was next up—apparently, they were all giving

statements. She answered the simple questions to the best of her ability. No, she had never met Brent Whaley before. There was nothing in the room—or any indication from anyone in the room—that there was a body buried beneath the floor. Yes, the rug was a bit off. When the rug was moved, it was evident that someone had somehow tampered with the floorboards.

Finally she returned to the table. Alistair Malcolm rose to pull back a chair for her. She was about to thank him and accept the seat when she noted something strange across the room.

A shadow...?

A silhouette...?

A man.

A dead man.

At first she thought she saw just a dazzle of light. And then she was certain that she saw him standing there. He was studying one of the portraits on the wall—a print of a famous Poe painting.

Indeed, it was Poe himself.

7

"The floorboards are the old floorboards. I believe a crowbar was originally used to lift them up, but we haven't found a crowbar anywhere. We have the nails used to hammer the floorboards back in, and we'll analyze them, but I believe we'll discover that they are nails that can be bought at any chain hardware store across the nation. We're really going to need to go through this entire place."

Amy Trent, perhaps thirty-five with dark hair prematurely graying just at her temples, was giving the report. She was lithe, spry and, according to Morris, a CSI who was very good at her job.

"How did someone get the man to just lie down in the floor?" Morris asked.

"Sir, I deal with evidence. I believe that the medical examiner may be able to answer you on that after the autopsy. If I were asked for an educated guess, I'd say some kind of drug was used. We have had something new here on the streets lately, a variant of GHB, called baby-baby."

"Date-rape drug," Griffin said. Morris looked at him and he went on to explain, "We've just been getting reports about it at the Bureau," he explained. "It's basically a roofie, and the key element is that it makes a person entirely pliable. They're awake and aware but have no energy, very little ability to move—and certainly none to fight back. Like Rohypnol, it takes away short-term memory, as well. It doesn't act as any kind of an aphrodisiac, it just renders someone a vegetable. If our killer has his hands on some of this stuff, he could have easily gotten Franklin Verne down to the cellar and Brent Whaley into the floor."

"I'll talk to our vice people," Carl Morris said. "God knows, maybe they can corner one of the peddlers on the street who can point to someone. Then again, it's damned hard to get the truth from the street dealers because it isn't like they ask for identification when selling their illegal crap."

"I'm sure Hatfield is testing for everything," Griffin said.

"I'm sure he is," Morris agreed. "Testing takes a bit of time, though. We'll get our officers asking around, whatever. When we have something definitive, all the better."

"We don't know that's the case, anyway," Amy Trent said. "I was just throwing it out there. I mean, I'm not a detective, but I'd say you just don't ask someone to lie down in the floor so that you can board them in."

"Most unlikely. I think we've all pretty much come to that conclusion," Griffin said.

Amy shrugged. "I wish there was more that I could

tell you. We're scouring the room for trace evidence, but the thing is…all the people you're probably looking at had business in this room and we've probably got trace on dozens more…"

"Do what you can, and tell us about anything you can get," Griffin said.

She nodded. "Yep, of course."

"Carl, will you excuse me, too, please?" Griffin asked. He needed to call in to Krewe headquarters and report the latest dire turn of events.

"Yeah, I need to call in, too. See what direction my lieutenant wants me to take."

As Morris turned to make his call, Griffin did the same. He reached Angela Hawkins in the main office.

"I'd have called you, soon," Angela told him. "You know, of course, that Adam Harrison is keeping his eye on this case. Franklin and Monica Verne were his kind of people—as in, they were very generous with Verne's income— philanthropists, much like our fearless leader. And now Brent Whaley. The police aren't letting out any information regarding his death due to the ongoing investigation. After the way Franklin Verne died at the same venue, I'm assuming Whaley's death was something along the lines of a Poe story, too?"

"Yep. Boarded into the floor."

"Jackson is out of the office. There's a fund-raiser for service veterans at Adam's theater today. I believe that we'll head up to you as soon as he's back. Even with traffic, it's about an hour and a half drive."

"Have we been officially invited in?" Griffin asked.

"Not yet. How are the cops on this?"

"At the moment? I'm working with the lead detective, Carl Morris. He's fine. But like me, he's calling this in to his superiors now. It could get stickier."

"I'll call Adam. He'll see that it doesn't," Angela assured him.

"Keep me posted on your ETA," he asked her.

"You bet."

He hung up. A flash streaked before his eyes. The crime-scene photographer had snapped a picture as Brent Whaley was lifted from the floor. More and more flashes popped across his eyes. Everything was being recorded: the body in the hole, the body out of the hole...

And the hole in the flooring itself.

Griffin walked over to peer in. It was just worthless space. The floor had been set up on cinder blocks about eighteen inches over whatever lay beneath—he couldn't tell. A layer of dirt and dust seemed to cover whatever the under-the-floor flooring was.

He frowned, thinking that the cellar should have been there.

"Why would there be this kind of space here?" he murmured. "The cellar isn't under this part of the restaurant?"

He was actually musing aloud. He was, however, overheard.

"I wondered about that myself," Amy Trent said, walking over to answer him. "Yes, the cellar is under us here. There's a subfloor and a crawlspace because of the water pipes and some of the wiring. When the last owner renovated, he chose to work it this way. Odd, yes, but effective, I suppose. I called a friend down at city hall—he looked it all up for me. That's how I know."

"Thank you," Griffin told her.

Odd.

So odd that…one would think you'd have to know about the structure of the place in order to plan to board in a body.

Poe.

Vickie sat at the table, glad that everyone around her seemed so self-reflective.

None of them noticed her watching the ghost, who seemed so at home in the restaurant as he studied the portrait of himself on the wall.

Apparently, he really enjoyed seeing images of himself. Maybe she was wrong. Maybe he was critical—or even wondering about the time he had spent alive on earth—perhaps he even wished that there were things he might have done differently. Maybe he knew there were situations when he had acted too rashly—hurt relationships with people who had cared.

The man did have an ego. But, Vickie thought, determining how she might best approach him with the others so near, his ego was about his work. As a man—to her, at least, and thus far as she had seen—he was polite, courteous and charming as well. In life—most of the time, she believed—he had surely been kind and solicitous of those he had loved and those he had called his friends.

He smiled suddenly, aware she was watching him, and he turned to look at her.

He knew that she couldn't really approach him—or, she could, but if she acknowledged him she'd appear completely insane or daft before all those who did *not* see him.

Especially after she had just helped Griffin rip up floorboards.

"Think I'll get a soda. Mr. Frampton," she said, hunkering down to stare Gary in the face, "may I go behind the bar and get a soda?"

"What?" he asked her, looking up.

"A soda, sir. May I go behind your bar and—"

"Of course, of course!" he assured her, waving a hand in the air.

"Would you like anything?" she asked Gary, and then Alistair Malcolm.

"I'm just fine for now," Alistair said.

Gary shook his head.

Vickie headed for the bar, passing by Poe. He turned to watch her, and then followed her. She was looking downward when he perched upon a bar stool and spoke to her.

"Did I see anything, do I know anything? You wish you could ask. Ah, well. I'll answer, anyway. It would only be fun to make people respond to you and look crazy to others when there aren't corpses piling up. So! No, I'm ever so sorry, I did not see what happened. Another man is dead."

"Yes," Vickie said, keeping her head down, pretending to study the spigot and choose a button between the offerings there. "I thought you intended to watch some of these people."

"My dear Miss Preston, I do believe that you're quite accustomed to seeing the dead, that you've known many of my number. You must, therefore, be well aware that not even a ghost can be in more than one place at a time. I have watched their Blackbird meetings, sometimes with gratitude that they remember me with such reverence—and sometimes appalled that they dare to think what was in my mind and my soul when I set pen to paper. I don't know who killed Franklin Verne, nor do I know who killed Brent Whaley. However! I believe they'll find that Brent Whaley died near the same time as Franklin Verne. It's extremely perplexing. Franklin in the cellar and Brent up here...boarded into the floor. And yet you heard those heartbeats, just as I heard them."

Vickie looked up at him, forgetting herself for a moment.

"Yes," he said, a wry expression on his features. "It was a ghastly, *ghostly* sound, don't you think?" he asked. "I heard it, too."

"Did you create the sound?" she asked.

He seemed amused again. "Don't you read any of those notes by the brilliant people who analyze fiction? Do we hear our own heartbeats, or is it an echo of what once was? Sometimes, perhaps, a man hasn't got the ability to come back as a ghost, but perhaps is able to bring those with special gifts or curses to their earthly remains. But seriously, as an amateur detective, I believe we might well find out that Brent Whaley was killed at *very nearly* the same time as Franklin Verne and that, given perhaps just a few more hours, the malodorous scent rising from the floor would have given all a clue that—as that man Shakespeare made us all fond of saying—something is rotten in Denmark, to paraphrase. If I had known what happened with the first, I'd know what happened with the second. Sadly, even we dead can't slip into the minds of heinous murderers to determine just when and where they will act, thus bearing witness to their deeds!"

She started to answer him, but then realized that—from across the room—both Gary Frampton and Alistair Malcolm were watching her.

They looked a little perplexed.

As if they were looking at someone who had helped rip up floorboards and was now talking to herself...

Making Liza Harcourt look almost sane!

She smiled, refrained from answering or even looking at Poe and shouted out, "Are you sure I can't get you anything?"

"Not me," Gary said.

"Okay, sure! Lemon lime," Alistair said.

She nodded. She looked up, hoping to imply with a stern stare that she wasn't going to chat with a ghost when others were watching, but it didn't matter. She wished she could convey to him that she did need to talk to him—she wanted to talk about her dream. Maybe he could remember *where* he had been when he had been attacked, even if he didn't know who had done the attacking.

But she wasn't going to be able to convey anything to the man.

Poe had disappeared.

Vickie poured herself and Alistair Malcolm sodas

and then headed to the table to join the two men. Griffin and Carl Morris were still in the private room with the medical examiner and the crime-scene technicians.

"I guess I should get on the phone and start warning customers who are on the way," Gary Frampton said dully. He rose, shaking his head and appearing extremely weary. "I'll get Alice. I mean, that's all right, right?" he asked Vickie.

"I believe that Detective Morris just wants some officers to be able to speak with everyone. Being here—anywhere—is fine," Vickie assured him. "If there's anything I can do..."

He seemed to brighten. "Yes, both of you, if you don't mind? Can you help me cancel what reservations we can?"

"Um, yes. Of course," Vickie said.

She looked up. Jon Skye was coming back toward the table, carrying the book that Alistair had asked Lacey to find, the Poe omnibus that included the story "The Tell-Tale Heart."

"There's Jon! An employee. I'm sure he'll help!" Alistair said.

"Of course, yes, an employee," Vickie murmured. "You won't mind, right, Jon?"

Jon Skye looked back at Vickie, his expression showing that he'd rather do anything but.

"Sure," he said weakly.

They headed with Gary to his office.

The body of Brent Whaley was out of the floor. Dozens of pictures had been taken. Forensic scientists had gone over the area with all the possible tools of their trade and now the corpse was ready to be brought to the morgue.

Brent Whaley had been placed with care and respect in a body bag on a wheeled gurney; at Hatfield's okay, he would be wheeled out to an ambulance and brought to the morgue.

Myron Hatfield spoke with Griffin and Carl Morris.

"I can't tell you right now. I will have to perform an autopsy. But here's what I'm thinking, and, of course, my professional opinion is just slightly—and I do mean *slightly*—skewed by our circumstances. I believe that he was set in the floor and buried there beneath the floorboards. And when the floorboards were boarded over him, he had a heart attack. Now, there are many conditions that can mimic a heart attack. Pulmonary thrombosis, a collapsed lung due to pneumonia or even some kinds of poisoning. Anyway, I'll find out. But what I believe is this—Brent Whaley was not in good shape, physically. He ate too much fat and salt. He weighed too much. He was, in truth, a heart attack waiting to happen. You two are the investigators, but I believe you'll discover that he was killed by someone who knew he most probably had a heart condition. Burying him beneath the floorboards just about guaranteed a heart attack." He eyed them both drily. "And, yes, of course, while it was possible that Franklin Verne died because of his own mischief and addiction, it is quite *improbable* that Brent Whaley nailed himself into the floor."

Griffin glanced over at Morris. "Yes, I guess we have made that observation. Dr. Hatfield, what do you think about the possibility of someone having used a drug to get him pliant enough to wind up in the floor? I didn't see any bruises on him or any signs of a struggle. Of course, I don't have a medical degree. One of the techs and Detective Morris and I were discussing that as a theory as to the physical act of getting a man into the floor."

"Sure. That's a possibility. No, there aren't signs of a struggle. I do believe it was a heart attack, but... I'll get him to the morgue. These murders will take precedence at the moment—barring something else perhaps even more bizarre and absurd, but we'll just hope that kind of event isn't coming," Hatfield told them. "Though I never discount that chance. You're more than welcome to join me at the autopsy. Give me four or five hours to handle some business and personal affairs and then you can meet me at the morgue. I'll get my assistants moving on this poor man right away."

Morris and Griffin both thanked him. Hatfield turned and nodded to his men, and they started out with the corpse.

"Sad and strange—two people dead. In this restaurant. Has to be someone involved here. One of those wacked-out Poe enthusiasts," Carl Morris said, watching the body leave. "Everyone who works here is under suspicion, as is everyone in that damned society. They knew about the cameras...about the back. But then again, none of that was really secret because Gary Frampton just isn't the sharpest knife in the drawer. And still, whoever did this... No prints. No footprints. No sign of a break-in." He swore softly.

"I'll leave you here with the techs," Griffin said, "And let the folks here head on home. I think, at this time, we need the place empty."

"Yeah, sure," Morris said. "I thought we might shake them up, making them stay. I guess no one is going to run in here with a confession."

"Nope, I don't think so," Griffin agreed.

Morris headed out. Griffin looked for Vickie and found her at the bar with Jon Skye, Alistair Malcolm and Gary Frampton.

Alistair had his nose deep in the pages of a book.

An open bottle of whiskey was on the counter between Gary and Jon.

Vickie looked up at Griffin. "We—we just watched them take the body out," she said.

Apparently, the whiskey was their way of coping, and she had been able to do little but indulge them while she waited.

"A good man," Jon said. "Good appetite. Really enjoyed it here. And…" He paused and flushed. "He tipped well. I mean, that's the least thing, but…said something about him, too. He was generous to those who were working."

"Good thing Liza, Lacey and Alice are in the back," Gary noted. "Good thing. Watching the body go… Well, that was sad." He proved his point, sniffing back a sob—and then hiccupping loudly.

"We're all so sorry," Vickie murmured.

"So, I guess I'm closed for a while, huh?" Gary said dully. He swept his shot glass in the air. "When might this restaurant be open again? What would the answer to that be? *Nevermore!*"

"You'll open again. You'll recover, probably be extremely popular. You'll have ghost-tracking groups from around the country plaguing you," Griffin promised him.

"She told me that… Your lady here…or your almost agent…or… Vickie… She's really a great kid!" Gary said.

"Yep, that's me," Vickie murmured, looking at Griffin with a silent plea for help. "Maybe we could get an officer to bring Gary home. I think he needs some sleep."

"It will be a while, though, huh?" Gary asked.

"A few days, I'm thinking," Griffin said.

"I gotta get away. I just gotta get away," Gary said. "Oh!" He turned to look at Jon Skye. "Hey, I'm feeling sorry for myself…but you, Jon! And the others. My servers and bartenders. How will they live?"

"The place won't close forever!" Jon Skye said. He glanced at Griffin and then Vickie apologetically. He'd been sharing the whiskey with Gary, just sipping instead of taking shots.

"I have an old house… We can spend a bit of time there, Alice and me. Lacey, she just works for me because she loves the society and the books and the shop. She'll be fine. It's my other people… Lacey'll want to come out and hang with us, I'm sure. Jon…well, you can hang out, too—if you don't have to find a way to make money," Gary said, shaking his head morosely again.

"Everyone will be fine," Jon Skye assured him. "It

won't be that long, and we all know places where we can fill in for a day or so for friends, pick up extra shifts. Not to worry." He grinned. "Mr. Frampton, if you have some kind of cool old place, trust me, we'll all find a way to hang out with you at one point or another."

"Cool? I'm not so sure. But no mortgage, and in the family, mine—all mine. For taxes each year, of course," Gary said.

Alice came striding into the bar with Liza and Lacey.

She stopped dead, sighing softly as she saw her father.

"Oh, dear," she said.

"Alice, baby, we're going to get out of town!" her father told her.

Alice looked at Griffin, arching a brow. "Dad," she said quietly. "I don't think that we're supposed to leave town right now."

"We're going to leave town without leaving town!" Gary announced, waving his shot glass. He reached for the bottle to refill it.

Alice grabbed the bottle first.

"Dad, I think you need some coffee. And a long nap."

"Baby, we have to go." He grinned and started laughing. "No, not out of town. Well, kind of out of town. To the border land!"

Alice sighed deeply, shook her head again and looked at Griffin. "We have an old family house just down in Glen Burnie. It's always been a nice hideaway for Dad. He loves the old place, although it's old. Needs work. But we do a little when we go. And…it's still within easy reach of Baltimore."

"I'll check with Detective Morris, but I'm sure it's all right if you go out there," Griffin said.

From the bar stool where he had been sitting silently, engrossed in his book, Alistair Malcolm suddenly looked up. "Frampton Manor! Interesting history to it!" he said. "Feel free to invite me out for dinner while you're there!" he told Alice.

"Certainly, sir," Alice said politely.

"Can we go home now?" Liza asked. "I've had a very traumatic day, raising the dead! I need some rest!"

"Yes, you can all go home," Griffin told them. "In fact, Gary, if you don't mind, I'd like to get all of you out—including you and your daughter—and see that the place is sealed up tight. The police will want to come back tomorrow for a fresh look at the place."

"Sure. Alice, sweetheart, Daddy will get the car," Gary said.

"God, no! I'll get the car, and you'll behave, and—"

"I can have an officer drive you both home," Griffin told her.

Alice shook her head. "No, I'm fine. I just need to get him to the car."

"I'll help you," Vickie said. She glanced at Griffin and then Alice. "Please—I'm feeling a little bit responsible. He asked us to join him at the bar, and..."

"We'll all get him out!" Jon Skye said cheerfully. He grinned at Vickie. "Go figure! You two in here just the other night when all this happened. Just customers. And now...wow. You're one with all of us." He broke off suddenly. "And men are dead. I am so sorry. Come on, let's get Gary to the car."

"I can help," Griffin said.

"We're fine," Vickie assured him, and, he realized quickly, they were. Jon Skye was tall and fairly lean, but appeared to be well built and in good shape. He was in his mid-twenties to thirty, perhaps, and he could easily support Gary's weight while Vickie did the guiding.

They left the restaurant. Lacey and Liza followed them toward the door, but apparently felt the need to stop and talk to Griffin.

"I'm going home—and you know where to find me. I might well be of more use, you know. We can try again to reach the other side," Liza said.

"I'm also going home," Lacey said, "and while you probably know where to find me, too, no offense, but please don't. I don't want you at my house, so don't come for me unless you need me!"

She went on out.

Liza let out a grunt of air and looked steadily at Griffin again. "I repeat, Special Agent Pryce, I am available if you need me."

Griffin forced a grim smile. "Thank you so much," he told her.

When they were out, Alistair Malcolm spoke from the bar. "I've been reading and it's quite extraordinary. Of course, any of us in just about any Poe society knows about the mysterious circumstances surrounding his death and how there never was any kind of decent investigation! Now I'm thinking that our killer is a player—but not an excessively good player, as one might expect. He knows about Poe—I mean, doesn't everyone? But he's not an expert. Not in the least. Take 'The Tell-Tale

Heart.' The narrator claims that he's not mad or insane. But he's obsessed. The old man's eye. He stalks his prey, and then snuffs the life out of him with a mattress. But in 'The Tell-Tale Heart,' the narrator dismembers his victim. Thank the good Lord that we didn't find Brent Whaley dismembered!"

Griffin had to agree with that, but still—dead was dead. He doubted if being dismembered would have mattered a great deal to Brent Whaley once his life had been taken.

"I guess I'll have to brush up on my Poe," Griffin said.

Jon Skye opened the door and held it so he and Vickie could re-enter.

"Quite a day. I mean, quite horrible." He paused, shuddering slightly. "And to think! I was rather touched and honored to be part of that séance. That one old bird—Liza—well, to say that she is a bit of a snob would be quite the understatement. And now, of course, I wish I'd never been invited."

"I'm sorry," Vickie murmured.

"Not your fault!" Jon said. He looked at Griffin. "Now what?"

Griffin smiled. "Now I say thank you. And then I ask you and Mr. Malcolm to leave."

"What?" Alistair asked.

"I need you all to leave. Everyone needs to be out now. The Baltimore crime lab has fantastic people working there, and they're going to go through the whole place. So..."

"Yes, well, Mr. Skye is a waiter. An excellent waiter! No offense, Jon."

"None taken, Alistair," Jon assured him, grinning.

"But I'm vice president of the Blackbirds!"

The man was truly indignant; as if he had somehow become one of Poe's detectives himself and therefore deserved to stay.

"Sir, we'll keep you informed every step of the way, and we'll come to you for any and all help that has to do with Poe," Griffin assured him politely. "But for now…"

"Well! Well. Well, of course. I'm not an officer. Of any kind," Alistair said, as if realizing that fact himself. "But… Oh, dear. I'm just like Liza. You know where I live. I do sincerely hope that you'll call on me if you need my help in any way. Liza is… Well, Liza is, quite frankly, a flake. Her and her belief that she can summon ghosts! Anyway, if you want facts and educated theories and not hocus-pocus, well, as I said, I am your man, at your disposal."

"And if you need a good waiter, give me a call!" Jon said, grinning. He slipped an arm around Alistair Malcolm's shoulders. "Come, good sir, I will see you to your car!"

He winked at Vickie and Griffin, and led Alistair on out.

"Are we leaving, too?" Vickie asked.

"Morris and the crime-scene guys are still here," he said.

"I know," she said. "Poe is here—or was here!" she added very softly.

"Perhaps," Griffin said, "if I can manage to be

around here until the end, we'll see him again. Although…"

"Although he doesn't seem to have any answers," Vickie said. "But I do have a few answers—or questions—for him. And you never know. Seriously, solving that murder from the past really might lead to solving these in the present."

"It might…"

"Or?"

"It could just lead us to more dead," Griffin said quietly.

8

They weren't going to have the restaurant to themselves.

Not for hours and hours.

The forensic crew was going to go through the entire place bit by bit. And it was going to take all day—and go into the night.

For a while, Griffin and Vickie sat quietly at a table together, going over what had happened and who they thought might have committed the murders.

At first, the list of possible suspects seemed immense. The link between the two murdered men seemed to be that they were both writers. Baltimore was a big city; there were many published and unpublished authors who might have felt bitterness or hatred toward Franklin Verne and Brent Whaley.

"But not really," Vickie argued. "They weren't at the same place in the writing world. Franklin Verne was huge—up there with Stephen King, J. K. Rowling, James Patterson and Nora Roberts. Brent Whaley was doing well, but he wasn't a megastar. It doesn't make any sense that they'd be killed because of their writing. Or, if it does, I can't figure out why."

"So, you're thinking the Poe-fanatic angle—which puts us back to there being dozens of Poe societies of one kind or another in Baltimore," Griffin said.

"And then there's the fact that both were found in the restaurant."

"Which brings us back to someone involved with the restaurant. Okay, two shifts, ten waitstaff and two bartenders per shift. Five maintenance employees, two chefs and four sous chefs. So far, we've concentrated on the Blackbirds. Maybe we need to start looking at staff."

"I guess Gary Frampton was very lax," Vickie agreed.

They could spin in circles forever, Griffin thought. He stood suddenly.

"Actually, let's leave the investigation here to Morris," he said. "I want to head to city hall."

"City hall?" Vickie asked.

He nodded. "The design in that private room is really quite bizarre, a floor built over a floor. The killer knew about it. I'd like to talk to someone in records and find out who might have known."

"Okay," Vickie agreed. "So…"

"I'll go tell Morris," Griffin said.

He smiled, leaving her at the table, hurrying back toward the area where Morris was now sitting and going through his own notes while sipping on a cola.

"Got a hunch—we're heading to city hall. I want to get all the specs on this place, all the info on renovations. Whoever has committed these murders knows the place backward and forward. You don't just happen on a crawlspace like that," Griffin told him.

Morris nodded. "I've got a theory going," he said.

"Oh? Anything you want to share?"

"Soon," Morris told him. "I'm working it out in my own head."

Griffin hesitated. "Maybe I can help."

"It's just the way I work—I've got to get this straight in my head. I'll bounce it off you then first thing. I promise. Go ahead—your idea is a damned good one," Morris told him.

Griffin almost pressed him, and then decided not to. At the moment, he was still working on the case only with the cop's direct permission—he wasn't there officially.

"I'll be back shortly," he told Morris.

"I'll wait for you here. We'll head to the autopsy together."

"Sure thing," Griffin promised.

Five minutes later, he and Vickie were on their way to city hall.

"Morris has an idea—but he didn't share it with you?" Vickie asked. "If you had some kind of an idea, wouldn't you want to put it out there in front of colleagues?"

"Maybe he doesn't consider us colleagues," Griffin said. "He called in to his lieutenant—perhaps he was even told to keep his ideas to himself. You never know. There is the possibility that someone out there is an obsessed Poe fan and has nothing to do with anyone at the restaurant—none of this would have been impossible. Gary Frampton was careless with anything that had to do with security. There were a number of employees who might have even said the wrong thing at the wrong time with a very wrong person within hearing distance."

"But you don't believe that. You think that someone directly involved with either the Blackbirds as a society or the Black Bird as a restaurant is involved."

"I do."

"Who?"

"I haven't the least idea right now."

Vickie was silent for a moment, but he knew her. "What?" he asked.

"I don't think it is Liza."

"Because she's small and because she's a woman?"

"I have no doubt that women can be every bit as spiteful, jealous, mean and conniving as men," she assured him.

"But she is tiny."

"Yes, but that has nothing to do with it."

"So, what does?" he asked, glancing her way, curious.

"Here's the thing. We don't particularly like her. She is more or less a snob, an elitist. She enjoys that she has money. She likes that she can use her privilege to enjoy the society of bright and renowned men. But..."

"But?"

"I think she does have a talent."

He looked at her and groaned. "Oh, no. Oh, no, no, no. She doesn't see the dead. If she actually saw the dead, she would have said so by now."

"I don't think she has what we have, what members of the Krewe have, Griffin. But she is one of those people who can *feel* them. It's true. She was leading a séance. And then we started to hear the *thump-thump, thump-thump*—as in the tell-tale heart."

"Alistair Malcolm is right. The killer isn't getting these at all right, at all exact to Poe," he grumbled irritably.

Was Vickie right? Did Liza Harcourt have something?

It was true that he really didn't like the woman. And so maybe he didn't want to share something that unique with her.

"Maybe we should let her have another séance," Vickie pressed.

Griffin groaned aloud again. "Oh, please. I don't think that any of us is up to finding another body at that restaurant."

"There isn't another body at the restaurant," Vickie said.

"And you know this because…?"

"A hunch. Everyone else is present and accounted for—I mean, as far as we know."

"I beg to differ. I'm sure a great deal of the population of the city is out and about and no one knows just where they might be!"

She made a face at him. "Griffin, I'm serious. I think that if anyone else is in danger of winding up dead—it's going to be someone we have met in the course of this. The restaurant is closed indefinitely now. Gary and his daughter are heading to their place on the edge of town, and Alistair wants to be invited there. Liza will be at her place… Jon Skye was with us today, and Lacey. I'm really afraid one of them will wind up dead."

"And at the hands of one of the others," Griffin murmured.

"Yes."

"A séance wouldn't hurt. You heard the heartbeats. I heard the heartbeats. *Poe heard the heartbeats!*"

"He's just a wonderfully helpful ghost, right?" Griffin asked. He glanced at her.

"I have a real feeling that I need to help him. And once I help him, I think that somehow he'll manage to help us. You doubt that, don't you?" she asked him quietly.

He reached over and squeezed her hand.

"I know that you feel you have to help him. So, yes, let's hope that Poe will become a master sleuth for us as well!"

The first gentleman they encountered in the offices of public records seemed harried and not much in the mood to help. If they were only capable and knew what they were doing, he implied, they could find anything they wanted online.

Not so, Griffin told him; they wouldn't know if local residents had actually been into the offices, if they'd asked to see original blueprints or if anyone had got an impression that someone was doing research for the wrong reasons.

They weren't after frivolous information; they were working murder investigations, and any attempt to waylay their investigation could be met with criminal obstruction of justice charges.

Vickie had noticed now through several situations, Griffin was always nice.

Until being nice didn't work.

Then he pulled out his government ID and asked to speak with a supervisor in a manner that somehow made people instantly regret that they hadn't helped to begin with. He never raised his voice, she decided.

It just became harder and deeper.

Something good to remember—icy-cold stares and precise language were far better tools than a voice screaming at high-octane level brought on by frustration.

The blustering young man immediately saw they were brought to a woman—his supervisor—who was very helpful.

She was, in fact, pleased to meet them. Her name was Mrs. Hermione Warren. She knew Gary Frampton and had known his parents, and had been very enthused about the opening of the Black Bird.

"I do love the idea of a restaurant with a library," she told them. "But I've never joined one of those Poe societies. Are you a fan?"

"Love the man's work!" Vickie assured her.

"Of course," Griffin agreed, smiling. It was time to be nice again.

"Gary Frampton was down here quite often while he was planning the restaurant," Mrs. Warren told them. "He and his daughter and, of course, a number of the workmen involved. You see, Gary and Brent Whaley

were friends. Shocking, horrible—we've just gotten the
news. Anyway, I'm delighted to help you in any way
that I can. Well, this is over murders. *Delighted* is not
a good word. Horrible, horrible—of course! If we can
do anything to bring a killer to justice..."

Her voice trailed.

"What we need can't really be seen through statis-
tics or the internet. I can't tell you how happy we are
to meet you—Baltimore is a big city. I can see where
there are dozens of people working and where there are
constantly hundreds of projects. But you love the city,
too, don't you, Mrs. Warren?" Griffin asked.

"Oh, I do! Preserving history here is so important!"
Hermione Warren said.

"So, what we're looking for," Griffin said, "is just
who might have been in during the last year or so, intrigued or interested in what renovations were being
done to the Black Bird building."

"One in particular," Mrs. Warren said gravely.

"Oh?" Griffin asked.

The woman nodded. "Why, here's what is so very
strange. None other than Franklin Verne himself was
in here," she said. "That's why... Well, when we first
heard that he had been found dead there, why, I have
to admit, I thought myself that he had chosen that way
to die. But then, of course, Mr. Whaley has now been
found there, so... So sad!"

"But he was looking into the Black Bird?" Griffin asked.

"Oh, yes. I was working that day, and I am a huge
admirer of the works of Franklin Verne. Hey, I even

love his TV commercials! He said that even with the TV commercials, people seldom recognized writers, and that I was very kind and that I had flattered him tremendously. You don't forget meeting a man like Franklin Verne!"

"Of course not," Griffin said. "So, remembering others might be much harder."

"Well, Gary came in many times."

"Of course," Vickie murmured in agreement.

"Anyone else you can think of?" Griffin asked her.

"Hard to tell, because sometimes people just come in to look up public records, and we don't always know just what they're up to," she said. "Public records are—public! And honestly, we talk about a 'big brother' society, but it's still the US of A! Oh! Well, I don't know exactly what she was doing, but the head of that society was in here. Now, she might have been looking something up regarding her own property."

"You mean Liza Harcourt?" Vickie asked.

Mrs. Warren pursed her lips. "Yes, exactly."

"Interesting, thank you. Any others that you know about?" Griffin asked.

She shook her head. "At one time, there were contractors, painters, electricians—you name it—in and out on that property. That would mean a lot of young men and a few women in the construction trades. Gary and his daughter—and that Lacey woman who works for him. I wish I could help you more, but…"

"Do you know Alistair Malcolm?" Griffin asked her.

"I do! His family has been quite influential in this city. Old money—from way back. His family were sea captains and traders. They are legendary here. And he's a very nice man."

"Has he been in lately?"

"Not that I know about. You can't possibly suspect... Oh! You do suspect!" she said, her mouth a huge O after she spoke.

Griffin smiled. "No, actually, I don't suspect anyone at the moment. That's why we're out looking for anything we can find."

"Oh, well, that Alistair. He's a lovely man. Old money and still just as fine and nice and feet-on-the-ground as a man can be. I'm so glad you don't suspect him."

"You've been a tremendous help," Griffin told her.

When they left, Vickie wasn't sure at all that anything had been of any help.

"Well, we can probably eliminate Alistair Malcolm, although even that I wouldn't do as of yet—Mrs. Warren is so enamored of him, she might have kept back information if she had seen him in there. Other than that, we've learned that just about everyone could have found out just about anything."

"So what did we learn?"

"That this was very well planned. And, of course, something very curious."

"That Franklin Verne was intrigued by the place himself?"

"Precisely."

Myron Hatfield's voice droned on as he recorded his vocal notes, working over the body of Brent Whaley.

There was just no way for an autopsy to be kind.

Brent Whaley appeared like a large hunk of blood-ied, puffy flesh on the silver gurney. He'd been washed and ripped open.

His incision had yet to be sewn.

It was not a pretty sight. Standing a short distance back from the body, Griffin had to wonder if they hadn't imagined the *thump-thump* of a heartbeat and been informed of the body because of the odors that had been emitted from it. Here, with no floorboards, with the corpse naked and dissected, the scent of death seemed to fill the air—quite unpleasantly. But then he was just inches from the cadaver, which now seemed to be stripped of everything that had made Brent Whaley a human being.

He'd been to many autopsies. It was possible for Griffin to slide into a protected place in his mind as he observed the procedure.

And in that place, he now wondered how in God's name anyone had come up with such a truly horrid plan, luring two men to the restaurant—two big men—and getting one down to the cellar to drink wine and another into the private room to lie down under the flooring!

Baby-baby. Newest street drug. And yet, it must have been horrible. The two men wouldn't have been able to protest, but each man would have known what was happening to him as it happened.

He was almost startled when Hatfield finished and stepped around the table, leaving the body for his dernier to stitch up.

"Detective, Special Agent," he said gravely, address-ing Carl Morris and then Griffin. "Naturally, we're having all kinds of tests done, but at this point, I believe I'm safe to say that the actual cause of death was a heart attack brought on by trauma, and I'm assuming that trauma to have been the fact that the man was boarded into the floor. As soon as possible, of course, I'll give you reports on toxic substances, stomach contents and so on."

"Thank you," Griffin said. They all looked at each other for a moment. There were no surprises in what the ME had discovered.

"Do you think—" Morris began.

"A street drug, making our victims pliant?" Hatfield asked. "I think so, yes—though we will wait for lab results, as I said. I can't imagine that either Franklin Verne or Brent Whaley just decided that they'd head to the restaurant and let someone kill them. There is, however, something I believe might be important—though I'm still waiting for lab results there, too. Just to verify what seems obvious to nose and eyes."

"What is that?" Griffin asked.

"Both Mr. Verne and Mr. Whaley enjoyed the last same meal—at, I estimate, the exact same time. Maryland crab cakes—trust me, you can't miss crab cakes even when they've been in the stomach. Crab cakes, tater tots and broccoli, if I'm not mistaken."

"Great!" Morris murmured. "It's Maryland! Where do they serve crab cakes? Everywhere!"

His phone buzzed and he turned to answer it. "Forensics!" he muttered briefly, before giving his attention to the caller. "I see, I see. Yes, of course. We'll head back in."

He hung up and looked at Griffin. "They've matched some fingerprints—very interesting fingerprints—on the raven souvenir that we found in Franklin Verne's hand. At the very least, we have reason to bring in a suspect for questioning. And, really, we can all guess who it is. Where does one always look first in a murder case?"

It was late in the day but there were still a number of visitors to Poe's grave. Vickie had come to the site, hoping that the ghost would show himself.

Some of the dead who remained in the physical world never frequented the place where they had been buried or interred; they loathed the very concept of a burial ground or a graveyard.

Some came now and then, just to remember their time on earth—or to see who might be there to visit their mortal remains, and even try to comfort them at times.

Poe, Vickie was pretty sure, stopped by his memorial now and then because he loved to see the people who came to honor him. Of course, he could stop by almost any time and find someone there. She wondered if he ever marveled at just how much his work was respected so many, many years after his death.

Dusk was coming, and Vickie knew that the graveyard would close when darkness began to fall. She glanced at her watch, admired the monument again and then headed out.

As she did so, she saw that he was there; he'd been watching her.

"Miss Preston. I see you are alone."

"I am."

"Where might your federal lawman be?"

"With Detective Morris. They're at the morgue."

"Ah." Poe seemed to shiver. "Dreadful places, morgues."

"Well, they are important."

"Indeed! Had they had half the medical acumen they have now when I died, I'm sure someone could have explained exactly how it came to be."

Vickie hesitated. She indicated the street. "Want to wander? You do have a talent to make me forget that it appears I am talking to myself. I could wear headphones as if I were talking on a cell phone, but then I'd feel ridiculous myself and it just isn't comfortable!"

He grinned at that.

"But I'm here to help you."

"I believe that. But I also believe that you want my help."

"I do," he agreed. "Let's wander."

Vickie started down the street, walking at a leisurely pace. The ghost of Edgar Allan Poe fell into step beside her.

"I don't know how or why, but I believe I'm dreaming what happened to you," she told him. "Maybe there are things deep in your mind that my mind is touching, memories that you've repressed, and things that happened when you were... I don't really know yet."

"You think I was hit on the head or drugged or something?"

"Maybe you suffered an injury to your head—"

"Ah, but not fair! As I don't actually have a head anymore, or any other body part. Well, of course, they existed, but…"

Vickie interrupted him quickly. "I believe that you were kidnapped. But you were walking down a street— a Baltimore street. I'm not sure where you were, but it was dark and late—I think that you were going to meet with someone."

"Yes, possibly," he murmured. "It's so hard to remember now. At the end…" He paused and looked at her. "I know that my biographers have been harsh. But I do remember what was going on before I left Richmond. I meant to marry again. I wasn't a saint. There had been other women in my life, often writers…women who intrigued for a day or so. Believe me, I did love my Virginia—and I had the deepest respect for my mother-in-law as well. I was going to bring her to town to live with me. You have to understand—I really loved Elmira as well. She was truly my first love—and, as you know, I imagine, her father destroyed all my letters to her." He paused, looking back in time. "Sarah Elmira Royster—of course, at that point in life, Sarah Elmira Royster Shelton. We weren't children anymore. We weren't at all young and silly. We knew about the seriousness of life—and how her family and her late husband's family might not be at all pleased about our marriage. But she was my first love, and my last love, and the inspiration for much of my work! She wanted me sober, so I was ready to join the temperance society. I didn't walk around with my head in the clouds all the time. Yes, I was a binge drinker, and I was not at all a pleasant man when I was drunk, but…I loved Elmira. And I meant to stay sober. A heinous enemy wrote my obituary—Rufus Wilmot Griswold! Of all the injustice!"

"I'm truly sorry."

He nodded and sighed. "Elmira… Such a dear, good woman! Before I left, she made me see a doctor. He advised me to stay a few more days in Richmond. They say that I didn't look well."

"But you left, anyway."

He nodded. "In Philadelphia, I was to meet with a woman. I had an editing job there. And I wanted to bring my mother-in-law, Maria Clemm, home. You know—from New York to Baltimore, where I'd live with my Elmira. Maria was my aunt as well as my mother-in-law. Elmira understood that. She was, as I said, an incredibly good woman. She had no jealousy of my poor dead wife, Virginia, nor did I feel any for her deceased husband."

"The doctor in attendance when you died—John Moran—claimed that you were not drunk, that you hadn't been drinking. But…"

"But no one believed him!" Poe said.

"Well, here's the bright side. People are still fighting over it all—politely, in an academic way—and they probably will be fighting over it for years and years to come," Vickie told him.

"I'm afraid I am a man of pompous ego, my dear, and that does somewhat bring a gentle balm to my soul!"

"Do you remember getting on the train out of Richmond?"

"Of course!"

"And Baltimore?"

"Yes, I remember getting off the train!"

Vickie studied him carefully and sighed. "History gives us little but speculation for the days you were missing. And a number of fun stories and movies. But from the time you got off the train there, most of anything is speculation."

"And yet…you saw me kidnapped?"

"You were walking down a shadowy street in Baltimore. It's as if…" Vickie paused, and then realized that she was worried about telling a *ghost* something that he might not believe. "It's as if I'm *you*—I feel your fear. I heard what was behind me. I—*we*—felt it when a bag went over our head, and then…"

"Then?"

"Then I woke up."

"Most annoying and irritating!" he told her.

"As is the fact that you're apparently helping us—but saw nothing!" she said.

"Actually, there is something I didn't mention to you."

"Something important?"

"Under the present circumstances, it would seem."

"So—what is it?"

"I believe that Franklin Verne and Brent Whaley had their supper together on the night they died—like a late supper."

"Where? I saw the security footage from the restaurant—Brent Whaley was at the Black Bird in the afternoon."

"I'd say six-ish, maybe," Poe said.

"And where?"

Poe smiled. "They both dined at Franklin's house." He sighed softly, grinning at her slightly. "They say that Monica Verne is an excellent cook."

Vickie's phone began to ring. She fumbled in her purse for it, looking at Poe.

He smiled, and faded away.

She answered her phone.

"Where are you?"

"Near Poe's grave. What's up? Should I get you?"

"No, Detective Morris has a car; I'm still with him. He's bringing in a suspect. Meet me at the police station."

"Who is the suspect?"

"Monica Verne."

They had Monica Verne sitting in one of the interrogation rooms; there was a cup of what Griffin assumed to be very bad station coffee in front of her. She wasn't touching it. In fact, she was just sitting silently—looking like a deer caught in the very bright headlights of a monster truck.

Griffin felt the urge to hurry out and take her comfortingly in his arms.

Not likely at the moment. He was looking at her through the one-way mirrored glass.

"I'll ask you to observe, please," Carl said to Griffin.

"Sure. Vickie is on her way in. Will someone bring her here, please?" Griffin asked in return.

"No problem."

Morris left him alone to observe and opened the door to the interrogation room.

The detective was polite as he took a seat in front of Monica Verne.

"What am I doing here?" she demanded.

"I need to ask you some questions, Mrs. Verne."

"You don't think that I've been asked enough questions? My husband is barely cold—and you choose to harass me with questions?"

"Mrs. Verne, you know that we found the body of Brent Whaley at the Black Bird today, too."

"Yes. I have ears and eyes and a television set," Monica said.

Morris smiled with no emotion. "Mrs. Verne, were you at that restaurant with your husband?"

"I have never been at that restaurant, period, Detective Morris."

"And yet your fingerprints were found there."

"My fingerprints? That's not possible," she said.

"Science doesn't lie," Morris said.

"But it can be misinterpreted. Wait a minute! Am I being accused?"

Near Griffin, a door opened and closed. Vickie had arrived. "Hey," she said quietly.

"Strange turn of events. Monica's prints were found on the little raven that Franklin Verne had in his hands when he died," he explained quickly.

"On a souvenir?" Monica was saying. "Are you kidding me? We've had dozens of those little ravens through the years!"

"Maybe he knows about Brent Whaley having had dinner at the Verne house," Vickie murmured.

"What?" Griffin asked. He turned his attention from the view through the one-way glass to Vickie—completely.

"What did you say?"

"Dinner. Friday, early evening. Well, that's what Poe said. Monica is supposedly a very good cook. The two men had dinner together the night they were both killed," Vickie told him.

Griffin swore softly. He didn't believe for a minute that Monica had killed her husband or Brent Whaley.

Monica was speaking. "I see. Now Brent is dead, too. He ate at our house on Friday. I must have killed them both. Did I poison them somehow? It was probably easy to poison my poor Franklin. Let's face it, his physical condition sucked. And Brent, now. He was a decade younger and in decent health. But the man was big, and that can put a strain on his heart, all right. He didn't look after himself, and that made him possibly vulnerable. But then, of course, they would have both trusted me, right?"

"Shut up, Monica, shut up!" Griffin said aloud.

"Oh, no!" Vickie murmured. "He will suspect her. I think it's ridiculous, but..."

Griffin's phone buzzed in his pocket. He pulled it out. He was grateful to see that the caller was Jackson Crow.

"Here at the station. Jackson, Morris has Monica Verne in an interrogation room. I'm observing. And she's busy damning herself...Okay...Excellent!"

He hung up the phone. Vickie was looking at him.

"All is well!" he said softly.

"It is?"

She frowned, looking into the room. The hallway door to the interrogation room opened; Detective Morris's lieutenant—a small, wiry man with snow-white hair—stepped in. He was followed by another man, middle-aged, broad, with steel-gray hair and dead straight demeanor.

"Barry!" Monica Verne said with relief.

"Good afternoon, Detective!" the man said.

"This is Barry Kenyon, Mrs. Verne's attorney," Morris's lieutenant said.

"Are you arresting Mrs. Verne?" Barry Kenyon asked Morris.

"No, sir, not at this time," Morris said.

"Then, we'll be leaving."

"We were just questioning Mrs. Verne, hoping for help in the investigation," Morris explained.

"Yes, well, you can question her in my presence from now on," Kenyon said.

"I don't mind helping at all—I want the killer caught!" Monica said. "But this oaf is suggesting that I put my fingerprints all over a raven and stuffed it into my poor Franklin's hands. Oh, and that since Brent Whaley is his friend and has been to my house, I killed him, too!"

The door to the observation room opened.

Jackson Crow stepped in, followed by Adam Harrison and Angela Hawkins.

"We're in officially," Adam said. "The mayor has asked for our help."

Griffin smiled and turned to Vickie. "The cavalry has arrived!" he told her.

9

Adam Harrison had to be the most dignified-looking man Vickie had met in her life—except, of course, for her own father, but then, Adam could have been her grandfather, rather than just a generation above her, and he'd done much to earn her admiration.

She'd gotten to know him, Angela, Jackson and a number of the other agents with the Krewe over the last month or so. She'd met them all when she applied at Quantico—and when her application had been given special consideration because of her specialty.

"History," as Jackson had said, not blinking, when they were in the offices for admissions.

Other departments speculated about the Krewe; some liked to tease and call them *Ghostbusters*.

But the Krewe came up with results, and therefore they were respected; often, those mocking them most especially wanted to be among their number.

After her lawyer escorted her from the police station, they brought Monica Verne to her house. Once safely inside, she broke down.

She and Adam went and sat by the pool, him comforting her. They must have really been good old friends, Vickie decided—closer than she had realized. Monica Verne had been giving them all a brave act; she had actually given way with Adam. She was sobbing hard as he soothed her. She needed that cry. It was great to be strong, but everyone needed to break down now and then.

"Poor woman," Jackson murmured, looking out. "Her husband found dead bright and early on a Saturday morning, and then Brent Whaley. And then..." His voice trailed.

Adam Harrison was such a good man. His interest in unusual people stemmed from his son, Josh, dying many, many years ago now in a car accident. But Adam had once told Vickie that he'd always tried to hold tight to Josh, perhaps somehow knowing himself that Josh wasn't meant to be in his mortal shell on Earth for too long. When Josh had died, his abilities had seemed to slip into a friend, and she had been one of the first people Adam knew of who had acknowledged speaking with the dead. For many years, it had been a frustration to Adam that he had no abilities, gifts or curses whatsoever himself. It had never turned him bitter or mean; it had just made him realize that the right people were out there for certain mysteries, and he had started putting people and situations together. Then he had formed the Krewe.

While he never gained the scope of abilities that were so often "gifts" of those around him, he had come to a point where he could see his own son.

Josh's ghost was often with Adam. Like Dylan, he was young. The dead never aged. But like Dylan, Josh had gained his own kind of wisdom. He seemed to be a very old soul.

Vickie had met Josh, too. He was charming; a little more bookish, perhaps, than Dylan had ever been, and yet, still similar to her own resident ghost. They were both fiercely loyal—and committed to those they had chosen to stay and protect. Josh seemed to appreciate that his father had found his true meaning in life, and also the fact that Adam hadn't given way to his despair, but had rather made something good of his loss.

Josh wasn't with them now. When it had been just Krewe members, Adam had mentioned casually that he had chosen to stay back at the hotel.

Vickie still marveled at the whole group—headed by Adam, and by Jackson in the field. They were just so amazing. So easy with the truth when they were alone together. So accustomed to living in a world, too, where most people walking down the streets didn't know that they were often actually crowded with the dead.

She was excited about striking out on her new life; the people with whom she would work were extraordinary and she sincerely liked everyone she had met so far. They made it easy to feel like family. She'd already worked with Special Agents Devin Lyle and Craig Rockwell—agent friends who had happened to be in Boston at the right time during a recent situation. They'd welcomed Vickie's help, even though she had still been a ways from making her decision to apply to the academy and the Bureau. They were wonderful.

Jackson Crow was an amazing individual as well, Vickie thought. He was a striking man; his Native American heritage was evident in the contours of his face. His eyes, in bright contrast, were light. And beyond that, he was the kind of man who seemed to command attention just by walking into a room.

Griffin, of course, was a lot like that, too. She thought that aspects of their manner were certainly innate, but possibly gained through the rigors of work as well.

Jackson led the Krewe in the field while Adam was the power behind the politics. Angela was Jackson's wife, but she had been among the original six people selected by Adam for his first experiment in creating the Krewe. She had, Vickie knew, an uncanny ability to choose what cases the Krewe should accept—as in, where they could be the most helpful—and she was also able to fathom when a Krewe member stumbled into something—as Griffin had with Vickie.

Vickie also simply *liked* both Angela and Jackson. There wasn't a way to turn off who they were and what they did, as some people could when they left the office at 5:00 p.m., but Jackson and Angela seemed to believe that it was important that they lived lives as normal as possible. Especially given that they used their strange gifts to work on cases that often centered on heinous killers.

Angela was blond, tall, slim and shapely. She was quick to smile and laugh. She was also extremely intelligent, could diagnose any situation and also whip information out of a computer with uncanny speed.

She was busy tearing into the little laptop she'd pulled from her bag, sitting at the dining room table with Vickie.

Vickie had done her best to bring Angela up-to-date on what was happening with the ghost of Poe—and with his determination to help them solve the current murders.

Angela turned to her. "So, Poe is hanging around, claiming he wants to and can help. But what about your young resident ghosts—Dylan and Darlene?"

"They managed to get here, too. But I haven't seen them since the other night. I'm going to assume they're off sleuthing on their own."

Angela looked back at the computer. "All right, well, it seems that Brent Whaley and Franklin Verne were better friends than most people knew."

"The police have Franklin Verne's desktop computer. But Monica said his laptop was still missing, I believe. The police haven't said that they've found anything on the desktop. In fact, it seemed he hardly used it for anything other than as a glorified word processor. He must have done all his emailing and social stuff on his laptop."

"Sometimes it's not the glaring clues that we're looking for," Angela murmured. She studied her screen, pushed keys and studied the screen again. "I'm sure the police checked out the social sites, but they might not have gone to the 'pro' pages. Each time one of the men posted something, the other made some kind of a complimentary comment."

"It's quite possible that when Brent Whaley was here

for dinner, he made plans with Franklin Verne to meet later in the night," Vickie mused. "At the Black Bird?"

"They were definitely good friends—not just associates or lip-service friends."

Vickie shook her head slowly. "There was something intriguing to both of them—something or someone. And it drew them out. And Franklin Verne didn't tell Monica because he knew that she would stop him from whatever it was he planned on doing."

"Yes, maybe."

"Maybe?"

Angela shrugged. "Oh, possibly Monica is involved."

"No! She can't be... I mean..."

"We've all learned that the person we least want to believe could be guilty just might be," Angela said.

"Yes, but you all came to her aid. You called her attorney. Adam is out there with her now."

"Yes. And I certainly hope that she's as innocent as she seems. Until we know who did do it, we don't forget that it might be just about anyone," Angela told her. "We've seen a lot through the years. When one Krewe member is emotionally involved, well, the others have to keep a little bit of armor on."

"We're only involved in this case because of Adam Harrison's friendship with Monica."

"Yes. And we will find the truth—because of Adam's friendship with Monica."

Monica and Adam were outside; Griffin and Jackson were by the back windows looking out. The men quietly exchanged words now and then.

Vickie wouldn't be overheard. She still lowered her voice.

"You really think that it could be *Monica*?" she asked incredulously.

"I don't suspect her more than anyone else close to the situation at the moment," Angela said. "I don't suspect her any less."

"Adam—does he know this?"

"Of course," Angela said, smiling and turning back to the computer again. "So—what was it that brought Brent Whaley from his home and Franklin Verne from his bed to the Black Bird in the middle of the night? They knew what they were doing when they left their homes."

"They haven't been able to find Franklin's phone," Vickie said.

"Nor have they found Brent Whaley's phone," Griffin said. Vickie started, turning to see that Griffin and Jackson were now by the table. "Naturally, the police are tracing the calls through their providers."

Vickie looked around at their group.

"And," she said, "they're going to find out that both men were contacted through a pay-as-you-go phone, bought with cash, with no record to trace."

"Yes, that's what they'll find," Griffin said. "It will have been purchased through a common chain store that sells thousands of items, and even if we were able to zero in on which store, it's completely unlikely anyone will remember having sold it."

"But," Angela said cheerfully, "that's when it's great that we have our own small army of street power. We can call on extra forces. And while we try to use tax-payer money prudently, Adam is wealthy—no matter how often he gives money away—and he funds extra help when necessary. We're now here officially. Of course, it's great that Griffin managed to keep such a cordial relationship with Carl Morris. We'll continue the co-investigation, but with a little more power behind the punch, so to say. Anyway, we'll get on all the tedious details. Griffin, you can…"

"Enjoy a few days at a mansion," Griffin said.

"Oh?" Vickie asked.

Griffin lifted his phone. "I've just received a message from Gary Frampton. He and his daughter are heading out to their property on the edge of the city—in the woods. We've been told that we're more than welcome to join them out there tomorrow, after they've gotten the place opened up. In fact, Gary will feel a great deal more secure if we're there."

"Ah," Vickie said. She looked at Angela. "Now, that should mean that Gary Frampton should be innocent of any wrongdoing. But no—not among suspicious minds. It just means that he wants witnesses for something, that he might be using us in one way or another…?"

"You're going to love the academy," Angela told her. Her smile faded as she looked over at the back door.

Adam was coming back in the house with Monica Verne.

"Monica is all right now," he told them. "It's been a very long day. Time to call it quits. Hotel, room service and sleep," he said.

"You all are more than welcome to stay here," Monica said.

"Maybe a few of us will come over tomorrow, Monica, if you're worried about being here alone," Adam told her. "At the moment, we're checked in to the hotel for the night. Of course, if you are nervous, I can have someone run things back to me."

"No. Tanya, my housekeeper, is here with me. The house has an excellent alarm system And I own a small hand gun and happen to be a crack shot," Monica said, wiping the last of her tears from her cheek. "I'll be fine."

Adam appeared uncertain for a moment.

Then Monica grinned. "Don't worry. Tanya is a crack shot, too." She shrugged. "Franklin wrote about cops and lawmen, historic and current. We went to shooting galleries fairly frequently. We're going to be fine."

"Excellent, then," Adam said. "But when we're gone, please set the alarm."

"Of course," Monica promised them.

She bid them all good-night at the door. Vickie was surprised when the woman suddenly hugged her.

"Thank you. Thank you so much," she said.

Vickie smiled, accepting the hug.

Then she realized Angela was right; it was always good for one member of the unit to remain doubtful.

Because Vickie knew she didn't want Monica to be guilty.

And that made her vulnerable.

* * *

Dylan and Darlene were in the room, watching HBO, when Vickie and Griffin returned that night. It was almost like having a pair of younger siblings, Griffin thought, aware that he let a weary breath escape when he saw the two of them sitting there. They had a habit of showing up when it was time to rest at last—and they were full of bubbling energy.

"Hey, glad you guys are finally here!" Dylan said, rising. "We've been trying very hard to keep our eyes open and on everything. We hung around outside the Black Bird for a while. And then we followed Gary Frampton."

"And what did Gary Frampton do?"

"Not much, really," Dylan admitted. "He went to his house."

"And packed," Darlene offered, rising as well. "But we watched Alice Frampton, too."

"And?" Vickie asked.

"Well, she's a little liar, but then again, I'm not sure it's in a bad way."

"What way is lying not bad?" Griffin asked her.

"Her dad is kind of hard on her. He knows that she's seeing Jon Skye now. But I guess he's like all dads, with a sterling image of his little girl. Anyway, she slips Jon into the house when her father has gone to bed for the night," Dylan said.

"She is twenty-one," Darlene offered. "I think that she doesn't want to upset or disappoint her dad."

"Thing is, of course, as Darlene said—she's an adult. She could walk out of the house if she wanted, see anyone she wanted… That's why it's not such a bad lie," Dylan said.

"She's sleeping with Jon, I take it?" Vickie asked.

"We can't swear to that," Dylan said.

"You know we would never hang around!" Darlene said.

"Right. Of course not," Griffin said, glancing over at Vickie with a grin. "And so now…"

"Well!" Dylan said cheerfully, reaching for Darlene's hand. "We're off! Have to change rooms. Those friends of yours—Krewe associates—checked in to the empty room we had claimed."

"Jackson and Angela?" Griffin asked, and teased, "How rude of them!"

"I found a better empty room, anyway," Darlene said. "We're going to have a suite tonight!"

"Nice," Griffin assured her.

"Good night then," Dylan said. He paused and looked at Vickie, and Griffin thought that he really had taken on a role as a brother to her. "Love you!" he said.

"Love you, too!" she assured him.

And then their ghostly guests were gone. They looked at one another for a moment and burst into laughter.

Griffin was still laughing when he walked across the room to her and took her into his arms.

"I must have a shower," she murmured. "And I am exhausted."

"And starving," he said.

"How romantic," she murmured.

"I meant…"

"Yes?" she teased.

"I meant, starving to meet you in the shower… Yes, soap, steam… Delicious!"

She grinned. "You can order dinner, too, though. That would be nice."

"Okay, what would you like?"

"You can choose."

"Cool. Dessert?"

"How about champagne and strawberries?"

"On the government's budget?"

"Indulge me. We'll pay. The hell with the government."

She kissed his lips quickly and escaped his arms. "I have no idea why—I just feel like something decadent!"

He called down to room service, then he followed her into the bathroom where her clothing lay suggestively strewn on the floor. The water was beating down, and steam was rising all around. She poked her head out of the curtain. "Champagne and strawberries?"

He laughed softly. "Beer and chocolate-covered pretzels," he told her. "It's late on a Sunday night."

"Ah!"

He stepped into the shower and teased, "Think of me as your champagne and strawberries!"

She laughed, running soap down his flesh. "I think something like that should be my line!"

"Don't be sexist!" he told her.

"I wouldn't dream of it. I'm far too fond of your sex…"

She moved closer to him. And made an absolute truth of her words.

* * *

Vickie was right back where she had been, in the alley. Or the street… She wasn't sure which. It was a different day, a different time, a world she had only learned about in books.

Gas lamps glowed, but illuminated little.

The shadows seemed to move like monsters, ready to pounce.

Poe was at her side. He was walking…and growing nervous.

They're coming, she thought. They were coming. And she and Poe would be one, and the burlap bag would come over her head as the attack took place…

And there was nothing—nothing!—she could do to stop it.

"Go back!" she said, looking at Poe.

But he didn't hear her. He was her; they were one being that night.

And a warning wouldn't have mattered; Poe was already frightened. He knew he shouldn't have been in the darkness…

The flurry of sound! The footsteps.

She—they—tried to whirl around, to ward off the attack, whatever it was going to be.

Too late!

The canvas bag was over her head, darkness was raging…

And there was nothing.

Yet, Vickie was still aware. She was even aware that she was dreaming. And she wanted to fight the darkness, all the shadows that surrounded her and her dream world. But she could not.

She could hear a sound. It was faint; she couldn't begin to comprehend just what it was. But then…

It grew louder. It was like a horrific howl and gnashing growl all in one. As if…

She blinked, at first, still seeing only darkness. Then, a prick of light, a pale glow…lamplight that afforded so little. So little except…

She heard screaming; it was Poe.

It was herself.

Then she saw the eyes, like demon eyes. Horrible, yellow, blood-flecked. She could only think that she had entered a realm of pure make-believe and horror. It was a devil, a demon; it was some kind of a werewolf, or…

"Vickie!"

She realized that Griffin was straddled over her— and that she had been screaming.

The reality of the room clicked into her mind; the reality that she was there, that he was with her.

She gasped to inhale.

Screaming in the middle of the night wasn't exactly new for her.

Her dreams recently were often tortured nightmares.

She fell silent, staring up at him.

"What was it?" he asked her, his dark eyes concerned.

"Poe. Poe…before he died."

"What happened? Did you see who was with him, who did it—whatever it was?" he asked.

"The devil!" she said.

"The devil?"

She shook her head. "I just saw the eyes..."

There was a tentative knock at their door. Griffin winced and rose. He grabbed a robe and Vickie leaped up to do the same.

Griffin opened the door.

A nervous-looking little man stood there.

"I'm sorry to disturb you. I'm Sonny Smith, the night manager. We had a report about a disturbance in this room," he said.

"We apologize. Vickie had a horrible nightmare," Griffin explained.

"And you're certain she's all right?" he asked.

Vickie strode quickly to the door. "I'm fine. I'm just fine. I'm just so sorry to have awakened people!" she said.

He looked her up and down and seemed satisfied. "Well, thank goodness. Please forgive me, but we can't have this kind of disturbance here. We value all our guests, but..."

"Not to worry, we understand," Griffin said. "And, actually, we are checking out tomorrow."

"Excellent! I mean, well, we're sorry to see you go. We hope you've enjoyed your time here!"

Flustered, the little man was ready to leave. Vickie felt so bad for him.

"I'm truly, truly apologetic!" she assured him.

With one last anxious smile, he hurried away down the hall.

Griffin turned to Vickie as he shut the door. "A devil? A demon? That's how Poe...died?"

"No! I don't think so. I mean... I don't really know what it was. I wish that I hadn't screamed myself awake. There was...more. There was sound, a guttural howling...or something like that."

"A werewolf killed Poe?" Griffin asked.

Vickie was still shaky, but she had to smile at that. "No... I'm not sure what I was seeing. I woke myself up."

"Did you tell Poe what you saw before?"

"Yes."

"And?"

"Whatever was done to him seemed to have stripped away his short-term memory. He doesn't remember anything at all. That's a kindness, I guess. He doesn't remember the hospital—anything. All he does know is that the man who wrote his obituary was his enemy and because of that, everyone remembers him only as a tormented drunk who was his own worst enemy." She fell silent. "I believe him when he tells me that he was older, wiser and in love again. He hadn't been well to begin with, so..."

"An attack by a werewolf couldn't be fought off easily!" Griffin finished.

"Amusing."

Griffin was suddenly silent. "Maybe not so amusing—maybe real."

"A werewolf?"

"No, not a were-anything. But a dog or a wolf."

"You think that he wouldn't remember such an attack?"

"In retrospect, one of the theories regarding Poe's

condition when he was found before his death was that he'd contracted rabies."

"Oh!"

"If he was attacked—bitten by a rabid dog or other creature—it could readily explain his apparent dementia."

"It is a theory!" Vickie said. "And maybe… Well, it would explain everything. Except…"

"What?"

"Why he was walking in a dark alley. And who attacked him. Because before he was attacked by the growling dog or animal or whatever, he was taken by someone."

"You're having the dream every time you go to sleep. The truth is in there somewhere. Trying to explain any of this absolutely defies science, but maybe Poe's subconscious mind is somehow manifesting through you. After all I've seen you do, the other dreams you've had, I don't doubt many possibilities."

She grinned. "Then, maybe a werewolf did get Poe."

"And maybe werewolves are man's creation to explain rabies."

"Maybe. I might have heard that theory, too," Vickie said. "And following that idea, all we have to do is figure out…"

"Who kidnapped him—and let him be attacked by a rabid animal," Griffin finished for her. "And we have to figure out what that has to do with what's happening now."

"You think that the two are connected?" Vickie asked.

He shrugged. "I can't be sure. But I do believe Poe is here because he's looking for vindication. Many biographers and scholars have helped restore his name—and the doctor who saw him definitely helped by stating that Poe was not under the influence of alcohol when he was found. But even if we can't prove what happened—just reinforce a theory—I think it will mean something to Poe. And because of the way our current murders have been committed, yes, I believe they are connected, even if it's a tenuous bond."

Dylan and Darlene had found Josh.

Downstairs in the sunny breakfast room, the three were engaged in conversation at the end of the buffet; Darlene leaned against the wall, the two young men facing her. Dylan paused now and then to reach out and touch someone who went by with a plate of food.

Vickie saw that he smiled each time he startled someone.

Griffin went to choose a table in the bright room on the east side of the old mansion and Vickie headed for the buffet. Taking care that no one noticed, she rebuked Dylan, "Cute, real cute," she told him.

"Oh, come on. It's a bit of fun," Dylan said.

Josh smiled at her. "Good to see you, Vickie."

"You, too," she assured the ghost. And then, of course, she realized that others had gotten into the buffet line and an elderly gentleman was staring at her.

Dylan laughed softly.

Vickie rolled her eyes and headed to the table, where

she and Griffin were soon joined by Jackson, Angela and Adam.

"So, Vickie, we were right," Griffin said. "Both Franklin Verne and Brent Whaley were called by the same number several times in the days before their deaths. The same number just showed up in their feeds for the first time that week. Each received a call from that number at 10:00 p.m. on the night they were killed."

"You did nail it," Vickie said. "But the number is from a pay-as-you-go phone, cash purchase?" she asked. "So how does it help?"

"It is a big needle in a haystack," Jackson said. "But we're going to canvass every store around here with pictures of the suspected players. We'll have a posse of agents, and the local police will have out an equal number of men and women."

"There is a chance that we'll get something with old-fashioned legwork," Angela said. She smiled. "It works now and then. We have people narrowing down the assigned number to the batch of hardware, so at the least we'll have an idea of where it was bought."

"That's great," Vickie said. She glanced over at Griffin. "Are we on patrol?"

"Oh, no, you're popular with the locals," Adam told her.

"Really?" Vickie asked.

"Gary Frampton did ask you out to his estate," Adam said, smiling.

"You'll be watching the key players," Angela said.

"I see. But…" She hesitated a minute, looking from

Angela to Adam. "Do you feel that you've eliminated anyone yet?"

"Monica," Adam said, shaking his head and smiling as he looked at Angela.

"We haven't eliminated anyone yet," Angela said, looking back at him—and shaking her head.

"But we will soon," Adam said. "I will be heading out to stay with the widow," he said.

"And we will hope that we can eliminate her soon. Jackson and I will also be looking more into Brent Whaley's life. One of his friends might know something. The police have pulled apart Franklin Verne's computer, but not Whaley's, and now that we're officially in, I want one of our experts to take a look at both computers. And the security footage. Hopefully fresh eyes will see something new."

"Hopefully," Vickie murmured. "So…" She looked over at Griffin.

"We're heading out to Frampton's in about an hour," he said.

"Do you think that the invitation was sincere?" Vickie asked him.

"He asked me again this morning," Griffin said. "He's definitely making it appear that he's afraid—without saying it. So, as we figured before, either he really is fearful, or he's playing it as a gambit in a game. We'll find out."

"All right," Vickie said.

"The children," Adam said with a sigh, "will be coming with me."

Vickie smiled. Adam was watching their three adolescent ghosts. Now they were all playing the touching game—seeing who totally ignored them and who reacted.

"They are good at exploring their environs," Vickie said.

Adam stared at Angela. "Exactly. So, if Monica is hiding something, we'll discover that soon."

Angela wagged a stern finger at him. "Do not let your guard down."

"I will not, Angela. I promise," he told her.

"Everyone, stay on point," Griffin said. He rose. "Vickie—let's get packed up and ready to get on the road."

"We're all within thirty minutes, tops, of one another," Jackson said. "Obviously, any information is important information."

He was looking at Vickie.

She realized that the others didn't need telling—they were accustomed to close communication at all times.

"Any information is important information," she said.

Jackson nodded and leaned toward her, and she realized that Griffin had told them all about what seemed to be a "serial" dream for her.

"Even what some people wouldn't accept as *real*. Anything that you even perceive as truth—awake or asleep—may be very important."

"Okay," Vickie said. "Do you think, too, that the dreams, Poe and the murders might all be related?"

"I don't see how they're not," Jackson said. He rose,

too. "Guess we should all get going. Adam, we'll drop you first."

"There's a plan," Adam said.

He smiled, looking at Vickie. "My dear, I think you are going to top all the rest for cases you've helped with as a civilian. Which is to your advantage. It has certainly given you time to consider whether you really do or don't want to be part of the Krewe. What do you think, what do you feel?"

Vickie rose to stand by Griffin. "With all my heart and mind, sir, I know that it's an incredible, life-changing opportunity to work with the Krewe. I couldn't be more determined to pass the academy."

"Good!" Adam told her. He winked, something that he got away with easily because he was such a distinguished older gentleman. "There are days when you are going to need that dedication!"

"To get through the academy?" she asked.

"The academy—and the life we live!" he added. "Excellent, excellent, excellent!"

He smiled and turned away. Breakfast was over; the day was beginning.

"We're on the legwork and the cyberwork," Jackson assured them as they split up. "You're on the people and intuition side of the equation."

"Yep. We'll be in touch," Griffin assured him.

Griffin was quiet as they went back upstairs for their belongings.

"What are you thinking?" Vickie asked him.

"It's our third actual day on this," he said. "Oh, we were here Friday night. But that was before. Saturday morning, a body. Franklin Verne. Sunday, a body. Brent Whaley. And now..."

"Monday."

"Yes."

"And you're concerned...we're going to find a third body? But we're not going to be anywhere near the restaurant. The police have combed it over and over."

"Yes, I know."

"You think that there is a body out at Gary Frampton's country house?" she asked.

"Not necessarily."

"Good."

Griffin looked at her and gave a slight shrug. "But," he said quietly, "yes—the idea is there in my mind. I do think that, somewhere in the great Baltimore area, another body will be found today." He attempted a smile for her. "But hey, that's just me. You might actually enjoy what we're doing—Gary Frampton has assured me that his house is extremely historic. It was used as a headquarters by several generals in several wars. It's just the kind of place you love."

Vickie nodded.

She refrained from telling him that he was wrong...

She really wasn't at all fond of places where she was afraid she would find the bodies of the recently deceased.

10

"Oh... Oh, my God!" Vickie breathed, staring.

Gary Frampton's house in the outskirts-slash-woods of Maryland was—as he had said—old.

But it was more than just old.

It was both magnificent—and straight out of a Poe story.

It had an air of decaying grandeur; it spoke of elegant bygone days. Vickie quickly estimated that it had been begun before the first shots had been fired in the American Revolution. It had continued to grow; the outline of the original saltbox could just be seen by a slight discoloration in the sad gray-beige paint that covered the house. A grand porch with chipping columns had been added at some point, along with a third story and an attic.

Whoever had added on during the early Victorian days had seen to it that the extensions or wings on each side were the same in size. They'd added balconies to the second story, and someone, somewhere along the line, had given both wings bay windows in the front.

It was beautiful.

It was morose.

Vines trailed over the house and over the brick wall surrounding the overgrown lawn. A wrought-iron gate opened to the immediate surrounding woods. A groundskeeper had evidently not been about in years.

Unpruned bushes with a few withering blooms suggested the remains of a rose garden to the front, and awkward shapes to the left were an indication that sometime in recent history—perhaps as close in the past as Gary's parents—someone had kept a topiary.

"It's right out of 'The Fall of the House of Usher!'" Griffin said.

"Exactly! I mean…it looks like it could fall down at any time. All the vines…the paint, the columns…" Vickie said.

The gate had been left open; Griffin drove on through. The front door to the house opened even as they were maneuvering the overgrown drive.

Alice came running out. She seemed overjoyed to see them.

Strange. Vickie hadn't been certain that the girl had even really liked either of them.

"You're here!" she cried, her voice bright with pleasure.

Alice was closest to Griffin as he stepped out of the driver's seat. She threw her arms around his neck, hugging him.

She surely took him by surprise. He looked over her head at Vickie, a little bit helpless.

Vickie just smiled.

But she needn't have felt neglected. Alice came racing around to the passenger side of the car, throwing her arms around Vickie as well.

"Hey!" Vickie said. "It's nice to see you, too. What have we missed, a day?"

"A day is forever when the cracked-out virago is on the property!" Alice said.

"Cracked-out virago," Griffin repeated. "You don't mean—"

"She doesn't mean drugs. She means crackpot. As in Liza?" Vickie asked.

Alice nodded dully. "She's chasing my father. Oh, not romantically—my dad is no spring chicken, but she has him by more than a decade, I'm certain. No... she just has to be near him! She's afraid for him. And if the dead are around and trying to get a message to him about who to watch out for, well, she's the only one who can help him."

"I see," Griffin murmured. He looked up at the house. "So, it's you, your dad—and Liza?"

Alice flushed. "And Jon."

"Jon is here, too?" Griffin asked.

Dylan and Darlene had told Griffin and Vickie that Jon and Alice were a couple.

Griffin evidently wanted to hear Alice say it.

Alice's flush deepened and Vickie laughed.

"I see," Vickie said, as if she was only just "seeing" what was going on.

"Ah, you two are dating," Griffin said.

Alice nodded. "We had been keeping it on the down low, you see, just because...well, my dad owns the restaurant, I'm his daughter and Jon is an employee. But I told my dad I wanted Jon out here with me. I mean..." She paused to shudder. "I know that this house is family property. Historic and cool. I know I should be grateful that my dad belongs to the Sons of the American Revolution. Yeah, it's all special, huh? But as you can see, we haven't been out here a whole lot lately. And at night? There are no timers or anything—you have to make sure you have lights on before it gets dark. It's a stygian pool inside if you don't. There's a nice full moon tonight, which is cool, because I actually freaked myself out the other day when we were inside and I came running out. Then Dad got the lights on...and I was okay. But besides crazy séance lady, it's creepy—and it's good to have Jon here."

"Well, then, great," Griffin said.

"Lacey is coming out. She's another hanger-on. She can't let my dad get too far out of her sight. And she's bored, I guess. She has plenty of money, so...we have Liza and Lacey—and I can almost bet one of them has called Alistair Malcolm and asked him to come out, too," Alice said.

"Well, Liza did speak to us about a séance out here. Maybe she wanted the same grouping—especially since she is convinced that she contacted the dead," Vickie said, glancing at Griffin.

His quick stare made her smile. Griffin simply wasn't fond of Liza Harcourt. He didn't want to believe she was capable of summoning so much as a living puppy.

Gary Frampton appeared on his porch. He was

beaming—definitely looking ten times better and certainly more cheerful than he had appeared the day before.

"Hey! I'm so glad you two made it. Miss Preston, I hear that you're quite the historian—in fact, I hadn't realized that I'd read one of your articles in one of the museum magazines I have a subscription to—you are something. 'Adams and Hancock—two very different men who came together to make a difference.' Excellent, excellent. You're going to have to attack Maryland history now."

"Beautiful state, great history," Vickie said cheerfully.

Gary walked down to meet them at the car, slipping an arm around his daughter's shoulders. "I wish Alice loved it all the way you do. In fact, now that you're here, I'm embarrassed. I should have been paying so much more attention to this property. The house is special."

"So special," Alice said. "It needs paint. Oh, wait—it needs decent electric. And plumbing."

"There's nothing wrong with the plumbing," Gary said.

"If you're into nice cold showers," Alice said drily. "Honestly, Dad, it's almost rude to ask people out here when they have to freeze to bathe!"

"You don't freeze," Gary protested.

"Not to worry. We're both from Boston. We're good at freezing," Griffin assured him.

"Well, the electric sucks," Alice said. "The lights are always switching on and off."

"We'll just have to make our way around in the

dark," Vickie told her. "It's okay, really. I can see your problems—it's difficult to live with history over modern conveniences. But it really is incredibly cool."

"Okay, so it is," Alice agreed. She swept an arm out as they headed up the porch steps. "It was built in the mid-1700s."

"This is the center of the main house, as you can see," Gary explained, pointing out the wings to the sides. "The main house has a date etched into a brick— May 7, 1750. Baltimore was just beginning to get on her feet. Like most of the East Coast, the history of European settlement goes way back. And John Smith took a trip up the Chesapeake Bay, but in general, the city itself isn't as old as Jamestown or Plymouth or some of the other sites of original colonization. Of course, the city was named for Lord Baltimore, and it's an incredible harbor—"

"And Baltimore has Fort McHenry! 'Oh, say can you see!'" Alice announced, showing unexpected enthusiasm. She blushed suddenly. "See, Dad, I'm not that big a jerk. I do have pride in my home. Anyway! This house was first owned by General Hamish McCartney—and he reported directly to General Washington during the Revolution."

"Washington slept here?" Vickie asked, smiling.

"You bet! Or so they say," Gary told them. "Supposedly, Washington was here. The house is quite secluded. History claims the British never even knew that it existed, making it a key meeting place for generals and leaders when the army was near."

"So, we dine where great leaders of the Revolution dined?" Griffin asked. "Nice."

"See—there's a man who has it right. Appreciate it all—but don't live for it!" Alice said. She tossed back a long lock of hair. "Anyway, it badly needs renovations. Dad had started, but then he became fixated on opening the restaurant."

"*Fixated* isn't a fair word," Gary argued. "The restaurant makes money."

"I'm sure we could sell this place to a history hound and make a small fortune," Alice argued. "And then you wouldn't have to worry about a restaurant. Where people have been murdered," she added, wincing.

"This has an amazing heritage!" Gary told her.

Alice looked at Griffin and shook her head—she seemed to think that he was on her side. "What's heritage without an in-ground swimming pool?" she asked. "Other friends even have diving boards. Me—I get a creepy old family cemetery!"

"Wow. Cemetery, huh?" Griffin asked Gary.

"Yes, we have a family cemetery," Gary said.

"Not to worry, Dad, I'll make sure you're in it— one day, a long, long, long time from now!" Alice told him. "As for me—I want to be cremated, and my ashes thrown into the Atlantic!"

"Hey, I'd just as soon not talk about what we'll do when we're gone," Gary said. "Not…not today. Not here. Not… Just not! Anyway, let's bring our guests up to their room, eh?"

It wasn't going to be quite so simple to get to their room. They had packed small overnight bags, and it was easy enough for Griffin to grab both out of the car, assuring Gary he needed no help. But once they were inside the house, a number of others descended upon them.

"How awesome that you came!" Jon Skye said, greeting them. "Let me help you!" he told Griffin.

"I'm good, thanks," Griffin told him. "We're traveling really light. Literally."

"Okay, sure," Jon said. "I'll let you get upstairs then—"

But as he spoke, Liza Harcourt came hurrying down the stairs. "You're here! How delightful. It's wonderful to have *the law* in the house."

Griffin glanced at Vickie with surprise before asking Liza, "Why? Do you think that there's some kind of illegal activity in the house?"

"No! Of course not," Liza said, frowning. "But you must know, you must see! Obviously. There is evil afoot. Franklin is dead. Brent is dead. This is a darkness that hangs over all of us. Brent Whaley is trying to speak with us. Perhaps Franklin would like to speak as well. We must pray that they can bring us to the truth. And we must be on guard should the evil follow us here, and you mark my words, that evil very much exists!"

Alice Frampton was standing behind her. She made a motion with her fingers, indicating that she thought Liza was insane.

"We really should get our things upstairs, and then we can come down and talk," Griffin said.

"Yes, it's just about lunch—we waited for the midday meal for you, hoping that you'd make it out here in fairly good time," Gary said.

"That was very nice of you," Vickie told him.

"Who is the chef?" Griffin asked.

"Me," Jon told him proudly. "I love restaurants—noticeable by the fact I'm a waiter, I assume. But I am an excellent cook, and one day—as soon as there is an opening—I hope to start working in the kitchen at the Black Bird."

"If there still is a Black Bird," Gary said, his shoulders hunching.

"There will be, Gary. There will be," Liza told him.

Griffin cleared his throat. "Well, excuse me, if you will. Where am I going with these bags?"

"This way!" Alice said, sliding around Liza and hurrying up the stairs. Griffin followed her; Vickie excused herself and did the same.

Alice turned left once she was up the stairs, leading them by three doors before stopping at one at the end of the hall.

"It's the old master's quarters," Alice said proudly, throwing open double doors to a very large room.

"The master's quarters? Should this be your dad's room, or your room?" Vickie asked.

"Oh, no, not while you're here. My dad has the room at the other end of the hall—it's cool, too, has a massive dressing room and private bath and all."

"What about you—and Liza?" Griffin asked.

"Not to worry—someone in the family had a major pack of kids. There are actually ten bedrooms up here, just on this floor alone. There are 'servants' quarters upstairs, not that we have the servants to fill them. There's just Hallie."

"Hallie?" Vickie asked.

"Hallie Long. She looks after things when we're away, the best that she can. And she hires in a cleaning crew when we're on our way out. She's impressive— about six feet even, slim and pretty, and strong, like a bull!" Alice said, laughing. "Her boyfriend, Sven Moller, does a lot of the patching up of the place for my dad. Anyway, they live upstairs. You'll meet them somewhere along the line."

"Hallie and Sven. Okay," Vickie said. "Still…this room is really lovely."

Alice laughed. "That's the point! We want you somewhere lovely, of course. These wings were added on about ten years before the Civil War," she said. "My ancestors were entranced by the homes they'd seen deeper in the South. They just loved the whole plantation thing. Of course, they had no plantation—or farm. This was just kind of a wilderness retreat—my family made their money in shipping back then. I honestly don't think we ever owned slaves—there's no record of it, but I do believe we were pretty brutal to some indentured Irish servants back in the day. The Civil War era… It really was still the South, but the Union kept troops here so that the state wouldn't secede. Maryland was all split back then—the state never did leave the Union, but my Lord, there were dozens and dozens of Southern sympathizers. You know, of course, that John Wilkes Booth was from Maryland and that a bunch of the stuff in the conspiracy to kill Lincoln and others came from

Maryland? Whatever—my great-great-whomever was never actually a traitor, but he might have been, given the opportunity. They say that he hid escaping prisoners here at the house. Some people get to be nice and proud—they were part of the Underground Railroad. Not us—we just helped the Rebels escape."

"It's not as if they were all bad men," Vickie said. "They were just convinced of a different cause."

"Nice of you to say so—being a Bostonian and all," Alice told her. She grinned suddenly. "Anyway, the South did produce better generals. So there. Whatever. It's over now. Even if there are weirdos who like to dress up and do it all over again. Me—I'm far more into the future, but… Anyway…the grandest part of this room is the view. Voila!"

She walked across the expanse of the room to the French doors that led out to the balcony. They were covered with drapes—which Alice dramatically threw back. "Come, come over! Please. Even I love this part of the estate."

They quickly walked over to join her, Vickie stepping in front, Griffin standing behind her, looking over her head, his hands on her shoulders.

The view *was* fantastic.

An extended wooden porch stretched out behind the house. A tangled garden was to the left; a winding path lined with statuary was to the right. The garden was edged by columns and several ponds—only somewhat filled with algae from this viewpoint. The path laden with the statues led to a little fence, beyond which was the family graveyard. There appeared to be a tiny chapel and a number of small mausoleums. There were all kinds of graves.

The family had been buried at the estate for quite a while. Vickie assumed that employees and their children might have been buried there as well.

"Personally, I like my room. It looks out over the overgrown front and the gates. This view…well, this one is just a wee bit too creepy for me." She perked up suddenly. "Actually, I'm surprised that old Liza Harcourt didn't scream at you and scratch your eyes out— she was really miffed that Dad insisted you two have this room instead of her. But what the heck, she is next door. She just doesn't have the French doors to the balcony. She has a window. God knows, the foolish woman will probably crawl out the damned thing!"

"It is all impressive," Vickie assured her.

"Yes, you'll be happy here?" they all heard.

Spinning around quickly, Vickie saw that Gary Frampton was standing in the doorway.

"It's terrific," Vickie said. "Really, your house is wonderful."

"And you're thinking it's a crime that I own something that is such an incredible piece of history—and I treat it so badly," Gary said.

"Not at all, sir. We're not here to judge."

"No, you're going to catch a killer, right?" Gary said. "And you came out here because you think you'll find him or her here. Well, maybe you will."

He stared at his daughter.

Alice stared back at him.

"What's your problem?" Alice demanded.

Gary Frampton shook his head. "I love you, Alice," he told her softly.

"And I love you, Dad. But give it a rest. Let the cops do their job. We'll survive," Alice said. She grinned. "Even if I'm dating a would-be cook rather than a lawyer. Okay?" she asked. Then she looked at Griffin and Vickie, flushing. "Sorry!"

She turned and fled the room.

Gary looked after her helplessly. "Lunch is just about on. Come on down as soon as you're ready!" he said.

He left the room, closing the door behind him.

"So, Gary Frampton thinks Jon Skye is involved in the murders," Griffin murmured.

"And what do you think?"

"I think the jury is still out," he told her. "But lunch is almost on. And, joy of all joys, Liza Harcourt is here. I'm sure we'll be having a séance. And really, what could be better here? This house is, beyond a doubt, the perfect setting for a gothic ghost story."

"All right, so, here's the thing. All these foods that are suddenly so popular," Jon Skye said, "really come in fads. I mean, seriously, who actually looked for a kale salad a decade ago?" He lifted a hand. "I'm not saying one or two people weren't out there, I'm just pointing out the fact that it wasn't on many menus. Same thing with quinoa. And some of the wild hot sauces. How often did you used to hear the words sriracha sauce? Now, there's nothing wrong with all these new culinary delights, but a menu should also include comfort food made well, made right. This is Baltimore—of course, crab cakes must be on a menu. But also, some simple pleasures. Shepherd's pie, turkey and potatoes—meat loaf!"

"Normal meat loaf," Alice said. "As in, just meat loaf. No weird things in it."

"A little honey, and a little oatmeal. Salt, pepper, ground beef, ground pork, a bit of tomato, onion and bell peppers. I think it's really good—I hope you do, too!" Jon said.

There were six of them gathered around the table—Gary and Alice Frampton, Liza Harcourt, Jon Skye, Vickie and Griffin.

Jon looked straight at Griffin as he spoke, as if it was his approval he was seeking.

Jon wasn't seated. He was serving. Besides his meat loaf, he had a nice-looking Caesar salad on the table, too.

"I'm sure it's going to be great," Griffin said. "Not to mention, it's just so nice to have you do this, and serve us."

"Hey, well, ask my boss. I'm good at the serving kind of thing," Jon said lightly.

Griffin looked over at Gary Frampton, still curious. Gary wasn't happy about Alice seeing Jon, he thought, and yet, Gary didn't really seem to be any kind of an elitist. But he barely acknowledged Jon's comment.

Maybe he just disliked the idea that something had apparently been going on beneath his nose that he hadn't seen—until he'd been forced to.

And it might have been more. Did Gary suspect Jon of illegal activity—something more than a father's suspicion regarding anyone seeing his daughter?

"Food! What does food matter?" Liza murmured, looking around the table.

There were two extra place settings.

"Where is Alistair?" Liza asked. "And that woman from the shop?"

"They've both been invited, Liza," Gary said.

"I thought they both said that they were coming!" she said.

"They will come. Liza—there were no time limits on people arriving," Gary said.

"How can we have the séance?" Liza asked.

"Maybe we shouldn't have a séance!" Alice exploded. "My dad is here to escape. Very bad things happened. Maybe we don't all want to be reminded of them over and over. Jon worked hard, if you don't mind…"

"The meat loaf really is delicious," Vickie said brightly. "Excellent. Thank you, Jon. And Liza, think about it—don't you really prefer the nighttime for your séances, anyway?"

Liza shrugged, still looking unhappy. Griffin wondered just what it was the woman must have over Gary; he'd invited her out to his place when he had supposedly come here to escape, just as Alice had suggested.

Money? Influence in the city?

Or was he afraid that she did know something, have some kind of connection with the dead? And if something was going to come out—some piece of information, a clue, anything that had to do with the two dead men… Did he want to make sure he was there for it?

"Really?" Jon asked Vickie anxiously. "You're not just saying that?"

"Nope. And I understand what you were saying. There is nothing wrong with trying fresh new things, but sometimes traditional is awfully darned good. This is wonderful, as far as my taste buds are concerned. The honey gives it just a touch of sweetness, and I think that the oatmeal makes it richer than just bread crumbs... Well, I'm not sure what does what, but it's excellent, Jon."

"It is almost...good," Gary said. He looked at Jon, nodding slowly.

"Thank you!" Jon said drily, his tone not quite sarcastic.

A very tall and handsome blonde woman strode into the room, waving cheerfully to all the guests. "Hello! Do you need some help at all?" She had a broad face and a wide smile, and seemed delighted to see all the people in the dining room. She walked over to Vickie and Griffin and offered them handshakes. "I'm Hallie. Sven is right behind me. We're so happy to have you. It's great out here, but lonely sometimes, too. Don't tell Sven I said that."

Griffin had stood as soon as she'd come in. Vickie had done the same, and told Hallie what a pleasure it was to meet her.

"And here is Sven," Hallie said, pointing as a very tall and attractive blond man walked into the room.

"Hello, all," he said, only a trace of accent in his voice.

"Sven, I'm Griffin, and this is Vickie."

Sven beamed as well. "Yes! You are from the FBI. How very nice. Welcome. So happy to meet you. We've never met a government man before. G-man, right? Like Elliot Ness, the Untouchables and all?"

"Kind of—and not really at all," Griffin assured him. "Norway?"

"Exactly! You nailed it. Most people say Sweden. But I have been here, in the United States, since I was a boy of about fifteen."

"I just look Scandinavian," Hallie said. "Born and raised in DC. A city girl, but I love it out here."

"And they do wonders with the little we give them to keep the place up," Alice said.

"Yes, really, Gary, it's disgraceful," Liza said.

"There are more guests coming, too, right?" Hallie asked, looking around. "We've been in town—picking up some groceries—but I thought that there were a few more people coming."

"They're expected soon," Gary said.

"I hope you guys are hungry," Jon Skye said. "There's a lot of meat loaf."

"May we join you?" Hallie asked, pulling out a chair.

"Of course!" Jon said, enthused. "Hang on, I'll—"

"You sit, we'll help ourselves," Hallie said. "And then you must relax. Cooks do not pick up after themselves, not when we're around, right, Sven?"

"Right!"

Apparently, there was just too much cheer going around for Liza Harcourt. She stood suddenly. "I'll be in my room, if the others ever show up."

"Hallie and Sven are here now," Jon said, "If you need eight people…"

"I need the right eight people!" Liza snapped. "And

really, Mr. Skye, you're not among the right eight yourself, not fully in our Poe society, so, please, if you will, don't make suggestions!"

There was silence as she left the room.

Hallie cleared her throat and portioned out some meat loaf for Sven.

"Bitch," Alice muttered.

"Alice," Gary said.

"Well, she really is one of the most unpleasant people, Gary," Hallie said quietly. "I'm not sure why you let her come, but...hey. It's your place."

Hallie was certainly no ordinary housekeeper. But she wasn't really a *housekeeper*, per se. She was a property manager more or less, and she evidently had no problem telling Gary what she thought of things.

"Bitch!" Alice repeated. "Honestly, Dad, you should tell her. She just has no right to speak to Jon that way."

"Or anyone," Sven said quietly.

Everyone looked over at him and he looked up with a flush. "I'm sorry. It's not my place. But it's true, she's just not a very pleasant woman."

"She's just..." Gary began, and then he shook his head. "I've known Liza forever. We were in a book club together before I had any idea of opening the restaurant—before the building became available. And when I knew that I wanted to open it, I really, truly, shamefully used Liza Harcourt. I got her to form the Blackbird Society. She promoted the restaurant—she put us on the map."

"Hey, Gary, it's okay," Jon said. "Some people are rude. That's their problem. She doesn't bother me."

"Well, it is a problem," Gary said.

"The meat loaf! It's wonderful!" Hallie said.

"Isn't it?" Vickie agreed enthusiastically. "Really nice."

"So wonderful!" Sven agreed. He smiled. "So, what will you do now?" His question was addressed to Vickie and Griffin.

Vickie answered.

Griffin, however, knew exactly what she would say.

"Oh, the family graveyard," she said. "That's a wonderful old graveyard out there. Gary, I was hoping you'd give us a tour."

"A tour sounds great," Griffin said.

"There's no underground crypt or anything, is there?" Vickie asked. "Sorry, I was thinking 'The Fall of the House of Usher' and the like."

Alice laughed. "No! God help us, at least all our old family corpses are outside. Ugh! I don't think I could stay here, no matter what, if they were downstairs."

"I wouldn't mind a tour, either," Jon said. He added, explaining to the others, "This is my first trip to Franklin Manor. I've had a great time seeing the house, but I haven't been out to the graveyard myself. I'd love to go."

Alice groaned.

"And Dad loves to give tours. You guys go ahead. Hallie and Sven and I will pick up."

"Oh, we can all help," Vickie said.

"No, no. Out. Make my dad happy," Alice said. "Please."

"Okay," Vickie said, rising. "Jon, thank you for a great meal."

"Come on, I'll tell you about the statue trail and then

the cemetery. We can head out the back door," Gary
told them. "Just go back out to the hall and to the end.
The original house was a little shotgun cottage, front
door, back door—you could shoot straight and go right
through the place. I guess you know more than I do
about Colonial times, though, Vickie. It's my understanding that you are respected in your field."

"She's very, very good," Griffin couldn't help but
say.

"But I'm sure you're the expert when it comes to your
family home on the outskirts of Baltimore," Vickie said.

Gary grinned, pleased. "Okay, so the statues!"

The path was badly overgrown. Vines covered the
handsomely crafted marble statues of Shakespearean
and other literary characters. A rusting gate and broken
brick wall surrounded the family cemetery.

"These are real marble. Very cool!" Jon said, admiring a life-sized statue of Shakespeare's Juliet.

"Beautiful," Vickie agreed.

"I think I like the Ophelia at the end best," Griffin
commented.

"Ophelia, yes—pointing the way to the end!" Jon
said. "So sad—that statue is even more amazing. I'm
assuming one of your ancestors commissioned these,
right, Gary?"

"Yeah, a great-great-great…something. The artist
was an Italian immigrant. You'll see his work other
places in the area. I think it is really worth something
now. Poor bastard, worked his ass off during his life-
time. He just made a living, so I've heard. Antonio

Baldi—that was his name. Oh, and he's in one of the mausoleums, by the way."

"Cool," Jon applauded. "And here...the cemetery!" he said.

The name Frampton was worked into the metal of the arch that sat high above the gate.

"I probably should take that down one day. It disturbs Alice," Gary said.

"In this day and age, most last names have been around—and they'll be found on a tombstone somewhere," Griffin noted.

"True," Gary agreed.

"It's really not as overgrown as it could be," Vickie noted.

Griffin glanced over at her. "No?" In his mind, it was heavily overgrown. He *was* a Bostonian by birth, and he was accustomed to visiting very old graveyards and cemeteries. Of course, in the city of Boston, they were pretty well kept up. Yet there were dozens of really old towns in Massachusetts. Dozens of towns where Mother Nature wanted to reclaim her dead.

"Hallie has a lawn guy come now and then. I think he rips out the worst of the weeds," Gary offered. "It's not that bad, is it?"

"Very atmospheric," Vickie assured him.

"There are, of course, more than Frampton family members in here. Friends... A few dead Southerners *and* a few dead Northerners. Servants. And pets! That section over there is dedicated to our four-legged friends. Cats and dogs, mainly, though I believe there are a few raccoons the family became attached to as well," Gary told them. "But for you, I guess, some of our earliest graves are the most significant. The oldest stones are from the 1760s. The oldest family vault is back there—looks like a medieval castle, doesn't it? A small one, but a medieval castle."

The oldest Frampton vault had been built in the Gothic style, and it resembled a miniature Notre Dame. Vines crawled around it and it was surrounded by slanted, ancient tombstones, broken-winged cherubs and more.

"Antonio Baldi, the sculptor, is in there!" Gary said.

"How many burials and interments are there here?" Griffin asked Gary.

"Oh, I think around eight or nine hundred, if I remember right," Gary said. "They first settled here right around the Revolution, so generations, friends during the generations. Slaves," he added unhappily. Then he said, "See that building over there? That's a little chapel. I guess, at one time, they held services for the dead right on the property and in the graveyard. Anyway, there's an old Bible there with all the inhabitants of our estate listed. Don't worry, it's not just rotting away. I did get a reinforced glass case for it. And the key is up in my study. No one knows where it is," he assured them. He waved a hand in the air. "I just never thought to be that paranoid. I mean, I had an alarm system at the restaurant. Who would have ever thought that I needed to be worried that some psycho wanted to murder people there?"

There was no answer for him.

They walked along a path with broken flagstones

leading the way and Gary pointed out another of the haphazard mausoleums that dotted the graveyard.

"That mausoleum isn't the oldest in the cemetery, but to me, it holds one of my most important ancestors—General David Frampton. He was one of the leaders when the colony went against the British during the War of 1812. The Battle of Baltimore was won on September 13, 1814—and my ancestor was key in repulsing the attack by land and sea. Francis Scott Key wrote 'The Star Spangled Banner' right after that battle. Anyway, General Frampton died in 1850 and, as you can see, his name is etched into this mausoleum, even though there are about a dozen people in there—great-aunts, uncles…they did a lot of propagating back then. Me, I just have Alice. When my wife, Elyssa, died, I just never…" Gary Frampton broke off and shrugged. "She's here, Elyssa is here, buried in the newer vault my grandfather put up in the 1920s," he added.

He pointed across the graveyard. Vickie nodded and smiled at him. "Very art nouveau!" she told him.

Griffin studied the mausoleum. He wasn't sure that he could have pegged it as art nouveau, but it was a very handsome building with a clean style to the marble facade and stained-glass windows that looked as if they had come from Tiffany's.

"I'm sorry about your wife," Vickie told him.

"It has been a long time now. Over a decade," he said, flashing her a smile. "I'm sorry, too."

"I'm very sorry, too," Jon Skye said.

Gary didn't seem to hear him. But then they were all suddenly aware of another sound.

A distant roll of thunder growled, and a jagged flash of yellow lit up the sky.

A breeze suddenly picked up, and the sky seemed to slip into darkness after the slash of light.

"I guess it's going to rain," Griffin said.

"We should get back to the house," Gary said.

"A sound plan, I'd say!" Jon agreed, and started on the return trek.

Gary followed him.

Vickie had paused. The breeze lifted her dark hair and it swirled around her; for a moment, she looked like an extremely beautiful Ophelia or Juliet herself.

"Vickie, you coming?"

She nodded.

"What is it?"

"I was just thinking."

"Just thinking what?"

She smiled at him.

"It was a dark and stormy night!" she whispered.

And then she hurried ahead of him, and he rushed as well, wanting to get back before the promised rain began to fall with a vengeance.

11

They were just back in the house when it seemed that the sky split open; a truly brilliant flash of lightning lit up the heavens, a massive crash boomed and the rain began.

"Now, that's a storm," Jon announced, panting slightly as he stared out the back door; they'd all done a bit of running to get in before the deluge.

As he spoke, lightning flashed across the sky again. There was another tremendous clap of thunder.

And the lights inside the house went out.

For a moment, it was very dark—Vickie couldn't see the people around her. Then what was left of the light of day managed to trickle in. They stood in the storm shadow of the afternoon, near the back door. When she turned, the main hall of the old house seemed like something out of a movie—light tried to make its way in the front windows; it could only manage a few weak streaks.

"Oh, ouch!" Alice said, meeting up with them in the back hall. She shivered and hurried over to Jon and slipped her arm around him. "Great, just great. Good thinking, Dad. We're not just out in the nowhere 'burbs, we're out in the nowhere 'burbs without cable or Wi-Fi!"

"Oh, we'll survive," Gary said.

"No lights, no television…with the Queen of Mean upstairs!" Alice said.

"Shh!" her father warned.

"Hey, it's not even full dark yet. It will be pitch-black later," Alice said. She looked around at them all. "This place used to terrify me when I was little, when we lost power because of a storm. Even when it's at its best, the furniture is older than sin and the spiders around here seem to work double-time."

"The power could come back on by tonight," Griffin said. "That's possible, right?"

"Sure. They rush to get the power back up where there's only one house," Alice said bleakly.

"You've never gotten a generator?" Griffin asked.

"No, we're just not here that much these days," Gary said.

Vickie thought that even Griffin was startled when they heard a massive slam and then a banging against the door.

"Alistair, or Lacey, or maybe both," Gary muttered.

Griffin turned and headed toward the front door, then opened it. A very soaked Lacey Shaw stood there, shivering, a paper still over her head, though she stood beneath the cover of the front porch.

"Oh, Lord! What a storm. Let me in, let me in, please!" she begged.

"Of course, of course," Gary said, hurrying to the

door and drawing her inside. "You poor thing. You're utterly soaked. It will be dark and shadowy, but maybe you want to hop right in a shower while there's still some hot water, Lacey."

"Sounds great, but my things are out in the car," Lacey said. "I can't brave the rain again. A fire! We should all head into the parlor or the music room and put on a fire. That would be wonderful."

"I'll be happy to get your things," Griffin told her. There was an umbrella caddy by the door. Griffin helped himself and assured them he'd be right back in. Lacey thanked him effusively.

Hallie and Sven arrived in the hall.

"Welcome to our storm world!" Hallie said. "When it rains here, it really rains!" She was carrying a big mesh bag and she went from person to person, handing out flashlights and candles, with Sven working as her assistant. "These are the coolest flashlights," she assured them. "Three settings, and you can stand them on end, like a lamp in a room. Low, for a night-light, medium to softly illuminate a room and high for some real light! And candles…just because. Candles are just so nice, huh? Like a roaring fire."

Just as Griffin came back in the front door with Lacey's bag, Liza Harcourt came running down the stairway, looking at them all. Vickie realized she wasn't upset by the storm or the loss of power.

She wanted to see who had arrived.

"Lacey! You're here," she said, pleased. "This is actually quite nice—the powerful storm, the wind, the lack of modern electrical interference. Perfect!"

"Perfect?" Alice muttered.

"For my séance. Lacey, did Alistair come out here with you?"

"And here I was thinking charades," Gary said. He suddenly seemed to brighten. "Actually, I love charades. We're still hoping that Alistair will make it out… While we're waiting, why don't we play charades?"

"Dad, tell me you're kidding," Alice begged.

"Alice! Come on, parlor games can be fun—really fun!" Jon said.

She looked at him and smiled.

"Okay, if you're game…"

Lacey looked over at Griffin and Vickie. "What about you two? I don't mean to be rude in any way here, but…would a game of charades be something you two would enjoy?" She let out a sigh, looking around. "Let's face it—I'll be honest. It's fine that you two are here. Vickie—not to be insulting, but you don't do much for me in terms of protection, but we're all glad to have Griffin out here—a muscle-bound man with a gun."

"We're out of the city!" Gary said, sounding both testy and frightened. "We're away from whatever sick criminal has been using my place for his or her even sicker intentions."

"Yes, but you're happy they're here, too, Dad," Alice said. "Let's be blunt here. They're obviously just here to protect us—or figure out which one of us is a killer."

"There is that," Griffin said.

"Which? You want to protect us—or find a killer?" Alice demanded.

"Both," Griffin said. He seemed to be getting impatient.

"I personally love charades," Vickie said. "It will be a lot of fun. And we haven't even seen the parlor or the music room yet."

"East wing!" Gary said happily. "Come on. Hallie, Sven, you'll play, right?"

"Sure!" Hallie said. "But first, what can we get people? I have coffee on. There's tea and hot chocolate. I'll get everyone settled while you draw up teams."

Vickie looked at Griffin. He raised his eyebrows.

Playing along is part of the job. Okay.

Charades it was.

"Into the parlor," Gary said, urging them all along.

At one time, Vickie thought, it had been a grand old Victorian parlor. There were several beautiful love seats, wing-back chairs, carved buffets and secretaries and a massive double fireplace that served the music room as well.

"Eastern end of the house," Griffin murmured to Vickie. "Our room is right above."

She nodded.

The upholstery on the furniture was all but threadbare. Someone had cleaned, and so the floor was swept and everything had been dusted, including the many fine lamps around the room.

"Split 'em up, shake 'em up. No couples together," Lacey said. "It will be more fun. So, I'll take the lead with one team—and I'll take Griffin and Alice and Hallie. Gary, you take Vickie and Jon and Sven, and…"

Her voice trailed. There was one "odd man" out—
Liza Harcourt.

"Not to worry. I will sit in judgment, call foul when
it is necessary," Liza said. "I'm rather anxious. I want
Alistair to get here!"

"Has anyone talked to him?" Vickie asked.

They looked around at each other.

Griffin pulled out his phone. "I'll call him."

He walked away as he put through the call.

They could all hear him talking. With Griffin, of
course, it was impossible to tell from his inflection or
his expression just what was going on.

He hung up and came back over. Watching him,
Vickie quickly lowered her head to hide a frown.

Griffin hadn't just called Alistair Malcolm. He'd
made a second call.

Had something else happened?

"Well?" Liza asked anxiously. "Actually, you know,
I am the president of the Blackbirds. And Alistair Malcolm is the vice president. He really should have had
more courtesy. He should have let me know what was
going on with him."

"He was a little bit nervous about coming," Griffin said.

"Nervous? Why?" Gary asked.

Griffin smiled then, looking at Liza. "Well, he believes in our medium, of course."

"And that makes him nervous?" Liza asked, frowning.

"Some people don't like the concept of connecting
with the dead," Griffin told her.

"That's just silly. The dead don't come back to hurt people," Liza said.

"No—just give them heart attacks!" Jon said.

"Alistair didn't look so good when we found Brent, did he?" Alice asked.

"It's our duty to help the dead!" Liza said.

"But for now we'll play charades!" Vickie said.

The strange thing was that their game of charades was actually fun.

They all quickly had the knack of book, movie, TV show, two of the above or all of the above. Alice got into her father's game, showing them all her way of giving the clue to a group as to whether their chosen subject had been a comic before becoming anything else.

Liza became very involved as well. As a "timer," she was a positive dictator. But she kept them all laughing with her buzzing sounds and absolute tyrannical determination not to give anyone a break.

Griffin wasn't really great with charades. Vickie whispered that he needed to think of it as undercover work. Of course, it wasn't the same—not in any way, shape or form. But he had to give it a try.

He pulled Hemingway's *The Old Man and the Sea* when it was his turn. Old was easy—the rest not so much, but his team got it before Liza chimed in with one of her buzzing sounds.

Vickie was excellent. And she was constantly cheerful, keeping everything going well. When she drew her paper, however, she seemed to freeze for a minute and reflect hard on what she had drawn.

She turned to her group.

Book and movie.

She began to act it all out. They quickly realized that she was pretending her death. And then the fact that she was walking again.

Two words, book and movie.

"The Ghost in the Machine!" Alice said.

"Beetlejuice!" Sven suggested.

"The Ghost and Mrs. Muir!" Jon called out.

"Not your team, Jon, and no! That's not two words!" Gary protested. "And none of those is two words. What's the matter with you guys?"

"Ghost Story!" Alice cried. "Peter Straub—and there was a movie, too! I saw it on Netflix. Old dudes were in it... Red Buttons, I forget who else!"

Lightning flashed hard against the sky. The wind shifted.

There was a slam at the door.

Everyone jumped.

"Alistair, of course!" Gary said, shaking his head.

"Let's get him in here!" Lacey said, and they all hurried out to the hall, ready to greet Alistair.

At first, he appeared as some kind of monster, or weird creature of the storm; he had himself pressed against the window by the door, his mouth was open and he seemed to be screaming.

It was, indeed, Alistair. He was soaking wet and startled by their reception.

Gary threw open the door.

Alistair the monster was no more. The man stood

there, large and smiling. "Damn, it takes you people long enough to answer the door."

Alice and Lacey laughed, a little nervously, Griffin thought.

Gary begged him to come on in. "We're sorry, so sorry! Get in here!"

Alistair noticed Griffin, and Griffin smiled.

Alistair Malcolm was truly frightened. Brent Whaley had been killed, Franklin Verne had been killed. They were both men, both writers...both involved with Poe in one way or another.

He had not wanted to come out to Frampton Manor— he had only agreed because Griffin had promised him that extra agents would be watching the house—unknown to the other visitors.

And then Griffin had called Jackson Crow.

Jackson promised he and Angela would shadow Alistair Malcolm. They could leave the tediousness of door-to-door and finding anyone associated with the dead men to the police and other agents. Yes, the weather sucked. Not to worry—they'd all worked in bad weather before. They'd be close, Jackson promised. And he'd make sure that Alistair knew that they were on hand.

The dynamics of such a situation could be advantageous, Jackson had determined.

So now they were all there. The original group who had gathered around for Liza's séance when they had found the body of Brent Whaley. They had Hallie and Sven as well.

"We were playing charades," Alice told Alistair. "It was fun, honestly."

"Yes. You all can finish your game," Liza said firmly. "And then we can have my séance."

"Great. Perfect. Now that it *is* dark!" Alice said.

"Alice, it's okay!" Hallie told her. "We may not have a generator, but Sven and I are used to the fact that the electricity fails in a storm. There are tons of lights and candles."

"I don't want to raise the dead," Alice said petulantly. "I'm tired of all the old and the dead. Jon and I will sit out."

"Why? Did you and Jon have something to do with killing Franklin and Brent?" Liza demanded.

"Oh, this is ridiculous!" Alice said.

"Honey, let's just humor everyone, okay?" Jon said.

"She keeps insulting you, and…"

"It's all right," Jon said. He yawned. "Let's do it, huh? I'm exhausted. We have the séance, we can make up some sandwiches or leftovers for dinner…"

"Fine!" Alice announced. "It's dark, it's rainy and we have our very own creepy family cemetery just outside. Hell, yes, let's scare ourselves to death," Alice said. She wagged a finger at her father. "Don't you even think about having some kind of a fit if Jon sleeps in my room!"

"Alice," Jon murmured uncomfortably.

"As if she hasn't slept with him a zillion times already," Liza said. "All of you, this way. Hallie, I can't let you and Sven be part of my séance, but you are welcome to be in the room. Let's get this thing set up and going!"

* * *

Vickie made an excuse about getting a sweater and ran up to their room; she knew that Griffin would follow.

He did.

"What the hell is going on?" she asked him. "Alistair— the way that he looked at you. He is freaked out, right? He doesn't want another séance. Alice doesn't, either."

"Boy, though, Liza does!"

"Which should make her innocent," Vickie said.

Griffin hesitated. "I think that Liza is innocent. She is so passionate about this. But I also think she believes that someone here did kill those two men."

Vickie shook her head. "So hard to believe! I mean, why would Gary do it? He's had to close his restaurant. Why would Lacey? She loses her work, and she loves the place. Alice? Jon? Alice is Gary's daughter—Jon is a waiter and he wants to work in the kitchen there."

Griffin was quiet a minute and then he shrugged and set his hands on her shoulders. "You're just coming into this, but you've seen a lot, Vickie. The sick son of a bitch who nearly killed you when you were in high school, and the legacy he created. And the twisted minds of those who kidnapped one of your best friends. It's almost impossible to follow the human mind. We can have dozens of theories as to what makes someone tick, or what their motivation is. I think this could go two ways—either someone wants people dead, and they're using the Poe thing as a cover, or someone has a fixation on Poe, and perhaps a desire for revenge for one reason or another." He hesitated. "Adam is convinced that Monica is innocent, and she's not here now. I can't help but believe that she would have found a way to be here if she'd had anything to do with the murders. I also believe that she really, truly loved her husband. One down."

"One down, two dead," Vickie murmured. "Anyway, I think that Liza does have something."

"A nasty, elitist attitude?" Griffin asked.

"Well, that, too. But I think she does have a sense of things around her. Maybe she did do something that allowed us to hear the echoes of Brent Whaley's last heartbeats."

"And maybe we just heard them because we are who we are. The thing is, Whaley's body would have been discovered. This is indelicate, but the smell would have become noticeable very soon."

"Yeah, well… Want to go speak to the dead?"

"Sure." But Griffin still hesitated. "Did you get anything from the family graveyard?"

"Not a thing," Vickie told him.

"Interesting. Gary Frampton gave us a tour, and he told us about his wife's interment—but he didn't actually bring us to the grave."

"It's probably too painful."

He nodded. "Maybe. Well, anyway, we do have people checking out the mausoleums."

"Oh?"

"Jackson and Angela."

"They're in the graveyard?"

"Yep."

"And Alistair Malcolm knows that they're near. I

hope I'm putting together something that will cause something else to happen."

"Let's hope it's not another murder!" Vickie said.

"That's our role, Vickie. We have to stop the next murder. And have a séance in a creepy old mansion. Why the hell not, huh? Shall we?"

"All right, ready if you are." Vickie couldn't help but pause again for a minute, walking over to the French doors that went to the balcony. She looked out over the sculpture-garden trail to the cemetery.

The rain was still coming down. It had given way to little more than a trickle.

Dusk had fallen. There was still just enough light in the sky to make the world before her appear shadowed and eerie.

The marble statues looked as if they could move.

The cemetery looked haunted, as if cherubs might fly...as if the dead might arise.

"Séance," she murmured. "Great. Just great."

And she wondered just where, out in the realm of the dead, Jackson and Angela might be.

"Actually, you're right—it's all really nice and lovely, with all the candles. And dusk has come and gone—it is dark now!" Liza said happily.

She'd brought something else to the table for the séance that night, making Griffin think more than ever that the woman was a total nutcase.

Liza had packed and brought with her the crystal ball from her home.

It was very large and heavy. She had a wood pedestal for it, and she'd set it in the middle of the table.

"Are we going to have a séance or tell fortunes?" Gary asked her.

"Crystal is simply very powerful as far as the universe is concerned," Liza said, not about to be rattled. "Really, Gary. Two *friends* died. We need to reach them. We need to have them tell us what was done to them."

"Liza, Liza!" Gary said. "They are not going to pop out of your crystal ball like a pair of genies, ready to talk."

"I think they will talk," Liza said.

"I think I should have stayed in town," Alistair Malcolm said, shaking his head. He rubbed his hands together as well. "Dark, dank, chilly! What are we doing? Have we all gone mad?"

"Hey, you want to be a writer, Alistair," Liza said.

"I am a writer," he told her flatly. "I write—and writing makes me a writer! Not to mention that I have been published in a few prestigious places!"

"This should give you lots of inspiration for great stories, huh? A séance, a dark, stormy night—candles wavering?" Liza asked.

"I think what you're doing is dangerous," Alistair said flatly.

"But you're here—you've agreed to be here!" Alice pointed out.

"I'm not going to be the one to deny anything that might help," Alistair said.

"You're a big guy, Mr. Malcolm," Jon pointed out.

He added quickly, "As in strong, sir, that's what I mean. No one is going to mess with you."

"If only that was the case!" Alistair said sagely. "Size can help—but when someone has a gun or a knife…"

"Or a drug," Lacey said, and shivered.

"Or a drug," Alistair agreed. He looked over at Griffin and Vickie. "You're going to be here, right? You're going to be here through the whole thing. You won't disappear or anything if all the candles suddenly blow out."

"We're here, Alistair," Griffin assured him. "We're right here. If one of my team members has promised you something, it will happen."

Alistair nodded. "Then let's get this sucker over with. You wait for me to get here to stop the fun stuff like the charades, huh? Then we have to have a séance all over again!"

"Everyone around the table!" Liza ordered.

Griffin looked around. Maybe it was the candlelight, but everyone looked a little pale.

A little ghastly, really!

Jon sat by Liza, and Alice sat by him. On the other side, Gary took the chair by Liza, Vickie sat next to him and Griffin sat next to her. Lacey sat between him and Alice.

Hallie and Sven were there as well, standing awkwardly for a moment.

"Take seats, take those extra dining room chairs by the door," Liza commanded.

The two did so.

"Settle in," Liza said softly. "Feel the night. Watch the flicker of the candles. Let your minds and your souls be open to those who have lived…and gone to the great hereafter. My friends!" she said suddenly. "Dear, dear friends! Brent Whaley, Franklin Verne—I know that you are there. I know that you are near. I just need something from you. Some sweet sign. We won't give up. We are your friends. We will try for as long as it takes to reach you. We will find the truth about the night you died. Just give us a sign, please!"

There was silence.

It stretched out.

"Please!" Liza whispered. "Please, let us know you are with us. We will help you. We can find a way to communicate. Let the candles flicker… Let us hear a tap on the wood."

Again, silence.

And then a breeze seemed to pick up in the room.

The candles flickered.

"What the hell?" Hallie gasped from the corner of the room.

"Even a broken clock is right now and then!" Gary muttered. "There's a draft. Guys, come on, it's been raining all afternoon."

"They're here!" Liza insisted. "I feel them. I feel them both!"

Griffin squeezed Vickie's hand and looked at her. She shook her head slightly.

No, I'm not feeling as if the dead are in the room, she silently let him know. *What about you?*

He shook his head, no—he wasn't getting anything, either.

But then Griffin did see something—someone. It was the wrong dead man.

It was the ghost of Edgar Allan Poe.

He walked in, smiling a mischievous smile. He brushed Hallie's cheek with his fingers. She appeared to shiver and gulp in a breath of air.

"Something…" she whispered aloud.

"Are you here, are you here?" Liza called out. "I summon you, please, in the name of all goodness, in the name of justice?" she pleaded.

"Really!" Poe said. "How can you let that poor woman go on that way?"

"Stop it," Vickie said.

"No, no, I can't stop, we're going to reach them—I know it!" Liza cried.

"I'm sorry," Vickie murmured, "I didn't mean…"

She let her voice trail. Griffin saw that she was glaring at the ghost of Poe.

Poe was having a good time; he wasn't about to stop.

"A sign," Poe said. "She needs a sign. I'll give her a tap…no, a bunch of taps. I'll tap on the wall."

He didn't get a chance to do so.

Someone else—someone alive or dead—did it before he could.

Everyone in the room jumped—in one way or another.

"God help us, not another corpse!" Gary screamed.

Griffin stared hard at Poe. "You, sir, were looking straight at me! I didn't do a thing," Poe protested.

"Then what the hell was it?" Vickie demanded.

"She's good. She's actually really good!" Jon Skye said, admiring Liza.

"Stop, shush! They're trying to communicate. Come on, please, hush, get it all back together again, and we can ask them what's going on," Liza said. "Please, please! Let's go back now."

"I think that someone in this room did it!" Alice said.

"It? Alice, darling—we don't even know what *it* is," Jon said.

Gary made something like a choking or growling sound. Griffin wasn't sure if the man was upset by Jon calling Alice *darling*—or if he was disturbed by what was happening with the séance.

"A tap!" Alice said. "Everybody knows that fakers tap. They make tables wiggle and they make tapping sounds. Easiest sound in the world. People don't come back. Brent Whaley isn't going to walk in here and tell us what happened and neither is Franklin Verne!"

"Please, Alice…" Hallie murmured.

"Stop it, stop it, stop it!" Liza commanded.

"I'm shaking!" Alistair told them. "I'm shaking. There is something going on, I know it!"

"Yes, you nitwit," Poe said. "I'm standing right behind you."

"Don't be so rude," Vickie whispered.

"What? Was I being rude?" Alistair asked.

"We really need to just break this up," Lacey said. "Everyone is getting uncomfortable."

"Because men were murdered!" Liza snapped. "Come now." Her voice rose high. "Franklin, Brent, we feel you. We know that you are among us. We can hear you—you gave us a sign! Thank you, thank you. Yes, we're nervous. We're afraid. But we want to help you! We need another sign."

Everyone waited; they could have heard a pin drop in the room.

Poe let out a snort of derision.

"Did someone kill you? Someone that we know? Let us help you!" Liza cried.

There was silence again.

"Give us a sign! A sign! Tap if you know who killed you—tap twice if it was someone that you knew, someone we all know…"

At first, once again, there was silence.

Then there were two thunderous claps.

The sound was so strange that even Griffin sat silent as Lacey and Alice let out screams, as Alistair seemed to choke, as…

"Dear Lord!" Griffin said, rising. "Please, people, get a grip!"

"You heard it, you heard it—I know you heard it!" Liza cried.

"Yes! And we're all about to hear it again," Griffin said. "Think, people…!"

The thunderous sound came again.

"It's the door, people. Someone is at the door!" Griffin said. And shaking his head, he hurried out of the dining room and toward the front door.

"She asked for a sign…she asked for a sign," he heard Alistair saying.

"Yes, and now someone is here and…"

As Griffin reached the entrance, he heard the others racing out behind him.

Candles in the hallway flickered wildly as he opened the door.

Monica Verne was standing there. Adam Harrison was right behind her.

"Monica!" Liza exclaimed.

"Mrs. Verne?" Gary said, evidently very surprised.

"Yes, Mr. Frampton. I believe we've actually met— casually, at an autographing here and there."

"I'm so sorry for your loss. Come in, please, and you…" He paused, looking at Adam Harrison, a little lost. "Please, come inside!"

"Oh, my God!" Alistair said. "Liza asked for a sign… and here she is!"

He backed away slightly, as if suddenly seeing a terrible truth.

Never to be outdone in any way, Liza Harcourt stepped forward. "Oh, my God. A sign indeed. Monica! It was you. You—you murdered them both!" she declared.

12

Monica Verne stepped deeper into the hall, staring at Liza and shaking her head with disbelief and disgust as she wriggled out of the raincoat she'd been wearing.

"Liza Harcourt!" she declared. "You self-absorbed, self-important, self-aggrandizing bitch! What on earth is the matter with you? I loved my husband dearly, and Brent Whaley was an exceptionally good friend. I can understand that people are willing to indulge you, to see what you might come up with in your insane games, but I don't believe you could summon the remnant of some dead spy who might have said something evil regarding me or my feelings for my husband and a friend. Trust me. My husband thought you were an arrogant ass!"

Liza gasped. "Oh! Just because you were married to a great man, there is no reason in hell for you to think highly of yourself! Oh, my God! He was the brilliant one. You're just a shrew, Monica, just a horrible shrew—"

"Please, ladies," Adam said.

"But there was an unknown tapping sound!" Alice Frampton said, speaking up, wide-eyed.

"Most things that are unknown," Griffin said, "are simply unexplained." He paused to smile at Monica and then Liza. "But please! Ladies, obviously, you know one another. Everyone else, this is Adam Harrison, the brains behind my special unit at the Bureau. Adam, Gary Frampton, owner of the Black Bird, and his lovely daughter, Alice. Lacey Shaw, who runs the gift shop there, and Jon Skye, restaurant staff and rising young chef. Alistair Malcolm, vice president of the Blackbirds, and Liza Harcourt, president of the society. I'd also have you meet this lovely, young, tall and golden couple," he added, smiling over at Hallie and Sven and turning Adam in their direction. "Hallie and Sven. They take care of the property when Gary is busy in town, which, until lately, as we all know, was where he was most frequently busy. And," he added, looking at Vickie, "you both know Vickie."

Vickie stepped forward. "Let me take your coats!"

Monica handed over her coat; Adam held his coat a moment longer, getting a hug from Vickie as he handed it to her.

"What's the matter with us!" Hallie said, shaking her head. "The lights go out, a few candles, some hocus-pocus and we forget our manners. Vickie, please, let me hang those up. And we'll get you something to drink… hot, cold, coffee, tea or something stiff!"

"Thank you," Adam said.

"Let's move back in the parlor," Vickie suggested.

"We'd been playing charades at one point tonight. It wasn't a bad thing."

"I'm not sure they want to play charades. Is there a reason you came out here now?" Griffin asked Adam.

His director's arrival had been quite a surprise—even for him. And they were usually in frequent communication.

"I knew everyone was here," Monica said. "I made Adam bring me out. I'm going insane," she explained. She looked at Gary. "I knew my husband—and Brent. You know the Black Bird and the people who know the restaurant inside and out. I need the truth about my husband. I'm desperate."

"But we don't have any answers. I wish so badly that we did!" Gary said.

"Let's go sit comfortably, shall we?" Vickie said.

She urged them all into the room where the fire was still blazing and where candles burned, getting lower now. Some of the heavy-duty flashlights were set up to shine light around as well. The room was fairly well illuminated, and more important, it was warm and felt good. Hallie and Sven went to the kitchen.

"What can I get you?" Vickie asked, getting Monica seated in a chair.

Griffin noted that Alistair Malcolm hadn't taken his eyes off Monica. He chose to sit in a wing-back chair that was opposite the spot she had taken on the love seat.

Lacey had followed immediately as well, and took a seat in a chair by Alistair. Liza had turned in a furious whirl and gone back into the dining room.

Apparently, while the others might have been somewhat on edge, they weren't ready to take up with Liza against Monica Verne—she was on her own.

There had been a strange sound; it hadn't been Poe.

Griffin looked around suddenly; he wondered how the ghost had come to be among them, exactly when and where he had been.

He had forgotten him in all that was going on.

But Poe was there. He was standing by the fireplace. He seemed to be watching what was happening with both keen interest and dry amusement.

Hallie came in, pushing a kitchen cart. "I feel like a flight attendant!" she said. "But this is great. Sven's idea. We have coffee, tea, a bottle of red, a bottle of white, some sparkling water and a few sodas. Hopefully something for everyone," she said cheerfully.

"Very nice, Hallie. Thank you," Gary Frampton said.

They were all settled in again, except for Liza Harcourt, who, it seemed, had chosen not to join them.

"Should we play another game?" Gary asked.

"I have a better idea," Monica said.

"What would that be?" Alistair asked her.

"Well," Monica said, "You, Alistair, are vice president of the Blackbird Society. Gary Frampton owns a Poe-themed restaurant. Alice may or may not love Poe, but she does work at the restaurant, as does Jon Skye. And Lacey—I know Lacey, because she ordered all my husband's books—is truly something of a Poe gourmet. I will use that word since we are talking about a restaurant."

"Okay," Alice said. "I'm not as much into dead poets

as some of the others here, but…what are you suggesting, Mrs. Verne?"

"Well, a meeting on Poe, of course," Monica said. "It feels appropriate to the situation."

At the fireplace, the ghost of Poe straightened and smiled pleasantly.

"A Poe meeting," Vickie murmured. She glanced over at Griffin. She looked uncomfortable.

Vickie, of course, had noticed Poe leaning against the mantelpiece.

"Yes. So, my husband was only nominally a member of your society, giving lip service more than anything else—affording the Blackbirds the privilege to be seen as a respectable society," Monica said.

"Now, Brent Whaley was a published author, too!" Lacey reminded her.

"Yes, of course. Brent. Good man, talented writer. But he had nowhere near the respect or following that my dear Franklin had. So, the society was dedicated to all things Poe. Let's start with you, Lacey. Poe's unaccounted absence before he died. He left Richmond a mature man in love and ready to marry a mature woman, who also happened to be his first love. Quite charming, really. But Poe disappeared in Baltimore. No one knows what happened for five days. Then he is found at the polling place, the tavern. He is delirious and—most curiously—wearing someone else's clothing. What do you say happened to him?"

Vickie rose, walking behind the chair where Adam Harrison was sitting, toward the end of the room—

kitty-corner from Monica Verne. Poe was now staring at all of them, tension causing his ghostly form to quiver.

"My real opinion?" Lacey said. "Bear in mind I love his work. I'm impressed by everything I've ever read about the man. I think he was a good man. Artistic—and therefore temperamental, but a good man."

"Lacey, you're talking in circles. How do you think he died? What do you think happened to him? There are all kinds of theories," Monica said.

Griffin glanced at Adam. His director was watching everyone in the room, keenly and subtly. Obviously, he had known what Monica had planned.

He had brought Monica here. So, whatever it was, Adam wanted to go with it.

"I'm just telling you, I have the utmost respect for the man," Lacey said.

"So, what do you think happened to him?" Monica persisted.

"All right. Yes, he swore to temperance, but he was an addict. He saw a friend in Baltimore. He couldn't resist. He wound up drinking with his friend. But his body couldn't take it anymore. Like any addict, he drank too much, and yet not enough. He sold his good clothing and bought the rags he was found in so that he could buy himself some more liquor. And then, at the end, he went to the polling place because the men there would buy him more drinks—they would be buying his vote!"

By the fireplace, Poe had a single word to say. "No!"

He looked ill.

If it was possible for the dead to look ill.

Monica smiled icily. "And that's what you think happened with my Franklin, right? He just couldn't resist? He knew how to slip into the delivery entrance to the Black Bird, and so he let himself in, and he drank until his body gave out?"

"No!" Lacey protested. "I didn't really know Franklin Verne. Just through conversation. He seemed like a very nice man. But you can be a good man, a nice man, and fall prey to addiction. But no, I don't believe that I really have an opinion. I don't know, it's just so strange."

"Let's be honest. At first," Gary murmured, "we all did think that maybe Franklin thought it a fitting thing to come into a wine cellar and…let life end dramatically."

"You can't fault my father," Alice said protectively. "Or any of us. We didn't know. We just didn't know. But then there was Brent…" she added, swallowing.

"And he didn't nail *himself* into the floor," Lacey said.

"Okay," Monica said. "So, now—because of Brent Whaley *not* nailing himself into the floor, we can be pretty sure that Franklin didn't just drink himself to death."

No one responded to her. She shrugged and turned to Gary Frampton.

"What do you think happened?"

"Oh!" Gary said. "To your husband? Or do you mean Edgar Allan Poe?"

"Let's start with Poe," Monica said.

"Oh, well, there were so many theories," Gary said. "Even his family members, who were called, thought that he might have slipped. I mean, times were different. No cell phones, no DNA testing, no way to check up on what was going on… I mean, an election day back then would have been deplorable! Men manipulating other men…"

"You believe that he was kidnapped so that he could be forced to change up his look and vote over and over again?" Monica asked.

"To me, it's the most possible of the theories. For one, him not being found in his own clothing," Gary said.

Alistair suddenly sat forward. "Yes, you see, it does make the most sense to believe that he was first more or less seduced!"

"Seduced?" Vickie murmured, frowning as she glanced at Griffin. They were both aware of Poe, tense, watching, listening—getting ready to bang on something.

"Yes," Alistair said, "you see, one of the pollsters—his name lost to history—tempted Poe. He made him have that first glass of wine or whiskey. And then another and another. And they had him vote first in his own clothing, maybe a couple of places. They forced him then to change clothing—probably selling his finer garments and giving him the ragamuffin stuff. It was called *cooping*, and Poe would not have been the only victim of such a practice. He was fed alcohol, and then made to vote repeatedly—and he was left then at the tavern, the last place he voted. Poor man, used and abused. But his vice made it easier for those out to get them."

"Not true, not true!" Poe protested.

"Not true!" Vickie said aloud.

Alistair stared at her, startled. "What? How do you know? It's all speculation!"

"Right, of course," Vickie agreed quickly, "but... I believe—from everything that I've read—that Poe was in love. And I don't think that he was as much a drunkard as those biographers who did not like Poe tried to portray. His obituary depicted him as a drunk, and therefore, that's what's been remembered through the ages. There's recently been a strong case made by a young writer named Peters suggesting that the brain-tumor theory might be the right direction. Poe's body was moved to where it is now a few decades after his death and, apparently, someone who saw the body then commented on the state of his brain. Normally a brain—soft tissue—decays quickly. But a tumor could have caused calcification."

"And that's your theory?" Monica asked her.

Vickie was quiet for a minute, looking at Monica.

"No," she said.

"So, what is your theory?" Monica asked.

Vickie hesitated, glancing at Griffin again. He nodded slightly, just for her. Adam had obviously brought Monica to stir the pot; Vickie might as well play the game all the way.

"I believe that he was kidnapped. He did not drink. He was taken against his will, and he was attacked by a rabid dog. Whoever took him had an agenda of his own," Vickie said.

"There is a theory that he was murdered by the brothers of the woman he loved," Monica said. "Is that what you're suggesting?"

Vickie hesitated again.

"Victoria is not merely a young woman about to enter the FBI academy," Adam Harrison said. "She is a brilliant researcher and writer. And more. She has a very special affinity for the dead."

Everyone in the room was very still.

And then, suddenly, Liza Harcourt was back.

"Oh, please! You're making fun of my abilities when we've all seen results! But this young woman supposedly has an affinity with the dead. Let's not be ridiculous."

"I think that we should hypnotize Vickie," Adam said.

Griffin frowned.

Liza swore in disbelief and flounced back out of the room.

"Hypnotize the young lady?" Monica repeated, obviously intrigued with the idea.

Vickie stared over at Adam. He gave her an encouraging nod.

She looked at Griffin. His look back at her tried to convey that she must do what felt comfortable to her—say no, if she wished.

Go with it, if she wished as well.

"And who will hypnotize her?" Alice asked suspiciously.

"I will," Adam said. He told Alice, "I've lived a long life. I've been and done many things. Lately, the study of psychology has become exceptionally important to me. I've studied with some of the best. I believe that I can safely lead Vickie through what she is thinking, what she sees and thinks, deep down in her subconscious."

"What would be there that could explain how Poe was killed?" Jon asked.

"Ah! Well, her deep reservoir of knowledge. Vickie has read more books than I've probably ever even counted, not to mention the historical sites she has visited, the academic papers she has read, the personal diaries of those long gone, and more. The unfettered subconscious might be free to make associations, draw conclusions from all that knowledge. So... Vickie, up to you!" Adam said.

Everyone was looking at her. Griffin knew that on the one hand, she probably longed to explore what might happen. She was likely also afraid. There were so many people around her.

But that was the point. If Franklin Verne and Brent Whaley had been killed over something to do with Poe, hypnotizing Vickie could definitely shake up the killer.

And when shaken up, killers had a tendency to give themselves away.

Or act in haste. The good thing here was that Adam was in the house; Vickie and Griffin were in the house. And unknown to anyone else other than them and Alistair Malcolm, Jackson and Angela were outside.

Cold, wet and miserable, Griffin was certain. But then again, they were pros. They were accustomed to being cold, wet and miserable in the pursuit of justice!

"Sure," Vickie said finally. "How will we do this? Do I follow a pocket watch, or something like that?"

"No, no. I'm just going to get you really comfortable

and take you back. And try to see what went on, what we're seeing through your eyes," Adam said.

"That sofa, there," Hallie suggested. "The love seat with the pillows. It's so comfortable!"

"Okay."

Vickie moved over to the love seat. Adam followed her, pulling a chair close. The others flocked around, but not too near.

Everyone seemed fascinated.

"Adam, I'm not sure this can work with this many people staring at me," Vickie said.

"I think it will work, and work well," Adam said. "But we'll see. No pain, no gain, huh?" He glanced at Griffin. "Sorry, sorry, I'm not putting Vickie in any pain. That's just a saying. We'll give this a try—see if it works."

"It's up to Vickie, not me," Griffin said.

"Completely. So, Vickie…?"

"Go right ahead. Do your best," Vickie told Adam.

"Okay. Just be comfortable. Think of the crackle of the fire. It's so nice, huh? A warm fire is one of man's greatest comforts. And the love seat, it's soft. The pillows beneath your head…they're so fluffy and comfortable. The rain outside is refreshing. Violent, and then sweet as it washes away so much heat and all else. Think about the cascade of water, think of the sweetness of darkness and rest when you're weary. Close your eyes…"

Adam continued to talk. His voice was soothing, Griffin thought that he could probably doze off himself.

Some people could be hypnotized, he knew, and some couldn't.

He thought that with Adam leading her, Vickie might well be a good candidate for hypnosis.

She trusted Adam.

"Vickie, always listen to the sound of my voice," Adam said. "Rest well, but if I say that you're to awaken, you will awaken."

Vickie's eyes were closed. She nodded and her lips moved slightly. "I will awaken," she said.

"The year," Adam said, "is 1849. Horses are pulling carriages through the streets. They move with the clip-clop sound of their hooves on the pavement. You can hear great carriage wheels as they turn, tumbling over the brick pavement. Hawkers cry out to sell newspapers in the street; orange girls offer up refreshment outside music halls and theaters. There is a lot of shouting in the streets. Baltimore is coming up on an election day. A train rolls into the station. Edgar Allan Poe is on that train," Adam said.

"Yes," Vickie murmured.

"His work was in Philadelphia. He was then to see Mrs. Clemm in the Bronx. But he detrained in Baltimore. On his own?"

"Yes, I am getting off the train."

Vickie's voice had changed. It was deep. Masculine.

Griffin looked across the room.

Poe was no longer present.

He stared at Vickie, frowning. She looked relaxed; she appeared to be sleeping. Her lips moved.

And yet it was as if she was really speaking as the dead man!

"You're getting off the train. Why? Has someone tried to urge you to a tavern? Are you meeting friends for drinks?"

Vickie twitched, looking distressed for a minute. She shook her head. "No. No drinks. I have joined the temperance society. I want to marry. I want a home and a family. I love Elmira."

"But you chose to get off the train. Why?"

"I am to meet a man."

"You're to meet a man?" Adam asked, trying to keep the surprise out of his voice.

"No, he was supposed to be in Philly—to work for a woman!" Alistair said.

Adam didn't shush him, but neither did he pay him any attention.

"I was supposed to meet Reynolds," Vickie said.

"Reynolds!" Alice gasped. "Dad, when Poe was dying, didn't he keep asking about Reynolds?" Alice asked.

"Well, that's what's in the record, but...he was in a hospital, having delirium tremors and all kinds of other problems," Gary said. "I always wondered if the doctor heard the name that Poe was saying wrong—if Poe hadn't been using a different name—but it has come down to us through the ages the way his doctor heard it."

"Why were you to meet this Mr. Reynolds?" Adam asked Vickie.

"A mutual agreement would be made. I would help him. He would help me."

"But you didn't meet him," Adam said.

"I went to meet him. I went to meet him as we had arranged."

Vickie suddenly began to twist and turn on the love seat, appearing to be seriously distressed.

"Adam?" Griffin murmured.

"A minute, just a minute," Adam implored. "What happened when you went to meet Reynolds?"

"The street. I am there. I am walking down the street. The lamps are poor here. They don't illuminate well at all. They create shadows. Everything seems to move. Everything forms like a monster in that shadow land. I remember the sound. Just subtle. And I knew that someone was behind me."

Griffin clutched his hands together, aware that his knuckles were growing white.

The voice coming from Vickie wasn't hers. It was masculine; it had a Southern timbre to it that wasn't Vickie's.

Griffin started to move forward; Vickie still seemed to be so distressed.

"Bastard! Sneaking, manipulative bastard. I can hear the footsteps coming, furtive, menacing. And I turn and… Ah!"

Vickie suddenly jerked straight up, looking around at all of them. Griffin could see that her pulse was racing.

He pushed his way to the love seat, drawing her up and into his arms.

"That—that was a heck of a performance!" Alice said awed.

"Incredible. I didn't know that Miss Preston was an actress," Jon said.

"She's not an actress!" Griffin said irritably. "I think, Adam—"

"Vickie, what did you see?" Adam asked her. "Right before you bolted up."

"The same thing I've seen before," Vickie said.

"And that was…"

"Burlap. A burlap bag coming over my head," Vickie said.

"And who…?"

"I don't know. I didn't see. I believe that Poe thought, however, that it was this mysterious Reynolds that he was raving about when he died," Vickie said.

"Whoa, freaky. I mean, really far freakier than a séance," Sven said, standing up and shaking, as if he could shrug off what he had seen.

"I've never seen anything like it," Hallie murmured.

"Very cool," Alice said. "And scary as hell," she added. She grinned. "Boy, Liza should have been here for this. Sadly, she's so impressed with herself she just can't see anything else. But wow. Are you sure you're not some kind of an actress?" she asked Vickie.

Vickie shook her head. She looked at Adam. "What do you think it means? Everyone has wondered and speculated forever on just who Reynolds might have been. But what if he was someone Poe intended to meet? He went to meet him and he was attacked—either by Reynolds, or by pollsters." She hesitated and then continued, "I think that after he was kidnapped, he was also attacked by a rabid dog. He wasn't drunk—he was suffering from rabies. I mean, I do understand that Poe having a brain tumor might be a possibility, but it doesn't explain why he would have been wearing different clothing."

"Miss Preston, do you do this often—this channeling thing, or whatever?" Monica Verne asked her. She looked perplexed, whether she wasn't sure if she believed what she had just witnessed or not.

"No. Never before, nothing like this," Vickie said.

"Well, she is a writer!" Alistair Malcolm pointed out. "A good one, from all that I've ascertained. It's natural that such a man as Poe would find a beautiful young woman to speak for him!"

"Poe is long gone," Alice said. "But that…was…"

"Freaky!" Hallie said. "Scary—and amazing. Was that real? How could that have been real?"

"How could it not have been real," Alistair asked. "That was Poe! That was the master. My God, you could hear his voice. Amazing."

"Amazing," Gary agreed.

"We have a new dilemma now," Adam said.

"Exactly!" Alistair Malcolm said. "We're back to a question that has plagued scholars for ages, for decades upon decades. Just who was this Reynolds? And why was Poe meeting him?"

Vickie turned to look at Griffin.

He smiled at her gravely.

They just might be able to discover the answer to that question!

* * *

Vickie knew that Griffin was worried.

She'd been worried herself. She'd never—even in her dreams—experienced anything the way she had when Adam had hypnotized her and led her through Poe's experience. It felt once again as if she was there, but as if she was literally sharing herself with another person.

It had grown late. While a few of the others had determined to cook on a small gas stove, Vickie had begged off, saying that they had a few power bars and would like to get to sleep. She'd tried very hard for just a few minutes alone with Adam Harrison; he and Monica had arrived without the little horde of ghost adolescents who had been with them.

Adam briefly explained to her that Dylan, Darlene and Josh were staying at Monica's house; they were going to make certain that no one came to create any kind of mischief there.

Gary had said that he was going to go to bed as well—as soon as he and Hallie and Sven had set up two more rooms, since Adam and Monica had arrived pretty much by surprise.

When they reached their room, Vickie turned and threw her arms around Griffin's neck, holding him tight. "I love you!" she whispered.

She felt the pressure of his arms pulling her closer. "I love you." Then he drew away from her, looking at her anxiously. "You're all right? You're really all right?"

"I'm fine," she said. She hadn't been—but now she was. Whatever it took. She wanted to be one of the Krewe. That meant using her talents. She believed in

Adam—and he had made incredible things happen. She trusted him—and she believed that it had been important.

"You've definitely shaken things up," Griffin said. "They don't know whether they just witnessed a spectacular magic show, or if you really channeled Poe."

"Have you seen him since?" Vickie asked anxiously.

"No, I haven't," Griffin said. "Maybe it's hard for him when he speaks through you. Maybe he has to rest afterward—I don't know. We've never really figured out the physical—or lack of—realm of the dead. I'm sure he'll reappear when it's the right time."

Vickie nodded, staying close to him. "I'm not frightened, Griffin. You're warm."

"Fear isn't a bad thing. How we deal with fear can be. Be afraid sometimes, Vickie. Fear can keep us from terrible danger, or make us deal with it wide-awake and aware."

"But I'm really not afraid. Not of… Not of trying to help out. Griffin, we can ask Poe about Reynolds! People have wondered why he was asking for a man named Reynolds forever and ever. And since he knew he was supposed to meet with the man, there was a reason, and so help me, I believe that he will explain when we do see him again!"

"Hopefully," Griffin agreed thoughtfully. He walked over to the French doors to the balcony. He peered out. The rain had stopped. The moon had risen; stars twinkled in the heavens.

He wondered if Jackson and Angela had taken refuge

in their car somewhere—of if they had chosen to wait out some time in one of the little family mausoleums.

Jackson would do as he deemed best, Griffin knew.

He closed and locked the doors. "Hey, you!" he said to Vickie.

"What?"

"Let's get some rest."

"Yes, rest will be great. Lying next to you… The only thing…"

"What?"

"I'm still cold," Vickie told him.

"I'll fix that!" he swore.

He was already in the bed, patting the spot for her to join him.

She did so. He held her, and pulled her close. The warmth of his body seeped into her.

Warmth…that grew and grew…

She relished the simple feel of him beside her; but they were both tense, lying awake.

Listening.

They heard Adam in the hall bidding Monica Verne and others a good-night. They heard Alice telling her father to go to bed—and not worry about her and Jon.

They heard Hallie and Sven heading up to their room in the attic, and they heard Lacey and Alistair arguing about Poe's life and death in the hallway—before they, too, split up to go to their own rooms.

They lay there, listening as the house grew silent first, and then as the old floorboards creaked and settled.

It felt like only moments after they'd finally closed their eyes when they heard a scream.

Vickie bolted out of bed, raced to the French doors and threw it open. The scream had come from below, from the sculpture garden.

She looked out.

A woman in a white gown was racing down the trail, heading into the cemetery.

"Griffin!" she gasped.

He was already by her side, pulling his jeans on. He dived across the bed again, gathering up his shirt and the holster that held his Glock.

Vickie grabbed her clothing and went racing after him.

The hall was suddenly filled with people.

"What was it? Who... What's going on? I heard a scream... I heard... Oh, my God!" Gary exclaimed, looking around. "Alice! Where is Alice?"

Jon Skye was just coming out of a room, rubbing his eyes. He was shirtless, in jeans.

Gary Frampton rushed over to him, taking him by the shoulders, shoving him roughly. "Where is she? Where the hell is Alice?" he demanded.

"Alice? She's out here somewhere... She got up. She's not in bed," he said, as confused as a man who had just woken up might be. "I don't know when she left. I just realized she was gone. I was coming out to look for her when I heard..."

"Alice!" Gary screamed.

Griffin cut through the group crowding in the hallway, racing down the stairs.

Vickie followed close behind him.

Griffin was on his phone, she realized, calling Jackson Crow. Wherever Jackson and Angela were, they would be on the chase, too.

Because it was Alice who had run into the cemetery.

Griffin burst through the gate; Vickie followed. They rushed around to the newest of the Frampton-family mausoleums.

Alice was standing in front of the art nouveau mausoleum where her mother had been interred.

"Alice!" Griffin said gently.

She didn't hear him. She just stood there, ethereal in a long white gown.

Gary Frampton burst upon them. But then he froze, calling out a different name.

"Elyssa!" he said. "Oh, my God, Elyssa!"

"His wife? Is that his dead wife's name?" Vickie murmured.

"Has to be," Griffin said.

He swirled around quickly to speak to Gary.

"No, Gary. No, it's Alice."

"My wife… It looks like Elyssa. We buried her…we buried her in white!"

The man had to know better, Vickie thought. But out here, in the moonlight, in the cemetery, it was easy to see where shock and fear had played with his mind.

Alice didn't appear to notice them at all. She just stood in front of the mausoleum, moving from side to side, staring out. She looked like a trapped animal, terrified and unaware at the same time. Her hair streamed down her back in long blond locks. She appeared ghostly in the white gown, and her behavior was both erratic and somehow gracefully eerie.

"Elyssa?" Gary said again, but it sounded more like a question.

"No, sir, it's not your dead wife, it's your daughter," Vickie said softly. She hurried to him, catching him by the shoulders, making him see her. "It's Alice. We'll call paramedics. We'll get her to the house."

"My God!" Gary breathed. "Yes, yes, all right."

But then Alice suddenly shrieked again; she threw her arms up to the heavens…and seemed to pose, like one of the marble Shakespeare characters in the sculpture garden.

And then she collapsed.

Just as she did, another scream, shrill and piercing, sounded from the house.

13

Griffin pulled his phone out and dialed 9-1-1.

Gary Frampton hadn't seemed to have heard the scream that came from the house.

He raced toward his fallen daughter.

Vickie did the same, sliding to her knees by Alice before her father could reach her, feeling for her pulse.

The girl was alive.

Vickie nodded an okay to Griffin. He turned his attention to his call, asking for paramedics and police out at Frampton Manor. He left Vickie with Alice and Gary and turned to head back to the manor, almost crashing into Lacey Shaw.

"Police and medics are on the way," he said curtly.

As he made his way through the statuary trail, he was stopped by Hallie and Sven—both looking worried and addled. "Which way?" Hallie asked him. "We want to help, but there was a scream in the cemetery and a scream back at the house!"

"House!" Griffin said. "Help is coming."

He raced through the back door of the house to find

that Jackson and Angela were in there already; Angela was urging Monica Verne into the parlor along with Adam and Jon Skye and Alistair Malcolm. Jackson was headed for the stairs.

"What room?" Griffin asked him. "The scream?"

"I only know that it came from upstairs," Jackson told him. "We saw you with Gary and Alice and hurried in here as we heard the scream. I'm pretty sure it came from upstairs. But I don't believe anyone is still in their room, sleeping."

"Don't know and don't care," Griffin said. "He was ahead of Jackson by about two steps; they reached the second-floor landing. Griffin indicated he'd take the left side of the hall; Jackson took the right.

One by one, they tore into the rooms.

They were hasty at first, anxious to find someone who might be in trouble.

But the rooms were empty.

"No one? Nothing?" Griffin asked Jackson.

He shook his head.

"Who is unaccounted for?" Jackson asked Griffin.

"Gary and Alice are out in the cemetery. I passed Lacey while I was racing back to the house, and then Hallie and Sven. The people still in the house should be Adam and Monica, Alistair Malcolm, Liza Harcourt and Jon Skye. I think that's everyone. Including you and Angela, Vickie and myself and Adam and Monica, there should be twelve people here all told."

They heard sirens; help was arriving.

"I'll get the EMTs out to Alice," Griffin said.

"And I'll make a head count again. Let's corral everyone back into the house."

"Yes, and we need to see that Detective Carl Morris has been personally notified."

"On it already," Jackson assured him.

Griffin didn't pause to pay much attention to those seated in the parlor; leaving Jackson to explain the situation to the local police, Griffin met the paramedics at the door and hurried them out to the graveyard. Gary was on the ground next to his daughter.

Vickie had Alice's head in her lap; she was checking her breathing. She looked up as Griffin led help through, telling him, "Her pulse is steady but weak. She's breathing fine on her own. She hasn't opened her eyes yet."

The two emergency medical technicians immediately went to work. They'd brought a portable gurney out, and they opened it smoothly while learning that their patient had just collapsed inexplicably a few minutes ago. They secured her on the gurney while starting an IV and reporting her condition to the hospital where they'd be taking her.

They headed back through the cemetery and the garden trail, and then through the house. The medical technicians were talking, explaining where they'd be going.

Gary said he was Alice's father, and that he had to be with his daughter.

That was all right. Gary was going to go in the ambulance; Vickie would follow right behind, accompanied by Angela. Jackson and Griffin and Adam would stay at the house.

They hurried through the back door into the hallway and straight out the front.

They reached the yard when Jon Skye came bursting out of the house. "Take me, please, you have to take me!" he begged Vickie.

Gary was getting into the ambulance, but he crawled out.

Griffin was pretty sure he intended to give Jon Skye a right hook to the jaw. He stepped quickly between the two men.

"Alice needs help," he said simply.

"You! You did this!" Gary screamed. "You stay away from my daughter. You get the hell out of my house and don't you come near me or my daughter again. Do you hear me?"

"I did nothing!" Jon shrieked back. "I woke up and she was gone. Don't lay this on me. I love Alice, too. This is the doing of one of your sick Poe-fanatic friends! Don't blame me, Gary!"

"Get out—get away!" Gary screamed.

"The ambulance is going to leave," Vickie pointed out. She set a hand on Jon Skye's shoulder. "Go in. Go back in the house. Let them get Alice to the hospital. Then we'll all find out what happened."

Gary turned and jumped into the ambulance.

Angela came hurrying out of the house and Vickie excused herself to Jon, looking at Griffin to take over.

Griffin set his hands firmly on Jon Skye's shoulders. "Let them go," he said.

"I love Alice. I love her," Jon said.

"Then let them tend to her," Griffin said. "And come

in and answer some questions with everyone else. That's the best we can do for her now."

Griffin watched the ambulance and the car go, then he physically steered Jon Skye back toward the house.

The sun, he saw, was just beginning to rise.

Vickie and Angela sat close together in the waiting room, Angela explaining to Vickie just where she and Jackson had been during the past hours. She spoke softly; they were both keeping an eye on Gary Frampton.

He had been forced out of the emergency room as the doctors had worked over Alice, trying to ascertain just what was wrong with her.

Gary had been so miserable and desperate that they'd given him a sedative; now he leaned against the wall in his chair, his eyes closed.

"The weather was horrible. You stayed out in the back all that time?"

"We were in the car some of the time, but it also seemed prudent to explore the cemetery. The family mausoleums are very interesting. They all have gates, and you can actually go inside all of them, including the small ones. They aren't well kept, but they aren't falling apart, either. The last interment in the cemetery was Elyssa Frampton, Alice's mother. I assume that Alice must be a spitting image of her. It's a really fascinating place, and I think that the preservation of the cemetery and that great statuary garden has to do with the fact that it has remained in one family."

"Did you find anything—unusual?" Vickie asked her.

Angela shook her head. "No ghosts seemed to be wandering around. We didn't find anything out of place that might suggest someone intended to play games out there."

"But something was planned—and somehow, what happened to Alice Frampton was set in motion," Vickie said.

"And, obviously, Jon Skye comes up as the main suspect," Angela said.

"He said that he was sound asleep and she left him."

"Do you believe him?" Angela asked.

"I don't know. And, of course, here's the other thing. Where the hell did that second scream come from?" Vickie asked.

"Hopefully, they'll figure that out while we're here," Angela said. She stood suddenly, and Vickie did the same. The doctor was coming out of the emergency room doors to the waiting area. He was a somber middle-aged man with a pleasant and controlled manner.

Vickie noted that Gary Frampton had apparently sank into a deep sleep or passed out from the sedative he had been given.

He didn't see the doctor, and he didn't rise.

"Her father is sleeping?" the doctor asked. "And you are?"

Angela produced her FBI badge. The doctor glanced at Gary; he knew they had all come in together.

"She's going to be fine. She's sleeping right now."

"What happened to her? She was delirious…running into a cemetery at night and then collapsing," Vickie said.

"Drug overdose," the doctor said. "Not lethal, thankfully. We've done blood tests. I don't have everything back from the lab yet, but I believe she was soaring on a comparatively new drug that's hit the streets lately."

"Would the street name for it be baby-baby?" Vickie asked him.

"Yes, exactly," the doctor said. "It can cause hallucinations. It leaves a person entirely pliable to what others want. It's definitely a date-rape drug, but I consider it even more dangerous than most. It puts extreme pressure on the heart. And the person taking it becomes prone to suggestion. Almost like a hypnotic. It also causes memory loss—really a dangerous concoction," he said, shaking his head. "The good news is that she's going to be all right. I'd like to keep her in the hospital today and overnight for observation."

"Of course," Angela said.

"May we see her yet?" Vickie asked.

"She's in a deep sleep, but yes, you may come in." The doctor cleared his throat, indicating Gary Frampton.

"We'll get him up and in to see her," Vickie assured him.

The doctor nodded and waited politely. Vickie and Angela walked over to Gary Frampton. "I'll stay here and watch over her," Angela said.

"You think she's in danger?" Vickie asked.

"I don't think she dosed herself with this baby-baby stuff," Angela said.

"No, I guess not. Gary Frampton is ready to rip Jon Skye apart, but Jon Skye claims that she was just gone—that she left the room while he was sleeping."

They'd reached Gary; the doctor was waiting. They woke him and explained what the doctor had said.

"That bastard, Jon. He did this. He did this to my girl."

"Gary, it might have been someone else. At the moment, let's just worry about Alice, okay? They're going to keep her overnight."

"Then, I will be here overnight, too," Gary said. "And when I'm out...that bastard better be out of my house and he'd better plan on staying away from my girl!"

"I'll keep you posted if she wakes," Angela told Vickie. "And I'll want to know as soon as you know about anything at the house."

The scream...

Who had screamed?

Why?

Where were they...?

And suddenly she knew.

What had happened with Alice Frampton had been a diversion, nothing more.

Vickie fumbled for her phone as she hurried to the car. She dialed Griffin's number; he answered tersely.

"I think I know what's going on!" she told him.

"'Ligeia,'" Alistair said sadly. "Alice running around in a white gown like that, looking just like her mother, and nearly giving her poor old dad a heart attack, I say," he added.

"But she wasn't killed," Lacey said. "Thank God! She wasn't killed. She was just... She is going to be okay?" she asked Griffin, who had hung up after speaking with Vickie.

"Yes, Alice is going to be okay," he said.

"What about Liza Harcourt?" Jon Skye asked dully. "She's gone. She's just gone. And there was that horrible scream we heard."

Griffin had begun to figure that what had been done to Alice Frampton had been a ruse—something to distract them all as Liza was taken.

She was still missing.

Everyone else was present and accounted for.

But Liza was not.

She wasn't in the guest room she'd been given. The room she had apparently seen as a haven when she'd been angry with everyone after the séance.

And there was still no answer to the scream they'd all heard, though the police had come—with Detective Morris quickly following the patrolmen—and all of them searching the house high and low.

Could the sound have come from outside the house? they'd all wondered.

Had it been some kind of a recording?

Had a feral cat let out that horrible piercing shriek?

"I feel terrible," Lacey Shaw said, shaking her head. "I mean…Liza can be such a witch! I'm sure I've said things about her, but…I wouldn't want anything happening to her."

"The thing is, she went upstairs a long time before the rest of us. She could have been angry enough to slip out and go home last night," Alistair said.

"That doesn't sound like Liza," Monica Verne said.

"She would have been very dramatic about the way she left. But the point is, she's just not here. The police searched the house, we've searched the house... Where is she?"

"Her suitcase is upstairs," Griffin said. "But I didn't see any kind of a purse or a handbag up there."

"Oh, my God!" Alistair said. "The cemetery! Do you think that someone dragged her out to the cemetery and locked her in a mausoleum? 'The Premature Burial'! 'The Fall of the House of Usher'!"

Before Griffin could answer, Jackson and Carl Morris came back down the stairs to the parlor, followed by Hallie and Sven.

"We've searched the attic—totally ripped it to shreds," Hallie said.

"She's nowhere. Dead or alive," Sven said. "Sorry, sorry! I mean...something didn't happen to her, at any rate. We'd have found the body, right?"

Would they?

Franklin Verne had been easy enough to find—he'd been left there, sitting in a chair.

Brent Whaley? Not so easy to find.

Griffin looked over at Jackson and Carl Morris, who both shook their heads.

"We don't know—we seriously don't know—that any harm has come to Liza," Alistair said. "She's, as we've said over and over again, just Liza. If she was mad at everyone, she might have walked off. She could have called an Uber or a taxi. She isn't here. Everyone has searched. Has anyone tried her cell number?"

"Of course!" Lacey said. "Yes, I've called and called. It goes right to voice mail."

"Can we get a track going on her phone?" Adam Harrison asked.

"Yes. Although officially, she's not a missing person," Carl said.

"But we suspect foul play. Under these circumstances, I think we're fine. We can initiate, or the Baltimore Police Department can," Griffin said.

"I'll get it going immediately," Carl told Griffin. "And we'll get an APB out on Liza. Hopefully, she'll show up soon. Maybe she went to her house. I'll send a patrol car by just in case."

"I doubt that," Griffin said. "Let's go over this. Hallie and Sven—you were upstairs in the attic until you heard the screaming, right?"

"Absolutely," Hallie said.

"And you have no idea of how Alice was drugged, who screamed and where Liza might have gone?" Griffin asked.

"Not a clue!" Sven assured him.

"Okay... Alistair?"

"I came out when I heard Gary yelling at Jon," Alistair said. "And no, and no. I didn't drug anybody. I don't even know how to get illegal drugs. And as to Liza... I think she walked off somewhere to drive us all crazy. She's dramatic like that."

"Monica?" Griffin asked quietly.

"Oh, please, Griffin. I just got here with Adam. We said good-night up in the hall. Like everyone else, I came out of my room when I heard the shouting," Monica said, looking to Adam for help.

"He has to ask," Adam said.

"Okay," Monica said. "I didn't drug anyone. Like Alistair, I don't think I'd even know where to get illegal drugs. And as for Liza... God knows. I'm not so sure I believe she walked off—we don't have a great track record here. What about you, Lacey—what were you doing in the middle of the night?"

"Sleeping! I came out to the hall, too," Lacey said.

"And last!" Griffin said quietly. "Jon. What the hell happened?"

Jon looked torn, as if he was about to weep. "I don't know! Why doesn't anybody believe me? I love Alice, I love her so much! We went to sleep together. That's the last thing I know."

"Was she wearing that gown when you went to bed?" Griffin asked.

Jon suddenly straightened, looking around. He frowned. "No...no! She was wearing one of those long T-shirt kind of nightgown things. She wasn't in that gown at all."

Hallie gasped. "The gown! The gown was in a trunk in the attic. Do you know what that was?" she demanded. "I know, because Gary showed me one day. The trunk. It had everything that he'd kept that had belonged to his wife. The white gown... She wore it when they went on their honeymoon. He was keeping everything there for Alice. He figured she'd want something of her mother one day."

"We're really just stating the obvious," Jackson Crow

said quietly. "Whoever did this wanted to haunt Gary—and he did it with a Poe theme. Make someone look like a man's true love, and how much easier could it be than to dress up a daughter who is the image of her mother?"

"Which brings us back to the main question," Griffin said. "Where is Liza?" He glanced at Carl Morris and added, "People, we're going to have to search through all your personal belongings."

"What?" Monica asked.

"That's not very American!" Sven said.

"Don't you need search warrants?" Hallie asked.

"I'm sure we have Gary's permission to search the house," Griffin said.

"But—our belongings! Like—like our underwear?" Jon Skye protested.

"I don't think we want to search your underwear, Jon," Griffin assured him. "But we do need to find out who had that drug. And, yes, warrants might be in order."

"But not if you give us permission to search your belongings," Carl Morris said.

"And, of course, if you don't give us permission, we will hold up your belongings until we do have a warrant," Griffin said.

"All right, all right! You want to search? Come on up—you can start with my room. That room I share with Alice!" He was angry and walked past them all, starting up the stairs. He looked back at them. "Oh, my God! You don't think…you really don't think that Alice could have had that drug, and that she would have done something like that to herself on purpose…to get to her father?"

"Let's see what we find," Griffin said quietly. "Maybe nothing. Let's go ahead and start with you— and then we'll get to everyone."

Vickie was startled to find Poe by her car.

He was pacing just outside it.

"How did you get here?" she asked him.

"I rode with you—you just didn't see me. I didn't care to be seen—I was… Frankly, I was exhausted. I mean, that whole thing you do. It's almost as if I have a body again. But…but a rather useless body, I'm afraid."

"Hey!"

"Sorry, it's just that, well, you're just lying there, and it's all a mind or soul manipulation or a miracle— a curse as you might see it—or…or, I don't know! And so strange. But it makes it so that I can't make myself seen or heard, even by you. Because, as I said, I'm just so…exhausted. Drained! But I could see, at the house, anyway. I could observe… Alice, running into the night. That scream. And then the confusion! The police, the paramedics! And then… I just slipped out to the car with you and that lovely blonde—"

"Angela."

"Yes, truly an angel! Anyway, now…well, I've some strength back. And I still am so little help to you. And I'm so angry! Seriously, who would do this with my work? Yes, you know, of course, with my story 'The Mystery of Marie Rogêt,' I based it all upon the death of beautiful young Mary Celia Rogers, who was murdered most cruelly in New York. I chose to study real life for the creation of my detective. But you must understand, that while scholars have said, 'Oh, this woman is Poe's Lenore, or that woman was his Ligeia!' I wrote fiction, Victoria, fiction. I based my characters on people in life, yes, but on others as well. This killer… I don't understand. Why does he use my work so heinously?"

"I don't know. Until we discover the killer, we'll never break through to his—or her—mind. But sir, tell me, please—who exactly was Reynolds and why were you to meet him, and why, in delirium, would you call out his name?"

"Reynolds?" He stared at her hard, and then sighed deeply. "Reynolds!" he said softly. "Walter Reynolds—or his name as he gave it to me."

"You were to meet him in Baltimore."

Poe nodded. "We met on the streets of Richmond one day, soon after I joined the temperance society. He told me that his home was in Baltimore, and that we might work there."

"If you were going to work in Baltimore, why didn't anyone know about it?"

"Because it was to be a grand surprise. He claimed that he had a family inheritance, and that he was a tremendous fan of mine. He was a writer himself—but he knew talent when he saw it, and he was convinced that I knew far more than he ever could. He wanted to publish a literary magazine, and he wanted me to be editor. I would choose the material while others were chosen for more menial editorial work. That way, I would have time to continue creating my own stories."

"And you went to meet him, but you were attacked. The burlap bag was thrown over your head," Vickie murmured. "Did you ever *see* Reynolds?"

"No."

"How did you know where you were to go to meet him?"

"A boy met the train and he gave me the address. Now, as I went there, I became quite curious and a wee bit concerned, for—as you have seen—the address was down an alley."

"Was Reynolds the one who attacked you?"

"I don't know. You know I don't know!"

"Right," Victoria murmured. "Well, I'm going to have to find out about this Reynolds. He never appeared at the hospital when you were ill."

"I only know that with what he promised, Elmira and I might have lived happily. There would have been no dissension from her brothers or her children, for it would be my income and no inheritance that supported my household. I told you—I loved Elmira. I swore to temperance. I meant to make our lives sober and dignified."

Vickie nodded. "All right. I am, somehow, going to find out about this man. Now I must get back to Frampton Manor. I believe that a life may be at stake."

There was nothing to be found in the room that Jon Skye had shared with Alice Frampton.

They searched meticulously.

And then it was time to go through the belongings of

everyone who had stayed at Frampton Manor through the night.

Because someone, somehow, had drugged Alice Frampton.

And because Liza Harcourt was still missing.

But before they could move on to another room and another suspect, Griffin could hear car wheels on the gravel drive outside the house.

Vickie had returned.

"I'll see if she's gotten anything else, anything at all," Griffin told Jackson and Carl Morris.

"We've got this," Morris assured him wearily.

Griffin hurried out to meet Vickie.

"Nothing yet? No Liza?" she asked him anxiously.

"No."

"The more I think about it, the more I'm convinced that Alice's situation was created just to throw everyone off."

"Morris has an APB out on Liza. I didn't see a handbag in her room. But her other belongings are still there. As far as the situation with Alice, Jon definitely appeared to be the most suspicious—after all, he was sleeping with her. But we tore apart their room and his things. Jackson and Morris are upstairs now, going through Alistair's stuff. We will do it with every person who was here. We will find out if anyone has any sign of drugs or anything suspicious whatsoever in their personal belongings."

"And then?"

"We will keep looking until we find something."

"Griffin, no."

"No? We have to solve this."

"Yes, but we can't waste time. Liza is somewhere."

"Taken by the killer, you mean?"

"Yes."

Griffin looked at her steadily. "Do you think she's already dead?"

Vickie inhaled and exhaled slowly and deeply and then shook her head. "I don't know. I really don't know. But I do believe that she was the real victim, and that we were drawn out to the cemetery on purpose. And here's the thing, Griffin. The killer didn't kill either Franklin Verne or Brent Whaley immediately. He used Poe-inspired methods. That meant drugging and then putting the victim in a position where they died on their own. I believe that the killer has Liza Harcourt. And that she's somewhere she is meant to die. We have to find her before that happens, Griffin."

"And where do you think she might be? Vickie, I'm telling you, we've gone over this place thoroughly. Are you thinking the cemetery? A Poe place, where the women who were loved sometimes seem to rise from the grave? Vickie, Alice came running out to the cemetery. Jackson and Angela spent most of the night among the tombstones. Even if the killer is something of a magician, I don't know how he could have gotten Liza out there."

"Not the cemetery, Griffin. Somewhere in the house."

Griffin paused for a moment. "All right, in 'The Fall of the House of Usher,' there was a crypt. This place has a cemetery, but not a crypt. It does have a basement."

"And," Vickie reminded him quietly, "we have experience with basements—and people who like to bury their victims."

He nodded, tempted to pull her close. His heart was beating a little too hard. He knew that he had to accept that he was going to be afraid for her; he always would be.

He had to accept that she would be afraid for him as well.

"I'm fine!" she said, as if reading his mind. She smiled at him. "I'm with you!" she reminded him. "Now, you looked in the basement, but did you really tear it apart? Should we get the others, get some kind of help from them?"

"No," he said. "I'll let Jackson know, but not the others. If we're right—if we're close—we don't want to warn the killer that we just might find the victim alive. Morris can keep searching and we'll get Jackson down with us."

"All right," Vickie said.

Griffin called Jackson and told him about his conversation with Vickie.

"We might find a living woman," Griffin said.

"Or we just might find a dead one," Jackson said.

Griffin didn't argue. One way or the other, he hoped that they found Liza Harcourt.

Quickly.

14

Jackson joined Griffin on the stairway.

He explained that they really didn't want any of the others to know what they were doing.

"We did search the basement," Jackson reminded him.

"Yes, but we didn't knock on walls, try the floors or any of that. And with what has been going on, it seems the next logical step."

"I agree," Jackson said. "But no one here is a prisoner. I'll go talk to Adam quickly and make sure he knows that we need that group to stay in the parlor, the kitchen or the dining room. With the cops and us searching personal belongings—they've pretty much all huddled together there, waiting, to the best of my knowledge."

Griffin agreed.

"I'll see Adam. You two head down and start searching."

Griffin nodded and joined Vickie at the foot of the main stairs. "Through the kitchen," he told her.

He'd already visited the basement; he'd been down when they'd first tried to find out who had emitted the horrible scream.

Vickie hadn't been there.

He led the way down rickety wooden stairs.

Even when the electricity worked, the basement was certainly a dark and dank place. Although he'd had a flashlight when he'd come down the first time, Griffin had already cracked his head against the single bulb for the place, which hung from a cord on the rafters.

The basement smelled of earth, a rich, redolent, but almost overpowering scent.

The space was filled with spiderwebs.

While the rest of the house was seldom used, he had a feeling that—other than today—the basement had been untouched for months.

Perhaps years.

It was truly a kingdom for the spiders.

While the walls were mainly bare brick, at some time in history, wood paneling had been added to parts of the walls. There, the spiders had enjoyed a heyday. Webs tangled in fantasy knots, almost glistening when Griffin hit them with the glow from his flashlight.

As the spots of light swept around the dismal space, Griffin couldn't help but worry about Vickie.

During the Undertaker case, when he and Vickie had met again after so many years apart, she had been buried alive. But then, as now, Vickie was a fighter. He knew that if he ever tried to stop her from going to the academy, from joining the Krewe, he'd be tearing the two of them apart. The Krewe had become so important to Vickie. In her mind, it made no sense to be tormented by the souls of those gone who now needed help—or intended to help. Using their very strange abilities to help was a way to stay sane.

And he still couldn't help himself.

"Are you okay?" he asked her.

She turned and smiled at him. "I'm fine. I'm with you. Jackson and Adam are upstairs. No one is going to bury me. And," she added quietly, "the more I go through all of this with you and other Krewe members, the more comfortable I feel. Except that man's inhumanity to man will always hurt. And that's why we stop it as much as we can, right?"

"Right," he told her. He hesitated. "You're right."

She moved ahead in the basement.

It was cluttered with luggage trunks that appeared to be well over a hundred years old, fishing gear that was nowhere near that old, hockey sticks, tennis rackets, household tools and garden implements.

Vickie walked through something of a trail to the rear where the water heater stood. She shined her flashlight all around it.

Griffin realized that he was just watching her.

He began to go through the basement methodically, keeping to the left, while he suggested that she take the right.

"I can't find anything—or see anything—that suggests that a wall might have been rebuilt or that the floor might have been dug up," Vickie said. "And I was so convinced that she was being held here somehow."

Griffin had moved back through an area where a

number of old dressmaker's dummies were crammed together. He ran his hands over the wall there; nothing was new.

He got down on the floor, sliding a trunk to one side, thinking that they were going to have to move everything in the basement.

It was going to be quite a task.

"Griffin," Vickie said.

"What?" He was concentrating on the floor.

"Griffin!"

"What?"

He felt Vickie by him and saw that she had her light shining on the dressmaker's forms.

He stared at them…and saw canvas and resin and metal. Then he realized that in the middle of the headless mannequins was one with a head.

She was propped up on a metal towel rack, so close in with the dummies that she seemed a part of them; many were draped in swatches of fabric and seemed to blend haphazardly into one another.

But Liza was there, her head hanging down, her arms propped around the rack as if she were a scarecrow. There was no way to tell if she had been set there or if she had come to the basement herself, running and scared, and got caught up on the rack.

"My God!" Griffin breathed.

He hurried to her, hastily pushing dummies out of the way. Vickie had turned to race back up the stairs, dialing 9-1-1 for another ambulance even as she ran.

Griffin slid out the towel rack; like the dress forms, it was on wheels. Things around the rack seemed to spin eerily in the shadowy flashlight beam that was all that illuminated the basement.

He lifted Liza from the rack, knowing that he might be destroying evidence.

But she might be alive.

Life came first. Always. He felt for a pulse; she still had a heartbeat, though she was extremely cold and her pulse was very weak.

Griffin lifted her, hurrying up the stairs and calling for a blanket, even as Jackson and Vickie started running back down the stairs.

"She's alive, she's alive!" he cried.

Vickie and Jackson moved out of the way.

"Blankets, blankets...we need blankets," Vickie cried, hurrying through.

As he reached the kitchen with Liza Harcourt in his arms, Griffin saw that those remaining in the household had gathered around the door to the basement. "Excuse me, excuse me, move, please!" he said, hurrying through the kitchen and then the hall and into the parlor.

He laid her down on the love seat, where, just the night before, Vickie had been hypnotized.

Vickie reached him with blankets.

Adam brought water. He lifted Liza's head, trying to allow her to drink. Her lips moved; she seemed to take a sip.

"What the hell happened to her?" Monica demanded.

"Where was she?" Jon asked.

"Oh, my God, did she trip and hurt herself?" Lacey asked worriedly.

"I don't know," Griffin said. "I just honestly don't

know. But I don't see where she could have hurt herself. There's no blood on her that I can find. We've called the paramedics. I'm afraid that she's been drugged, though. She's limp and nonresponsive, and her pulse is steady but faint."

"Liza is very dramatic," Monica noted. "She might have gone down there and screamed to get us all to pay attention to her—and then tripped or fallen."

They could hear the wail of an ambulance in the distance.

"Thank God! Help—fast," Adam said. He looked intently at Griffin. Griffin returned his gaze, hiking his shoulders ever so slightly.

Had she run to the basement and tripped?

Unlikely.

Then again…

"She was angry with all of us. Thought we were making fun of her," Sven said.

"Which we probably were," Jon muttered.

"And so she ran down to the basement? Right when Alice was out running around the cemetery in a white gown?" Lacey asked.

"Don't be ridiculous. There's a killer here, and the killer lured her downstairs. She's alive, and Alice is alive, and one of them is going to be able to tell us something about who is doing all these horrible things. The women both survived, but who knows what was intended," Monica said.

"Everyone back off!" Carl Morris said wearily. "EMTs are on the way. Go sit down. We need to talk all over again."

"We've talked!" Alistair Malcolm exploded. "We've talked and talked. You've gone through all our things. We've been searched and our privacy violated. I can't stay here anymore. I have to get out of here. I didn't want to come. You thought I should come!" he said, pointing a finger at Griffin.

Before anyone could answer, the wail of the ambulance reached the front of the house. Emergency technicians poured in; Griffin told them how he had found her and they'd done nothing but try to give her sips of water and warm her up.

One of the EMTs was on the phone with the hospital, giving a description, receiving instructions. In a matter of minutes, Liza Harcourt was on a gurney and being rushed out.

"I'll go with her," Jackson told Griffin. "I'll fill them in the best I can. And then Angela and I can stand guard at the hospital and let you know the minute anyone wakes up and says anything."

As Vickie and Griffin stood there watching the ambulance depart, one of Carl Morris's men came hurrying down the stairs to whisper in his ear.

"No one knows what happened to Liza Harcourt, right?" Morris asked, his tone hard and sarcastic.

Griffin saw that everyone there just stared at him blankly. He watched Carl, irritated, because something was going on and the detective hadn't looped him in.

"Of course not," Morris said. He offered them all a grim smile. And then, to Griffin's surprise, he turned to Alistair Malcolm. "Sir, I'll need you to come with me for questioning down at the station," he said.

"What?" Alistair seemed stunned.

Griffin was surprised himself.

"We found a number of suspicious pills in a tiny tin box among your toiletries, sir," Morris said.

"I take pills for my high blood pressure!" Alistair said. "Which is rising right now, as we speak!"

"What's in the tin isn't for blood pressure," Morris told him. "Please, Mr. Malcolm, just come along with me."

Alistair began to sputter. The others stared at him. Then backed away.

The man seemed truly bewildered. He pointed a tense finger at Lacey and then at Jon and then at Adam and Monica and on to Sven and Hallie.

"You! One of you. You're doing this. One of you has done this—not me! I wasn't even here at first. I didn't want to be here at all. I came because you were supposed to protect me!" he railed, turning on Griffin.

He was a big man. He walked toward Griffin as if he wanted to hurt him. Making a judgment call, Griffin just stood still. The man was scared. He didn't know what was going on, and he was lashing out defensively.

Alistair Malcolm stopped in front of Griffin, not touching him, just staring at him—as Griffin had thought he would.

"Mr. Malcolm, you can straighten things out at the station," he said.

"You betrayed me. You have no idea what you're doing, and you betrayed me. I didn't do this." He spun around to look at Hallie and Sven. "You know the house—you did this. You got Liza down to the cellar and you drugged that idiot girl and she raced out to the cemetery. And you put whatever it is they think that I had, that I was giving people, in my things. You're the ones who know the house!"

"Please," Hallie protested softly. "I don't know if you're innocent, Mr. Malcolm, but Sven and I—we weren't even in the restaurant. We haven't been into town in weeks. Please, we didn't do anything to you."

"I'm going to kill you!" Alistair told Griffin.

"At least he's giving you a warning," Jon said darkly.

"That's a federal offense, threatening a federal officer!" Morris warned Alistair. "Sir, if you'll just come with me..."

Griffin looked hard at the man, who was still staring at him, blaming him. Griffin said flatly, "You'll be safe. You'll be out of the house," he said quietly.

Alistair held his stare for several seconds and something in his expression changed. In that moment, Griffin determined that the man was innocent.

He'd rather be arrested than killed.

Griffin wasn't sure exactly what Morris had found, and, if he had found strange pills, how he could be sure that they were what had been used to drug Alice or Liza.

But he didn't think that it was a bad thing for Alistair Malcolm to be out of the mix.

The household was growing smaller at least.

"And you, sir!" Morris said, addressing Jon. "I'll need to talk to you again, you do realize."

"I was sleeping!"

"Yes, with Miss Frampton, who is now at the hospital, recovering from a drug overdose," Morris told him.

"You don't need to worry. You'll be able to find me," Jon said.

"Let's go," Morris said to Alistair. He looked at Griffin. "I'll be in touch."

"What about us?" Monica asked. "Officer Morris. What about us? Do we have to stay here? Do we go home now?"

"You do what you like," Morris said. "But…"

"Don't go far," Jon said dully. He hesitated, looking bleakly at Griffin. "Don't leave town. That's the story, right?"

"You got it. Don't go far," Morris said.

"You're horrible people!" Alistair said. "You're all horrible people. I am an innocent man. And you'll pay for not defending me! This is so bad, so ridiculous!"

Detective Morris ignored Malcolm. He nodded to Griffin and walked Alistair Malcolm out the door. The police officer who had come down to talk to him hurried after them, carrying Alistair Malcolm's big black overnight bag.

For a moment, there was silence in the old Frampton Manor.

Then Jon Skye spoke. "The police have arrested Alistair. Can you tell that to Gary Frampton? Get him to let me see Alice? This hasn't been fair."

"Life isn't fair, so I've been told," Griffin said. "I don't know what Gary feels, and I don't know the hospital policy. Alice is only due to be in overnight for observation."

Jon looked at Lacey Shaw. "This all sucks," he told her. "Big-time."

"Yes, Jon. Probably most for Franklin and Brent. They're dead," she said. Lacey turned to Griffin. "I'm leaving."

She turned and headed up the stairs for her things.

"I guess we might want to head back to my house, too," Monica told Adam.

Adam was thoughtful for a minute. "Griffin, thoughts?"

"I think that, at this moment, we're probably still deep in the dark. But if Monica wants to head home, that's fine. Gary, Alice and Liza are at the hospital. Lacey is leaving. Alistair is with the police now. I'm sure it's fine."

"You're all welcome to stay," Hallie said. "I'm sure that Gary would say that, except for..."

She broke off, wincing as she looked at Jon.

"Well, you will have to speak with Gary, I'm afraid, Jon. He is blaming you for Alice's condition, so it seems."

Sven set a protective arm around Hallie's shoulders.

"Yes," he said firmly. "You will have to speak with Gary."

Jon looked at Griffin. "But how could the man still be angry with me? The police just found drugs in Alistair Malcolm's overnight bag."

"Well, here's the thing, Jon," Vickie said quietly. "How did Alistair get to her to give her the pills?"

"Please! People do fall asleep! Easy," Jon said. "Alice could have gone downstairs for a drink of water. He could have been down there. I mean, maybe it wasn't so much a plan as it was a crime of convenience. I love Alice. I wouldn't have hurt her."

Griffin's phone rang; he excused himself to answer it.

On the line was Dr. Myron Hatfield.

"There's still more details for the lab to discover— as in, sometimes we can even trace the specific chemical makeup of a drug to a certain street vendor—but I wanted to let you and the police know as soon as possible. Both victims received heavy doses of baby-baby. In the case of Brent Whaley, as we know, he suffered a massive heart attack there, nailed into the floor. Franklin Verne died more slowly, a case of alcohol poisoning, considering the condition of his heavily damaged organs due to his years of abuse."

"Whoever did it had to have known Franklin Verne, or about him—and known about his condition, right? If he had been a strong and healthy man, he wouldn't have died as he did, correct?" Griffin asked.

"Correct," Hatfield agreed.

Griffin told him about the two women who had been taken to the hospital. Hatfield agreed to speak with Jackson and the staff there; testing on the afflicted women could possibly tell them, once again, just what the composition of the street drug had been, and where they might possibly find who was manufacturing it— and who was selling it.

As he turned back to the others, they all looked at him anxiously.

"Yes?"

"Anything else?" Lacey asked him.

Griffin shook his head; there was definitely nothing else he was sharing with them at the moment.

"I'm going to the hospital," Jon said. "I'll just sit there and wait until Gary Frampton realizes how much I love his daughter."

"How melodramatic," Monica said. "Adam?" she asked. "May we leave?"

"Yes, as you wish," Adam said, looking over at Griffin. "What is your plan?" he asked.

"I believe we have some research to do, Adam. We'll all keep close what we learn," he said. He looked at Vickie. "Shall we?" he asked her.

Hallie and Sven were left alone at Frampton Manor.

Jon had gone to the hospital. Lacey had gone home. Alice, Gary and Liza were still at the hospital, and Adam had taken Monica back to her house.

Vickie had been anxious to speak to Griffin with none of the others present. As soon as the guests were out of the house, he told her about Dr. Myron Hatfield's call, and then he sent text messages to Jackson and Adam to convey that information to them as well.

She was eager to tell him about her conversation with Poe. "I really believe that this is incredibly important. If we can find out just what did happen to Poe, we'll know what's going on here. And this may be ridiculous—another theory to go with dozens of other theories—but what if this man Reynolds just pretended to want to hire Poe? What he really wanted all along was to do the man in. He'd have to do it very carefully, or else be caught and prosecuted for murder. But if you were to do something like what was done to Poe…"

"You mean that he was kidnapped and then set before a rabid dog on purpose?" Griffin asked.

"I think it's possible," Vickie said. "This man, Reynolds. We have to be able to find some kind of information on him. If I could just go through archives, see his notes, or…"

She paused, frowning. "Franklin Verne's laptop," she said.

"Whoa, wait," Griffin said. "We just went from Poe archives to Franklin Verne's computer."

"Yeah, sorry. Okay, here's what I'm thinking. Poe was killed because someone was jealous of him—or because someone believed that he received a serious affront from him."

"From what I understand, he did, at times, insult just about everyone out there."

"He could be quite a critic," Vickie agreed. "But I think it was something more serious than that."

"What? How? In what way?"

"I'm not sure. I mean, it could have been some kind of a perceived ill instead of something real," Vickie said. "Maybe the killer even thought that he was being plagiarized. Which, of course, is why I'm thinking the same thing here. The two men who are actually dead were writers—published writers. Franklin Verne had a soaring career—and Brent Whaley had a good one. Franklin was only nominally part of the society, but Brent was in it, and who knows? Perhaps someone was sharing work…and thinks that one of the men stole an idea or even pages of prose or something like that."

"All right, so where do you want to start? Franklin Verne's laptop disappeared with him."

"The police have his home computer—he just didn't use it for his communications. Maybe he also had a tablet or something else."

"No phone has been found yet, either," Griffin reminded her. "I don't know why—they should have traced it by now."

"Unless the killer was smart enough to totally destroy it. We do know from the phone company that the same person called the two of them and lured them out. And that same person has been out on the streets—procuring baby-baby."

"The restaurant," Vickie said.

"The police have been through it and through it," Griffin said.

"But maybe they didn't realize what they should be looking for. There are computers at the restaurant, used for seating and reservations, for orders and bookkeeping."

"True. Okay. Let's go see what we can find."

"Something! We have to try—we're spinning our wheels here."

Twenty minutes later, they had driven into town and parked near the Black Bird. There was nothing going on; a patrol officer was watching the street and the restaurant. Griffin produced his credentials, and the officer let them in.

It was eerie being in the empty restaurant. The bar

carried a slight scent of drinks gone by, just as the whole of the place retained a slight aroma of food—both good and bad.

"And where did you want to start?" Griffin asked Vickie.

"I don't know. I guess…room by room."

"All right. I'll start with the bar, you look in the gift shop."

"Devices are so small these days, they could easily be shoved in somewhere under or between things. I'd swear that Franklin Verne carried a laptop or tablet. And we'd figured stolen, but…"

"As you say, it could be hidden here. Okay, I'm on it in the bar. I will move all the bottles, look under the ice and the plumbing fixtures. Then I'll start on silverware, plates…you name it. Nothing unturned, I promise," Griffin assured her.

"Thank you, sir, thank you," Vickie told him.

She felt that the ghost of Poe should arrive now, while they were there.

She paused for a moment, and then she moved on into the shop. Poe's picture seemed to be just about everywhere.

Yes, the man definitely should make one of his ghostly appearances!

While she was in the gift shop, she found herself standing in front of a basket of the little ravens like the one that had been clutched in Franklin Verne's cold, dead hand.

Vickie picked up one of the little birds, hoping it would give her a sense of something, or someone.

It did not.

She set the bird back down and looked at the rows and rows of modern compilations of Edgar Allan Poe's work.

His voice had been so unique.

She was getting nowhere, and so she forced herself to forget about the ravens and the stories and she went methodically through the checkout counter, the storage bins, the boxes in the storage room and every drawer and nook and cranny she could find.

There was nothing to be found in the gift shop.

She walked out, wondering just where Griffin had gotten.

Then she knew; she could hear him going through all the cabinets and cooking carts, drawers and probably even the refrigerators and ovens in the kitchen.

The basement seemed to beckon to her.

She headed down the stairs.

There was the desk—and the chair where Franklin Verne had died.

And there were the rows and rows and rows of wine.

Determined, Vickie started with the desk. Every drawer, under, beneath.

Nothing.

She looked at the rows of wine and started going down them, one by one. It was something like traveling through a maze, but the construction of the wine holders allowed for numerous little nooks and crannies here and there where one just might stow a computer.

She kept going.

She realized that all she could hear down there was her own breath.

The light—in the midst of the many rows—did not seem to penetrate well and she wished for a flashlight. But it was fine—she could certainly see well enough to find a computer.

She'd nearly come to the end and was feeling tired and aggravated when she saw something that just might be what she was seeking.

Against the silver edging on the last rack, she saw something else silver that seemed to blend right in, but was just that little bit different.

She reached for it.

And it was just then that the lights went out, and the room was plunged into darkness.

Vickie could hear breathing.

Breathing that was not her own.

She held dead still for a minute. She listened carefully, goose bumps breaking out on her skin.

Someone was there; someone was there with her. She wondered if they, too, had come for the computer.

She reached into the rack as silently as she could, trying to pull the computer from the edge of the rack. It wasn't a big computer; the screen was probably about fifteen inches. It wasn't heavy; it was an MacBook Air, she thought.

The breathing was coming closer.

And she could hear footsteps. So quiet. Someone knew that she was there; someone was coming after her, moving in the darkness, step by step.

She didn't know how someone could have gotten

down to her—not with Griffin there. The place had been locked up tight until they had arrived that day.

They had been alone...

But someone had come in by way of the delivery door on the night that Franklin Verne and Brent Whaley had been killed.

Someone had lured them both here. Big men, led to their deaths. That someone knew the restaurant, knew the entrance where there was no camera...

If they hadn't been lurking in the restaurant, hidden somewhere when they had arrived, this someone had snuck in through the delivery entrance, just as before, slipping around the false wall.

That was it—the false wall.

They had come in by the back. Maybe they had seen Griffin and Vickie arrive!

Sound was deceptive in the basement. She could hear the eerie breathing, though her pursuer was trying hard to be silent.

Could he or she hear her as well? Each breath that she took?

She wasn't armed. She could do one of two things: stay silent, try to creep away, try to ascertain where the person was and go the other way...

Or she could scream. Scream as loudly as possible, and hope that the sound could be heard up the stairs, and wherever Griffin might be...

She finished sliding the computer off the rack and held it close to her chest. Then she began to back up, just inching away, thinking that she should head toward the stairs that would lead to the restaurant.

Lead up to the light, to Griffin…

To help.

Suddenly, the breathing seemed to have changed. Softer… She was hearing something that was so close, barely there.

And much nearer.

Almost upon her.

15

The only reason that Griffin noted the light changing down in the basement was that by pure happenstance he walked by the ground floor door to the stairway down. It hadn't been open before; that meant Vickie had opened it and gone down.

She wouldn't have descended into pitch darkness.

And that meant...

He tried not to give in to fear. But logically it meant that someone had turned the lights off.

Vickie hadn't cried out for him; he couldn't hear her at all. She was hiding in the darkness that had been meant to trap her.

Griffin made his way down the stairs, tension ruling his every movement and his every breath. He walked carefully.

Listening.

Yes, Vickie was down there, and she hadn't screamed or come running up the stairs—or straight into the arms of whoever else had made his or her way into the basement.

He was proud of her; she was going to make such a good agent. She was smart, savvy, cool under fire…

And in danger now!

Step by step, around the rows of wine, Griffin moved so, so tenderly, reaching out, trying to ascertain his exact position with each movement, and not rattle the racks or wine bottles in any way.

Breathing…

Yes, he could hear breathing.

The harder he listened, the better he could hear it. He was closer to Vickie because he had entered from the restaurant above. Vickie had been going shelf by shelf, working from the front to the back. Her pursuer had come in by way of the delivery entrance and the false wall.

Breathing…

It seemed to grow louder and louder. Just as the heartbeats had grown louder and louder once when he had listened.

But this person wasn't dead.

They were far more dangerous.

They were living.

He paused; Vickie was there, right in front of him.

He knew that he had reached her by the subtle, faint, familiar scent of her. She was just ahead of him.

But someone else was still down in the darkness of the cellar with them.

And so he reached out, quickly drawing Vickie into his arms, a hand over her mouth—and he prayed that she would recognize him as readily as he had known her.

There was just one fleeting instant when she stiffened, and then she nodded. She knew it was him.

Now they were the ones in control. Vickie hadn't carelessly given herself away, running blind. And Griffin was armed; he was armed at all times.

He held still again. He was aware of her heartbeat and of his own.

And aware, still, that someone else, believing they had the advantage, was still slipping around, trying to find Vickie. Trying to...

He didn't know.

And he didn't think about it.

He concentrated on every little tick of sound. In the cellar, in the darkness, the least thing seemed to ricochet loudly. There was a scurrying; an insect, perhaps. Or a rat. Not the person who had brought about the darkness. That was a different movement.

He pressed Vickie gently behind him, and then turned, using the pressure of his hand to indicate that she needed to go back around the row the other way and get up the stairs.

She understood; she knew what he was doing. He felt her leave him, felt her first movement. And so he breathed deeply, very deeply, and shuffled his feet.

Just barely.

Just enough to keep the killer moving toward him, and allow Vickie the time to get up the stairs.

He moved forward, just an inch. He listened again. The person was moving again, coming through the wine bottles.

Vickie was past him; she was nearly to the stairs, he was certain.

And the killer had not heard her; just him.

He stayed still. And it was excruciating, waiting, each second an eon.

The breathing grew louder and louder.

And, yes, he could hear another heartbeat.

The killer was in front of him. In a swift movement, Griffin drew his gun, aiming directly where he knew the person would appear.

And then it happened. Vickie had reached the top.

The lights didn't come on in a flood, in a brilliant flash of light.

But they did illuminate clearly against the depth of the darkness.

The killer stared straight at Griffin.

And screamed.

The closest police were immediately dispatched and Vickie was quickly put through to Carl Morris. She explained where they were and her position and what was going on.

Naturally, she heard the scream of shock that emitted from down the steps, now cast in a weird glow that was a misty yellow-beige color.

It sure as hell hadn't been Griffin who had screamed. The sound had been high-pitched and startled, that of someone not expecting a man with a gun to be standing before them.

Vickie was still on the phone with Morris and quickly explained, "The lights were thrown out while I was down in the cellar. I heard someone. Someone apparently looking for something—just as I was looking for a place hidden in plain sight where the killer might have stashed Franklin Verne's laptop," she said. "Griffin is down there. He's with them now... I think it's a woman!"

Morris assured her that he'd be right with them.

She realized then that she actually had the computer. She had found it; she had not dropped it. She hadn't had a heart attack when Griffin had reached out for her—or a panic attack or any kind of an attack. She hadn't thrown it straight into the air.

It was in her arms.

She now could hear Griffin's voice, sharp, demanding.

He was the one in charge. It was safe to go down. But as she started down the stairs, she felt someone next to her.

She turned. Poe's ghost was with her. He was looking at her with his large, soulful eyes, and it was almost as if she could feel something living and real as he held her elbow gently.

"You have it? That's it? That's Verne's computer?"

"I believe," she said.

"It's in there. The why. I know that it's in there."

Vickie nodded and said quietly, "If there is an answer in here, I will find it. I'll figure it out. And I'll search for Reynolds, too, I promise."

He nodded, and then he seemed to fade away, and Vickie hurried down the steps.

She stopped as Griffin was coming up. He was leading Lacey Shaw out of the wine cellar.

"You don't understand," Lacey was grumbling. "I have every right to be here."

"Sneaking around in the basement?" Griffin asked her.

"I wasn't sneaking around!" she protested.

"Really? So, why didn't you come in by the front door? Why didn't you identify yourself?" Griffin asked her while leading her into the main hall of the restaurant.

Lacey cast a baleful glance in Vickie's direction. "I came in by the delivery door because there are so many cops around here all the time. Because they might have stopped me."

"Why were you carrying a gun?" Griffin asked her.

Vickie stared at Griffin, startled. She hadn't realized that the woman had been carrying a weapon; Griffin had evidently taken it from her.

"Well, I'm scared, of course!" Lacey said.

"Of what?"

"Of whoever killed Franklin and Brent—and drugged Liza and Alice and nearly killed them as well."

"Detective Carl Morris is on his way," Vickie said.

"You mean—you mean I'm going to be arrested for this?" Lacey demanded. "But I work here! I'm supposed to be here."

"So you turned the lights out and snuck into the cellar through the service entrance—because you work here?" Griffin asked her.

"What?" Lacey returned, seeming genuinely perplexed by the question.

"The lights, Lacey. The main lights were off and the switch for the emergency lights had been turned to an off position as well. That should never have happened."

Lacey looked as if she had been hit across the face.

"I didn't!" she said. "I swear, I didn't. I didn't have anything to do with the lights being turned on or off!"

"Lacey—" Vickie began.

"Oh, no. Oh, my God!" Lacey said.

"What?" Griffin asked her drily.

"There had to have been somebody else down there. There had to have been!"

The door banged open; Detective Morris came striding in, meeting up with the three of them right by the top of the stairs that led downward. He looked irritated.

"You're under arrest!" he told Lacey.

"I have a right to be here!" Lacey protested.

"You have all kinds of rights, but at this moment, one of them is not to be in this restaurant when we're still sorting through the circumstances regarding two dead men!" Morris said. "You were carrying a gun?"

"I...just had a gun because it can be a very dangerous world. What is the matter with you people?" Lacey said. "Two of my friends are dead!"

"Yes, and I believe they got that way because of a so-called friend," Morris said. "Turn around."

"You're going to cuff me?" Lacey said.

"Yes. Get it straight—you are under arrest."

"For what?"

"At this moment? Tampering with evidence in a homicide investigation. And you had a firearm. You have a permit for it?" Morris demanded.

Lacey pursed her lips. "It's not my gun."

"Who owns it?"

"Gary Frampton."

"Did you steal it?" Morris demanded.

"Go downstairs again, you idiots!" Lacey insisted. "There was someone else down there. You're up here, harassing me, and I'm just trying not to become another victim!"

Officers had come in behind Morris.

He cuffed Lacey, and turned her over to them.

"How did she get in?" Morris asked as the officers walked a still-protesting Lacey away.

"There's one false wall down there that I've found, which the owner knows about. Lacey probably has keys to the delivery door. Once you're in, you can't be seen behind the false wall. Most people arrive and just come from the delivery area into the main section of the cellar—you can roll liquor deliveries straight over to the desk, where, I'm assuming, they were usually logged in. If you slip around the false wall—you can't even see that it is a false wall unless you have really glaring light—you come right into the racks of wine. There may be more strange building quirks that we haven't discovered about the place," Griffin said. "I'm getting the main lights back on, and I'm going to go down and tear the cellar apart."

"All right. I am arresting Lacey. A good attorney will have her out by tomorrow morning, but at the rate things are happening..." Morris broke off, his hands in the air. "You want help here? You want officers?"

"No, but I do need to know—is Alistair Malcolm still in custody?" Griffin asked.

"Yes, he is," Morris said.

"And what about the hospital?" Vickie asked.

"That I don't know," Morris told him. "You have people there, right? We don't have officers watching over the women who went in. Our forces are spread thin at the moment."

"Yes, we have people there. I'll be in touch," Griffin said.

Morris stared at Vickie.

"What is that?"

He meant the computer, she knew.

"I believe that it is Franklin Verne's laptop," she said.

He stared at her a long moment. "I should take that," he said.

"The FBI is officially on the case," Griffin reminded him.

"Yes, but…"

"I'll be extremely careful. Carl," Vickie said in a rush, "the FBI does have priority right now, though of course I know we're all working together. But I think I can find something. I really believe there is a correlation between these murders and the death of Edgar Allan Poe. And if I can discover what it is, I'll have a lead on what has happened now."

"Poe died in 1849!" Morris said.

"Yes, I know. But years don't make killers any less active. There's something going on. I'm extremely good with computers. I will be very careful. I'll get it to you by tomorrow morning, latest."

"I am with the FBI," Griffin said quietly.

Morris threw up his hands. "Sure. Tomorrow morning. Great. It's night and I'm still working—again. I'm taking someone else into the station. Great, great, great. You know what, Special Agent Pryce? I'm damned glad that—while we're working in tandem and cooperation

and all that bull—this is really your case! Good night!"
he said. "And, God help me, make this your last call to
me for today, huh?"

Vickie realized that Griffin was trying to hide a grin
as Morris walked away from him. But then, as the officer left them, he shook his head and looked down
the stairs.

"I'm getting the lights on—I'm going back down
there. She might have been lying or she might have been
telling the truth. I just don't know with Lacey. But…"

"There just might be someone else down there,"
Vickie said.

"Exactly," Griffin said.

"I'll come with you."

"No. Start on the computer," he told her, pulling out
his phone.

Vickie knew that he was calling Jackson.

He looked at her as he made the call, and as he spoke.

"Hey, are Gary Frampton and Jon Skye still at the
hospital?" he asked. "I see. Huh," he murmured.

"What?" Vickie demanded.

Griffin shook his head, telling her what Jackson had
told him. "Alice came to. She spoke to her father. She
doesn't know what happened to her, but she does remember that she got out of bed. She swears that nothing happened to her in her room, that Jon Skye would
never hurt her.

"But Gary left the hospital?" Griffin asked Jackson. He put his phone on speaker so that Vickie could
hear the answer.

"Yes, he was going to get some things and come

back," Jackson said. "I asked an officer to follow him, but he lost him right away. He's not at his home in the city. As to Jon Skye, yes, I did see him—but he left almost right away, too. He saw Alice. They had a teary reunion. But then Jon left. He wanted to speak with Gary Frampton and clear the air. Why? What's going on?"

Griffin explained to Jackson.

"Lacey swears she didn't turn off the lights," he said. "She suggests that someone else was down there."

"It is possible," Jackson said. "And as for Lacey…"

"Yeah?" Griffin asked.

"Just don't be fooled. We have seen women kill. You should try questioning her yourself, Griffin. You may discover something that Morris doesn't."

"Well, one way or the other, she'll spend the night in jail. They won't be able to arraign her until tomorrow morning. I'll search this place again. And then I'll try my luck with Lacey."

Jackson went on to tell them that Liza Harcourt was stable, but that she hadn't come around yet.

"And, yes, by the way—lots of the street drug baby-baby was found in both women," Jackson told them.

Griffin thanked him; Jackson said that he and Angela would be standing guard at the hospital for a few more hours, and then see if Morris could replace them with some of his officers.

He didn't want to lose any more people.

Griffin hung up.

Vickie looked at him and waited.

"I'm going back down to the cellar," he told her.

She nodded, and went to find a table where she could set up and get going with Verne's laptop.

It was rather amazing, Griffin thought, that in all that had happened down in the cellar, not a drop of wine had been spilled.

He now had lights glaring everywhere. He walked to the desk, paused. He retraced his steps over and over and over again.

Nothing. He went through the false wall to the back. He frowned, noting that the delivery door was still standing ajar.

Simple. Lacey hadn't closed it.

But…

Was Lacey the killer? Was she capable of it? Could she have gotten a man the size of Brent Whaley into the floor?

Apparently baby-baby was strong enough to make a monster pliable. But still…

How did a man lie right down to die? How did he crawl into such a horrible situation?

Griffin retraced his steps again.

This time, he found something.

It wasn't much, but it was something.

Caught on the wire cork-cage of one of the champagne bottles was a bit of fluff.

Griffin reached into his jacket pocket for tweezers and a little evidence bag. He snagged the fluff with the tweezers and studied it.

Black wool, he thought.

Lacey had been wearing a pale blue pullover and jeans.

But then again, maybe this had been here; maybe it had been overlooked.

He didn't think so; the forensic science teams were very good. After Franklin Verne's death, they had inspected every inch of the wine cellar.

They had missed the false wall, he reminded himself.

But that was architectural.

Griffin bagged the fluff and turned back into the cellar.

If there was one false wall...

There just might be another.

16

Vickie found it was incredibly easy to hack Franklin Verne's laptop.

He used his wife's name for every password. On one account, he used her name with the number one. He apparently hated passwords.

Vickie was surprised and touched to discover just how active the man had been on his social media. He was funny, nonpolitical and to the point. He advised readers on great new books coming out that he'd had the opportunity to read.

Facebook didn't give her much.

His email account was different.

She discovered that he'd kept a running conversation going with Brent Whaley.

One note read, "Brent, I understand your feeling of frustration. This is one of the reasons that while I am a member of many societies and groups, I keep my distance. I know this individual myself. Nothing overt, ever, nothing in front of others. But this writer will corner you and demand to know how you *stole* from their work. Stole! My dear friend, we both know that we do not need to steal from any other writer, nor, for that matter, does the greenest beginner who loves the craft. I keep my temper because of the very interesting bits and pieces of history our friend is able to glean and give out upon occasion. Hold your temper, but know, if need be, I will be there to defend you."

Vickie sat back. She let out a long breath. She hadn't been far off the truth at all—someone out there had accused a man like *Franklin Verne* of stealing.

Verne had found such a possibility laughable— almost to the point of being nothing at all.

But obviously, whoever it was had come after both men.

Then again, there was another puzzling dilemma. If the person had just been after Brent Whaley and Franklin Verne for stealing, why also attack Alice Frampton and Liza Harcourt?

She was pondering the question and all but losing her mind when she felt a whiff of cold air and felt someone heading her way.

Poe.

She smiled at him gently. "I don't know who yet, but I believe I have found proof that someone believed that Brent Whaley and Franklin Verne were stealing prose. Plagiarizing," she said.

He frowned. "And you think that… Yes! You think that Reynolds thought that I was stealing from him? But I barely knew the man. And I never stole a line in my life!"

"I don't believe that Verne or Whaley ever plagiarized as much as a line, either," Vickie said. "But what's real doesn't always matter. What people think has been done to them can be just as serious as what really happened."

Poe nodded thoughtfully. He looked up at his picture on the wall.

"No matter what you discover, you'll be able to put forth another theory. But at this stage, more than a hundred and fifty years later, there will be no proof," he said.

"It's likely that there won't be proof," Vickie said. "Still, I'm going to do all the research that I can. I'll do everything in my power to find out what happened."

"When will you start?"

"I'm going to go through more of these emails and see if Franklin Verne left us anymore clues. And after that…"

"After that you'll start on Reynolds?" he asked hopefully.

"Yes. I promise. I…"

She paused, afraid to really put her finger on just what might be happening.

Happening now…with two deaths already.

Perhaps more that needed to be prevented.

"Vickie?" Poe said softly.

"I think Reynolds killed you in jealousy over a belief that you stole from him. And I believe that whoever murdered these men did it for the same reason—and actually knew what was done to you and who did it. How and why… Well, I have to figure that out!"

* * *

There was something Griffin knew he was missing; the thing was that everything had happened so quickly, and the situation had been so tense minute after minute that they were all exhausted. It was time to head back to the beautiful historic hotel they'd first checked in to—now with a new reservation—and get some sleep.

He found Vickie upstairs, sitting at one of the restaurant's booths; she was excited and wired.

She'd been far more successful than he had. He'd gone over the walls in the cellar of the restaurant for hours, tapping, listening and pushing—and he'd found nothing else.

Vickie told him about the emails she had discovered—one from Brent Whaley and another from Franklin Verne to Brent Whaley. They were all about the "person" or "writer" who seemed to believe that they had been wronged.

"We're back to 'The Cask of Amontillado,' Griffin. The victim is made drunk and walled up—for having insulted the narrator. The narrator gets away with it."

"Poe wasn't walled up," Griffin pointed out.

"No, but he was kidnapped—and I'm certain that his attacker set him up to be bitten by a rabid animal. A dog, if my dream is right. The man who was after Poe claimed his name was Reynolds. He lured Poe with a promise of work and a lot of money. And once he had him...well, it wouldn't work to wall him up."

"Why take a chance of leaving him alive?" Griffin asked her.

"Rabies, Griffin! Poe was not going to recover from rabies!"

That made sense; he believed Vickie. But he needed some sleep. "We're going to the hotel for now, okay? Bring the computer. You can keep digging. I have to sleep. I'll be useless if I don't."

He could tell that she was happy to go to the hotel, even if she didn't have the least intention of sleeping herself. She was fixated on the laptop.

They stopped for a quick meal of sushi. From the restaurant they chose, they could see Fort McHenry.

"Baltimore is really an amazing city," Vickie murmured. "I've done it before, of course. When we're settled…"

"We'll come back and visit the fort," he promised.

She laughed. "It always makes me think of the flag! And Francis Scott Key and 'The Star-Spangled Banner.'"

He agreed, and found himself thinking that he loved the fact that she found such tremendous pleasure in every place they went, in every historic event that was relevant.

And, of course, she made good use of that love of history.

"We will have to turn that computer in as evidence. It should have been cataloged. But I think that Morris meant what he said—he was glad that the majority of the case was falling on us."

"He'll have this computer tomorrow," she promised. "I think I've actually gotten what I need from it. Neither man actually names the writer who is being so vicious toward them both, certain that they were stealing his work. Neither even makes a mistake and alludes to it being a man or a woman. But it's there, and I believe we will figure out who it was."

"Gary Frampton just owns the restaurant. Sure, he loves Poe and literature. The man had to, in order to open a place like the Black Bird. But he doesn't write. And he was damned distraught about Alice."

"So was Jon Skye."

"Alistair Malcolm is in custody, and now, for the night, at least, Lacey Shaw is in custody as well. All should be quiet. Adam is with Monica, so she's well, but…"

"Only Gary Frampton and Jon Skye are really out and about," Vickie said.

"They'll wind up back at the hospital," Griffin said with confidence.

"You're so sure."

"Yes. As long as Alice is in there, they'll return. As for us…are you all set? I've got to go to sleep."

When they reached their room, it was her own computer that Vickie pulled out. "I'll be quiet, and I won't be long," she promised.

She started working. On what, he wasn't sure.

Griffin stripped down and stretched out on the bed. Vickie turned off all the lights, using just the glow of her screen. She seemed to be going from site to site, frowning here and there, hurriedly keying in another search.

He watched her for a while. Then he crawled out of bed and stood behind her. She eventually looked up.

"I've heard that a shake-up in activities sharpens the mind," he told her.

She smiled. "I'm so close."

"Yes, you are," he whispered. He spun the swivel chair she was sitting in around. Reaching for her, he pulled her up into his arms.

"I don't really mean to interrupt," he said. "I just needed to save you. You were looking incredibly frustrated."

"Frustration is a terrible thing," she said.

"I know. I was suffering from it."

She laughed; she was in his arms.

Life was magic.

Vickie was there, and yet she wasn't herself anymore. Poe was with her.

They weren't separate; neither one of them watched the other. They were as one person.

Hands tied behind the back...

Burlap bag over the head, blinding. And yet they could hear. Two speakers. Both men, or so it seemed. The one voice was coarse and scratchy. Male or female? It was the voice that spoke first.

"I started with the opium. He's had enough. I shut him in the yard."

"Have you loosed the dog yet?"

"Any minute. Did you do what I asked?"

"He's voted three times. Now you must do as I ask. Then a few days...and we've both got what we want, and the infamous Poe will go down in history as the wretch he is!"

"No…"

Vickie heard the word as a moan. A protest. And she saw glimpses of a life—good memories flashing by. She saw Elmira playing the piano in her parlor, flushing as she turned to smile.

Gone!

"He's awake!" said someone. "Get the bag off. Let him see what's coming!"

Vickie was seeing what Poe had seen. And he hadn't seen who pulled the burlap bag from his head and face.

He just saw the terrible and tormented creature before him, howling, wailing and gnashing its teeth, specks of drool tossing here and then, and…

Eyes of hell and pure fire, coming at him…

Vickie woke with a scream. Griffin was at her side, holding her, pulling her close.

"I will find it! I will find out who did this. It's all related somehow. That's why this is happening, why Poe is with us!"

As always, he soothed her, smoothing back her hair, rocking with her. Just holding her. He never tried to tell her that it was just a nightmare; Griffin knew that it was not. He never discouraged the dreams, even knowing that they sometimes ripped her apart. They were something that she lived with; he just had a knack for bringing her out of them, studying them and using them.

She turned in his arms, telling him earnestly, "I'm all right. I'm really all right. I'm going to embrace all this—and find out what it means! Two people—I take it Reynolds and one other—kidnapped Poe. They drugged him with opium. And then they set a dog on him… I don't know how he wasn't torn to shreds, but I guess he was in such bad condition when he was found that it was difficult to define any mark on him. After he was attacked… Well, I don't know where it went from there, but it could so easily be made to look as if he had either gone on a binge—or as if he had been attacked by a rabid dog. Both were true—and neither were true." She gasped suddenly. "The baby-baby, Griffin. Even that is part of it. Poe was given opium and alcohol. Franklin was drugged and given alcohol. Who knows about Brent—he wasn't an addict, so it wouldn't have mattered to the killer. Franklin, though, had to smell like alcohol! It had to appear that he betrayed the promise he made to Monica about temperance!"

Griffin was thoughtful. He leaned back, pulling her with him. "That's what you've been looking for, isn't it? Records about someone writing like Poe. Someone publishing similar stories—once he was dead."

"Yes."

"I doubt if Reynolds was really his name."

"Probably not," Vickie said. "I think I'm going to have to dig up every mention of Poe in any paper that came out right after his death—and in the years that followed. There's going to be something there, and it will help us, I'm certain of it."

The phone rang suddenly, a strident sound. Griffin rolled over to answer it. He listened for a minute. Vickie heard him say, "Yes," and then "Yes," again.

He hung up and looked at her. "Okay, I'm going to go to the police station. Carl Morris has kept Lacey Shaw in a tank overnight. He did have legal grounds to hold her and I think he does intend to charge her with obstruction of justice. But even though she was down there, we can't charge her with murder—a good attorney would have a judge laugh a prosecutor right out of court. We just don't have the evidence."

"She was down in that cellar—sneaking around. I don't think that I believe her about the lights. If she didn't turn them off, who did? And if someone else was down there, how the hell did they get out?"

Griffin shook his head. "I never did find anything. But he wants me to talk to Lacey. I don't think it's a bad idea. I may just get something." He grimaced. "Good cop, bad cop. Carl will have either worn her down or aggravated the hell out of her by now."

Vickie pushed past him, looking at the clock. It was nearly 7:00 a.m.

"And," Griffin continued, "Jackson has suggested that you meet up with Angela at the hospital. They're going to hold Alice one more night—apparently she got a real good dose of baby-baby—and they're hoping that Liza Harcourt will come around soon."

"But Alice has been conscious awhile, right? Has she said anything else?"

"I doubt if she's going to—not now, anyway. Remember why date-rape drugs are so effective—the victims can't remember that they were raped. They may have an odd feeling of having been manipulated and violated, but they don't remember any details. Half the time, sadly, they don't remember people or names. So I don't think we'll get much out of Alice."

"But Liza was given the same thing, so they say."

"Yes."

"So what are the chances she remembers anything?"

"We can still hope, and still try speaking with them," he said. "And you're good at that. You and Angela. And while you're sitting around, you can get on with your research. She excels at that, too, and she'll also get the department going back at headquarters."

He rolled out of bed. "Hey, get to it!" he teased. "Early hours!"

"I spit on your early hours!" she retorted, leaping up. "They are nothing to me! In fact, I will race you into the shower!"

"Hey. You know, we could share."

"That doesn't work out so well," she told him. "Not if we're supposed to be moving quickly."

"Things done quickly can still be tremendous fun."

Vickie laughed and headed in. She left it up to him as to whether he chose to follow or not.

"This is quite ridiculous," Lacey said. "You've thrown me in a cell. You've now dragged me into an office for the third time to talk to me. My answers haven't changed. They aren't going to change. You want to charge me with breaking and entering? Go for it—Gary still owns the place and he'll make you drop the charges. And whatever it is—obstructing a criminal investigation! How did I obstruct anything?" she demanded.

She was good, Griffin thought. Good—or completely innocent. But if she was innocent, what had she been doing prowling around in the wine cellar?

"Lacey, what did you expect?" he asked her. Carl was watching from behind the two-way mirror; Lacey was seated. Griffin moved slowly around the room, walking behind her and then coming around to look at her, his arms crossed over his chest.

"What do you mean? I work at the Black Bird."

"Which, as you know, is closed, under lock and key, until the police decide that it's time to reopen. It's the scene of not just one, but two crimes, Lacey."

She fell silent, pouting.

"You were there for a reason."

"Yes, I work there."

"You work in the gift shop. And the gift shop was closed, as was the restaurant. Come on, Lacey, quit playing stupid."

"I'm not playing stupid. I do stock with Gary or whomever now and then. It's a family business. We all work all over. At a restaurant, a lot of people come and go. Waiters and waitresses, bartenders, kitchen staff. I'm really part of the family," she said.

Griffin stopped pacing and leaned on the table, his face close to hers. He didn't raise his voice.

"Why were you in the cellar last night? There was no reason for you to be there. Unless, of course, you were looking for Franklin Verne's laptop, and if so—why?"

She swallowed in a gulp, staring at him.

"Yes," she said.

"You were looking for the laptop. Why?"

"I had to see… I had to see what he was doing."

"What do you mean, what Franklin was doing?"

Lacey let out a long breath. "For me, I just wanted

to know. Our group…the Blackbirds…we have so many discussions on what made Poe's work so good, so fantastic. For one, he had a true talent for seeing what was going on around him—as in the case of Mary Rogers, 'the beautiful cigar girl,' the girl murdered in New York while he was living there. Anyway, we all talk, and we talked about great cases once when Brent Whaley was at a meeting, and he said that we were all brilliant, that he was going to be talking to Franklin Verne, and surely, Franklin would want to use one of our ideas. So, you see, I had this great idea that centered around Poe's suicide, because, you see, I actually think that Poe brought about his own death, that he was completely self-destructive. And I…I wanted to see what Franklin Verne was doing—if he chose to use my idea."

"At this Blackbird meeting, what else was going on? Who was there?"

"Oh, a few of our out-of-town members were here that day, but they haven't been back in the city," Lacey said. "A couple of retirees from Florida. Wonderful people. A lady from Tampa, and he retired to Daytona Beach."

"But they haven't been in Baltimore lately."

"No, they only come up around the early summer," Lacey said. "Brent was here—of course, I said that. And Liza and Gary and Alice, and I don't remember who was waiting on tables or tending bar. People were in and out…it was fun. It was a great meeting. It was all a what-if kind of a thing, and it was great."

"But because of that meeting, Lacey, you were willing to break the law and try to take a computer that is considered evidence in *murder* cases?"

"It just wasn't that big a deal."

"Really?" Griffin asked. "Not that big a deal—and what about murder, Lacey? It's where Franklin Verne was brought and killed. Was that no big deal?"

"No!"

"Was it important enough to get that computer, Lacey, that you would have killed to get it?"

"Oh, my God! No. This is all ridiculous."

"Okay, Lacey, then who would kill over all this?"

She let out a long breath, staring at him.

"Gary," she said. "Gary Frampton. He's not even a has-been, he's a never-was! He wants to write, he's always wanted to write. That's why he has the books in the restaurant, that's why he has the pictures of Poe... That's it, yes! Gary Frampton is a murderer. Or Alistair! Yes, of course, it's Alistair! Alistair is the one, he secretly wants to be famous—he wanted that book he's eternally working on to be published. He wants to write great fiction—to be like Poe. He wanted to be a Franklin Verne!"

Griffin turned away from her, aware that Carl Morris had been watching him.

He shook his head. Lacey was just throwing out names. Either that, or she was really good at playing the naive idiot—and she was involved.

His phone was ringing. He answered it quickly, wondering if there had been any kind of a breakthrough at the hospital.

But it wasn't the hospital.

It was Adam.

"Griffin, get over here, please, now. There's some kind of screeching here—and it's coming from the walls."

Vickie kept concentrating on Poe, hoping that would help.

He had been murdered. He hadn't given into temptation; he had loved his intended bride and he had meant to keep his promise to her.

He'd been tricked by a man named Reynolds. Tricked into leaving the train at Baltimore, and then lured down a dark street. He'd been kidnapped, his clothing had been stolen and he'd been dressed anew—used by pollsters, men intent on getting their candidate elected.

They had arranged for him to be attacked by a rabid dog. Or had that been...before?

As Vickie drove to the hospital, she decided to question her smartphone. The system on her phone had been named Gladys.

Gladys had a lovely Kiwi accent, as if she were a New Zealander.

"Hey, Gladys! How long does it take to go into dementia from rabies?" she asked aloud.

"Hello, Victoria," Gladys said. "Rabies. Length of time for symptoms to appear depends on the area of the bite. An arm or leg, possibly a week. On the face or neck, sooner. If bitten, Victoria, go immediately to the hospital for a series of shots. If symptoms occur at a later stage and the victim hasn't been treated, there is no survival."

The timing was right.

"Gladys, what writers came to prominence in the horror and mystery fields in the 1850s? Writers who might have created works that resembled those of Edgar Allan Poe."

Gladys answered, "I know of no writer named Alice the Hoe."

Vickie winced. She had asked two questions at once. She rephrased. "What writers came to prominence along with Edgar Allan Poe in the 1850s?" she asked, enunciating as carefully as she could.

This time, Gladys went off nicely.

"*The Scarlet Letter* by Nathaniel Hawthorne, *Moby Dick* by Herman Melville, *Uncle Tom's Cabin* by Harriet Beecher Stowe, along with works by Walt Whitman and Henry David Thoreau. And then," Gladys continued, "we have lesser known work…"

Gladys went on to talk about a few of the near misses as well.

"Among those 'imitators' was Walter Randolph, a student of Edgar Allan Poe. His 'Lilies Cut From Life' made a brave attempt to capture the narrative style of Poe along with the overall atmosphere, failing dismally. Critics were brutal. The author, in fact, was shot down by police—but not before he managed to stab to death the editor of a Washington paper who had dealt harshly with his material."

Vickie almost drove off the road, but she managed not to do so. She was nearly at the hospital.

She waited until she reached the parking lot and put a call through to Griffin. He didn't answer. She quickly dialed Angela, even though the agent was just upstairs in the building.

Angela was a seasoned guru when it came to research, so Griffin had assured Vickie. If there was a way to find out more about the murderous Walter Randolph, Angela would be able to help Vickie dig it up—and quickly.

"I've don't know if this means anything or not, but there was a Poe imitator named Walter Randolph who put out some work shortly after Poe's death. I think he might have been the Reynolds who Poe was supposed to meet in Baltimore before he died," Vickie explained.

"Okay, I'm on it. I'm staying here, hanging out in Liza Harcourt's room," Angela said. "You might want to turn around. I just called Griffin and I was about to call you. Gary Frampton took Alice back to Frampton Manor. Jackson went with them. I thought you might want to meet up with them there and talk to Alice— maybe she can give you something."

"Thank you," Vickie told her. "I'm heading back around."

"I'll get on this research now. Hopefully, an answer will somehow help us…and if not, well, I'm doing my thing as guard duty here, anyway."

"Thanks, Angela," Vickie told her.

Angela said goodbye, and that she'd keep Vickie informed on anything at all that she discovered.

Vickie turned the car around and headed for Frampton Manor.

She was only about twenty minutes away, and she soon pulled into the driveway.

The door opened as soon as she arrived. Hallie stood there. She seemed to beam with surprise and pleasure as she saw Vickie.

"Hi!" Hallie said. "Gary and Alice are back with Special Agent Crow. I'm so pleased that you're joining them. It felt so odd—scary, even—here, with everyone suddenly gone. But Alice is okay—she's up in bed already, if you want to talk to her. And Gary is doing well, too. He's in his office with Special Agent Crow."

"Thank you," Vickie told her. "I guess I'll just check in with Jackson and Gary, and then go up and see Alice."

"You don't have any bags—an overnight case of any kind?" Hallie asked hopefully.

"No, I'm not—I'm not sure what will be happening later," Vickie said. "I hadn't known until a few minutes ago that Alice was being released."

"Well, she's fine. Doing very well. She's just extremely sleepy," Hallie said.

She opened the door wide for Vickie to enter. Vickie slid by her.

"I'll just run into the office," Vickie told her.

"I'm going to put some coffee on. I'll be in the kitchen. Oh, are you hungry? Should I make you a sandwich or something?"

"Sure!" Vickie said. Keeping Hallie busy seemed like a good thing to do. "Thank you."

"No problem!" Hallie said happily. She turned to head to the kitchen and then stopped. "Whoops, sorry. What kind of a sandwich? Turkey and Swiss okay? Are you a mayo-and-mustard kind of girl, or just mayo?"

"Sounds great, and sure, a little mayo and a little mustard," Vickie said.

Hallie smiled and went through the door from the central hallway to the right. Vickie watched her go, and then she turned toward the left wing of the house. Walking through the parlor back to the office, she couldn't help but notice details of the house and the decor, more visible now in daytime than they had been during her last stormy visit. Everything had an air of faded gentility, something once very nice but lost in time. It was almost as if the very air was composed of ghosts of the past, and as if a fine, ghostly gray mist hung over everything from the walls to the furniture to the floor.

Yep. "Fall of the House of Usher."

She hurried on through.

Gary Frampton's home office was much like the rest of the house—something out of a gothic novel.

The desk was a beautiful, heavy wood, oak, Vickie thought. Even antique and untended for decades, it had a beautiful natural patina. Naturally, Gary had a laptop on his desk and a small printer. But nothing else in the room showed any link to the twenty-first century. The phone on a small pedestal table by the door hadn't been connected in years and years; it had probably been installed in the 1920s.

An antique Oriental rug lay on the floor and the walls were covered almost floor to ceiling with bookshelves.

Many of the books appeared to be priceless—first-run, original copies of classics.

She wondered, however, how many were still in decent condition. They hadn't been a valuable collection when they had been set in the shelves—they had just been reading material. Fiction, at that.

Gary had been sitting behind his desk. Jackson was on one of the two Duncan Phyfe chairs in front.

Both men rose as she entered the room.

"Miss Preston," Gary said. "How very nice to see you."

"I'm glad that Alice is well, and out of the hospital," Vickie told him. "I thought that maybe I could speak with her and try to get to the bottom of what might have happened."

"I did try speaking with her," Jackson said. "But you might just come up with the right question to break through," he added.

Vickie nodded. She knew why Griffin loved working with him and Adam so much. Neither man either thought himself as more experienced or more certain to get results. They trusted those who worked with them and never micromanaged.

"I'll run up and give it a try. Hallie is making me a sandwich," she told them. "If she comes here, will you let her know I'll be right down?"

"Of course!" Jackson assured her.

She left the men and returned to the hallway. She could hear Hallie moving about in the kitchen. As Vickie started up the stairs, she noticed the art on the walls. There were framed paintings: pictures of famed writers, some alone, some together in imaginary groupings. There were also vintage Frampton family portraits.

One portrait had to be of Alice—or her mother. Vickie peered closely at it. She thought that the painting was of Alice's mother, definitely. The hair was feathered in a style popular in the 1970s and '80s.

The resemblance was startling. She had been very beautiful.

Vickie gazed at it just a moment.

Writers…and this beautiful woman. Alice's mom.

She could have lingered longer, but she hurried on.

The place still seemed so odd…bathed in a strange drab, gray mist.

She gave herself shake, paused and then ran on up the stairs.

On the second floor, she tapped on Alice's door, wondering what to do if the girl didn't answer. The door, however, wasn't really closed, and when she knocked, it opened.

"Yes?" Alice said. She was in bed, but sat up as Vickie entered.

She still looked way too much like her mother, Vickie thought. She was wearing a long white nightgown reminiscent of something from the mid-1800s.

What was it about the house? Did people forget what century they were actually living in?

"Hey, Alice, it's me, Vickie Preston. Do you mind if I come in and speak with you for a while?" she asked.

"Sure," Alice said. She smiled wistfully as Vickie approached her and patted the bed. "Sit here, is that okay?"

"Sure."

Vickie perched next to the girl on the edge of the

bed. Alice was curled up with her legs beneath her. She was pale and seemed thinner, but though her eyes were anxious, they were clear.

"You're doing okay?" Vickie asked her.

"More or less," Alice said. "My father is a jerk. Jon is a heavy sleeper. He doesn't know what happened— I mean, he really doesn't. But of course, he's my dad. He's not going to like any guy that I'm involved with. I guess it's the way fathers act—being fathers."

"They can be protective. I think it's a biological thing," Vickie assured her.

"Your dad is overprotective?"

"Oh, yeah. Of course." Vickie told her a bit about her parents, dear and wonderful people who constantly worried about her but had finally accepted the fact that, with her life, she was probably better off going through training and becoming an FBI agent rather than waiting for more strange things to happen around her.

"So, yeah, parents," Vickie said. "But…Alice, you remember nothing?"

"Well, no, not nothing. I do remember heading down to the kitchen. I was thirsty."

"But you don't remember getting anything to drink? Talking to anyone else in the house? That's all?"

Alice shook her head. "No, I'm so sorry! I'd give anything…to help, to know!" She inhaled a long breath, staring at Vickie. "They say that I was heavily drugged. That's why, even if I thought I remembered something, I'd be afraid of what I thought I remembered."

"Alice, do you think that you remember something?" she asked.

Alice was silent a minute.

"What? Please, whatever it is, you can tell me," Vickie said softly.

Once again, Alice inhaled deeply. "I came down the stairs and it was the middle of the night. This house is so weird—sometimes I wish it would burn down." She paused, looking at Vickie. "You're not going to tell me that's a horrible thought?" she asked.

Vickie shook her head. "Probably not the nicest thing to think, but...not horrible, unless you have people in the house."

"Oh, God, no!" Alice said.

"Then in my book, you're fine. A house—no matter how historic—is a thing. Sometimes things can clog up our lives. People, however, are different."

"I wish no ill on anyone, I swear!" Alice said.

"I believe you. So...the house was weird. You went downstairs. You were thirsty, and you were headed to the kitchen."

"Yes. And then I heard the whispering."

"Someone was whispering?"

Alice looked at her and nodded, casting her head at an angle and adding drily, "The walls were whispering. I know it sounds bizarre. But I could swear the walls were talking, and I could hear them."

"And what were they saying?"

"Alice... Alice..." Alice paused and looked at Vickie. Her eyes were enormous and suddenly damp with tears. "That's crazy, right? The walls...the walls were whispering my name. And it was so terrifying. It was as if they were reaching out for me. As if they wanted to drag me in. As if they wanted to make me part of the awful miasma of this place!"

17

"It stopped!" Monica Verne told Griffin. She was effusive as she hurried on to say, "That's why, forgive me, it needed to be you. I mean, try to tell the police that you're certain you hear screaming, but that there's no one in your house—other than your guest and your housekeeper, neither of whom are screaming. Or hear the screaming. The police already want me incarcerated forever, the key thrown away, convinced I'm the evil one who did in my husband. And Adam promised that you wouldn't just think that I was making things up."

Griffin had arrived at the Verne house; Monica stood with Adam just inside the doorway.

He looked at Adam. "So—you didn't hear the screaming?"

"I was sleeping," Adam said. He shook his head. "I didn't hear it, but Monica swears that there was screaming."

The ghosts of Josh Harrison, Dylan Ballantine and Darlene Dutton hovered behind Monica Verne. Griffin looked at the ghosts.

The three of them gave him grim, wide-eyed nods.

"We're going to need to inspect the house," Griffin said. "All right, so the alarm system has been on and working the entire time?"

Again, he received a number of very serious nods—from the living and the dead.

"No one has gotten in here—you're certain?"

"Not through the front," Adam assured him. "Or through the back door, for that matter. The alarm covers the entire house, including the windows."

"What about the basement?" Griffin asked.

Adam looked at Monica. "What about the basement?"

"Well, you get to it by the back stairs—through the kitchen."

"Is there an external entrance?" Griffin asked.

Monica looked at him blankly.

"Could you call the housekeeper?" Griffin said.

Monica did so, shouting, "Tanya!"

"And Tanya's full name is?" Griffin asked.

"Tanya Cermak—she is Czech, and in the country legally," Monica informed him. "My husband and I saw to that."

The pretty young dark-haired woman they had met on the first day they'd come to the Verne house appeared in the hallway.

Griffin smiled at her. "Miss Cernak, what can you tell me about the basement? I'm sorry, what I mean is, can you tell me if there are other ways into the basement? And, by any chance, did you hear anything at all that might have sounded like screaming?"

Tanya looked uncomfortable. "No, I did not hear screaming this morning."

"That's okay. If you didn't hear it, you didn't hear it."

"I—I heard it before, though," she said, looking at her employer uneasily. "I am so sorry. I didn't know anything. I thought that it was something that warned us about Mr. Verne. I cried when I thought about him, when I thought that I had heard the sound. It was like the walls were crying, as if they mourned for Mr. Verne. As if...as if the walls knew."

Griffin prayed that no human being had been walled up. If that was the case, they'd now been trapped for days.

And if not, what the hell made the noise?

"And what about the basement, Tanya? Do you know if there's any kind of an outside entrance to the basement?"

"There is storm door," Tanya said. "Near back of the house, with ladder into the basement."

"Okay. Thank you," Griffin told her. He looked at Adam. "I'm going to try the outside. I'll meet you down there. Put on every light down there, please."

Adam nodded. Griffin left the house and walked around it. He had a feeling that Franklin Verne and Monica had treated their alarm the way most people did. Sometimes, they remembered to set it. Right now Monica would definitely be making a point to turn on the alarm. But they had probably been careless in the past, as many people were. Unhelpfully, there was no camera surveillance.

He walked around the house. Bushes grew alongside

it, but there were breaks beside the wall. They were dwarf azaleas, he thought—something he knew, only because his mom loved them so much.

They were well kept, but they still seemed to run over what appeared to be a storm door.

He'd found it.

There wasn't even a padlock on it.

Griffin shook his head, threw the door open and looked in. Adam and Monica had already reached the basement and switched on lights.

Narrow steps, almost attached to a rear wall, led down to the floor.

It wasn't a finished basement—the floor was raw concrete. But there were rugs thrown here and there. Franklin Verne had used it to store all kinds of tools, and evidence of his life and work—there were some bookshelves, and there were boxes and boxes of books, labelled by country; Verne had been published in at least thirty languages, according to the boxes.

"You never noticed the steps?" Griffin asked Monica.

"Griffin, I'm so sorry, and I'm sure I sound like a terrible human being, but I just never came to the basement. The washer and dryer are down here—a whole laundry room," Monica said. "All kinds of things. But honestly..."

"You don't do the wash," Griffin said.

"No. I haven't done the wash in...well, at least twenty years," Monica said.

"There's nothing wrong with that," Adam assured her.

"No, it's okay. You don't need to apologize for success," Griffin said.

"Franklin's success," Monica said.

"He loved you. You were his everything," Griffin said. "That helped to make him a success. Don't undervalue what being an amazing wife can mean to someone."

Monica smiled at him and touched his cheek. "Thank you for that!" she said.

And as she spoke, Griffin heard it. The sound was terrible. It sounded like something straight out of hell, out of a horror novel…something terrible and eerie.

And it sounded almost as if it had come from the entire house, as if brick and mortar and stone had screamed from top to bottom.

"What is it? Oh, my God, what is it?" Monica asked, shaking. "You heard it, right? You all heard it, too, right?"

"Definitely," Adam said.

"Yes," Griffin agreed.

He looked from the stairs—where he had entered—across the expanse of the room to wall separations and the stairs that led up to the kitchen.

"How many rooms is the house divided into down here?" Griffin asked.

"Six," she told him. "Three here, three the other side. There's a Ping-Pong table in a room with some chairs and a few bookcases, the laundry room—and an ironing room, though, seriously, I haven't even asked anyone else to *iron* in at least twenty years."

He nodded curtly and hurried past structural pillars

to the other side of the house. The walls in the room with the Ping-Pong table were too visible—too obvious. In the laundry room, there was evidence of recent activity, and it was clear that the washer and dryer, folding tables and even a few clotheslines were easily accessible, but the walls appeared to have been as they were for years.

Griffin almost pushed past Adam and Monica—who had followed him—to reach the ironing room. There, he saw that wire shelving for luggage and cleaning supplies had been pressed haphazardly against the walls, and he suddenly realized that at least one of the shelves had been dragged from one area to another. He hurried to that point and pulled the shelf unit away from the wall.

He quickly saw that the brick here against the wall had recently been replaced. The mortar was not hard and firm like that around it.

For the second time in recent memory, he was certain that he looked like a crazy man. He searched the room. He didn't find a crowbar, but he saw a set of old building tools against the corner of the room that included something much better.

A sledgehammer.

He quickly picked it up and sent it flying against the wall with all his strength. Brick and mortar began to fly.

The terrible wailing scream seemed to tear through the house again.

And then echo as Monica picked up the sound.

And Griffin stared into the blackness of the hole he had just created.

* * *

*The walls called her name; the walls in the old house
called out to Alice.*

So very Poe! Vickie thought.

There was an explanation somewhere, she determined. On the one hand, the killer had pressed Brent
Whaley into a floor—and they'd heard a heartbeat.
His phantom heartbeat? A killer's heartbeat? Vickie
didn't know. Even a mutually *imagined* heartbeat—
once again, something à la Edgar Allan Poe. Fear was
in the perception. It was physical, yes, still it became a
far greater force when expanded in the mind.

But the walls here…

Whispering the word *Alice.*

"There's an audio player somewhere," Vickie said
flatly. "Alice, you know that you were attacked by
someone—plied with baby-baby. That's why you can't
remember anything clearly. But if you heard your name
called over and over—and in this house—I'm sure
someone is playing parlor tricks."

Alice's eyes were wide. "You think there's a player
in the parlor?"

Vickie sighed inwardly and started over. "There may
be a number of devices."

"So, you don't believe in ghosts?"

"I don't believe that ghosts are holed up in the walls,
calling your name," Vickie said. "I do think someone
very much alive is playing tricks—besides murdering
people. Maybe you were supposed to die—"

"Oh, God!"

"Sorry, sorry! Or cause someone to get hurt—your father to have a heart attack, for one," Vickie said.

"My dad, my poor dad. I mean, he aggravates me to hell, but he is my father!" Alice said.

"Of course. Okay, get some rest. I'm going to prowl around the house and see if I can find evidence of audio devices."

She smiled and stood, heading toward the door. Turning back, she told Alice, "Don't worry, stay here— rest. We'll find the truth."

Alice smiled wanly.

Vickie ran down to the office first. Gary wasn't there anymore. Jackson had a laptop out on the desk.

"Gary went up to rest—he's still pretty shaken. Not that old, but old enough, I guess, for this to have taken a toll on him, physically," he said.

"He should get some rest," Vickie said. "Jackson, Alice believes she heard talking in the walls. I believe someone has put some kind of audio device in a wall somewhere. She's convinced that 'ghosts' in the walls talk."

"And what do they say?"

"They say her name, Alice—over and over again."

"Well, there's an easy recording for you." He closed his laptop. "Let's start looking. I'll take the basement and downstairs and you can have upstairs."

"Okay. I didn't mean to stop you from whatever you were doing."

"Not a problem. I was doing research on your Poe writer. That fellow Walter Randolph. Angela told me what you'd discovered. She's got a few people working on uncovering just who he was and what his story was. And how he could have something to do with what's going on here and now. She's the best."

"So I hear. Okay, I'll head up."

"And I'll head down."

"Perfect," Vickie said. She started out of the room. Hallie caught her in the hall. "Your sandwich is ready!" she told her.

"Hang on to it for me for just a minute!" Vickie pleaded. "I'll be right back."

Determined, she headed up the stairs. But then she paused.

One of the paintings on the wall that she hadn't taken the time to really study earlier was a very old painting of a number of great writers, all who had lived and worked in the mid-1800s.

One of them, of course, was Poe. Around him were James Fenimore Cooper, Ralph Waldo Emerson, Henry David Thoreau and two others Vickie didn't immediately recognize.

She froze, however, staring at it. Arrayed at the bottom—in various odd positions—were three blackbirds.

They all appeared to be dead.

She had to show Griffin and the others!

She realized now that the painting wasn't hanging exactly flush with the wall; it seemed to extend just a bit too far.

Vickie studied it for a moment, then lifted it from the hooks that held it. The painting in its thick wood frame was heavy. She nearly dropped it.

Someone else had already dropped the painting. The frame was cracked in one corner.

And behind the painting, duct-taped to the back of the bottom of the frame, she discovered what she'd had a feeling she'd find. A small digital audio player. Vickie pulled the device free. There was only one file on it, unnamed. She pressed the play button.

"Alice…" a haunting voice whispered.

There was also a plastic baggie taped to the back of the painting.

Vickie turned the painting to look at it again. The great writers were all gathered around a table in an old tavern. Their names were written in tiny ornate balloons just over or near them.

She realized that there was a balloon on a man who appeared to be the bartender or tavern keeper.

Vickie nearly dropped the painting.

The name in the balloon was Walter Randolph.

"Jackson!" she shouted.

He came hurrying in from the eastern end of the house.

Hallie followed close behind him; she nearly crashed into his back when he stopped. Jackson turned, taking her by the shoulders firmly.

"Stay!" he told her.

He hurried up to the middle of the stairway to join Vickie.

"What is it?" he asked.

"Look! He's here. Walter Randolph is here—he's in this painting. And I found a player—right behind the painting."

"Oh, my God!" Hallie breathed.

Vickie and Jackson both turned to look at her.

"No, no, no! I didn't do it!" Hallie said. "I didn't, Sven didn't... We're not here all the time. This house doesn't have any real alarm system. Anyone could have snuck in. I swear to you, I don't know how that got there!"

Jackson ignored her. He looked at Vickie. "We may be able to pull prints."

"Oh, my God!" Hallie repeated.

Vickie turned to frown at her.

But Hallie wasn't looking up the stairs anymore. She was staring down the central hallway—through the shotgun center of the house.

Jackson trotted down the stairs and stood next to her, looking out. He swore softly and went tearing toward the back of the house.

Vickie chased after him, catching Hallie by the shoulders. "What? What is it?" she demanded.

"Alice...and her father. Again!"

Vickie spun around. She did so just in time to see that Jackson had taken off after Alice, who was still in a white gown, beckoning her father—who appeared to be in shock—out through the sculpture garden.

And into the cemetery.

The wall of the basement was remarkable for what they did find...

And what they didn't find.

"Oh, poor, poor kitty!" Monica cried.

And that was it.

The wall held a cat. Most naturally, a black cat. For a long moment, the terrified creature stood frozen, its hackles up, and then it tore off into the basement and up the back stairs to freedom.

Monice Verne swayed, catching hold of Adam's arm as her hand fell over her heart. "A cat!" she said. "A cat! Oh, thank God. A cat—no...no...human!"

"No, I don't believe so," Griffin said. He moved forward to study the hole he had created. No. There were no bodies in the wall.

Someone had simply torn it apart before to wall in the cat.

He looked at Monica. "When did you first hear the cat?" he asked her.

"When we called you. Right, Adam?" Monica said. "We called Griffin the moment we heard the screaming or wailing or...whatever word one might use to describe that sound!"

Something was bothering Griffin; he wasn't quite sure what it was.

He searched the wall. Monica and Adam stared at him as he did so.

"Maybe Tanya," he murmured.

"Tanya?" Monica said, then called, "Tanya!"

The girl didn't come downstairs.

"I do hope she's all right," Monica murmured.

"Maybe she can't hear us down here," Griffin said.

"I think that she can hear us!" Adam said. "She always seems to hear us, but..."

There was a sudden sound—like that of cans being cast down the cellar steps.

From above, they heard another scream.

"Down!" Griffin shouted, throwing himself at Adam and Monica and forcing the two flat on the floor—just in time.

Flames and debris shot through the basement as the canisters that had been thrown into it exploded, ripping into the wall, into brick, mortar and earth.

Fire shot all around them, and then burned in clusters around the room. Griffin came to his feet, wrenching Monica and then Adam up with him. They were all covered in dust and black powder. Monica was shaking and reeling.

Adam was black-faced, but stoic. And more: he was angry.

"We're meant to burn to death down here!" he said indignantly.

And he was right; the stairs up to the house were all but engulfed in flames.

Griffin looked to the rear—to the stairs out to the garden. He grabbed Monica by the arm and dragged her along; Adam followed. The top three rungs of the narrow, ladderlike stairway had been blasted away. Griffin hopped up to the top, pulling himself up on the edge of the storm door, and reached down to help Monica, lifting her out the exit.

"Too hard!" Adam told him. "Leave me!"

"No, sir!" Griffin told him. In the flames, he could see that the ghost of Josh Harrison had come to stand beside his father; Dylan and Darlene were with him.

"Not in this afterlife!" Josh whispered, looking at Griffin.

Griffin caught hold of Adam's arms. He pulled with all his strength; Adam wasn't heavyset, but he was tall. Griffin didn't know if he could have pulled him up and out on his own or not; he couldn't help but believe that the spirits of the three incredible young people had helped.

Adam shot up; Griffin almost threw him out past the bushes and onto the lawn. Crawling up behind the two, he lay on the grass for a moment, gasping for breath. As he did so, he thought he saw someone running through the thick brush.

Someone in black...

A black wool sweater?

They could already hear sirens. Someone, somewhere, had dialed 9-1-1. Whoever they were, he silently blessed them.

"Help is coming!" Griffin said. He rolled to his feet and drew out his phone and dialed.

Vickie didn't answer.

Then neither did Jackson.

At last he reached Angela Hawkins, still at the hospital, watching over Liza Harcourt.

"Griffin, they're at Frampton Manor," Angela told him. "Alice was released from the hospital. Vickie gave me the name of an author who published works very similar to Poe's, in inspiration at least, if not in talent, after Poe's death. She was right, Griffin—there is an association. I'm going to head on out to Frampton Manor, too."

"I'm on my way. I don't know what the next plan is

going to be, but get out there—because I think I have an idea of what's going on. And someone else is supposed to die."

Vickie caught up with Jackson Crow at the gates to the cemetery. He held up a hand, indicating that she be still and silent for a minute. Then he shook his head.

"Keep behind me," he warned her.

Vickie did as she was told.

Jackson was armed; she was not.

It appeared that Alice was under the influence of a drug again! She had just been speaking with Alice.

Jackson moved slowly and carefully through the graveyard. They twisted around small mausoleums and gravestones, cupids and angels.

And, finally, they saw them ahead.

They had come to the art nouveau tomb.

The tomb where Alice's mother lay. And there was Alice, beckoning to Gary, looking just like the ghost of her mother.

The great iron gate to the tomb stood open—making it appear that Alice had just stepped out from the grave.

It seemed that there was something wrong with Gary.

"My love!" he said shakily.

Jackson stopped dead in the clearing. His Glock was in his hand. But Vickie didn't think that he intended to fire.

He spoke softly. "Gary, stop. Gary, that's not your wife. It is your daughter."

"Come, come…come to me!" Alice said. "You must… you must come to me… I know that you must, I hear that you must. I hear the music, I hear the words that cry to me, I obey as I am told."

"Dial 9-1-1," Jackson said softly to Vickie. "And get back, quietly, carefully—and get down!"

I hear that you must. I hear the music...

Alice was manipulating her father—*as she had been ordered to manipulate him*?

If that was the case, then...

She instantly did as Jackson had ordered. Just as she ducked behind a tombstone, she heard a gunshot fired. There was a wild rush—Jackson hurling himself forward to bring Gary Frampton down to the ground.

Alice went running through the row of tombs, ethereal with her white gown flowing behind her.

Vickie didn't have time to think—another shot fired. Even as it ricocheted off a stone near her, she thought she knew who was shooting.

Plunging behind a now wingless angel, she shouted out, "Jon Skye, you started off with a plan, but you've destroyed it all now. Everyone will know that you've done this."

The cemetery was suddenly still. No shots; no movement.

Vickie decided to keep talking.

"You're a descendant. A descendant not of someone as celebrated as Poe, but of someone as ridiculous as Walter Randolph."

She hoped that by goading him, she'd get a response. She hoped that she'd show Jackson—who was armed— the killer's position, rather than showing the killer her own position.

Of course, she was doing both.

But she believed she had to speak.

"Someone who was as *poor* a writer as Walter Randolph!" she said.

"Poor! Why, you stupid, self-righteous bitch!"

It was Jon Skye who answered.

"You even look like him, you know," Vickie said. "I don't know how I didn't notice the resemblance between you two in the old painting on the stairway before. Actually, I only noticed the resemblance—and the painting, really—because you chose to hide your drugs behind it, too. And then, of course, there were the three blackbirds in the painting. You had to kill three of them to leave with Franklin Verne. Did you think that Alice or Gary would appear guilty if someone saw the painting and noticed the birds? I guess that was supposed to be cool and clever, too. What, you were so damned jealous of Franklin Verne and Brent Whaley that you couldn't stand it? You didn't really carry through so well," she told him.

"I carried through brilliantly!" he protested.

She tried to figure out his position. If she could just slither without being seen, she could get behind the art nouveau tomb.

Where is Jackson? What about Gary Frampton? And Alice?

"Throw down your gun!" Jackson shouted. She couldn't see him, but Jon fired at the sound of his voice. Vickie slithered around the tomb.

"Okay, so, your great-great-grandfather was Walter Randolph—who killed Edgar Allan Poe. Once Poe was dead, he tried to use Poe's work by turning it into his own words—and he failed abysmally. He didn't become famous—he didn't become a Poe," she called out. "And hey, you also botched it all. The way you killed Franklin Verne—not at all the way your great-great-grandfather killed Poe. And not even the way Montresor was killed—walled up—in the Poe story."

"No, you stupid woman!" Jon shouted back. "It was perfect—it was half Poe's death combined with a death like his character's."

"And Liza Harcourt didn't even die!"

"Ah, but she will," Jon said.

Crouched now behind an elaborate angel at the edge of the tomb, Vickie felt a chill.

"Once I finish here," Jon said.

"Drop your weapon!" Jackson shouted again, then fired toward where Jon's voice had come from.

Jon stepped out around one of the older tombs.

He had Alice held firmly in front of him.

"Shoot will you? Shoot at me?" he demanded. "Do it again and she's dead! In fact, Miss Victoria Preston, Miss Wonder-nonfiction-woman with no damned right to be a critic, you come out. You come out and show yourself, or I'll shoot her!"

"No!" Gary Frampton had heard the words. He'd been down on the ground; now he leaped to his feet, streaking out to race toward Jon Skye and his daughter. "No!" he screamed again.

Jon thrust Alice away to take aim at Gary. But Jackson Crow fired.

Jon was forced to spin around.

Vickie grabbed Alice. She dragged her, pulling her into the art nouveau tomb where Alice's mother lay.

She slammed the heavy iron door shut behind them.

And then she heard Alice begin to laugh.

Griffin arrived in time to hear the slam of a bullet against the marble of a tomb.

He fell back, his heart thundering.

"Jon Skye!" he shouted. "Jon Skye, throw down your gun. I'll let you come in alive!"

"Two of you assholes now, huh? Did you do any research? I'm a crack shot."

"Could have fooled me!" Jackson shouted from his location.

"What the hell do you think? That you're going to kill all of us? And then what? The research has been done at our headquarters, Jon. Everyone is going to know about your great-great-grandfather. And I have a feeling that as soon as she's threatened with deportation, Tanya is going to sing like a canary, Jon. All she's really guilty of doing is walling up a cat. And abetting you by providing information and helping you trick a few victims. Actually, that is conspiracy, but…I'll bet she's going to swear that she didn't know you were going to kill them."

A bullet bit into the shimmering granite tomb wall at his back. Griffin ducked low. As he did, he saw the ghost of Poe. Poe was heading toward a large mausoleum. He looked over at Griffin.

"That bastard! He looked at history, right or wrong, and committed murder. The son of the son of the son of the man who killed me. Here. He's right here," Poe said, and he pointed down behind the tombstone.

"Hey, Jon—Edgar Allan Poe is right next to you!" Griffin called out. "And he's really pissed off!"

Griffin didn't know what Jon Skye's reaction would be.

But apparently the man turned. And saw the ghost of Poe.

He let out some kind of strangled sound.

Griffin took that moment to streak across the open space between the stones. He slammed down on Jon with a hard tackle, and disarmed him.

Jon Skye screamed with rage.

"He was a lousy writer. He was a thief!" he cried. "Walter Randolph was so much better!"

Vickie listened intently, trying to discern what was going on outside the mausoleum.

"Oh, you are priceless, just priceless! You really are such a stupid woman!" Alice told her.

Stunned, Vickie turned to look at Alice.

The girl wasn't anywhere near as stoned as she had appeared.

"No one ever listened!" Alice said. "I love him. Don't you understand? I love Jon. And we're going to be together forever. I'm sorry about my father, but..."

Vickie realized that Alice was watching her with a sad smile.

And that she was reaching for an ax—one that had been left right behind the small wooden altar in the family mausoleum.

"Oh, no, no, no!" Vickie told her.

She wasn't armed, but she wasn't going down to a crazed young woman armed with a rusty old ax.

Alice swung; Vickie dodged behind the altar. The ax stuck into the panel of the altar and was pulled out of Alice's grip.

Vickie made a jab to get the ax before Alice could retrieve it. But the other woman was closer.

Alice had it back in her hands. She started to swing again. Vickie dived beneath the altar—which was quickly shattering to bits under the force of Alice's next slash.

"Alice, kill her, kill her, do it!" Jon Skye shouted from outside. A shot sounded. They were both aware of a tussle outside, screaming and grunts and groans.

"Alice, stop!"

Alice did pause—though Jon Skye was not the one to shout out the words.

Griffin continued, "Alice, don't do it for him. He's a liar and a cheat. He was sleeping with you to carry off what he told you was a prank—drugging you and hiding Liza Harcourt in the basement. Don't you understand? He was using you."

"He loves me!" Alice cried.

"And he must love Tanya, too, Mrs. Verne's housekeeper. He's been sleeping with her. He seduced her so that she would wall up a cat. So that he would get secrets that he could use to lure Franklin Verne to meet up with him. Alice, he's slept around—he doesn't love you!"

"I do, Alice! Kill her!" Jon Skye shouted hoarsely.

Alice burst past Vickie, heading outside—her ax raised high. She headed straight for Griffin—who now held a handcuffed Jon Skye at his side. Sirens were wailing with a fury from down the road.

Jackson was with Gary Frampton, who sat sobbing on the ground.

"My Alice! My Alice!"

"Kill her, Alice, vengeance, poetry!" Jon Skye called. "A true Poe story!"

But Alice wasn't planning to send the ax into Vickie's head any longer.

Alice had other intentions.

Vickie tripped her right before she could cleave Jon Skye's skull in two.

Vickie lay on the ground, panting, as Jackson strode over and drew Alice to her feet, cuffing her as well. Police officers suddenly filled the little family cemetery.

Griffin shook his head, standing over Vickie for a minute. He reached down and pulled her to her feet.

"You're okay?" he asked shakily.

She nodded.

Someone else had made it through the graves and mausoleums and cherubs to come quickly to stand beside them—and look at Vickie anxiously.

"You're all right?" Adam Harrison asked her.

"All right. I'm actually a mean tackle," she told him.

He smiled at that.

"A mean tackle," he agreed. "Griffin, how...how did you know what was happening here when the cat was found at Monica's house?"

"Tanya—she said that she heard the cat two nights

ago. She lied. She just put the cat in the wall herself. You or Monica would have heard something, too, if the cat had been there longer," Griffin said. "It wasn't too much of a stretch to guess *why* she was lying."

"He's in the picture—sorry, I mean, Jon Skye's ancestor is in the painting on the wall. Jon was trying to make up for what was done to him… Repeat history… I don't really know. But…the blackbirds were there— three dead blackbirds. If we'd seen the painting and realized…"

"Blackbirds, ravens…" Adam said. "I hope I don't see either, or a crow, now for…forever!"

"You had Angela looking it all up," Griffin said.

"And it all came together," Adam said.

Detective Carl Morris came walking through the graves. He paused for a minute, looking around. "No new ones?" he asked hopefully.

"No new ones," Griffin said.

Adam reached for Vickie's hand. "Well, shall we go and…breathe? And get through all the paperwork? And…"

"And?" Griffin asked him.

"I just have one more thing to say," Adam said.

"And that is?" Vickie asked, smiling.

"You're going to make one hell of an agent. One hell of an agent, Miss Preston!"

Epilogue

Vickie loved Griffin's apartment in Alexandria.

It covered the entire ground floor of a Colonial row house built in the late 1700s. Because his was the ground-floor apartment, it was surrounded by a beautiful porch, and beyond that, a handsome, well-manicured lawn and a tree—a cherry tree.

It would bloom every spring.

The apartment itself had a living room, dining room, back family room and two bedrooms. There were crown moldings throughout, and all that was modern had been beautifully blended with the old.

The events in Baltimore had come to an end; the guilty had been made to pay.

There would be more, she knew, in the future—as there had been in the past.

She was due to go into the academy in about a week.

She was exactly where she wanted to be.

Griffin had vacation time on his hands; they could have gone anywhere. But they didn't want to go away. They wanted to settle in. She'd have to be in training soon, and then their time together would be limited. It was wonderful to stay home, to add her touches to the apartment, to go to sleep every night at Griffin's side, to wake there every morning.

While the end of the Poe murders case had been terrifying, it had also taught her that she was really ready for the Krewe, and that she was ahead of the game. She knew so many things already that were incredibly important. It wasn't just all right to be frightened—it was smart. Fear kept one alert, aware—and prepared. It was all right to rely on other people. That was what Krewe members did—they had one another's backs. She didn't have to be a power unto herself.

And she and Griffin could make it with both of them being agents; it was fine, too, that you feared for your partner. That was human. How you learned to use your fear was paramount.

She woke up one beautiful fall morning in his arms and marveled at the way her life had changed, and how that change had really begun so many, many years ago; it had begun when a serial killer had first come after a young woman who was babysitting and the spirit of the baby's brother had been so strong, he wouldn't let harm come to them.

She'd learned to speak with the dead. And now she knew that talent meant so much, had an important purpose.

She smiled, rolling slightly to her side.

The dead, of course, could really be a pain in the ass!

But for now Dylan and Darlene were back up with the Ballantine family. Dylan would do what he had always done—spend his time between watching after his mom, dad and brother—and Vickie.

He had the train schedules down pat. He far preferred the train to flying!

She suddenly felt warm and she realized that Griffin was awake, that he was watching her. He smiled slowly. "And…you're smiling because you're thinking of me?" he asked.

"Of course," she murmured.

"Liar."

"Okay, I was thinking about the kids."

"The kids? Our kids? Are we having kids? How many?"

"Well, I'd like to think that we will at one point, but at the moment, I was thinking of Dylan and Darlene."

"Lovely. And I thought that smile was for me."

"Oh, but it was, you see. I was thinking how wonderful it was that we have absolute privacy since the kids are up with Dylan's family."

"Ah."

"And you're looking stern and perplexed," Vickie said.

"Sadly, I was thinking that I've just got you moved in—and you'll be moving out. To the academy."

"We won't be far away."

"The academy is serious," he said.

"I know." She stroked his face, as always slightly amazed that he was the man he was—and that he loved her so deeply.

"So…to that end!" She rose suddenly, straddling him. "I'm all settled in, the apartment is quite in order and, therefore, we need to use our time to the very best advantage!"

He smiled, reaching up, and lowered her against him.

There was such an incredible spark of heat and urgency just in the touch of their naked skin.

Especially when a man and woman were aware of just how fleeting life could be, and just how fragile all that was created of bone and blood was.

It was hours later before they rose; these days were definitely precious days.

And it was late afternoon when Vickie stepped out onto the back porch, surprised to see that they had a visitor there, a man with dark soulful eyes, who sat on one of the antique wicker rocking chairs there and looked out on the beauty of the lawn and the trees that stretched out before him.

He rose, seeing Vickie.

"Edgar! What are you doing here?" she asked him.

He smiled very slowly, studying her, and then she realized that his smile was somewhat sad.

"I've come to say thank you and goodbye," he told her.

"Well, you already thanked me, and we did say goodbye," she told him. "I'm afraid that there is no historical board who will say that what I saw happen to you was the truth, that history can be rewritten to change what it says."

"It doesn't matter—I know. And those I loved, well... I'm not with them yet, but they know. Maybe the truth is just something that we need to have for ourselves, and truth is what we see in our hearts or souls. Not sure if I have a heart these days, but I know I have a soul."

"A beautiful soul," Vickie assured him.

Griffin came out to the porch; he stood behind Vickie, his hands on her shoulders, drawing her back against him.

"Mr. Poe," he said.

"I've come to say a final farewell. It's time that I take my own dark journey, ever praying for the light. Having belief in the beauty of both life and death, and leaving behind the shroud that seemed to cover me while I drew breath."

"Oh!" Vickie said.

He walked to her, taking her hand, kissing the knuckles with a breath. He looked at Griffin where he stood behind her. "Know, sir, that you hold in your hands the most precious of all lovers, a sweet Lenore—none of my sirens who would taunt and tease but a brilliant beauty encompassing the purest love of the greatest light."

Griffin smiled. "I'm not at all sure I could say it that way, but rest assured, my friend, that I do indeed cherish this woman with every bit of life and breath within me."

Poe nodded, pleased. Vickie smiled.

And then he stepped away.

It was that time of day when the sun was just beginning to set. When streaks of gold tore through a sky that was pink and mauve, both pastel and brilliant.

Poe smiled a jaunty smile, tipped his hat and started off the porch.

And for once, Vickie thought, he walked entirely into light.

The sun seemed to flare; he was gone.

For a moment, she and Griffin just stood there. And then she turned into his arms and told him, "Poet or no, my love, that was quite beautiful."

"Thank you," he told her, and kissed her lips. He looked off into the yard. "I pray he finds peace," he said. Griffin set an arm around her shoulders to lead her back into the house.

But he paused, and she looked at him, and he shrugged a bit sheepishly.

"'Quoth the raven,'" he said. "'Nevermore!'"

* * * * *

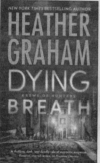  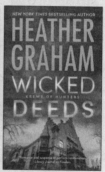

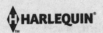

I N T R I G U E

EDGE-OF-YOUR-SEAT INTRIGUE, FEARLESS ROMANCE.

Save **$1.00**

on the purchase of ANY Harlequin® Intrigue book.

Available wherever books are sold, including most bookstores, supermarkets, drugstores and discount stores.

Save $1.00

on the purchase of any Harlequin® Intrigue book.

Coupon valid until December 31, 2017.
Redeemable at participating outlets in the U.S. and Canada only.
Not redeemable at Barnes & Noble stores. Limit one coupon per customer.

52614978

Canadian Retailers: Harlequin Enterprises Limited will pay the face value of this coupon plus 10.25¢ if submitted by customer for this product only. Any other use constitutes fraud. Coupon is nonassignable. Void if taxed, prohibited or restricted by law. Consumer must pay any government taxes. Void if copied. Inmar Promotional Services ("IPS") customers submit coupons and proof of sales to Harlequin Enterprises Limited, P.O. Box 3000, Saint John, NB E2L 4L3, Canada. Non-IPS retailer—for reimbursement submit coupons and proof of sales directly to Harlequin Enterprises Limited, Retail Marketing Department, 225 Duncan Mill Rd., Don Mills, ON M3B 3K9, Canada.

U.S. Retailers: Harlequin Enterprises Limited will pay the face value of this coupon plus 8¢ if submitted by customer for this product only. Any other use constitutes fraud. Coupon is nonassignable. Void if taxed, prohibited or restricted by law. Consumer must pay any government taxes. Void if copied. For reimbursement submit coupons and proof of sales directly to Harlequin Enterprises, Ltd 482, NCH Marketing Services, P.O. Box 880001, El Paso, TX 88588-0001, U.S.A. Cash value 1/100 cents.

5 65373 00076 2   (8100)0 12293

® and ™ are trademarks owned and used by the trademark owner and/or its licensee.

© 2017 Harlequin Enterprises Limited

HIBJDCOUPI017

She prayed for sleep, but her mind kept returning to that time
in the Sahara. Being part of the expedition had been such a
privilege. She remembered the way they'd all felt when they'd
broken through to the tomb. Satima Mahmoud—the pretty
Egyptian interpreter who had so enchanted Joe Rosello—had
been the first to scream when the workers found the entry.

Of course, Henry Tomlinson was called then. He'd been
there to break the seal. They'd all laughed and joked about
the curses that came with such finds, about the stupid movies
that had been made.

Yes, people had died during other expeditions—as if they
had been cursed. The Tut story was one example—and yet,
by all accounts, there had been scientific explanations for
everything that'd happened.

Almost everything, anyway.

And their find…

There hadn't been any curses. Not written curses, at any
rate.

But Henry had died. And Henry had broken the seal…

No mummy curse had gotten to them; someone had killed
Henry. And that someone had gotten away with it because

neither the American Department of State nor the Egyptian government had wanted the expedition caught in the crosshairs of an insurgency. Reasonably enough!

But now…

For some reason, the uneasy dreams that came with her restless sleep weren't filled with mummies, tombs, sarcophagi or canopic jars. No funerary objects whatsoever, no golden scepters, no jewelry, no treasures.

Instead, she saw the sand. The endless sand of the Sahara. And the sand was teeming, rising up from the ground, swirling in the air.

Someone was coming…

She braced, because there were rumors swirling along with the sand. Their group could fall under attack—there was unrest in the area. Good Lord, they were in the Middle East!

But she found herself walking through the sand, toward whomever or whatever was coming.

She saw someone.

The killer?

She kept walking toward him. There was more upheaval behind the man, sand billowing dark and heavy like a twister of deadly granules.

Then she saw him.

And it was Micah Fox.

She woke with a start.

And she wondered if he was going to be her salvation…

Or a greater danger to her heart, a danger she hadn't yet seen.

Don't miss
SHADOWS IN THE NIGHT,
available November 2017 wherever
Harlequin® Intrigue books and ebooks are sold.

www.Harlequin.com

HIEXP1017